THE SAGA
AMERICANS C
THE LAST M
WITHIN A DYIN
AND ARCTIC
NEW WEAPONS TO WAR AGAINST THE PEOPLE.

NE'GAUNI—Betrayed by those he loves, he is ready to yield his life to the River of Death . . . only to be reborn in a haunted forest. From there he will set forth on an epic journey to the ends of the earth, and discover the power of a "magic" new weapon.

M'ALSUM—Haunted by a secret shame, he will stop at nothing to avenge a wrong done to his one true love. Through treachery and murder, he will win back his pride—and hers—at any cost.

HASU'U—As M'alsum's woman, her happy songs bring joy to all . . . until cannibal raiders fall upon her band. Fighting for her life, she is given a desperate choice: to live as one of them, or to witness the slaughter of her people.

TUNRAQ—An interloper from the high Arctic, he speaks a tongue never before heard, uses a weapon never before seen, and hides his face behind a mask. Is he a protective spirit sent to save the People . . . or a demon bent on destroying them?

YOUNG ONE—A child of the Old Tribe, her forest world is a lonely realm of wolves and shadows, and secrets too terrible to share. Now, a stranger has entered her world. A forbidden love has touched her heart. And a legend will be fulfilled . . . in blood.

BANTAM BOOKS BY WILLIAM SARABANDE

BA Henderson

TIME
BEYOND
BEGINNING

William Sarabande

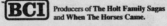

BCI Producers of **The Holt Family Sagas**
and **When The Horses Came.**

Book Creations Inc., Canaan, NY • George S. Engel, Executive Producer

❀ BANTAM BOOKS

New York Toronto London
Sydney Auckland

TIME BEYOND BEGINNING

A *Bantam Book* / *September 1998*
Produced by Book Creations, Inc.
Lyle Kenyon Engel, Founder

Canadian Museum of Civilization: Excerpt from *Canadian Arctic Prehistory* by Robert McGhee. Copyright © 1990 by Robert McGhee. Reprinted by permission of Canadian Museum of Civilization. University of Nebraska Press: Excerpt from *Midwinter Rites of the Cayuga Long House* by Frank G. Speck. Copyright © 1995 by Frank G. Speck. Reprinted by permission of University of Nebraska Press.

ISBN 0-553-57906-1

Published simultaneously in the United States and Canada

Bantam Books are published by Bantam Books, a division of Bantam Doubleday Dell Publishing Group, Inc. Its trademark, consisting of the words "Bantam Books" and the portrayal of a rooster, is Registered in U.S. Patent and Trademark Office and in other countries. Marca Registrada. Bantam Books, 1540 Broadway, New York, New York 10036.

PRINTED IN THE UNITED STATES OF AMERICA

OPM   10 9 8 7 6 5 4 3 2 1

To Charles

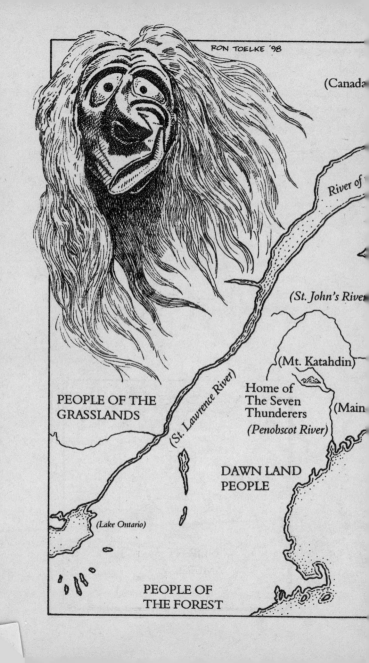

RON TOELKE '98

(Canada

River of

(St. John's River)

(Mt. Katahdin)

PEOPLE OF THE
GRASSLANDS

Home of
The Seven
Thunderers
(Penobscot River)

(Main

DAWN LAND
PEOPLE

(Lake Ontario)

PEOPLE OF
THE FOREST

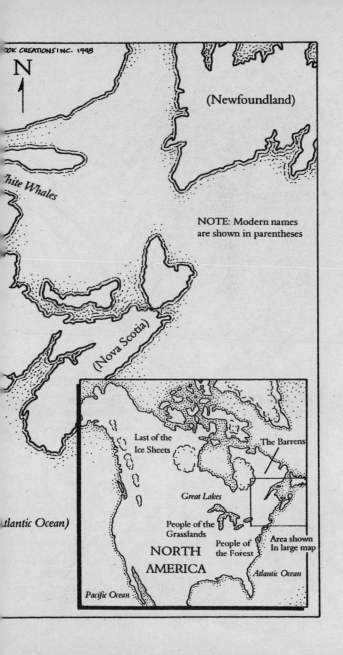

N

COOK CREATIONS INC. 1998

(Newfoundland)

White Whales

NOTE: Modern names
are shown in parentheses

(Nova Scotia)

(Atlantic Ocean)

Last of the
Ice Sheets

The Barrens

Great Lakes

People of the
Grasslands

People of
the Forest

Area shown
In large map

NORTH
AMERICA

Atlantic Ocean

Pacific Ocean

Come!

Let it be told in the old way

The dancers gather

Enter with them into the winter dark

Enter into the time beyond beginning

Enter into the firelit cavern that is the belly of all imagining

Here lives my story

Come!

Enter into this wilderness lodge of words

My story camps within

His fire burns steady and hot

He has been struck from good flint

He has been kindled from the splintered bones of man
and bear and wolf

From shavings of narwhal horn and mammoth tusk

From feathers plucked from the wings of the last auk

And from the spindrift hair of the wild woman

Who dared walk with Wíndigo, Great Ghost Cannibal of the North

Come!

My story waits

Within shrouds of winter mist and caribou moss

He is as ancient as the bones he burns

But there is blood and fat and marrow in him still

Feast now upon the conjuring that is to come

My story speaks

The winter dance begins

Enter into the time beyond beginning

Come!

Part One

GHOST ROAD

▼▼▼▼▼▼▼

"There was once a world before this, and in it lived people who were not of our tribe."

—TUGLIK, IGLOOLIK AREA
Canadian Arctic Prehistory, Robert McGhee

Chapter One

▼▼▼▼▼▼▼

The young one crouched within the trees. She was frightened. Her heart was beating fast. Much too fast. Casting a worried glance upward at gathering storm clouds, she chastised herself for venturing so far downstream. If only she had allowed the lengthening shadows to urge her home instead of inspiring her to check the last snare in her trapline! If only she had hurried back across the snow to the safety of Old One's den when she had first caught the stink of Strangers upon the wind! Now it was too late.

They were coming!

She could see them now. They were just emerging from the dark depths of the evergreen forest on the far side of the creek. Distance raised a thin shimmer of mist that obscured her vision. She growled, recognized mist for the trickster it was, and kept her gaze fixed and steady. In the cold vastness of this northern land, discerning eyes could easily pierce the substance of illusion and force reality into stark definition. And even in the fading light of this late winter day, the young one's eyes were as discerning as the eyes of the black wolves from whose loins Old One claimed the ancestors of their kind had sprung.

Another growl formed at the back of her throat. She was no wolf. But this was her hunting ground! And now, as she deftly strangled the winter-lean hare she had just withdrawn from her snare, she watched the Strangers driving their dogs and sled toward her across open snow. Her eyes narrowed. She counted four males, two females, a double hand-count of dogs. They were headed for the creek. *Her* creek. Never before had their kind ventured so deeply into her hunting grounds. Never! The wind brought her their strong, smoky stink. She snarled. They reeked of danger.

And they were coming closer, fast.

Her heartbeat quickened. If they kept to their present course they would soon be upon her. She looked around, worriedly eyed the surrounding copse of slender, bare-branched young birches, and knew that the trees offered no hope of continued concealment. She must run before she was seen!

Fighting panic, she hurriedly slip-noosed the warm, limp body of the hare to a hunting thong already laden with a cottontail and two larger hares. The combined weight of the uneviscerated animals was considerable; nevertheless, the young one slung all four carcasses over her bearskin-clad shoulder with little effort. She had not yet attained the full power that would be hers in maturity, but she was nearly fully grown and as strong as she was resolute. She would not abandon her kills to the carrion eaters of the forest. She would not dishonor her prey. She was of the Old Tribe! That which she had snared and strangled she would eat. Tonight she and Old One would feast. Later, when their bellies were full and the coals in the fire pit were sleeping beneath a blanket of insulating ash, they would take the skulls and bones of the hares and rabbit into the night. They would venture to the center of the sacred spruce grove. They would place the skulls and bones in a circle on the snow. They would hunker together inside the circle, wave their willow wands, raise their long pale faces to the darkness, and sing the ancient song of their kind, summoning the kami with their howls.

She held her breath, trembling as she thought of how it would be—of how it must be. When she and Old One had finished their song and gone back to the lodge, the spirits would come. For newly fleshed bones and skulls the kami always came. And in the thin chill of dawn, when she and Old One returned to the clearing, the bones and skulls would have vanished. By the grace of the kami, the hares and rabbit would be alive again, running and leaping along the slender hunting trails that their long-eared, high-flanked kind made through the winter forest, offering themselves as prey while the rabbit drummed upon the earth with its great feet and the hares danced the wondrous winter dance of their kind, asking to be stalked again, slain again, devoured again, and reborn again in the never-ending Circle of Life Ending and Life Beginning.

She exhaled. Her heart was still beating far too fast. Her mouth had gone dry. If there was to be a feast, if there was to be a singing in the forest, if life was to be renewed and endless winter brought to an end through the dance, she must make it back to the lodge with her prey.

The Strangers had reached the creek. Two of them were lagging behind, but the rest of the pack was continuing on, driving their dogs and sled fast across the ice.

The young one gripped the shaft of her bear-bone lance so tightly that the palms of her fur-wrapped hands ached from the pressure. Restraining a gasp of fright, she turned and darted toward a nearby snowbank. Clambering to the top, she slid down the lee side of the drift, scooted on all fours into the cover of a thick snaggle of deadwood, and sprawled flat on her belly.

The Strangers were still coming!

She lay motionless. The shock waves generated by their movement across the snowpack rippled beneath her. Hard. Pounding. Threatening. Closing her eyes tight, she uttered an involuntary sob of fright as she buried her face in the soft fur of her folded arms. Her mind flamed with a terrifying recollection of Old One's oft-spoken warning:

"Look not you upon the Strangers lest the power of your gaze they feel. Let them or their dogs set eyes upon you never. *Never!* If ever see or scent you them passing through our forest, conceal yourself within wind and trees and go your way unseen, leaving no track by which you may be followed. The Strangers are Enemy! Outside of the sacred circle do they stand. There is not one among their many tribes who will suffer our kind to live!"

A shiver went up the young one's broad, powerful back; the short, coarse hairs at the base of her spine prickled as her senses quickened with a loathing born of generations of enmity and alienation.

The Strangers were almost upon her!

The hackles rose on her skin. She heard a sharp crack of sound followed by the pained yelp of a dog, then felt the Strangers cresting the outer slope of the snowbank. They were passing directly above her now, moving fast along the narrow, elongated top of the drift, heading toward the deep woods that lay beyond. She listened to the runners of the sled sliding, bouncing, and slicing deep into hard-packed snow made nearly gelatinous by several consecutive days of clear skies and the frail, all-too-fleeting warmth of a pale winter's-end sun. She heard the creak of wood, the stress of thong, the strained suck and pull of human breathing, the heaving, slobbering panting of dogs.

Never before had she been so close to Strangers. Their presence was overwhelming; it reeked of power and arrogance. Their scent was revolting. And yet, impelled by a curiosity innate to her kind, the young one could not resist peering up at the beasts of Old One's warnings. Just one quick look was all she desired, to see if they were truly as ugly as Old One said. Surely one look could not matter, could not . . .

The lead dog felt her gaze. It rolled an eye downward. It saw her.

Trapped in a lake of shadow within a maze of tangled deadfall, the young one's muscular body tensed and resonated with a virulent loathing so overwhelming that she was momentarily transported beyond fear, beyond reason. Her upper lip quivered upward to display her canines as, growling deep in her throat, she warned the dog out of fixed and narrowed eyes.

Look away, foul and unnatural thing, for if to my enemies you betray me, I will find a way to gut you before I die!

Startled and intimidated by the unspoken communication, the dog yarfed, bucked sideways in its harness, spurted urine, yet kept on its way, inspired not only by the young one's warning but by the crack of a well-oiled thong whip.

The young one shut her eyes so tightly that her entire face hurt. The Strangers hurried on without so much as a sideward glance, and images of them remained burned beneath her lids as she lay trembling in a descending explosion of ice particles kicked up out of the snow by the runners of the passing sled.

Big dogs. Heavy-jawed. Slavering. Wolf-eared. Tails

curling high over blanketed flanks, exposed anal hair
stained from endless defecations. Hideous! Foul!

Strangers. All in caribou skins. All on snow walkers.
All hooded. All stinking! She knew their gender, not only
by the cut of their garments but by their scent. One female,
big, lagging slightly behind the males, bent double beneath
the weight of an enormous pack. Three males: one trotting
close to one side of the sled, another on the opposite side,
and the master of the sled loping behind, cracking his
whip, his hood blown back, his hip-length black hair flying
loose and wild in the wind, his profile strong, smooth, devoid of fur, broad-mouthed, high-nosed as an eagle, with
the black barred lines of a shrike running upward toward
his temple from the corner of a long, angular eye.

The young one caught her breath. The master of the
sled owned the face of a raptor. A predator's face. And he
was *not* ugly. He was the most singularly beautiful creature
she had ever seen. She shivered, not in fear of him but in
awe of his beauty, and in stunned recognition, for she was
also a predator, a stalker of prey, an eater of flesh, a gnawer
of bone, a sucker of marrow and blood taken hot from her
kills. And her face was broad-mouthed and high-nosed
and—so unlike Old One's—devoid of fur.

We are of a kind, this Stranger and I!

The realization burst into her consciousness. Sun-
bright, fire-hot, it was as appalling as it was enthralling—
until she recalled Old One's warning that Strangers were
like mist: tricksters, dangerous and deceptive and often
deadly in their endless and unpredictable transformations.
Yet now, with their scent lingering in her nostrils, the
young one found herself wondering if her own scent was
not also redolent of den smoke and if, were she ever to find
cause to journey many days beyond Old One's refuge, she

would not also take on a stink if she could not air her furs or bathe in clean, warm ashes.

But would she ever stink quite so disgustingly of fear?

The question pricked her. She remained motionless, eyes tightly shut, trying to understand the deeper implication of the information her nostrils had just sent to her brain. The Strangers were afraid! She had not thought it possible. Nevertheless, the sour scent of their terror was unmistakable. They were running from something. But from what? The wind was at their backs, blowing straight across the top of the drift. She doubted that they had picked up even the slightest scent of her. And yet, even if they had, she could think of no reason why a pack of Strangers would flee from a solitary member of her kind. It would be so much easier for them to set their dogs on her, to stand by and watch their beasts run her down and tear her to pieces as they had done to her mother when they had come upon her feeding alone in distant hills so long ago.

Her mouth tightened. She could feel the Strangers moving off the drift now, still heading toward the woods. Her heart hardened toward them. She was now confident that they were not running from her. Alone she was no threat to them. As long as they kept their pack together and moved warily through her forest, they were safe from her predations. Something else had frightened them. But in these last lingering days of the Cold Moon beneath which great bears still lay sleeping in the earth and lions hunted far to the south, what would set the Strangers running like panicked herd animals?

The young one's spirit went suddenly cold. As though in answer to her unspoken question, the wind rose and brought to her an intricate braiding of new, more complex scents. She opened her eyes, raised her head, and set her nostrils questing wide, scenting the air, pulling it deep, until, with a startled intake of breath, recognition burned her senses.

The Great One had returned!

Earth Shaker! Life Giver! Thunder Speaker! The Destroyer!

The ancient names of the giant rolled within her brain like thunderstorms threatening on a far horizon. But there were other scents on the wind. There were other trespassers in her forest. The Strangers were definitely not alone. Their stink had masked the scent of the Great One as surely as it disguised the closer, more pertinent danger that was now advancing through the deep woods on the far side of the creek. Another much larger pack of Strangers was walking in her forest! The young one could smell them and, by the subtle textures and gradations of their stink, knew their intent: They were stalking the smaller pack. A thin shiver of excitement burned beneath her skin. Death was stirring the wind and taking many forms as it moved at will through her forest this day.

Suddenly, again impelled by curiosity, the young one elbowed her way out of the deadfall and scrambled up the steep side of the snowdrift to cautiously peer over the top. She wanted to see what must happen now.

The Strangers were still heading doggedly into the woodlands, but the two members of the pack who had fallen behind were just now crossing the clearing and approaching the far side of the creek. She stared fixedly at them. They appeared relaxed, unaware of danger. A small female in heavy furs. A young male with a great load on his back and something bright, shining like a piece of dark sunlight, on the tip of his lance. The young one cocked her head to one side; Strangers often carried lances, but never before had she seen one quite like this.

A strange thought drifted across her mind: If she were to raise a howl now, the twosome might possibly be intelligent enough to hear the warning in it. If they did, there might yet be time enough for them to flee to safety across the creek. And if she put all her strength and skill behind the howl, the young male might be so startled and frightened that he would drop his bright-headed lance as he ran. It would be hers then, easily collected after Death had come and gone its way, unless one of the other pack of Strangers saw it first.

She cocked her head to the other side. Why should she wish to help any of their kind? Even in hope of taking for herself a bright-headed lance? They were Strangers! Mother slayers! They killed for pleasure as often as they killed for meat and by so doing deliberately chose to stand outside the sacred Circle of Life. If they knew she was here, they would not hesitate to hunt her. They would spear her. They would flay her alive as they had flayed what was left of her mother after their dogs had savaged her. And when they had fleshed her skin and staked it to cure in the winter sun, they would toss her meat to their dogs. Their filthy children would come close to gawk as whoever had slain her would proudly prepare to display her pelt as a war trophy outside his lodge.

She shivered. "Enemy they are." She repeated Old One's warning as she lay flat on her belly and, with a cold and unforgiving heart, prepared to watch them die.

▼▼▼▼

The winter forest was alive with spirits. Cannibal spirits. All men knew this. And yet the woman smiled and sang happily to herself as she kicked off her birch-framed snow walkers, upended them in the snow, and knelt before the ice-sheathed creek with a happy sigh. Winter was almost over. She was not afraid.

Her name was Hasu'u, One Who Sings Always. Under the wide, windswept gray of a lowering storm sky, the day was fast growing old, but she was young and strong and had come far without complaint. The deep pleasure of self-congratulatory pride filled her body; it allowed no space for caution as the fur-clad youth paused beside her on the snowy embankment.

"The trading band continues on without us!" he said sharply. Glowering down at her, he shook back his hood and commanded in a tone that was surlier than the growl of a riled wolverine, "You will not sing. You will get up! This is not a place to rest! You will follow the band across the creek and into the cover of the trees. My brothers are anxious to find a good, protected place to camp before the dark comes down. Why do you stop in this clearing? It is not safe!"

Safe.

Hasu'u's smile vanished, and the song died in her throat. All too soon she would remember the emphasis he had placed on that one small word. Now, as she looked up at Ne'gauni, youngest brother of her man, M'alsum, she was so irritated by his overbearing manner that she missed the uncharacteristic edge of anxiety that had sharpened his voice. It was the youth's habit to hurl words as though they were stones with which he intended to bruise flesh as well as spirit. Indignant, Hasu'u told herself that she would not be bruised. Upon Ne'gauni's haughty tongue the pleasantly polite dialect of her husband's forest tribe was invariably transformed into rudeness; she should be used to his impertinence by now. But this time he had gone too far. He had actually dared to command her. He had spoken as though he, and not his eldest brother, was headman of the band. As the headman's woman, she would not answer his question. She would not obey his commands. To do either would be to honor his insolence.

"Why do you stare?" he demanded. "Have you not ears to hear me when I speak? You must keep walking! You cannot stop! Get up, I say! *Now!*"

Hasu'u did not get up. Her mouth tightened. Her tattooed eyelids lowered. With his shoulders thrown back and his handsome head held high, the youth was holding himself as erect as a blustering bear. If he was fatigued in the least by the rigors of the day's trek or by the staggering weight of his antler-framed backpack, he gave no sign of it. Hasu'u vented a derisive little snort. She knew that Ne'gauni was deliberately attempting to appear big, bold, and invincible in her eyes. She was not impressed. Nor was she intimidated.

"You are not yet a chief in this part of the forest or any other, Little Brother," she reminded him curtly. "But I am our headman's woman and, in the Dawnland hunting grounds of my grandfathers, a hunt chief's daughter! I will stare when it pleases me to stare. I will rise and walk when it pleases me to rise and walk. And I will stop and sing when it pleases me to stop and sing. So go on your way. Follow your brothers. I did not ask you to stand guardian over me!"

"I will not allow you to be outside the protective shadow of a man."

"You are no man!"

"I am man enough to protect you!"

Again Hasu'u failed to recognize the anxiety in the

youth's voice. Mistaking it for his usual bombast, she snorted again and, through a curtain of well-greased lashes, took further measure of Ne'gauni's belligerent stance and arrogant expression. As one who needed only a scant three hands to sum the number of his years, he had yet to come to his Ordeal; his face was devoid of the high, lustrous scars and intricate tattooing that would one day enhance his already exceptional good looks and mark him as an adult male of his Inland clan. And he was clad entirely in the pelts of small, forest-dwelling carnivores. The garments were as exquisitely made as his snow walkers; nevertheless, they had not been cut and sewn of the soft, insulating skins of winter-killed forest caribou as were the coats, trousers, and legginged moccasins in which she and his brothers, M'alsum, Sac, and M'ingwé, and their burden woman, Kicháwan, traveled. Ne'gauni's clothing set him apart as an untested youth. Yet he carried a spear, a man's weapon.

Hasu'u frowned as her eyes took in the sleek hardwood shaft and the spearhead of darkly gleaming pounded copper. It upset her to see such a rare and wondrous weapon in the possession of one who was wholly unworthy of it. Ne'gauni's spear had not been made by his own hands. It had not been earned in the taking of his first bear, or wolf, or lion, as was the age-old custom among the People. It had come to him fully formed, the most prized possession of his father, used only in ceremony until, in a display of excessive paternal zeal on the day the trading band left the old chief's village, Asticou had presented it to his favorite son as a parting gift. Hasu'u had not approved then, nor did she approve now. M'alsum had told her that the spear had been made especially for his father by Sebec, a distant cousin and chief of a minor Lakeland clan in the country of the Copper People. It had been given at a clan gathering under the Coming Together Moon when Asticou had agreed to take Sebec's nine-year-old daughter, Wawautaési, to be his second wife. A man did not give away such a gift. Indeed, many would have said that it was far more valuable than the new bride. A man kept such an offering, kept it close all of his days, and, when at last his spirit left his body, took it with him to the world beyond this world so that he could hunt with it forever on the shores of the Great Sky River. Had it been a woman's place to speak, Hasu'u would have told all who would listen that Asticou was not wise to spurn the traditions of the Ancestors in order to lavish favor upon his youngest son. The old chief's openly preferential treatment of Ne'gauni, only son born to him of his child bride, bred resentment in the sons he had made on his first wife. It was no secret that the very name of the youth was an offense to his brothers: Ne'gauni, He Walks Ahead. As though a lastborn son might presume to be first in a father's eyes! It was unthinkable!

And yet here he was, standing before her as bold, brash, and obnoxious as ever, and all because foolish old Asticou had reluctantly put aside his misgivings and yielded to Ne'gauni's desire to join his older brothers on their trading venture.

"Guard his life with your own lives. And may the spirits of the far north smile upon Ne'gauni and ease the way of the youngest, bravest, and best of the sons of Asticou as he journeys for the first time through their forest!"

Hasu'u's frown became a scowl as she recalled the old man's words. It was also M'ingwé's and Sac's first journey to the Dawnland. Had Asticou no concern for *their* safety? Had the old man no admiration or respect for the restless daring and far-seeing ambitions of his firstborn son? Sometimes, as in this moment, Hasu'u found it very easy to understand why M'alsum had abandoned his father's village to take up the ways of a wandering trader. Surely this trading venture would not be taking place at all had M'alsum not decided to return home after many long moons away so that he might share his life once more with his mother, brothers, and band! Asticou's uncaring and insensitive words to his eldest sons upon their departure from his hunting grounds still rang harshly in her ears, as did the call of Ne'gauni's mother, Wawautaésie, the Lakeland Firefly.

"Do not return from the Dawnland without presents. Many presents. Bring me necklaces of shining shells! Bring me a wristlet of sea-dog fur and an anklet of golden seabird beaks! Bring me earrings of glistening beads! And bring me a cape sewn of many feathers gathered in the Cave of the Winds where Thunderbird makes his home above the Great Salt Water!"

Hasu'u could still hear Firefly's greedy shouts. No "Come back safely" from that one! No "I will not sleep or dare to dream until the safe return of my only son!" No. While frail, aged Meya'kwé, Standing Woman, first wife of Asticou, asked nothing of her sons save that she be allowed to draw strength from the sight of them until they went their way, the open avarice of Asticou's second wife was only slightly less insufferable than the arrogance of her only son. No matter how hard she tried, Hasu'u could not even begin to comprehend why M'alsum, Sac, and M'ingwé were so eager to bring Ne'gauni north with them.

"Go away!" Hasu'u told the youth. "I cannot stand the sight of you!"

Ne'gauni's eyebrows arched with surprise. Ignoring her statement, he insisted, "You will rise and cross the creek!"

"I will rise and cross the creek when I am ready! Now I will drink my fill of it!"

"You can drink later!"

"I thirst now!" Hasu'u's declaration invited no debate. A son had been born to her along the trail, a strong, lusty, two-fisted bawler of a son. She needed to drink often and deeply if her body was to provide nourishment for the headman's wonderful child. Her heart swelled with joy as she felt the baby sleeping against her back in its moss-lined cradleboard. She could barely keep herself from bursting into song as she imagined the happiness that must surely come to her and the child in the days that lay ahead.

Soon the little trading band would reach the Dawnland. Her people would come from their late-winter hunting camp on the bluffs above the river that emptied into the broad, shallow, saltwater bay where seals followed the opening leads and came to whelp on the ice to provide food for her people. They would welcome traders, as they always did. They would rejoice at the return of M'alsum and at the sight of a male infant at the breasts of their long-absent sister.

Then the sons of Asticou would order Kicháwan, burden woman of the trading band, to roll out the great brown bison hide, and when this was done, they would assemble their items of trade upon it: from the interior and southern forests, rare pelts, healing leaves and bark, fungi and tubers, and several small packets of rare powdered roots steeped in snake venom that, when released into water, were said to take the breath from fish and cause them to float to the surface so they could easily be speared and netted; from the land of great lakes, a few small nodes of precious copper and a cedar bag filled to bursting with parched kernels of mano'min, the much-coveted food that grew on water;

from the western hills, fist-sized nodules of translucent white quartz, out of which the stoneworkers of her Dawnland tribe could flake many fine tools; and from the heart of the deep woods in which M'alsum's people made their year-round home, several duck mandibles and birchbark cones and packets, makuks, all filled with the sweet, crystallized sap of the a'nina'tig tree, a delicacy that her people had come to crave.

And then, when the last of the items had been bartered and a meal of fresh-killed seal meat had been shared by all, M'alsum would take the baby into his strong hands and honor her father and mother by conferring with them as to the most auspicious name for their grandchild, his wonderful firstborn son.

Ah, what a reunion it would be!

"You will get up! You will put on your snow walkers! You will follow the others!" snapped Ne'gauni.

"First I will drink!" Hasu'u snapped back as she reached defiantly down with the side of a fur-mittened fist to crack the thin layer of ice that veneered the shallows at the edge of the frozen creek. She had finally heard the anxiety in the youth's voice, but it did not alarm her. She mistook it for frustration and was delighted to think that she was irritating him for a change. "You must not fear, Little Brother," she taunted. "M'alsum would not allow his woman and wonderful son to fall behind if he thought there was any danger to us . . . not with only an untested whelp such as you to stand watch over us!"

"I am the best and the bravest of the sons of Asticou!"

"Ha! Tell me that when you have made your own spear! Tell me that when you have stalked and slain something more dangerous than squirrels or hares or deer or the turtles that I have seen you so bravely roast alive! Tell me that when you have endured a man's Ordeal and dared journey alone, as M'alsum has done, to seek and find the Dawnland before returning home as a successful trader among many tribes! And tell me that when your brothers trust you enough to name you Headman and follow you on a trading venture of your own under winter skies! Ha! Until you have done even the least of these things, do not boast to me, for in my eyes you are the least of your brothers and unfit to walk in the tracings of M'alsum's sled dogs!"

"You are only a woman. It does not matter what your eyes see!"

"Ha!" She laughed again. Taking immense pleasure in baiting him, she bent to suck liquid through the intricately carved swan-bone drinking tube that her man had fashioned for her as a wedding gift. M'alsum! Her heart sang at the very thought of his name, for surely *he* was the best and bravest and most beautiful of the sons of Asticou! Not one of M'alsum's brothers, least of all this aggravating stripling who stood beside her, could ever hope to equal him.

"You will hurry!" Ne'gauni was emphatic.

Hasu'u did not hurry. The water was cold and sweet. She drank deeply, greedily, gratefully. After nearly a moon of journeying across a frozen land in which water for drinking had to be melted out of ice and was all too soon tainted by the boiling bags and by the bladder flasks in which it was carried, she allowed a low hum of contentment to escape her lips. Silently she thanked Halboredja, the wandering sun, for his gift of gradually lengthening days. The resultant warmth had been barely perceptible to her and her fellow travelers, but she knew that it was responsible for thinning the ice along this south-facing periphery of the creek just enough to allow her this moment of singular enjoyment. Surely, she thought, there could be no harm in taking a few moments to drink. Indeed, she was certain that the water spirits would be offended if she did not!

The youth exhaled in frustration, looked nervously around, then lowered his head and whispered imperatively, "Dawnland Woman of my eldest brother, I tell you it is not good to be out of the protection of our band in this country of many manitous where Wíndigo, Great Ghost Cannibal, is winter chief!"

Hasu'u's heart skipped a beat. Appalled, she choked and sputtered, then stared up at Ne'gauni in gape-mouthed incredulity. The drinking tube fell from her lips to dangle from the braided sinew necklet to which it was attached. Dread shivered beneath her skin. The manitous and their cannibal winter chief were the resident spirits of this far northern forest. All people knew this, just as all people knew that in the depth of winter these phantoms could turn into man eaters if not properly appeased. A day had not dawned or succumbed to night upon the long trail without M'alsum raising his fine voice in wordless chants of respect and invocations for sufferance. A meal had not been eaten before cuttings of each man's and woman's portion of meat were hung from the branches of trees as offerings to carnivorous forest spirits whose names were never uttered under the open sky lest they overhear and think themselves summoned to feast upon human flesh. And now, in a single moment, Ne'gauni had risked undoing all of M'alsum's meticulous efforts to win and sustain the goodwill of the manitous and their terrible winter chief.

"Are you so full of yourself that you have forgotten that it is against the laws of the Ancestors to speak aloud of these things, Little Brother?" she exclaimed, aghast.

"Your disobedience made me speak! And I . . . I did not speak loudly!"

Hasu'u was shaken. The youth was right. She had deliberately provoked him. But he had at least shown sense enough to whisper. Perhaps the forest spirits had not overheard him. Surely, she thought—and tried hard to find comfort in her reasoning—the very fact that she was here, kneeling beside a melting creek, proved that winter would soon be over and that Wíndigo, Great Ghost Cannibal, winter chief of the manitous, was in retreat.

Or was he?

A great roaring filled the forest. Not wind. Not thunder. Deep at first, rumbling, it came through the trees as from some vast resonating chamber to become a high-pitched animal scream that ululated across the world like the cry of a dying giant.

Hasu'u's blood ran cold. Never before had she heard such a sound. Never! As it ebbed, leaving the headman's child fussing in its cradleboard, she eyed the sky and storm clouds and surrounding forest with dismay. And then, suddenly, the wind rose to take her breath away.

It gusted hard from the north. A cold wind. It shook the winter-bare hardwoods and weather-blasted evergreens that grew on either side of the creek. An angry wind. It rattled the brittle bones of standing and fallen deadwood. An unforgiving wind. It set tree limbs swaying and cracking. And then, as suddenly as it had risen, it was gone.

A heavy silence settled upon the forest.

Hasu'u willed herself to breathe again.

A raven called. Another answered. And then a twig snapped in the gathering gloom between the trees through which the woman and the youth had come. It was a small sound. Dry. Thin. No louder than the breaking of a song-bird's wing.

Hasu'u tensed.

Ne'gauni whirled and, instinctively repositioning his spear, assumed a defensive stance as he glared into the thickening gray of the dying day.

Hasu'u remained motionless. All was quiet now. Within the soft, warm swaddling and furs of its sheltering cradleboard, the headman's child seemed to have relaxed once more into the easily found contentment of infant dreams. She smiled with love for her little son. Then ravens called again. Her smile disappeared. The birds sounded closer than before. And once again the wind was rising.

"You will get up now, Dawnland Woman! Raven speaks in the forest. We must go on! I do not like the stink of this wind! There is Storm in it. And something else. Something . . ."

Hasu'u's brow furrowed. Ne'gauni looked like a stranger. All signs of arrogance had vanished from his face and stance.

"Please, Dawnland Woman. I do not know what I sense in the wind," he admitted with obvious reluctance. "But M'alsum, Sac, and M'ingwé have taken Kicháwan and driven the dogs and sled so deeply into the trees on the far side of the creek that I can no longer see them. We must follow! I tell you, it is not good be separated from our band. Soon the dark will come. It is not safe for us here."

Safe.

Hasu'u cocked her head. There was that word again. So small, so sharply spoken, that somehow it made her know that it was not the dark that Ne'gauni feared. There was something else. Something that, in darkness, would be empowered to fall upon them unseen. There was panic in the youth's eyes. It startled her as much as the sudden certainty that there was something very odd about the communications the ravens were making. Something unnatural. Something almost human. She listened, recalling that in the lore of the People, Raven wore the reversible black robe of Trickster. One side of his robe named him Life Giver. The other side named him Death. One could never be sure which side he would show to the world. Sometimes Raven led starving people to meat. Sometimes he led predators to make meat of starving people. And always, cawing and chortling with laughter, Raven was there to pick the bones of the dead when his trickery was done.

Hasu'u's heart sank as she looked around to see that M'alsum had, indeed, led the others on without waiting for her. And Ne'gauni was right about the wind. It bore the threat of impending snow—and the rank stink of something else, something stale and subtly sweet. Something that made her think of old meat and open wounds. She tensed. Whatever the scent was, it reeked of danger.

Her head went up. Her eyes widened. She was acutely aware of the weight of the infant sleeping against her back—so small, so trusting, and so vulnerable. If Death were to take her baby now, without a name, its spirit would find no place in the world beyond this world. No star fire would be raised by the Ancestors beside which the little one might encamp until it was called to be born again into the world. Death would devour such a spirit, and it would be as though the headman's wonderful child had never existed!

Hasu'u's breath snagged in her throat. Her mind was aflame with lurid images born of ancient tales told in snow-bound winter lodges: tales of the uncounted and uncountable ways in which mortals might be slain by the many mysterious manitous and Wíndigo, their cannibal winter chief; tales of Gaoh, malevolent Master of the Winds; tales of Katcheetohúskw, mountainous five-legged monster who spoke with the voice of thunder and stormed through the forest to crush and eat careless travelers while they slept; tales of the hideous Djeneta and Djigáha, grotesquely deformed giants and demented dwarfs who danced under the midwinter stars in the skins of flayed human captives while Mowea'qua, immortal wolf woman of the far north, howled to the winter moon as she prowled the vastness of the forest in eternal search of human prey.

Hasu'u's breath escaped in a ragged sigh. The winter tales were of blood and death and of horrors too terrible to think of. Yet, with ravens cawing in the woods, her nameless baby asleep against her back, and the stench of the rising wind in her nostrils, Hasu'u could not keep herself from thinking of anything else.

"Come!" Ne'gauni was extending a hand to her. "We must follow M'alsum and the others across the creek. Now!"

"Yes!" Hasu'u agreed and, starting to rise, eagerly raised a hand to his.

But Ne'gauni did not take her hand. Instead, staring wide-eyed and slack-jawed toward the trees, the youth took a backward step, and then another, and another. By the time he paused on the ice in the middle of the creek, all color had drained from his face.

Something hissed in the air over Hasu'u's shoulder. She ducked and, crouching low, caught a fleeting glimpse of what seemed to be a slender branch as long as her forearm and as straight as a well-made lance. It was headed for Ne'gauni. He saw it coming and moved to avoid it, but its speed was the speed of lightning. As the object flew past him, the youth dropped his spear and grabbed at his face. Hasu'u gasped. Blood was welling around the edges of his mittens. So much blood! And then there was another hiss.

Ne'gauni cried out. He spun around. With his back to the woman he clutched at his right shoulder, staggered forward, then swayed on his snow walkers a moment before falling with his arms and legs splayed wide.

Again Hasu'u gasped. A deep, dangerous crack of sound rent the air as the ice was stressed beyond bearing by the weight of Ne'gauni's heavily clad body and massively loaded backpack. She could see blood begin to spread in an ever-widening red pool beneath his downturned head just before the frozen surface of the creek shattered and broke wide. Water erupted to the surface. Dark, roaring as though triumphant in its unexpected release, it powered free of its winter confines and began to flow furiously downstream, taking fractured plates of ice and the bleeding body of the youth with it.

Hasu'u leaped to her feet. "Ne'gauni!" she called in a wail of desperation, as though by speaking the youth's name aloud she might somehow restore his life and, perhaps, safeguard her own and that of her child. But in that very moment something small and hard struck the side of her head.

Light and pain exploded behind Hasu'u's eyes. Her knees buckled. The world went black, and then, slowly, light returned. Bright. Hurtful. Stunned, she found herself on the snow again, on all fours, fighting for consciousness and clarity of vision. She won the battle. But she won it much too late. Great Ghost Cannibal was coming from the trees. And the manitous of the winter forest were already upon her.

▼▼▼▼

Blood.

And cold.

And the sound of water running tumultuously over and around him.

Of these three things only was Ne'gauni aware as he lay sprawled on his belly in the shallows, bleeding, shaking with cold, too numb and shocked to move, too weak to prevent himself from retching.

With his head turned sideways, the youth opened his mouth and heaved the contents of his belly into the fast-running creek. The violent contractions loosed an equally violent measure of pain. He would have screamed, but he knew that to scream was to die.

They were there.

Upstream.

On the snowy embankment upon which he had abandoned his eldest brother's Dawnland woman to face them alone, the manitous and their cannibal winter chief had come from the forest to surround Hasu'u and her baby.

Ne'gauni groaned in despair as he remembered whispering the names of the spirits. Hasu'u had forced him to speak them! Her stubborn refusal to move on had compelled him to speak them! No—he would not blame her. It was his fault. He should have grabbed her by the hair, yanked her to her feet, and prodded her on at spearpoint if necessary. But somehow he had been unable to raise a hand against her, and the forbidden words had flown from his mouth before he could think to call them back. He had not intended to summon the manitous any more than he had willed his snow walkers to carry him backward into full retreat. And he could not understand how Great Ghost

Cannibal had struck him down from so great a distance when neither the winter chief nor any of the manitous carried a spear or appeared to hurl anything larger or longer than twigs.

He felt sick. The chill race of the creek numbed his bewilderment but did nothing to lessen his shame as, lying with his face partially submerged, Ne'gauni found himself taking in with one eye a scene that filled him with anguish and horror.

The cannibal spirits of the winter forest circled Hasu'u. Furred and fanged, they stood upright in the way of men. But there was nothing human about them. Led by a winged phantom with the head of a raven, they leered down at the Dawnland woman out of bloodstained animal faces. Then, as one, they swarmed together and pulled her to her feet.

Hasu'u screamed.

Ne'gauni winced. Pain took control of every quadrant of his being. He cursed it and succeeded in willing it away only because he knew what his brothers would say of him if he allowed himself to abandon Hasu'u a second time. He would not have them name him Coward! If he truly was the bravest and best of the sons of Asticou, this was his chance to prove it. He must rise to the defense of his eldest brother's Dawnland woman before M'alsum, Sac, and M'ingwé came bursting through the trees with their weapons flying to drive the cannibal manitous back into the spirit world where they belonged. He must be the one to save Hasu'u and her nameless infant. *Now.*

The youth shivered. His newly placed resolve was intoxicating. Mixed with his need to banish shame, he found it a heady brew. Disowning caution along with fear, he levered up with both hands and found strength as well as gratification in the knowledge that, although he had lost his father's spear, he still possessed his nerve.

It was not enough.

The ice-ridden creek had done more than batter the youth when it swept him downstream; it had brought him hard against and almost completely beneath a fallen tree. In his attempt to rise, Ne'gauni found his body pressed to the stony bottom of the creek by the rough, rock-hard musculature of a massive limb. Pain made him aware of every cut and bruise as he tried to wedge himself forward. The weight of his saturated garments was appalling. His pack was hopelessly snagged. His snow walkers were snarled in submerged branches, and no matter how hard he tried, he could neither move nor feel the lower half of his left leg. And there was something embedded in his chest.

Something. But what? He caught his breath. Whatever the object was, he could feel it lying buried at an oblique angle just below his right shoulder. Slender as the extended forefinger of a child, hot and hard as a fire-seared lance, a small portion of it protruded from his breast. He reached for it in hope of pulling it from his body and, too late, found it to be the source of some of his worst pain. A burst of agony took him into oblivion.

The cries of an infant brought him back.

Dusk grayed the world to near darkness. The wind continued to gust relentlessly. Ne'gauni's temples throbbed. He could taste blood and bile in his mouth. Never in his life had he imagined that it was possible to feel so weak, to hurt so much, or to be so cold.

Snow was beginning to fall. Flakes the size and texture of river sand stung the surface of the creek and scudded hurtfully across his face. He lay inert as a stone, watching them whirl and dance on wind-tattered tides of thickening mist. Then, slowly, it occurred to him that, if night had not yet fallen, only a few moments could have passed since he first saw the manitous and their cannibal winter chief emerge from the forest.

Where was M'alsum?

Where were Sac and M'ingwé?

The unspoken questions sparked hope within Ne'gauni. His brothers must be near, he thought. They must have heard Hasu'u's scream. Why, then, had they not come to her rescue? And his?

A sudden epiphany struck the youth. He wanted no part of it, yet it would not be denied. His brothers were brave men. M'ingwé was stronger than most. Sac was clever and cautious and given to innovative thought. M'alsum possessed the assets of the other two and at least one more: He embraced danger as most men embraced a loving woman. He feared nothing. A terrible coldness filled Ne'gauni's heart. There was only one thing that would keep his brothers from coming from the forest, and that was if they could *not* come. If they, too, had been set upon by manitous. If, of the four sons of Asticou, only he, Ne'gauni, was left alive.

Hasu'u screamed again.

In a daze Ne'gauni saw the manitous tearing at the moose-hide straps that held the cradleboard to the Dawnland woman's back. He could hear her begging for the life of her child even as the infant, still bound to the cradleboard, was hurled into the creek.

"No!" screamed Hasu'u.

The youth's heart lurched when he saw the baby carrier, infant side down, hit the water with an explosive slap. The impact was brutal. He heard Hasu'u cry out for her nameless little son, but the interest of the manitous remained fixed on the woman while the cradleboard, still upside down, began to bob and turn wildly as it was swept downstream toward him.

Ne'gauni knew what he must do. The excruciatingly cold run of the creek was beginning to work to his advantage; within his thick, sodden garments his body was so numb that he found the plight of Hasu'u and her baby infinitely more painful than his own injuries. He strained to move, to extend an arm, to make a grab for the infant carrier.

It was no use. Even if he had been able to overcome weakness, the constraints of his snarled backpack and snow walkers prevented him from extricating himself from the tree. As he watched, despairing, the cradleboard smashed into an outcropping of jagged rocks, was held briefly captive amidst a fountaining upsurge of violent current, then, still upside down, was swept downstream past him without ever coming within reach of his outstretched hand.

Hasu'u wailed.

Ne'gauni saw the manitous continue to maul the woman. They were ripping open her traveling coat, tearing at the laces of her deerskin shirt. All the while Hasu'u fought them, sobbing, not for herself but for the tiny son she would never again hold to her breasts.

A sudden soul-searing blend of anger and righteous indignation took hold of Ne'gauni. He told himself that his feelings had nothing to do with affection for the Dawnland woman. He knew that Hasu'u held him in contempt. From their very first meeting, although impelled to impress her with his boldest commands and most arrogant posturing, nothing he had ever said or done had succeeded in winning more than a sneer from her.

Again his heart lurched. He was shaking. His thoughts

were in tumult. He did not understand why the approval of one female should mean so much to a youth who was favored by virtually all females. But somehow, from the very beginning, to Ne'gauni it had meant everything. And still did.

Now, as he continued to stare ahead, the youth knew that he was all that stood between Death and his eldest brother's woman. The manitous were baring Hasu'u's breasts, gesturing to Great Ghost Cannibal, inviting their winter chief to bend his raven's head and be first among them to feed upon her flesh.

A raven called.

This time it was Ne'gauni who answered. "Stop!" he commanded the manitous as imperiously as he had earlier commanded Hasu'u. "You will not eat my eldest brother's Dawnland woman! You will let her go! Now!"

Great Ghost Cannibal turned his raven's head and set small, fire-red eyes questing downstream.

Ne'gauni was found. He felt sick again. Until this moment, despite all that had occurred since the manitous had first come from the trees, the very nature of youth had prevented him from even considering the possibility of his own death. Now, as he met the fixed, raptorial stare of the winter chief of the manitous, he saw his mortality reflected in the eyes of the phantom and knew that he had made himself as vulnerable to Death as a snared mouse that has been foolish enough to call itself to the attention of a hungry eagle.

All the phantoms were staring at him now.

The youth swallowed hard and willed himself to stare back. Bluff and bluster were his only weapons now.

Hasu'u moaned.

Great Ghost Cannibal, apparently seeing neither a

threat nor the potential of a meal in the sodden form that
had called to him from downstream, hefted the Dawnland
woman into furred arms, turned, and began to walk away.
At his side a bear-faced specter took hold of Hasu'u's snow
walkers, jerked them from the snow, slung them over
maned shoulders, then, with a nod to the other manitous,
followed the winter chief.

"Wait!" Ne'gauni called. Water rushed into his mouth.
A paroxysm of coughing roused a level of pain that, only
moments ago, would have been unendurable. The youth
barely felt it. Even as he fought for breath, he saw that
Hasu'u was no longer fighting her captors. Ensnared within
the grasp of Great Ghost Cannibal, her arms hung limp.
Her head had fallen back. Her moccasined feet dangled
like those of a carelessly held buckskin doll. She was dead.
He was certain of it. And now the winter chief of the
manitous was entering the gloom of the forest, within
which he would devour her.

"No!" cried Ne'gauni. "I am the one who spoke your
name! I am the one upon whom you should be feeding!
Come back! Come back for *me!*"

Great Ghost Cannibal paused and looked back. His followers stopped, listened as he spoke to them, then turned
as he turned and, striding out on either side of him, continued on their way into the trees.

A sob of anguish choked Ne'gauni. Night was falling
quickly now, conspiring with wind-driven mist and snow
to shroud the spirits as they moved ever deeper into the
forest. His heart was pounding—breaking, he thought—as
he summoned the last of his strength to rage at the vanishing specters. "I will follow you! I will come for my eldest
brother's Dawnland woman! I will not allow you to dishonor her spirit! I will find and gather her bones! I will

make lances of them! And then I will hunt you in this world or the world beyond! In the name of Hasu'u, this son of Asticou will make you regret what you have done this day!"

The threat must have reached them.

The youth waited for a reaction.

Great Ghost Cannibal and the manitous gave him none. With snow, wind, mist, and gathering nightfall as their allies, they had disappeared into the forest.

Ne'gauni sagged into the creek. The sheer force of his bravado had exhausted him. He knew that he was not going after them; the tree held him captive. His threats had been as empty and without substance as the wind.

Again a raven called, and again another answered.

The youth turned his face sideways, listening, breathing only because it was easier to breathe than to drown. He was beyond words now, beyond pain, beyond even the most lingering shred of hope for himself or the Dawnland woman. Hasu'u was dead. His brothers, their burden woman, Kicháwan, and perhaps even the dogs were slain. M'alsum's newborn child was drowned. And he was the one who had summoned the phantoms to kill them all.

Ne'gauni closed his eyes. He reminded himself that his summoning had not been intentional, but the reminder gave no solace. There was no excuse for the carelessness of his tongue, no reprieve from the consequences of his words, no forgiveness for the failure of his actions. The winter forest was alive with spirits. Cannibal spirits. All men knew this. He was only a youth, but he should have remembered. The ancient warnings and protocol had been inscribed into his brain as deeply as pictographs incised into stone during long winter nights when his people gathered within the warm, smoky lodge of Asticou to listen to the old chief recount the time-honored tales of the Ancestors: tales of First Man and First Woman; tales of epic wanderings across a savage sea of ice from which giants rose to feed upon the unwary among the sons and daughters of the Ancient Ones; tales of sacred stones and falling stars, of drowned lands and mountains that walked; tales of the tusked children of Katcheetohúskw, mammoth five-legged beasts that lived in the world no more; tales of great hunters and evil enchanters; wise and wondrous tales in which Ne'gauni had always seen himself as Hero.

"No more . . ." he sighed.

Somewhere all too near, a wolf howled, and even before he batted open his eyes, Ne'gauni felt the presence of the beast.

He looked up. It was there, crouching low, barely visible within a maze of tangled branches at the edge of the embankment closest to him. Yet he saw it clearly enough to know that it was no wolf. It was manitou. An amorphous thing of fur and fang, Mowea'qua, wild wolf woman of the northern forest, had, in her eternal search for human prey, found him.

He stared at the manitou.

The phantom stared back.

Then, in a sudden swirl of wind, snow eddied all around, and when it cleared, the specter was gone. Ne'gauni wondered if the phantom had been real or only a figment of his imagination. Strangely enough, he did not care. What was one more cannibal to him now? Closing his eyes, he felt his spirit waning within its all-too-vulnerable sheath of flesh and bones and sodden clothing. He knew that he was dying. He did not mind. Because of him, Death walked the winter world in the guise of Raven, slaying and consuming all he loved. He did not want to live in such a world. Indeed, he did not deserve to live in it! If the forces of Creation saw fit to end his days in the slavering jaws of a manitou, so be it; he would do his best to die well and without complaint.

A sigh went out of the youth. As he willingly yielded consciousness to the bitterly cold creek, he was grateful that his life was ending now, far from the distant village of Asticou, the beloved father who had so wrongly believed him to be the best and bravest and most worthy of his sons.

▼▼▼▼

"Listen, my brothers!" Sac's imperative whisper was a barely contained shriek. "Wolves!"

"I heard only one." M'ingwé kept his voice low as he hunkered close to the sled within the cover of the trees with his brothers, their hastily muzzled dogs, and Kicháwan, their burden woman. "But it could be the leader of a winter pack," he conceded.

"Yes!" Sac's voice was still a whisper, but it was sliding high, threatening to be broken by rising panic. "But what if it is no wolf at all? What if it is that which is spoken of in the winter tales . . . the half-human thing that howls in the dark and is drawn by the smell of blood to feed upon human flesh? It will feast upon our drowned brother! And then it will come for us!"

"Enough!" M'alsum's command issued as a snarl so deep and threatening that it withered his listeners on the spot. "Your quick mind and loose tongue outrun your wisdom, Sac! Would you summon the horror of which you speak? Or call back from the forest the even greater horrors that nearly served us all Death this day?"

Sac was instantly contrite. "No, Brother. No. Never."

M'ingwé's wide, sullen features were, like the faces of

his brothers, lost to view within the shadowed recesses of a projecting, fur-ruffed hood. Yet, when he spoke, his voice revealed his scowl. "I do not like the feel of this. If the wolf we heard is only a wolf, and if it is the leader of a winter pack, then there may be many wolves. Winter has been long. Too long. Snow lies deep. Too deep. Hunting may not have been good for their kind. Listen . . . another wolf answers the first. If they think us vulnerable, they—"

"Where men have easily found meat, no self-respecting wolf will starve," M'alsum interrupted on an exhalation of barely contained impatience.

"Still," insisted Sac, "wolves could prove trouble to us, M'alsum."

"No more trouble than we have just seen!" The headman's statement left the back of his throat as a growl that was somehow deeper, darker, and more dangerous than the growl of any wolf. "We have waited long enough. Come. We will cower within the cover of these trees like frightened women no more! I want to retrieve what we can of the trading goods in Ne'gauni's pack. And if I can find it, I want our father's copper-headed spear."

"Why?" asked M'ingwé. "Any of our stone-headed spears are just as good, maybe better, and those lustrous gray spearheads you brought as gifts from the north are the most beautiful I have ever seen."

"Stone is the old way!" M'alsum was adamant. "It does not gleam like copper when it is polished, and copper—"

"Breaks if it is hardened too fast after melting, and sometimes bends because it is too soft to penetrate the bones of a big kill," M'ingwé interrupted.

"Ask me and I say it is fit only to be pounded into trinkets for women," added Sac. 'There was good reason our father never used that spear save to catch the light of the rising and setting sun during ceremonies. Leave it, M'alsum. We have no time for—"

"It was his and I will have it!" The headman rose, a tall man, winter lean, tense and powerful as a stag set to break from cover. "The wind no longer carries the stink of those who have made an end of my Dawnland woman and son. They have gone their way back into the depths of the forest on the far side of the creek. If the legends of the Ancestors are true, they will feast now. I do not think they will return to trouble us, at least not for a while. So come. Follow me. Quickly and quietly. Or would you shame yourselves by making me go alone?"

Both Sac and M'ingwé grumbled, but neither man made the slightest move to oblige their eldest brother.

"Then stay with the dogs and burden woman," slurred M'alsum, "but know that whatever I manage to retrieve from Little Brother's pack will be mine to trade when we reach the Dawnland. I will not share it with those who are afraid to help me reclaim it!"

Sac and M'ingwé exchanged troubled glances. Each knew that the other was afraid. And each knew that the other was greedy. They got to their feet.

"You will remain where you are, Kicháwan," the headman told the burden woman as she started to rise. "Stay hidden within the trees, and see to it that you keep the dogs muzzled and tethered close to the sled."

"But . . . but after what we have just seen . . . after what has just befallen us . . . I am afraid to be alone in this forest!"

The headman was not moved to pity. "You will guard the dogs. If wolves come, you have your sling and braining club. You know how to use them. We will not be far, or long away."

"It is not only wolves I fear in this country of woman-eating spirits!" Kicháwan snapped to her feet and hugged herself like a frightened child. She was a big woman and, although well past youth, as strong as a bison. Her head went high. The admission of fear had not come easily. It was because of her strength of will and body that she had been chosen to accompany the trading band in place of the wives of Sac and M'ingwé, who, each with sucklings and toddlers to care for, had remained behind. She took great pride in the knowledge that the sons of Asticou had paid her husband generously in meat and hides for the use of his strong, barren, eldest wife. Each day upon the trail it had been her responsibility to attend to the headman's woman and see to the needs of the traders. She had been honored to serve as midwife at the birth of the headman's son and, later, to heft the new mother's belongings along with her own, although she already carried on her back whatever else could not be heaped onto the sled. Only young Ne'gauni carried a pack as heavy as Kicháwan's, not out of any gallant wish to lighten a burden woman's load but to prove his strength and endurance to the brothers who goaded him to his face, mocked him behind his back, and wisely kept their own loads light so that they would be free to see to the dogs, spear game, and protect the band if need arose.

Her face convulsed in an effort to control her emotions. Never again would the cocky youth trudge on under his load or pretend not to be fatigued at day's end while she gathered wood, made fire, prepared food, and saw to the many other evening tasks. And never again would pretty little Hasu'u settle into her bed furs to suckle her infant and sing happy songs of the Dawnland while Kicháwan massaged the tired muscles of the three eldest sons of Asticou before spreading herself for their sexual release while young Ne'gauni was made to stand aside and wait his turn.

The burden woman choked back a sob. Shivers ran up and down her wide, muscular back as she looked at the three surviving members of the little trading band preparing to go their way without her. Overwhelmed by recollections of the violence that she and the brothers had just witnessed from the cover of the trees, she could not bear the thought of being left alone.

"You will not leave me!" The statement burst boldly from Kicháwan's mouth. She was shocked by her own temerity. Not once upon the long, arduous trek northward through the cold vastness of the great forest had she protested the brothers' unrelenting demands or so much as hinted of her newfound delight in her big, strong body, for—although from the first day upon the trail she had been confident of her ability to look after the headman's woman and satisfy the needs of the sons of Asticou—she had not suspected until midway through the last moon that she was capable of being impregnated by any man. Now, certain that life was quickening in her belly for the first time, the aging burden woman could not bring herself to obey a command that might put the life of her unborn child at risk.

"I carry new life inside me!" Kicháwan proudly informed the sons of Asticou. Drawing courage from her certainty that the announcement must surely elevate her status and win their consideration and respect, she looked at the headman and allowed her emotions to overrun what little wisdom was innate to her nature. "I will not be left behind with the dogs in this dark forest where storm spirits gather and Raven is chief! I will not allow you to turn your back on me as you turned your back on Hasu'u. Sac warned you as we crossed the creek that he thought the dogs were scenting something. But M'alsum would not listen. M'alsum would continue on. And when the great roaring came through the forest, M'alsum would not go back for his woman or brother or son! Perhaps M'alsum was afraid to go back? Perhaps M'alsum was afraid to—"

A snarl tore the darkness as the headman silenced the burden woman with a furious backhanded strike that sent her sprawling. "I do not run from my fears! I face them! I destroy them!" The declaration was no louder than the hissing exhalation of a riled lynx as he moved to kick the downed woman again and again against the side of her head with the forward curve of his snow walker.

Kicháwan was making short, garbled gasps of pain as she clambered desperately to her knees, made a protective ball of her body, and, sobbing, covered her head with mittened hands.

"You will not again speak of the dead or presume to offer opinions to me, Burden Woman," warned M'alsum. He stood motionless now. Not once did he raise his voice as he spoke on, slowly, with venomous inflection. "Neither I nor my brothers care if you carry life in your belly. It is nothing to us if not an inconvenience. *You* are nothing to us. If you want to be fed and allowed a place at our fire, Kicháwan, remember that you are a burden woman, not a wife. You will stay and guard the dogs. It is where you belong, with the pack-and-pull animals that serve this band!" His anger sated, he turned and headed for the creek without another word to his brothers.

Once again M'ingwé and Sac exchanged troubled glances, but neither man spoke. Each avoided looking at Kicháwan as, leaving her in a whimpering, snuffling heap, they set their snow walkers in M'alsum's tracks and followed him into the rapidly congealing night.

The wind was down. Snow was falling heavily, silently, in large flakes that fell straight to the earth, blanketing the hard, rough, irregular surface of the late-winter snowpack, granting better footing to the travelers, lessening the danger of slipping, and improving the effectiveness of the small fur tassels on the outer frames of each man's snow walkers, attached for the purpose of muffling the sound of a hunter moving across the feeding grounds of potential prey. The brothers kept steadily on, grateful for the silence, knowing all too well that in this haunted forest they might yet become meat for the manitous.

The howling of wolves affirmed their fears. When the voice of a great horned owl came through the high canopy of the trees, both Sac and M'ingwé broke stride, albeit only for a moment. In the legends of the People, Owl announced the coming of Death, but they had seen Death come and go this day and, remembering that five long winter moons had passed since the last geese had flown south, knew that Owl would be nesting now. Under the insulating down of its broad wings, Owl would be warming half-grown fledglings against the cold of yet another snowstorm. Perhaps Owl was not speaking of Death at all but was only telling its hatchlings of all the soft, careless, sweet-fleshed young rabbits and rodents they would learn to hunt come spring.

The brothers hurried on. Using the sinew-webbed, hooped ends of their pointed snow prods for additional balance, they soon put the sheltering cover of the evergreens behind them and plodded back toward the creek through broken stands of bare birches. They could hear the race of open water and smell the sharp, bitter scents of wet

ice and rimed rock before they reached the clearing. Here
they stopped and scanned ahead to see M'alsum at the
creek's edge. He had found and retrieved their father's copper-headed spear and was moving downstream with the
weapon in one hand.

Neither man spoke as they followed their eldest brother
to where their youngest brother lay prostrate on his belly in
the shallows, his corpse help captive by the broad span of
an ancient fallen birch.

"Hurry," M'alsum urged, still holding his voice low. After removing his snow walkers and setting the spear upright
in the snow beside his snow prods, he clambered onto the
tree to crouch midstream, directly above Ne'gauni's body.
"His pack frame is snagged, but together we should be able
to free the carrying bags that hold the makuks. Hurry, I
say! Before water seeps through the seams and the sap
within is melted and washed away! I tell you, my brothers,
when you reach the Dawnland, you will see that the people
there will trade anything we desire of them in exchange for
sweet sap. Even though what we carry is the result of last
spring's sugaring, I want us to be the first traders to bring
sweet sap to the coast this year. The more we have of it the
better. So come! Take off your snow walkers! Help me!
Now!"

They did not refuse him, but while Sac balanced on the
same broad branch as M'alsum, M'ingwé positioned himself
on another limb and proceeded to help not his brothers,
but himself.

"What are you doing, Brother?" asked the headman.
"Leave Ne'gauni's snow walkers! They are damaged and of
no use to us!"

"I will salvage them. Never have I seen a finer pair! His
mother's hands worked magic in the things she made for

him and our father. Why should we not take at least some small share of the magic that was his? We could use a touch of it after all we have borne witness to this day!"

"It is forbidden to take the belongings of the dead!" Sac reminded him. "The trading goods in our brother's pack were meant to be shared equally by all, but our brother may need his snow walkers in the country of the dead."

"Why should we care for his needs in the world beyond this world? He never cared for ours in this one!" replied M'ingwé. "Besides, from what I can feel of it, his left leg is badly broken. He Walks Ahead will walk no more on that limb, ahead of us or behind us . . . in this world or any other. And if you can free his pack frame along with his carrying bags, we should take that, too, for it was made for him by Asticou of antlers cut from a stag that we sighted and brought down on our hunt together into the—"

"Always the best for the only son of our father's Lakeland Firefly!" M'alsum was snarling again, his voice low, tight, barely discernible above the sound of the creek. With the edge of the stone dagger that he had just drawn from a rawhide sheath at his side, he worked to slice through the thongs that bound the carrying sacks to Ne'gauni's pack frame. "And always the best for Wawautaésie!" He sawed through one thong, then turned his attention to another, muttering in a fever of resentment. "Even in lean times the Lakeland Firefly and her son were given much while we and our Grassland mother were given little!"

M'ingwé grumbled in affirmation. "And all so that Lakeland traders passing through our hunting grounds would see the honor in which a daughter and grandson of their clan were held and be generous when it came to trading their copper trinkets."

"A day will come when we will give our father cause to regret his ways," assured M'alsum. "So go ahead, M'ingwé, take Little Brother's snow walkers if you would have them. And yes, we will take his pack frame, too, if we can free it. It should have been for one of us, not for him!"

M'ingwé did not hesitate to act on the permission he had just been given to rob the dead, but a moment later he drew back with a startled exclamation. "Ah yah! Can it be? He breathes!"

Still again M'alsum snarled. He replaced his dagger in its sheath as he moved to confirm M'ingwé's revelation. "It is so. He lives . . . but not for long." There was a bite to the headman's statements; they cut the snowy night with the darkness of his intent and made it bleed an aura of foreboding even before he reached to press his youngest brother's face beneath the surface of the creek.

"M'alsum, what are you doing, my brother?" Greased by apprehension, Sac's voice was sliding high again.

"What I have longed to do since the day this one was born!" responded the headman.

"M'alsum, a man cannot take the life of a brother!"

A sound went out of the headman, neither a growl nor a fully articulated curse but something in between. "Have you forgotten our plan for him, Sac? Did we not secretly counsel together and agree among ourselves to barter him into slavery in exchange for whatever most pleased us when we reached the coast? It would have been worse than death for him. And better for us to see him shamed . . . degraded."

Sac was shaking his head. "But, M'alsum, to actually kill a brother with your own hand . . ."

"He was whelped more than a full moon early from between the thighs of our father's Lakeland bitch,"

M'alsum reminded him, his tone malevolent. "Who is to say that Little Brother is a true brother?"

"He carries the look of Asticou, and more than a little of you when you were his age," Sac offered without hesitation. "And if the blood of our father flows in his veins, then that blood is our blood. To have bartered him in exchange for goods, that would have been just retribution. No blood spilled. No killing done. But who can say if the forces of Creation will look kindly on a man who drowns a brother, or on those who stand by and watch?"

"Better to leave him as we found him—alive—to be meat for wolves or for whatever else hunts and howls in this forest," M'ingwé agreed.

"Better to take him from the creek," Sac disagreed. "Better to at least try to save him now that we know he still breathes!"

A spasm of loathing shook the headman. "My Dawnland woman is now meat in the jaws of the manitous! My son is drowned! Ne'gauni failed to protect them. It is right for me to kill him with my own hand!"

"No!" Sac's voice lacked all its earlier trepidation. It was strong now, direct, unflinching. And angry. "Let him breathe! He is only an untested youth. And of the four of us, only he displayed concern and courage enough to stay at your woman's side when she fell behind. Kicháwan was right. We should have gone back for them, or at least slowed our steps long enough to shout a warning to hurry on. We might have been able to drive off the—"

"It was too late!" M'alsum was adamant. "Too dangerous. Once they came from the trees, there was nothing to do but keep hidden and hold our ground for the good of the band!"

"We could have loosed the dogs on them," said M'ingwé.

"The dogs are valuable," replied M'alsum. "Why would I risk the pack unduly?"

It was Sac who answered. "For a brother . . . a woman . . . a son."

"I will make other sons! I will take other women! Do you imagine that I have not made new life on willing females in the villages and hunting camps in which I have wintered during the many long moons that I have been away from the hunting grounds of Asticou? Must I explain to you as I was forced to explain to our mother why a trader must secure alliances by setting his seed among many tribes? What better way to assure welcome and trust? And so why would I risk our lives for the sake of one woman? You are my brothers. We were outnumbered. We saw Ne'gauni abandon Hasu'u and my son. We saw him drop our father's spear. And now look at him. Most Favored Son of Asticou! His arrogance has brought him to lie where he is, bled out like a gutted deer with his spirit wandering away from us toward the world beyond this world, where—"

"Then let him go his way," interrupted Sac. "He needs no help from you. Let him breathe his last breath on his own, Brother. Do not give him cause to turn the forces of Creation against you as surely as he and his mother turned our father's affections against us!"

M'alsum did not like what he heard but, finding reason in it, took hold of Ne'gauni's hair and jerked the youth's head from the creek so savagely that, had he chosen to apply his strength to a sideward twist, he could easily have broken his neck. "Be it so, then. Breathe, Little Brother! I give you back your life so that you may live long enough to die with no help from me!"

Ne'gauni did not breathe.

M'alsum shook him viciously, until a sudden paroxysm of coughing had the youth gasping for air. The headman released Ne'gauni's hair with such a violent downward shove that the youth collapsed, retching and moaning in delirium. M'alsum slipped the rawhide packs from the sundered thongs that had held them to the backpack and, trembling against a storm of frustration, watched his brothers bending over Ne'gauni, working in unison to free the coveted snow walkers and pack frame.

"His face . . . did you see his face?" Sac's hood had fallen back. His long, foxlike features were contorted with revulsion as, rising, he leaped from the tree to the embankment with Ne'gauni's pack frame dripping in his hands.

"Even in snow and darkness I saw the wound," M'ingwé acknowledged. "It looks as though a spearhead sliced him from the top of one ear to the lobe of the other, but how could that be? We saw no spears in the hands of the—"

A shivering flash of lightning interrupted the man's words, illuminating the clouds above the brothers' heads and momentarily turning the night a bilious yellow.

"Enough talk!" M'alsum rumbled with the thunder as he moved to join Sac on the embankment. "We have what we want. The storm grows worse. We must find a safe place to take shelter. If the storm spirits allow, tomorrow we will travel on before dawn. The coast is not far. Two days, perhaps three. No more than that. If we can keep hard on the trail and the days continue to remain cold, we will see the Dawnland before the ice breaks wide on the big rivers. The winter hunting camp of Hasu'u's band will be the first we come to. And we still have pelts and dogs and, if the contents of these carrying bags are still dry, much sweet sap to trade!"

M'ingwé, Ne'gauni's snow walkers in hand, vaulted from the tree to stand beside his brothers. "And if Kicháwan is carrying life, we will be able to trade her for far more than we ever thought we could get for such a homely, sag-teated old bitch!"

"If M'alsum does not kick her to death first." Sac was shaking his head as he slung Ne'gauni's antler frame over one shoulder. "And how can we continue on to the coast without the Dawnland woman? What will Hasu'u's people say if it is discovered that we allowed a daughter of their hunt chief to be carried off and eaten by—"

"We share a common enemy now! A common grief!" M'alsum slipped his moccasined feet into the thong harnessing of his snow walkers and adjusted the lacings. "They will mourn Hasu'u's death. And we will make a great show of mourning with them. When we have mourned enough to satisfy them, we will trade our sweet sap and copper and pelts and healing leaves and whatever else they may want of us in exchange for her father's other daughters. There are many. You will see. It will be as I have promised. Life is good in the Dawnland. It is easy. Soon we will be living as chiefs in a land of weak men and many fat women."

"If we ever reach the Dawnland," Sac mumbled sourly.

M'alsum reached for his newly acquired spear. "Your complaints grow tedious, Brother. Big game is scarce in the dark forests of our grandfathers. Deer and caribou find little browse, and moose rarely come to the summoning horn of Asticou. Our father grows old. He inspires our people to a complacency that makes them content to feed on whatever 'little' meat can be taken in nets and snares and with birding slings and braining sticks, while our mother sickens and grows so weak that she could not journey north with us as I had hoped."

Sac shrugged. "Her days are nearly finished."

M'alsum's hand visibly tightened on the spear shaft. "Go back into the dark forest of our ancestors, Sac, if you are no longer content to walk with me! But M'ingwé and I will continue on to the Dawnland!"

"Where caribou still swarm like blackflies at the river crossings and big meat crawls up out of the Great Salt Water and calls out to hunters, 'Will you not take me to be food for you?'" There was a smile of anticipation on M'ingwé's face as he tightened the knots on his own snow walkers.

"It is so!" affirmed M'alsum. "We will take this meat. We will grow strong upon it. And the next time I return to the country of our ancestors, I will come to our father's village as a hunt chief with the wealth of the Dawnland in meat and hides and tusks cut from the fish-finned dogs and legless barking moose of the Dawnland sea. On that day we will take Asticou's lodge as our own. On that day we will make our father another lodge, one cut from the skin and bones of his Lakeland woman. On that day our mother, Meya'kwé, will live in honor once more. She will be strong again, proud again, as I have sworn it would one day be for her. And all will see the wisdom of M'alsum, her firstborn son, as I inspire them to leave the dark forest forever and take the hunting grounds of the Dawnland people as their own. So walk with your brothers, Sac, or journey back into the country of our ancestors alone. The choice is yours. But do not challenge me again. The storm spirits descend. I will linger in this place of death no more."

Chapter Two

▼▼▼▼▼▼▼

Death was a river.

Ne'gauni yielded to its flow. Cold, black, whispering, it took him deep. Adrift within an internal darkness as thick and viscous as the fluid that fills the center of an eye, the youth did not fight the deadly current of his fate. There was no need. In the realm of the manitous, Death was the only reality; this was where he belonged.

He did not see the two furred forms emerge from the forest. They came slowly through storm and darkness. Tentatively. Hunkering low. One cautious step at a time, they moved in tandem from the cover of the trees, advancing toward the creek as silently as falling snow. When they reached it, one paused and stood its ground on the embankment while the other leaped forward as sinuously and effortlessly as the wind. Springing onto the fallen tree, it advanced on all fours until, crouching over Ne'gauni's prone form, it stared down for a moment, then raised its head and uttered a thin, tremulous howl.

Consciousness rippled within the youth. His body gave no outward sign of life, but deep within the cortex of his brain the images of wolves took shape and, with them, a fleeting recollection of his brothers bending close, murmuring together, pulling at him, hurting him. The images faded along with the howling of the wolf. Other sounds drifted through his mind.

The low gurgling of the creek.

The lonely ululation of an owl.

The occasional rumble of thunder.

The pounding of a distant drum.

Ne'gauni listened. Gradually, awareness dawned. He fixed his mind on the sounds. The creek no longer seemed to be racing. The call of the owl came from far away. And the slow, hard, arrhythmic pounding of the drum was not coming from any external source; it was emanating from his heart.

Still beating? The premise seemed beyond consideration. Like an eel hopelessly undulating across the bottom of a freezing pond that has blocked migration to warmer waters, it moved through the turbid channels of Ne'gauni's dying mind, taking his thoughts ever deeper into the river of death until, at last, sound ebbed and the drumbeat stopped.

"Come! It is safe for us to take him now! The Strangers have all awayed! Good it is that you have come from the den. Until you answered, sure was I not that you my howls had heard!"

The voice, although soft, was sharply insistent. It cut through the waters of the river of death. Once again consciousness rippled within the youth.

Above Ne'gauni, on the fallen tree, another furred form now crouched beside the first, and then, suddenly, both were in the creek, one on each side of him.

"Mmm. Dead he is."

"No!"

"Soon so. And better for him."

"No!"

The voices swam down to Ne'gauni through an interior darkness. Female voices. One as light and ephemeral as the first breath of dawn, yet so earnest in its denial of the other that it was almost a sob. The other as heavy as the occasional roll of thunder, as cold as the creek, as ominous as the river of death.

"Come away, say I. Leave him now to be meat for Raven. Cold am I. Two packs of Strangers our forest roam this night. They may still close by be. And I have the voice of the Great One heard. Safe it is not for our kind to linger here. Leave this wounded one. Go now must we to shelter from snow and storm before we are seen."

"From water we must take him!"

"Why? We have meat enough to carry. This creek has swept him to a mating with this fallen tree. Beneath water my hands now feel this: Below his knee, bone is broken, and tendon, flesh, muscle, and skin all are cruelly torn. The limbs of this tree hold tight to this ruined leg that branches from the heart side of his body. One way only is there to break the coupling. And why, say I? By Strangers he was struck down, and by his own kind left to die. Come. Leave this dying one to walk on two strong legs into the country of the manitous."

The words—so unusually ordered and with every nuance and inflection at variance with the dialect of his own tribe—roused a subtle, undefined warning in some small, still sentient portion of Ne'gauni's mind. Country of the manitous? Was he not already "walking" there? Or was there still a choice for him? To live, to die: The distinction had been important to him once. No more.

The river of death ran on.

And then another voice spoke out of the darkness.

"You are not yet a chief in this part of the forest, Little Brother! Why do you linger in the country of the dead? Are you not man enough to stand guardian over me?"

"Hasu'u?" Did he cry the name of his brother's Dawnland woman? He was not sure. Logic told him that the dead could not speak. It also told him that the dead could feel no pain, but his face hurt and his body ached, and clearly he heard Hasu'u speak again.

"Why do you call to me in the country of the manitous, Little Brother? I am still a hunt chief's daughter and a headman's woman! I do not stop and sing where it does not please me to stop and sing! I do not rise and walk where it does not please me to rise and walk! And I will not swim in the river of death when the river of life is yet sweet and warm and welcoming! Surely M'alsum, Sac, and M'ingwé have found it so!"

Ne'gauni did not understand. The words made no sense to him. But as a vision of Hasu'u took form inside his mind, the drum within his chest began to beat again. She was not pale with fright or dressed in the cumbersome winter furs in which he had seen her meet her death. She appeared to him as she had been on that late summer day when M'alsum, in the company of a small band of traders, had returned from the Dawnland proudly leading his bride into their father's village for the first time.

Ne'gauni sobbed with longing for what he knew could never be again. Had there ever been a more beautiful day? Clear and hot and midway into the season when blueberries and craneberries were ripening in the marsh and the forest was festooned with flame-colored butterflies the size of hummingbirds—surely he would never again see its equal. And had there ever been a more extraordinary bride? Again he sobbed as, within his mind's eye, he saw his eldest brother's Dawnland woman begin to move toward him with one of the butterflies perched atop her head, fanning her brow as though it recognized her loveliness and chose to do her homage.

"Hasu'u!" Again he called her name, transfixed, not by the fragile beauty of the living adornment but by the radiant comeliness of the young woman who wore it.

Bare-breasted, with her nipples oiled and glinting in the sunlight like two unblinking brown eyes set amidst a circling of bold black tattooing, she was dressed in the summer style of a Dawnland woman. With the exception of the far-wandering M'alsum, no one in Asticou's small forest band had ever seen anything remotely like her. A knee-length skirt made entirely of black and white feathers parted with every bend of her knees to reveal the greased brownness of her flanks and belly. The small oval of her face was painted in vertical lines of white ash and red ochre. An intricately carved swan-bone drinking tube hung from a braided thong looped around her bare waist. Orange strands of the artfully arranged dried feet and beaks of some sort of rare birds adorned her neck and wrists. Her hair was twisted into two shining dark knots and fastened with combs of polished bone above each diminutive, shell-festooned ear. And a single bright bead of copper decorated the quill needle case that was inserted through the septum of her small, shapely nose.

"Ahh!" Ne'gauni exclaimed in an agony of remorse for having caused the death of such beauty. Once again he called to Hasu'u out of his delirium. "I would have given my life in exchange for yours! I would have saved your baby! If only the ice spirits had not opened wide beneath my feet! If only the water spirits had not taken me and prevented me from returning to your side! I would have fought the manitous! I would have been as brave and bold as the best of the sons of Asticou! I would! I know I would! For you, Hasu'u, I would dare anything!"

"Brave again you must be," said the vision.

Ne'gauni's heart leaped with joy. The Dawnland woman was doing something she had never done before. She was smiling at him! It was a sad, infinitely tender smile, and somehow he sensed regret in its tremulous curve, but it was a smile all the same, and it was just for him! Blood surged once more within his veins. The light of full consciousness flared brightly in his skull. He managed to raise his head. Suddenly the vision of Hasu'u blurred into another vision entirely.

Another face loomed before Ne'gauni.

He stared at it.

The face stared back.

A shivering screen of falling snow was all that stood between the youth and the apparition. Ne'gauni smelled the warm animal smell of its breath and body. And although its features were barely visible through falling snow and darkness, he saw enough of fur and fang to recognize the face.

"You have come back for me," he said to Mowea'qua, wolf woman of the northern forest. He knew that she was to be the deliverer of his death.

"Leave you could I not," she confirmed. "Soon now over for you will it be. Young you are, but strong enough to endure you must be."

Too long had Ne'gauni lain in the frigid waters of the creek. Too severely wounded was he to further resist or question his fate. It seemed to him now that he must have died and returned from the world beyond this world at least twice since Great Ghost Cannibal, winter chief of the manitous, had come from the forest. Now, once again, the black river of death awaited him. He was no longer afraid to swim in its depths. Indeed, as he looked into the long, pale eyes of Mowea'qua, he told himself that he should have known that the forces of Creation would not find him deserving of a gentle death after all that he had brought upon his brothers' trading band. "I will be strong enough to endure," he vowed to the manitou, and to himself.

"We will see," another voice said doubtfully—deep, unemotional.

Suddenly Ne'gauni was aware of the weight of something on his back. Whatever it was, it seemed to be kneeling on him, swaying and grunting to itself, working at some task of its own, pressing him hard. Now, for the first time since the ice had cracked wide and fed him to the creek, the youth felt distinct sensation in his lower left leg. It was a thin, superficial prickling in the skin, a dull, steady scraping, a slow, sure, downward pressure against bone. Pain? No. It was not quite pain. Not yet.

The weight on his back shifted, seemed to be centering itself, readjusting to some new purpose.

Ne'gauni attempted to turn his head to see just what it was, but he was too weak to do more than lay the side of his face back down into the shallows.

"Forgive?" asked Mowea'qua.

It seemed an odd request for a predator to ask of its prey. The youth had no chance to think about it. In an explosion of agony more excruciating than anything he had yet experienced, he heard as well as felt a horrendous, sickening crack. Fire burst from his left leg to sear every nerve ending in his body. His heart lurched in a wild, shivering leap, and for an instant he felt himself poised over some great, dark abyss. Then someone screamed. And as Ne'gauni plummeted once more into the black depths of the river of death, he did not recognize the high, frenzied shriek as his own.

▼▼▼▼

Sac froze in his tracks. "Did you hear that?"

Neither M'alsum nor M'ingwé offered a reply as they hurried back through the forest toward the place where they had left Kicháwan with the dogs and sled.

Sac remained where he was. He needed to rest for a moment. Just for a moment. And he needed to think. "We should have reached the sled by now," he muttered to himself, as was his habit when alone. "But M'alsum is in such a hurry to put distance between himself and the creek in which he has left a brother to die alone that he has taken a wrong turn through the birches. Not that he would admit to a mistake. No! Not even to one as obvious as this!"

He exhaled a harsh, ragged huff that was meant to lessen his intensifying uneasiness. The effort was in vain. If anything, Sac's feelings of disquiet grew worse. At the rising of this morning's sun he would have stood proudly before any man of any band or clan or tribe and sworn without hesitation that his eldest brother was incapable of making even the least error in judgment. Now, standing alone in snow and darkness, Sac knew that he would have been wrong. M'alsum was no longer infallible in his eyes. The knowledge seemed a betrayal somehow. It added to the weight of his worry and fatigue.

M'alsum was Firstborn! M'alsum was Eldest Son! M'alsum was Oldest Brother! And, although Sac and M'ingwé had never openly conceded between themselves that he was easily the best of the sons of Asticou, they had instinctively known and accepted the truth of this even though their father had seen to it that no one else had. How could it have been otherwise for them? M'alsum had gone out of his way to make himself the center of their lives in a world in which, since the birth of Ne'gauni, son of Wawautaésie, Asticou cared little about his sons by Meya'kwé. M'alsum had been both brother and father to them. He had given shade to the summer sun and warmth to the winter moon. When, at sixteen, he had stood before the band, unflinching throughout his Ordeal, enduring in stoic silence the pain and deprivation of ritual fasting and scarification, he had set an example by which they had thereafter ordered their days. And when he left the village without them, vanishing one night and making good his threat to take up with a band of northward-bound traders, something bright and elemental in their existence had faded. They had their women and children to comfort them, but without M'alsum the sun grew dull. Without M'alsum the moon was sapped of light. Nothing was the same until he returned.

And yet today, in order to save the dogs and trade goods, M'alsum had turned his back on his woman and infant and allowed them to fall prey to manitous. And he had nearly drowned Ne'gauni before agreeing to abandon him to die alone. Shaken, Sac tried not to think about the shriek that had brought him to pause. It was no use. The scream would linger in his thoughts and dreams forever; he was certain that it had been the death cry of his youngest brother.

"*Half* brother," he muttered in an effort to soothe his nerves as much as his conscience. He was not soothed. The hackles shivered up and down his back. Half brother or full brother, to Sac's way of thinking blood was blood, and no matter how he attempted to justify stripping Ne'gauni of his belongings and leaving him to be eaten alive by wolves or manitous, something seemed wrong about it. Totally, terribly wrong.

A howl went up in the night.

Wolf sound. Woman sound.

Again the hackles went marching beneath Sac's skin. "No wolf that," he whispered. Recalling the legend of Mowea'qua, he gritted his teeth lest he accidentally speak her name out loud or utter a careless word about her. He had no wish to summon a manitou. Squinting through falling whiteness, he imagined the wolf woman's man-eating presence lurking all around.

No! She will not come for me! She is feeding on Little Brother! But when she has eaten her fill of him, will not his spirit live on in her? Is this not the way of the hunt? The unfit falling prey to the strong so that they may be reborn in the flesh of the carnivore that has consumed them? Ah, M'alsum did not think of this! What will happen to the sons of Asticou if Little Brother lives on in the flesh of a cannibal manitou? Will he hunt us? Will he find us? Will he tear us to pieces and scatter our bodies across the land to be meat for carrion eaters as just punishment for what we have failed to do for him this night? If this happens, we might live on in a wolverine, or in foxes or martens, but more likely we would be reborn as rodents . . . as insects . . . as fungi sprouting from what is eventually left of our rotting bones . . . or as . . . The possibilities were too horrifying to consider.

"We should never have left him!" With a start Sac realized that he could no longer see his brothers. "Would you walk on and leave me behind, too?" Anger coupled with righteous indignation as he hurried on.

Snow was fast covering the tracks of M'alsum and M'ingwé. Within the sodden layerings of Sac's fawn-skin socks and knee-high moccasins, his feet were beginning to ache with cold, and the tips of his toes were tingling with the first ominous signs of the numbness that presaged frostbite. "So much for sloshing into a creek to rescue sweet sap in a blizzard! M'alsum had better find the sled soon and, with it, our dry socks and moccasins, or our feet will freeze and Ne'gauni will not be the only son of Asticou to die upon the long trail to the Dawnland!"

Sac leaned forward into each step. An inadvertent sideward glance gave him a view of his dead brother's pack frame hanging downward from his shoulder. Snow was accumulating on the gracefully curving tines of the paired antlers, but in his fear-ridden imagination they glinted as sharply as old bones splintered and defleshed by the savaging teeth of carnivores. He regretted the comparison, but not half as much as he regretted allowing M'alsum to coerce him into taking the pack frame. "M'alsum does not risk his own skin to the wrath of the manitous by carrying the personal belongings of the dead on his own back! Only M'ingwé and I have been foolish enough to do that. Only . . ." He stopped.

It was there again. That deep, terrible, disembodied animal roaring that had come through the forest just before Raven called to Death and before Great Ghost Cannibal, winter chief of the manitous, had come with his spirit warriors to slay Hasu'u on the far side of the creek.

Sac was suddenly giddy with terror as the monstrous sound came crashing and trampling into his brain to devastate his last reserves of self-control. A sob of horror went out of him. Katcheetohúskw, the legendary five-legged, man-eating monster who spoke with the voice of thunder and stormed through the forest to crush hapless journeyers beneath his tree-trunk limbs, was loose within Sac's mind. Panic had him now. He fumbled frantically with the frozen thong that looped his dead brother's pack frame to his shoulder, then flung it into the night as he set his snow walkers tromping madly after M'alsum and M'ingwé.

It seemed as though he would never close the distance between himself and his brothers, but this he did. Matching his pace with theirs, he blurted, "There are too many manitous in this forest! Big, hungry, man-eating manitous! We should never have come north. Never! You said there would be no danger to us, M'alsum, as long as we traveled under the Cold Moon beneath which great bears lie sleeping, as long as we made the proper sacrifices and chants. But now we are lost. Hasu'u and the baby are dead. And did you hear the roaring just now? Do you know what it was . . . who it was? Ah! I dare not even think of it, but, thanks to you, I could have been flattened beneath the pads of its great feet or thrown away into the stars by one killing kick of the fifth leg that grows from its face! And the earlier howling, ah! Whatever made that sound now feasts upon Little Brother. I know it does! Did you hear his scream? I tell you, M'alsum, our brother was still alive when whatever it is that now feeds upon his flesh came from the forest to devour him!"

"Good," said the headman.

"Good?" Sac was incredulous. "What if he suspected our plans to barter him off into slavery in the Dawnland? What if, before he died, he blamed us for not going back for him? He must have known that we abandoned him! He must have called out to us in the end! He must have suffered much pain! What if, after he is eaten, he is reborn as manitou and—"

"You must close your mouth and keep your fears to yourself, Sac, or you will also suffer much pain . . . at my hand!" warned M'alsum.

Sac shrank a little within his furs. He knew he was talking too much, but he did not like being threatened.

"Look! There are the dogs and sled!" M'ingwé was pointing ahead. "I had begun to think you were leading us in circles, M'alsum. But where is the burden woman?"

After a moment M'alsum said, "There."

Sac watched his eldest brother move forward in an obvious fury. Setting his snow walkers close on M'alsum's heels, he soon saw Kicháwan cowering within the meager cover of a thicket, rocking to and fro, holding her head in both hands as though trying to keep her skull from bursting.

"Did I not tell you to stay close to the dogs?" M'alsum demanded.

The burden woman uttered a garble of unintelligible mewing.

"Get up!" M'alsum commanded. "We have need of dry moccasins, liners, socks, and leggings. And fresh mittens, too. Move, Burden Woman, and move now, or with my own hands I will make sure that you never move again!"

Sac's brow furrowed. Another threat! Since when had M'alsum become so free with the use of intimidation? Since the wind had turned and carried the stink of unspecified danger through the trees. Since the great roaring had first come through the forest. Since Raven had called and Death had answered out of lowering storm clouds and, at M'alsum's insistence, they had raced for their lives with no thought to the safety of Ne'gauni, Hasu'u, or her infant son. Sac found himself scowling. If it had not been his eldest brother he was puzzling over, he would have been certain that he was in the presence of a man who was running from his fears.

Kicháwan tottered to her feet and came wading through the snow, still holding her head, still mewing, this time forming sound into words. "I was afraid that you would not return! So dark! So cold! Then Owl called. Had to hide! I heard wolves . . . and something else . . . a terrible cry. And my head will not stop hurting . . . so much . . . too much. I must rest . . . make the hurt go away . . . must sleep awhile and—"

"Sleep?" M'alsum was incredulous. "You will go to the sled! You will bring dry moccasins and—"

"Cannot," she mewed.

Enraged, the headman struck the woman a backhanded blow to her face.

Kicháwan went down with a *whoof*.

Sac was certain that M'alsum had killed her.

"Get up!" The headman kicked at the burden woman's crumpled form with the hard frontal curve of his right snow walker. "I will not command you again. If you will not attend the sons of Asticou, we will do for ourselves and leave you behind!"

Kicháwan moaned.

Sac was relieved to see that she was still alive, but as his brothers turned from the woman and hurried to the dogs and sled, their callousness troubled him. His feelings had nothing to do with compassion for Kicháwan. He knew as well as any man that it was sometimes necessary to be brutal with burden women, for only out of male dominance could such otherwise worthless females draw strength and any hope of courage. But, try as he might, Sac could find no logic in M'alsum's beating their only burden woman senseless when he and his brothers still had use for her.

"Come, Sac!" ordered the headman. "Why do you stand staring? You must get out of your wet moccasins. Take dry footwear from your bedroll and help us repack the sled. There is no fit shelter for us here. I want to distance ourselves from the creek and this part of the forest as quickly as we can . . . even if we have to travel all night."

Sac doubted that the intensifying snowfall would allow them to journey even halfway toward dawn before they were forced to stop and take shelter, but the idea of distancing himself from the creek and whatever howled and roared in this part of the forest was irresistible. Walking around the downed burden woman and toward his brothers, his mood lightened a little until he caught a familiar scent and knew that Kicháwan was bleeding from what M'alsum's blows had left of her nose. He did not pause to offer consolation, but as he came to stand beside the sled, he could not prevent himself from speaking his mind to his eldest brother. "Who will carry Kicháwan's load if you have damaged her so badly that she cannot continue on? You? Or must M'ingwé and I again share the weight of your bad judgment?"

"Bad judgment?" M'alsum was leaning against the sled. He flung off his wet foot coverings, pulled on a pair of fresh socks and oiled liners, then shoved his feet into a dry pair of heavily padded, knee-high moccasins. "If any dog of mine ever habitually balks in harness or refuses to obey my command, Sac, I will slay that animal on the spot and use it as meat to feed the others. How else would I make progress on the trail? How else would I keep order among the pack? Why should it be different with a burden woman . . . or with a brother?"

M'ingwé, taking the last words as a comment on the headman's dealings with Ne'gauni, nodded to himself as he changed his own footwear.

Sac, on the other hand, recognized another threat. He took it as he knew it had been intended—personally. "I grow tired of your threats, M'alsum."

"And I grow tired of your endless questions and complaints," replied the headman, lacing his moccasins and then standing to his full height. Appraising Sac, he asked, "Where is Little Brother's pack frame?"

"I . . ." Sac had almost forgotten the cast-off antler frame. Now, with M'alsum glaring and M'ingwé looking up at him expectantly, he knew that this was not the best moment in which to explain its loss. Nevertheless, he did not regret what he had done, and he did not hesitate to say so. "I have thrown our dead brother's pack frame away! To save our lives! To keep the manitous off our trail! As we should now be rid of Little Brother's snow walkers! I tell you again, my brothers, it is forbidden to take up the belongings of the dead!"

The silence that followed was so complete that Sac could hear the landing of each and every snowflake that alighted upon his furs.

After a moment M'alsum said to M'ingwé, "I think our brother Sac would be headman in my place."

Sac bristled. "I would counsel with my brother as an equal."

M'alsum did not deign to reply. Moving to the dogs, he spoke to them as though they, too, were his brothers. "I think our brother Sac would turn tail and run for home if he could," he said as he squatted, balanced on the balls of his feet, and braced himself for the welcoming onslaught of the pack. It came. M'alsum laughed at the buffeting. Addressing each animal by name, he tousled snow-dusted heads with open affection. The big, heavy-bodied dogs responded with a typically canine excess of warmth; grinning, whining, and thumping tails, they nosed the man with happy enthusiasm. He reciprocated, fondling ears and scratching under jaws and chests, speaking genially and confiding in them as though they were his most trusted hunt brothers. "Yes! Too long have you been tethered here! I, too, am anxious to be on our way. But I must tell you, my dog brothers and sisters, that I do not think our brother Sac understands that what has befallen our band may yet prove to be a good thing for us. I do not think that he appreciates the fact that with caution and cleverness we may yet turn adversity into advantage. No. Our brother Sac *does* believe these things. Our brother Sac has lost confidence in my ability to lead. He will not, I think, speak well of me when we reach the Dawnland."

"If we ever get there!" snapped Sac, thoroughly irked by his brother's taunting. "You have no cause to mock me, Brother. Not until the coming of this storm have I found cause to doubt any decision you have ever made. But now I will say this: Had it been my woman and my son, I would have gone back for them. I would have stood with Ne'gauni against the manitous. I would not have left a brother to die alone. And although I would have been afraid, I would have stood up to my fear as I now stand up to you!"

M'alsum rose.

M'ingwé's voice sounded pinched as he said, "Always you talk too much, Sac!"

"Yes," agreed M'alsum. "It is a bad and deadly habit."

Sac was furious. "You will not threaten me again!"

"No," replied M'alsum. "I will not."

Sac's mouth compressed. His brow came down. A sick, queasy churning loosened his gut. Defensive, he pulled his furs close around him and fixed himself stubbornly in place. "I will not cower from your threats!" he declared.

"Good," said M'alsum.

"You have given me cause to worry, Brother, and it is because of this that I have—" Sac did not have a chance to finish the sentence. M'alsum had come forward and placed his hands on his shoulders. Now, without warning, Sac found himself turned savagely around and pulled back against the headman's chest by the hard, unrelenting press of M'alsum's forearm across his throat. "Can . . . not . . . breathe!" he choked.

"Good," said M'alsum.

M'ingwé was on his feet.

The dogs were all up, ears back, tails tucked. One of the females was pissing in fright.

"M'alsum . . . let him go, M'alsum." M'ingwé's request was a breathy exhalation that fell far short of being a command.

"Why? Are you not weary of his endless wheedling and whining? Would you have him live to speak against us and then claim as his own our best share of the profits when we reach the Dawnland?"

Sac did not expect M'ingwé to hesitate. He did not expect him to suck air through his teeth and then exhale slowly, chuckling as though in gradually dawning appreciation of some subtle, obscene, and unexpectedly satisfying joke. He did not expect Mingwé to say,

"No."

The press of M'alsum's arm was unbearable. Sac fought against it. Hard. It was no use. Somewhere in the fading recesses of his mind, he heard the soft, unhappy mewing of a woman. Did Owl speak again? Did a raven call? He could not be sure. Death walked the winter forest in many forms this night. As Sac went limp in the killing grip of his eldest brother, he knew that M'alsum was one of them.

Chapter Three

▼▼▼▼▼▼▼▼

Deep within the forest there was a secret place, a hidden place, a lodge of bark and branch and bone, a refuge no men knew of but of which the old ones among the People whispered in the winter dark:

"Seek not the hiding place of Mowea'qua. Seek not the hidden den into which a man may enter as a man, but as a wolf emerge reborn."

It was to this place that they carried Ne'gauni. Bound and gagged, he knew little of his passage from the world of men into the realm of legend and nightmare. In silence they went, two darkly furred forms bearing him onward, hurrying across the snow, gasping their way through darkness, stumbling now and then under his weight, yet somehow bearing it until, at last, they were there—deep within a towering grove of ancient spruce, close by the silent, ice-sheathed tumult of a frozen waterfall that glazed an equally tumultuous fall of boulders carried to this place and then left behind by the retreating edge of a massive ice sheet whose remnant glaciers still scabbed the highlands of this rugged land.

Borne forward, shifted, lowered, and balanced and

rebalanced from below, Ne'gauni alternately tensed and relaxed within a relentless ebb and flow of pain as he drifted in and out of consciousness. He was not sure just when he became aware of a subtle change in the atmosphere around him, of a deeper, more confining darkness, of a lessening of cold, and of a potent combination of smells: rancid oil, smoldering ashes, wet leather, freshly cut balsam, dusty hides, canine urine, and the strong, musty scent of the skin and fur and dander of living animals.

Wolves?

The question swam through the youth's mind like a carnivorous little fish. He could actually see it moving inside his head, a wolf fish, finned and fanged, darting upward through the black currents of the river of death to nip and tear at the frayed edges of his consciousness. And then, suddenly, he felt himself tottering in midair, back at the edge of the abyss into which he had last fallen, but this time he did not plummet into mindless oblivion. Shocked into a near faint by the appalling intensity of pain that radiated from both his left leg and right shoulder, he rolled helplessly downward until he came to rest on his back on a tangle of thick furs and plaited reed matting. The latter gave off a disconcertingly familiar fragrance.

Bright memories of summer burst within Ne'gauni's skull: memories of warmth and sunlight, of sweet blossoms and tender leaves, of long-stemmed grasses and green reeds all gathered into the baskets and softly curving arms of the girls and women of his father's distant village—giggling girls with high-tailed puppies nipping at the fringes of their moccasins, laughing women with butterflies in their hair and the smell of the sun somehow caught up in their baskets and . . .

"Lives he still?"

"Yes!"

"Pity for him . . . and for us, too, think I."

"No!"

Ne'gauni flinched at the sound of the all-too-familiar voices. Female voices. Manitou voices!

"His fall, it has his gag loosened. Tighten it, Young One."

"No! Breathes he more easily without it."

The youth moaned. Someone—or something—was touching his face. Wanting to see just who or what was hurting him, he tried to open his eyes. It was no use. His lids were as heavy as stone; he was too weak to raise them. Inside his head, the bright memories of summer were fading. He felt himself fading with them. He did not care. His pain was fading, too, as, within his mind, Ne'gauni saw the girls and women of his father's village reaching out to him, inviting him to join with them in a joyous circling dance as they raised smiling faces to a receding sun and, laughing, tossed the contents of their baskets high. Amidst a descending cloud of falling leaves and stalks and blossoms, he saw Meya'kwé, his father's aged first wife, standing apart, as she always did, glaring hatefully at him, as she always did.

"Why will you not die?"

"I am dead," he told her.

She smiled.

He cringed. Meya'kwé's smile was a hateful thing. He was glad to see it fading along with the woman who wore it. And gladder still to see his mother take her place. Wawautaésie was not smiling. She reached out to him. He reached back. His mother took his hands. He felt a sharp pull and tightening at his wrists as she spoke in that special tone of wheedling petulance that she reserved for him alone.

"What are you doing in the country of the dead, Ne'gauni? He Walks Ahead must continue to the Dawnland! He must reach it before his brothers! And then he must come home again . . . before it is too late!"

"My brothers are dead! I am dead! How can you ask me to continue on?"

"You promised to bring me presents! Many presents!"

"Not all promises can be kept!"

"Where is my wristlet of sea-dog fur? Where is my anklet of golden seabird beaks? Where are my earrings of glistening beads and my cape sewn of many feathers gathered in the Cave of the Winds where Thunderbird makes his home above the Great Salt Water? Ah! You shame me before all, Ne'gauni! What kind of son are you? Surely not the bravest and boldest and best of the sons of Asticou!"

Ne'gauni began to shiver violently. Within his mind the sun went dark. An inner night absorbed the vision of his mother and, with her, all the laughing girls and women and bright butterflies and high-tailed pups. He was cold. So cold! His body felt strangely hollow. Again he shivered, felt darkness closing all around, listened to surging rivers of blood coursing in his veins, and, yielding to the flow, recognized the low sighing of distant winds to be the inhalations and exhalations of his breath. A great drum was sounding; its beat throbbed outward from the heart of ever-thickening darkness. Its rhythm, broken and erratic, was no true rhythm at all. And then, in a mad, wildly ascending flurry, the cadence quickened into a ferocious tattoo. Like the wings of a frenzied bird, the drum that was Ne'gauni's heart beat on and on. And then, suddenly, it stopped. All was silent. The youth's spirit collapsed inward into itself, into complete and total darkness. He heard and felt nothing at all. Until someone—or something—gripped him by the shoulders and shook him hard.

"Die you will not!"

"It will be so for him, Young One. Strong he is to have survived all that he has this night endured. But stop Death you cannot!"

"Try I will. Tell you I, perhaps the one promised by Kinap he is. A gift to me from the forest . . . no longer a Stranger, but one of the mikahmuwesu."

"An immortal? Ha! An aging fool is your father! And more foolish are you if his promise you believe. Forgets he the truth of our blood. And not since the first winter moon have we heard his howl or seen his ugly face. Maybe he will not again to us come. Maybe he cannot come. As for this wounded one, cuts and bleeds he far too much to be anything but mortal. Never to help you bring him here should I have agreed. He is no injured bird or beast that you can hope to heal and then set free to fly or walk away. A Stranger he is! An Enemy!"

"He is injured! And agreed you did! So save him now we must. His wet garments you must help me to remove. Like so."

"Hmm. Easier to stop the storm than your mind to change. But we, too, must dry garments have. Bring skins for us. Good. Now close you the smoke hole of our den with hides. Tight you must lace them. No smoke must escape as you now raise fire. Risk can I not drawing the Strangers to this place!"

Whatever—or whoever—had been handling Ne'gauni released him. He sagged with relief and, managing to open his eyes, saw a blur of dark fur slink away into an even greater darkness.

"Stones you must heat. And a hardwood brand you

must prepare. Yes, that one will do. Let it heat. Now light you must bring to us. And water and ash and healing fat and bark and clean sinew and needles and probes. Good! Now see we will if we are able to do what you so foolishly believe must and can be done."

The words were as shadows in the darkness. Ne'gauni tried to grasp them and failed. He lay inert, too weak to think or move as something—or someone—bent over him.

"Mmm," it growled as it gave a curious poke at the broken end of the flying stick that protruded from the youth's chest just below his right shoulder. "Well spitted you have been."

The youth lurched. "Spitted . . . ?"

"Mmm . . . like a hare or squirrel or a turtle for roasting ready."

Ne'gauni was suddenly aware of the scent of smoke. He heard the sound of tinder catching and then the rushing, crackling breath of newly born flame. He tensed. The manitous were making fire! A sick, sinking feeling gripped his belly. Was this how he was to meet his end? Not torn to pieces and devoured, but roasted alive like a turtle in the shell of his pain? Irony overrode dread. Surely such a death would be just retribution. His eyelids fluttered down as he wondered just how many woodland turtles he had snared, impaled alive, and cooked slowly over well-banked fires. How many times had he hunkered on his heels, watching in fascination, if not outright amusement, as the beaked mouths gaped and the gray necks extended and the red legs swam helplessly in space while the tongues swelled and the eyeballs whitened, until at last his victims went limp within their shells and their juices ran and sizzled? Perhaps one time too many?

He moaned, recalled old Asticou cautioning that in the

world beyond this world men were repaid in kind for their actions in this life. He had not listened. Indeed, he had found the premise of his own death ridiculous. It had pleased him to spit-roast turtles alive. It had delighted him to hold them over fire, to raise and lower them at whim as he alone determined just how long it would take them to die. He had not cared if his turtle roasts failed to win the approval of old Asticou. With only a smile and a few well-greased compliments placed here and there, he could always maneuver his father into granting him his way. And although Asticou had been unaware of it, Ne'gauni had long been fashioning his way after M'alsum's way.

He sighed, remembered tagging along unseen in his eldest brother's shadow, dropping to his knees amidst deep ferns, spying—as he often did—on the older brothers he so admired and emulated. He knew that they disliked him, but that was the way of older brothers, it seemed, and so he had followed, wanting to be close as he watched them crouching together in a circle in the deep woods that day, spitting a living box turtle, preparing a fire, smiling and talking low, thoughtfully.

"We must honor this prey and allow it to prove its valor before it dies. Then we will take it back to the village as a special gift for the Lakeland Firefly. You know what the old women say, the meat of turtles is irresistible to females!"

M'alsum's words murmured out of the past, and now, as then, Ne'gauni had trouble understanding why his brothers wanted to bring a gift to his mother. She was invariably so rude and dismissive toward them that he often winced. But now, suddenly, understanding dawned. He was almost a full hand-count of years older than he had been on that day. He knew now that in the time beyond beginning Great Turtle crawled up out of the boundless waters dragging drowned land with her so that Mother Earth might dry out beneath the sun and give birth to all Animals and People and Green Growing Things. Ever since that day turtle meat was said to make all females fertile. He smiled. Since giving birth to him, Wawautaésie had not given Asticou another child. His brothers, in their boundless generosity, had been making an effort to help her! Again he sighed, still smiling as he recalled the moment so clearly. Grasping it as yet another chance to shine in the eyes of his brothers, he had stepped boldly forward to remind them that it had rained the day before and they had forgotten an important lesson. He, on the other hand, as the best and boldest and surely the brightest son of Asticou, had not.

"Have you forgotten that snappers like that one feed on toadstools after a rain? The flesh of that turtle could be deadly to anyone who eats it. I am sure you would not want to be caught making such a mistake as that!"

His brothers had not thanked him. Indeed, after grinding the turtle under his heel and kicking earth onto the fire, M'alsum had led Sac and M'ingwé off without a word. Ne'gauni had not been offended; quite to the contrary, he had been immensely gratified to know that he had prevented them from making a terrible mistake. And from what he had overheard of their low talk, he had learned something new, not only about "honoring" prey, but about a subject that had been of gradually increasing interest to him. From that day he had gone out of his way to snare turtles in dry weather, confident that his invitations to share this meat with the girls of his band would be accepted and appreciated, that they would gather around his mother's cooking fire to ooh and aah as he honored his turtles and enabled them to prove their valor until the very moment of their deaths.

Light flared in the darkness.

It filtered through Ne'gauni's closed lids and hurt his eyes. The smell of smoke was strong now, and although the manitou was no longer poking at his wound, agony closed around him as surely as it must have enclosed the turtles within their carapaces before they died. "No way out . . . no way out," he exhaled in acquiescence to his fate. Once again he recalled old Asticou looking askance at his method of turtle cookery and warning that in the world beyond this world men were repaid in kind for their actions in this life. If this was true, thought Ne'gauni, it was going to take him a very long time to die.

"Drink now of this he must!"

"Yes. Surely so. Here . . . I will his head hold up . . . and be careful you! Choke not must he!"

Ne'gauni did exactly that. With someone—or something—gently lifting the back of his head, he could feel the smooth rim of some sort of vessel being pressed to his lips. He gagged on the scent of the liquid within even before the vile substance was poured into his mouth. As viscous as warm mucus, it slid down his throat as though motivated by a will of its own. Never before had he experienced a smell or taste as revolting. He sputtered and spat and blew what he could of it out of his mouth.

"Yah!"

The outcry startled him. He opened his eyes and, in the sputtering light of a pair of birchbark torches that had been placed upright on either side of the place where he lay, looked straight up into the face of the manitou that had been attempting to make him drink.

"Be it so, then!" The apparition was grimacing as it backhanded slime from its snout. "Drink you not! But no cause will you have to say that we did not try your pain to ease!"

In the shivering illumination of twin torches Ne'gauni's weakness would not grant him clarity of vision. The darkly furred face of the manitou was a blur. One moment it looked like a molting, gray-bearded, mottle-eared old wolf. The next it looked like a wolfskin-clad old woman peering at him out of a face as worn and haggard and hairy as a lichened rock. Was this the face he had seen watching him from the tangled branches at the edge of the creek? Was this the specter whose warm animal breath he had smelled and whose loathsome name he had spoken before he had plunged into the black river of death for the second time? "Mowea'qua . . . ?"

The apparition snorted derisively. "Mmph! See what you will!"

He did.

Above the wolf-faced old woman—or woman-faced old wolf—the rib cage of a giant seemed to be holding up the night. At the bottom of this vault of bones, Ne'gauni lay staring up at greasy black shadows that pulsed like bats' wings on the moss-lined walls of some sort of arching, elongated lodge of bark and moldering thatch. Beyond the fall of light, the interior was immersed in darkness, but from the corners of his eyes he could make out familiar forms.

Neatly stacked rolls of furs and hides.

Several pairs of snow walkers of varying styles upended against a curving wall.

A large woven fishing trap hanging from a tritonged antler along with neatly folded snare nets and lines.

A fire pit surrounded by blackened stones with cooking

and eating implements of varying shapes and sizes stacked near, and baskets piled close by, and a great ball of twisted willow twigs tied and ready to be used for kindling.

A wolf sleeping on its side with its nose tucked beneath its forepaws.

A wolf? Inside a lodge? Yes, surely it was that; a wolf as black as his dreams, a manitou wolf, for no dog ever possessed such long limbs or massive paws.

Something moved in the darkness above his head.

Ne'gauni looked up and slightly to his right. A white-headed eagle was eyeing him from its perch on a crudely hewn, unpeeled beam. It ruffled its feathers, stretched its broad dark wings, then resettled itself and resumed staring down at the youth out of a single fixed and golden eye. Ne'gauni stared back and, when the great bird turned its back to him, could have sworn that it spoke and said,

"Soon now over for you will it be."

A thin sting of apprehension threaded through his veins; it left dread burning in its wake. The eagle was no longer watching him, but, in the absence of its unnerving stare, Ne'gauni saw that the raptor was not alone. His gaze fastened on the eviscerated carcasses of many small birds and beasts hanging upside-down by their feet from the framework of the bone-braced roof. He felt sick. Somehow the sunken, empty eyes of the slain creatures communicated a warning. Understanding flared bright within his head. A wave of weakness carried him into despair as, closing his eyes, he realized that there was nothing he could do to prevent himself from joining them.

Something—or someone—was working at his wrists, tightening some sort of strictures, jerking his arms out and down, holding them fast. He tried to resist, but his mind could not quite find purchase in the moment, much less direct his body to obey his will.

"Strain not against your tethers," advised a soft, earnest female voice. "Soon now, truly, over for you will it be."

The words seemed to hang in the air above his face. He breathed them in. Caught a familiar, warm, living animal scent. Opened his eyes. And saw, not the ugly, wolfish face of a haggard old manitou, but the pale-eyed, smooth-fleshed, tender-mouthed face of a smiling young girl. In a sudden daze of hope and bewilderment, Ne'gauni saw only what he wanted to see and cried the beloved name. "Hasu'u!"

The face, no longer smiling, drew back.

Another face swam before his eyes.

The old manitou straddled him. She glared down, snarling, eyes fixed with terrible purpose. "Now see we will if man enough to endure you are."

And suddenly the phantom was tearing at his flesh, and he was screaming. A pair of hands—or paws—attempted to reposition his gag. Mad with pain, he felt the press of bare flesh against his mouth and, raising his head, bit down hard. Tissue gave and tore. Blood flowed. The gag remained loose as, shrieking against the relentless attack of the manitou, he managed a single upward lurch before collapsing.

The numbing currents of the river of death welcomed him once again. He swam deep. He sought the forgiveness of his slain brothers and of M'alsum's Dawnland woman. But it was Hasu'u's name he called before he lost all sense of being. Again and again he called it. But although Ne'gauni searched for her in the country of the dead, he could not find her. Hasu'u was not there.

▼▼▼▼

And yet she heard his call.

Snow was still falling, silent, heavy. Somehow, in some mystical inversion of color, it was drawing into itself the substance of the night and refracting its blackness in glistening white. Falling straight to the earth, it sifted downward through the trees in a slow, sure rain of crystals that, at any other time, would have been beautiful to Hasu'u's eyes.

Now, sitting behind a windbreak of bowed birches to the lee of which the manitous were hastily setting up leantos, the Dawnland woman raised her head from her bent knees. She turned up her face to the falling snow and, in its all too ephemeral beauty, saw only a cold reflection of her own devastated heart.

Had someone called her name?

No, she thought. *It cannot be. The manitous do not know my name, and my own band is no more. If M'alsum and the others were still alive, he would have led them to come for me by now. I know he would! I have sent my thoughts to him in the darkness. Again and again my heart has called. Come for me! Come for the one who still lives! But he has not come. He cannot come. Only Death could keep the boldest and bravest and best of the sons of Asticou from coming for his woman. The manitous have slain him. Ah! I hear only what I long to hear.*

Listless, bruised, and hurting to her very spirit inside the pale bearskin robe that the manitous had insisted she wear, Hasu'u buried her face in her knees. The bearskin robe was *his* robe! Great Ghost Cannibal's robe! She closed her eyes. She wanted to sleep; in sleep there might be some small hope of forgetfulness. Rocking slowly from side to side, she began to hum softly to herself, crooning the old

Dawnland lullaby that since the earliest days of her childhood had proved to be a pathway upon which she could
send troubled thoughts walking away into the realm of
dreams.

"*Hay ya, ya.*
Sleep, little one, sleep, sleep.
Hay ya, ya.
Sleep, little one . . ."

Hasu'u's throat constricted. She choked off further
words. It was a mistake to recall the old lullaby. With the
familiar cadence came a flood of memories: of the warm,
nurturing arms of her Dawnland mother; of the doting care
of plump aunties and graying grandmothers; of baby sisters
held in the curve of her own strong young arms in an
ancestral homeland she would never see again; and of her
newborn son, M'alsum's wonderful child, that sweet,
tender, nameless infant whose life spirit was now lost to
her forever.

Tears stung beneath her eyelids. Aching to hold her
baby, Hasu'u's arms tightened around her knees. As she
drew in a deep, steadying breath of pure wanting, she found
that she could actually smell the sweetness of her drowned
infant at her breast and feel the weight of him and—

"Hasu'u!"

The distant cry shattered the moment.

The Dawnland woman's head went up. "Little
Brother . . . ?" Her heartbeat quickened at the sound of
the familiar voice. It was gone before she could fully grasp
it, and when it did not repeat itself, she told herself that it
could not have been real. She had seen Ne'gauni struck

down. She had seen the youth swept away by the creek. And with him, her infant.

My baby . . . my firstborn . . . my unnamed son!

Confusion swarmed within Hasu'u's head like summer blackflies droning over the coastal salt marshes and forests of the Dawnland. She cocked her head. If her infant was dead, what was sucking so aggressively at her breast?

She shuddered. Now she remembered! Staring down into the warm darkness that filled the hollow between her bent knees and torso, she could just make out the baby lying there, its tiny body swathed in moss and cupped in the leather sling that hung suspended from around her neck, its mouth at her nipple, pulling hard, drawing the milk of life into itself, rousing a maternal tenderness that she could not—would not—allow.

"You are not mine!" she hissed to herself as much as to the newborn upon whom she now focused her loathing. "You may look and smell like a baby, but I will not be tricked! The life spirit of my unnamed son is lost forever. I know what you are! You are manitou! And I will not take the place of your dead mother. I will—"

"You will do as you are told."

Startled, Hasu'u turned her gaze to the heavily furred woman who sat beside her. She had been so absorbed in misery that she had forgotten that she was not alone with the infant. The manitous had chosen Amayersuk to sit watch over her, and now the woman was speaking to remind her of all that she had been trying so hard to forget.

"Your baby is dead. We have killed it. Now we have milk for our own newborn! You will suckle this infant as your own. If you do not and this baby dies, it will be as I have promised. We will take you back through the forest. We will seek and find those from whom we took you, and before you die—slowly—you will see us send into the world beyond this world every last living member of your pathetic excuse for a trading band!"

"They are already dead."

"Are they?"

"They would have come for me by now if they were not!"

"Would they? When they are few and we are many? When they know that they are only mortal men and we have made them see and believe that we are manitou? Would you truly have them come for you? Do you want to see them die?"

Hasu'u was shaking. Her mind was a quagmire. Her thoughts waded into it and promptly sank into despair. The woman who had just spoken was no manitou. Her short, muscular, compactly built form was that of a fully human female, and she was clad in foul-smelling furs cut and sewn in a style that Hasu'u had not seen since she was a little girl and a small band of odd-looking strangers from the far north had visited briefly among her people. The manitous called the woman Amayersuk and smirked as though at some perverse secret whenever they spoke her name. Hasu'u had not asked its meaning; something told her that it would be best if she did not. It was enough to know that Amayersuk's greasy face had been the first thing she had seen when she awakened from her faint and found herself lying in a heap with the manitous standing all around. A dirty face. A tattooed face. A tense and watchful face. Hovering close, looking down like a fur-ruffed brown moon, the unremarkable features had stretched wide to display a paucity of small, sharply filed teeth in a smile obviously calculated to be taken as a sign of intended friendship.

"You must not be afraid," Amayersuk had advised Hasu'u. "Do what is asked, and no harm will come to you or to those from whom you have been taken."

"No harm?" Hasu'u echoed the words now as she had echoed them then. They lay bitter on her tongue, ludicrous in light of all that had befallen her. At first, stunned and hurting and bewildered beyond bearing, she had not been sure how to respond to Amayersuk. Now she knew. The woman was of the People and, if she was to be believed, dwelled among cannibal spirits of her own free will. She spoke their language nearly as well as she spoke her own and had quickly proved herself to be as loyal, obedient, and eager to please the manitous as the most subservient of dogs. Indeed, that was how Hasu'u had come to see her: not as a woman at all, but as a watchdog, a human watchdog. Her watchdog! It had been so easy to come to loathe her.

"You must learn to be happy in your new life," advised Amayersuk. "If you are not happy, your milk will cease to flow. If you have no milk, the little one we have put to your breasts will go hungry. If this happens, it will not go well with you."

Hasu'u cringed. "Has it gone well with me? I had not noticed this! With my band slain and my infant drowned, better for me had the manitous eaten me!"

A guffaw broke from the moon-faced woman. "You were not taken to be food, gullible woman! You were taken to give food! For this purpose you have been taken by the manitous. For this purpose you will now live as one of us. A great honor has been given you, woman of my own kind. Why do you refuse to see this? Why do you sit here like one of the Noqumiut, a hang-headed ghost moping in self-pity as though you had no hope of ever again seeing the bright light of day?"

"It might as well be so for me."

Amayersuk rolled her eyes and shook her head as though in response to the foolishness of one who has refused meat under a Starving Moon. "Our Waseh'ya is dead. The forces of Creation have brought you through these dark forests to walk with us in her place. It is as though you were asking to be taken! With every fine chant and fragrant smoke that your band raised to the spirits, with every cut of meat left hanging in trees to mark your passage through the forest, and with every strip of soiled swaddling moss so carelessly left behind, you called us to you! And now that you are one of us, you will do what our Waseh'ya could not do—nourish the newborn son that she has given to our tunraq at the cost of her own life. This little one is now tiguak to you—an adopted son. Truly, woman of my own kind, you have lost nothing in the death of the infant you suckled before!"

"Nothing?" Hasu'u bit back a response. She had learned hours ago that it was no use trying to win Amayersuk's sympathy. The woman had lived too long among the cannibal manitous of the winter forest not to behave and think as they did. "One life cannot be replaced by another," she said coldly.

Amayersuk suddenly snapped to her feet. "Ah! He comes! You will rise to your feet, woman of my own kind! You will show respect to Tôrnârssuk, our tunraq! He is One Who Gives Power, Guide and Guardian and All-Knowing Spirit! Without him not one of us would live to see the rising of another sun."

Hasu'u was too weary to rise. She did not want to live to see the rising of another sun. And yet, as she looked ahead, she swallowed hard and knew just how much she was afraid of dying. Amayersuk was right. Tôrnârssuk, Guide and Guardian, All-Knowing Spirit, headman of the manitou raiding band, had parted from the ranks of his fellow phantoms. Hasu'u shivered. She knew him by another name: Death. In the guise of Wíndigo, Great Ghost Cannibal—Slayer of Youth, Slaughterer of Wayfarers, Destroyer of Dogs, Stealer of Women, Drowner of Infants—the winter chief of the manitous was coming toward her.

A tremor of fear and revulsion racked her. There was no mistaking him for another. Even though falling snow and darkness conspired to obscure the unusual cut of his garments and all but the most definitive contours of his powerful form, the length, rhythm, and absolute authority of his stride were uniquely his own. His was the long, sure, boldly splay-legged gait of one who has spent an eternity leading others across the world on snow walkers.

Hasu'u stiffened. Having no wish to give him the satisfaction of knowing how thoroughly he had cowed her, she willed herself to show no fear. But she had never been very good at concealing her emotions. When he paused before her, she recoiled, both sickened and afraid. His looming presence was as overpowering as his stink. He was not tall, but he was as broad across his chest and shoulders as two men, and he reeked of sweat and smoke as well as of the rancid fat and putrid meat that she had seen him and his kind devour with animalistic zeal.

She shivered, revolted by her recollection of their ways, and by his nearness. Even though he had long since taken off his mask, a grotesque, hideous beaked thing of brightly painted wood crowned by a dead raven with wings extended as though in flight, his face remained hidden within the circular projection of his sealskin hood. For this one small thing Hasu'u was grateful. She did not want to see the short, tusklike fangs that protruded from his lower lip, or look again at the thin dark hair that grew all around his mouth, or set her gaze into his long lifeless eyes or upon the wide, emotionless span of his broad, flat, not-quite-human features. Indeed, as she frowned up at him now, she was not in the least convinced that the strangely sallow face he had earlier chosen to reveal to her was not also a mask, a finely chiseled, cleverly carved disguise behind which he wisely hid his true visage lest, with the first glimpse of the monstrous reality of his manitou face, her heart stop with dread, her breasts grow instantly dry, and his spirit infant starve for want of a living woman's milk.

He spoke.

Hasu'u winced. His voice was a bludgeon to her ears. The language of his kind was so alien that, although each word was softly spoken, the oddly broken cadence of every syllable raked her senses.

"Our tunraq says that I am to tell you his words," Amayersuk informed her. "He says that his lean-to is ready. He will sleep close to the little one. The infant is all he has of his Waseh'ya now. He will keep it near. He will keep it safe from the great tusked one that walks in this dark forest. You will share his sleeping furs. You will suckle the little one when it hungers in the night."

Hasu'u was so revolted that she fought down the need to retch. "And what of my infant?" she asked, surprised that she managed to speak at all. "Who will feed my little drowned spirit when he hungers in the night?"

"The dead do not hunger," replied Amayersuk. "You must forget that one. You have another baby now. A better baby. It is Inuit! Someday it will be called Inuk, as is Tôrnârssuk, its father, White Bear, a man—I mean, manitou—preeminent, superior to all others. Why mourn for another when you have such a tiguak as this?"

"Because it is not mine!" Hasu'u fought back tears as, concentrating hard, she kept her hands alternately flexing and relaxing around her knees in an effort to prevent herself from smothering the unwanted thing at her breast. It would be so easy! A palm cupped to the curving back of the fragile skull, a slight pressure forward, a gentle pushing of the tiny face into her breast until the new life that had been so cruelly forced into her care went lax in its moss-lined sling and was soon alive no more! Wíndigo and his manitous would kill her then.

A sob formed at the back of her throat. With M'alsum slain, his wonderful child drowned, and her future as a slave to the cannibal spirits of the forest assured, she had no wish to live. Only Amayersuk's unsettling threats and lies about her band still being in existence—and her own disgraceful fear of dying—had kept her from smothering the manitou child before now. As long as she held even the slightest hope that M'alsum and the others might still be alive, she could not bring herself to do anything that might bring them to harm. But now, with Great Ghost Cannibal demanding that she share his foul sleeping furs and the manitou changeling tugging hurtfully at her breast, a deep, soul-numbing weariness engulfed Hasu'u as the last vestiges of hope bled from her heart.

No matter what Amayersuk said, Hasu'u was certain that M'alsum would have come for her had he been able. He and the other bold, brave sons of Asticou would have fought the manitous and at least tried to take her back from them. But they had not come. And now she knew that they never would. M'alsum was dead and, with him, clever Sac, and strong M'ingwé, and bold Ne'gauni, and big, kindhearted Kicháwan. Never again would she marvel at the older woman's strength or smile with gratitude as Kicháwan laid out her bed furs and cooked her meals upon the trail. Never again would she lie with her man and love him as she had never loved another. Never again would her face flush with pride as she observed the adoring ways in which his brothers and burden woman followed him without question or complaint. Never again would she delight in frustrating the arrogance of young Ne'gauni or daydream about returning home to the welcoming embraces of her parents and sisters and aunties and old grandmothers. And never again in this world or any other would she hold her own wonderful little son to her breasts.

Ah, my little lost child, if I cannot nourish you, I will nourish no other! And I will not lie down beside the manitou who has slain your father and taken you from me forever. Ah! May the forces of Creation give me the strength to die!

And it was so. She closed her eyes and moved her hands from her knees to shape her palms around the back of the infant's head and press the tiny manitou face into the warm, suffocating moistness of her breast.

"Hasu'u!"

Ne'gauni's cry broke through the forest like a startled deer. It was faint. Weak. And it came from very far away. But this time, before it fell away, it was unmistakable.

Hasu'u withdrew her hands from the back of the infant's head so quickly that, had the movement been visible outside the fall of the bearskin robe, it would have appeared as though the flesh of the manitou child had scalded her.

"You hear it clearly now!" proclaimed Amayersuk. "It is the voice of one of your own! I have not lied to you. Your band lives! But if you call out again—if they hear and follow—you will see them die!"

Hasu'u could scarcely breathe. Amayersuk's warning had been given with such unabashed enthusiasm that it was obvious that the moon-faced woman yearned to see her threat fulfilled. Hasu'u hated her, but her feelings toward the human watchdog were unimportant now. With hope surging once more within her body, she suddenly found herself on her feet with the bearskin tumbling from her shoulders and her thoughts running wild. If Ne'gauni, whom she had seen struck down and swept away by the creek, was still alive, then the others must be alive, too! Amayersuk had been telling the truth! And if Ne'gauni was calling her name, then he and the others must believe that there was a chance that she was alive.

"Ah!" Hasu'u exclaimed. "They will come searching for me! M'alsum will lead them! M'alsum will—"

"M'alsum?" Great Ghost Cannibal reached out to catch the bearskin and place it firmly back around her shoulders. "He is headman of your band, this M'alsum?"

Hasu'u gaped in stunned amazement. The specter had spoken, not in the clipped, growling tongue of the manitous but in a halting version of a dialect of her own Dawnland tribe.

"You will answer Tôrnârssuk, our tunraq!" prodded Amayersuk with a poke and a shove.

Hasu'u flinched. "M'alsum is the best and bravest and boldest of the sons of Asticou. M'alsum is headman of my band. M'alsum will not abandon his woman to the manitous. M'alsum is—"

"He has shown us what he is!" the phantom interrupted contemptuously. "We have given him a few names of our own. We call him Smells Danger and Runs and

Hides. We call him Abandons Woman and Never Looks Back. We call him Coward. Unlike the young one who was felled by our arrows, he would not risk himself for you even when he saw you fighting for your life. Why would he follow and fight the manitous for you now? No. He will not come. He will sit out the storm on the far side of the creek. When the skies clear and snow falls no more, Smells Danger will look to the safety of his own skin. Never Looks Back will go on his way, journeying into the rising sun, to this Dawnland you speak of. I have wintered among bands there. I have learned their ways and tongues. Abandons Woman and his band will live a soft fat life among the soft fat people who dwell in that place. They will not long remember you."

Hasu'u was shaking uncontrollably. Her heart was pounding. The bearskin lay heavily upon her shoulders. Too heavily. It was a robe fleshed from an animal that, when living, must have stood upright to twice the height of the tallest man. It was so heavy that it seemed to be driving her feet straight into the snowpack. She squared her shoulders. She told herself that she would not be driven. M'alsum was alive! And no matter what the manitou said, she knew that her man had not turned his back on her. If he believed that she still lived, he would come for her. He never ran from his fears; he took his greatest pride in meeting them head on and vanquishing them. But, as headman, his first responsibility was to secure the safety of his band, goods, and dogs; she had known this when she had so foolishly chosen to lag behind. If she had heeded Ne'gauni's warnings to hurry on, she might be with her man even now, and their wonderful child might still be alive.

The realization was almost too much to endure. She

braced her limbs lest they buckle beneath her. As the phantom's broad, hard hands closed painfully around her shoulders, the combined weight of guilt and regret was far greater than the weight of the skin of the white bear. Nevertheless, she clenched her fists at her sides and forced herself to proclaim to the specter, "M'alsum will remember me. He will not forget that you have drowned his son. He will not allow that death to go unavenged. He will come for his woman. He will find a way to free me from you. In this hope alone will I live."

"Then you may well live for many a long winter," said the winter chief of the manitous. As Tôrnârssuk spoke, his words were transformed by the frigid night air into mists that lingered like malevolent ghosts in the snow-riven darkness before his unseen face. "You are my woman now. Soon we will put this dark and endless forest behind us and return into the far country of my ancestors, where we will hunt once more under the open sky. You have been taken from your band to give life to my son along the trail. This you will do. If he perishes, you will perish. If he thrives, you will thrive. If, when the time of suckling him is over, you prove a life maker and otherwise useful, you will be fed and granted warmth. If not, you will finish your days at the killing end of a braining club, and it will be of no concern to me. So be strong and obedient in all ways. And do not speak again of your man or your people. Forget them. They are soft. Forget your child. It is dead. And forget the one you call M'alsum. You will grow old waiting for him. That one will never find courage enough to follow you. Not into the barrens. Not into the far country where great white bears come hungry from the sea and white wolves hunt with foxes under rivers of dancing light upon a land of ice that breathes and shifts as restlessly as the stars that sing.

Not into the feeding grounds of whales. Not into the spawning place of storms and hunting grounds where Wíndigo, Great Ghost Cannibal, is winter chief."

Hasu'u's heart went cold. "I will soon die in such a place."

He huffed derision, his patience done. "You will soon learn, woman, that to all but the manitous, you are already dead."

▼▼▼▼▼

"Do you think they finished her quickly?"

"What?" M'alsum was brought short by M'ingwé's question. They had been plodding along in silence behind the sled for so long that the headman had almost forgotten that he was not alone.

M'ingwé stopped beside him.

An owl was sounding somewhere close.

M'ingwé cocked his head, listening. "The spirits do speak in this forest, Brother . . . dark spirits . . . fearsome spirits."

M'alsum made no reply as, scowling into snow-dappled darkness, he looked back to see Kicháwan plodding toward him. He snarled—not at the burden woman, but at what he saw following her. They were still there! The ghosts of Sac, Ne'gauni, Hasu'u, and her unnamed infant were leering at him from behind the trees. He shivered. For hours now he had imagined them following, watching him, accusing him.

Do you truly think that you can ever hope to outdistance all that you have done this day and night, M'alsum, Firstborn and Eldest Son of Asticou?

The headman flinched. The ghosts vanished. He

snarled again, knowing that they and their query existed only within his troubled mind.

"I have been thinking," M'ingwé revealed in a hushed and worried tone, "about what Sac said before he died . . . about Little Brother blaming us for not going back . . . about how it must have been for him . . . and for Hasu'u, too, until the very end. Do you think she suffered, M'alsum? I do not like to think of it. She was such a happy, pretty little thing."

"Forget her! If she had not chosen to fall behind, she would be with us now. And so would Little Brother. So count yourself fortunate, M'ingwé, and stop looking back. What is done is done!"

"Still . . . do you not sometimes wonder if maybe . . . somehow . . . she could still be alive back there . . . with them?"

M'alsum was stunned. "Impossible!"

"Yes . . . but we did not actually see her die."

The headman did not like the direction in which his brother's words were leading. "Are you suggesting that we go back for her?"

"Me? No! Why would I want to risk myself? She was your woman, not mine."

Kicháwan, moaning under the weight of her pack, came to pause between them. "We will encamp now? So tired. Head hurts. Feel sick. Must sleep. Must—"

"You will sleep when I tell you to sleep," the headman snapped. Smarting against restlessness, he clicked his tongue to signal the dogs up and on.

The owl called again.

M'alsum grimaced as he strode ahead. The cursed bird sounded closer than before. The winter forest *was* alive with spirits. And not only the spirits of his dead relatives.

He ground his teeth, trying to understand just what he had done—or failed to do—to cause the manitous to turn against him. He had entered their forest with the utmost respect. He had made the required chants of propitiation. He had raised the necessary smokes to carry his invocations into the spirit world. He had offered the expected sacrifices. And all for nothing!

Still again the owl called.

M'alsum gripped Asticou's spear tightly in one hand and waited in angry expectation for M'ingwé to offer up yet another disquieting observation on the sounding of the bird. But, until their last pause, M'ingwé had been keeping his own counsel since consenting to the killing of Sac. If the man was troubled by the continued calling of the owl, he kept his feelings to himself.

M'alsum was grateful. Fatigue was weighting his every step. Given the intensifying black morass of his mood and the deteriorating state of his nerves, any more implied criticism from M'ingwé was likely to win the man a killing blow from Asticou's spear. The headman growled. He reminded himself that he had already killed one brother and left another to die alone this night, and, given the stubborn nature of the continuing snowfall, he was still a good three sleeps from the Dawnland. Only the forces of Creation could say what might befall him in this haunted forest before he reached the coast! And M'ingwé had proved loyal and brave beyond fault this day; his presence might mean the difference between life and death for them both.

A shudder rippled through the headman. There were no words for what he was feeling now—none that he would acknowledge. They all had too much to do with shame. And so he held his jaws clamped tight and his eyes fixed ahead as he kept his dogs, brother, and burden woman moving steadfastly into the night.

On into relentlessly falling snow.

On into ever-deepening cold.

Again and again Kicháwan stumbled under the weight of her massive backpack. She sobbed. She pressed the sides of her browband with mittened palms as though attempting to keep her skull from bursting. M'alsum ignored her pleas for rest. He shoved her forward when she faltered, jerked her upright by her pack straps when her knees betrayed her, and, setting her firmly on her snow walkers, kept her on her way. Away from the place where he had insisted they leave Sac in a lifeless heap, stripped of all useful belongings, decapitated and dismembered lest his life spirit remain intact to speak against his brothers in the spirit world. Away from the clearing where he had abandoned Hasu'u and their nameless infant to the cannibal manitous. Away from the creek where he had left Ne'gauni to die alone. Away from that part of the forest where he had come face to face with a part of himself that he had thought long vanquished until, in one appalling moment, the wind had turned and the great roaring had come through the trees and he had taken one look at the manitous and been so afraid for his life that, forgetting all else, he had driven the dogs on in a state of blind, mindless panic.

He would not think of it. He would not look back. He would not allow himself to stop or rest long enough to face his shame. Other men, lesser men, could yield to fear. He, M'alsum, could not. Would not! It was a pact he had made with himself in childhood on that terrible day when his father had first turned a cold and hostile eye to Meya'kwé and her firstborn.

"You do not cry out when he beats you, my mother."

"No, M'alsum. And you must never ever again cringe and hide when he strikes out at you for standing to my defense."

"But why does he hurt you?"

"He claims a husband's right and tries to break me, but I will not be broken. And though he falls upon me like an angry gale, I will not bend to him. As you must not bend. You must not be afraid. You must be strong, my son. You must be brave. You must make him know that you are a part of me that he will never own. Your strength will shame him in the end and make me proud. Someday you will be chief in his place. You will take me back to the Grassland of our ancestors. Or to the Dawnland of my grandmother's people. Ah! To live once again beneath the sun before I die!"

The recollection of that brief exchange of words was so hurtful that the headman ground his teeth as though to crush his memories between them. It vexed him to be able to recall his yesterdays so clearly. Every word! Every moment! Every sensation! It was a gift, Meya'kwé had assured him, a rare power inherited through the ancient shamanic line of her Grassland ancestors. And yet the power brought pain to him now. He could hear the past, smell it, sense it alive and extant all around as he walked on, back into time it seemed, straight into the snug little milk lodge within which he had passed so many days and nights with his mother.

▼▼▼▼

He was in her arms. A child again. A long, shivering sigh went out of him. The sweet smell of her bare skin and the warmth of her breath against his face and body seemed as real to him now as the voice of his father speaking out of time:

"How long must you insist on lying apart from me while you suckle my son, Meya'kwé? There is talk in the village. *Gossip*. It is not natural for a woman to make a man wait so long after the birth of a child before joining with him again in the pleasure of life making."

"Your pleasure is not mine, Asticou. And I have made a life. As long as my son has need, I will be a milk lodge woman. This is the way of my Grassland people."

"You are a Forest woman now!"

"By your will, not mine! And in the Grassland it is wisely said that the longer a son is nursed, the stronger and braver his spirit will be!"

"This son has been at you so long that he has sprouted all of his milk teeth! Look at him, woman! Nearly three summers have passed since his birth. No other woman keeps to the milk lodge as long as you do, Meya'kwé! I tell you again, it is not natural. Not natural! So come to me, Mother of M'alsum. It is time for you to remember that you are also Woman of Asticou! I, too, have needs! This son we have made together is strong and brave enough!"

M'alsum's mittened hands flexed, one around the shaft of Asticou's spear, the other in what he could have sworn was the loving embrace of his mother's fingers as she led him from the milk lodge to greet the sun on that fateful morning that was to forever change his life.

His father was waiting for him, as he waited each morning to greet his son. Smiling, he waited. Nodding in approval of the fine, strong milk boy he had made, he waited. Was it possible that there had been affection between them then? "Yes." It had been deep and true and boundless.

M'alsum scowled as he walked on, seeing the tight brown crinkles of a smile folding up around Asticou's small black eyes as he knelt back on his callused heels and reached out to welcome his son into his strong arms. M'alsum could feel the bony slope of his father's narrow shoulders as, with his limbs wrapped tightly around Asticou's sinewy neck, he was carried high above the world to begin the day with a ritual immersion in the cold waters of the stream that pooled close to the village. Shivering and gasping and laughing together, father and son rubbed each other dry with moss before returning to the village for food. There were games then, each designed to teach a little one the most elementary skills of hunting:

To listen and truly hear.

To look and truly see.

To walk in silence.

To run without faltering or falling.

And to fall without crying out.

"May the firstborn son of Asticou always know the favor of the Four Winds!" His father's invocation came across time. "May the forces of Creation grant to the firstborn son of Asticou the eyes and heart of Eagle! May this firstborn son of Asticou grow to be a great forest hunter like his father! May this firstborn son of Asticou know that in changing times brave men must learn new ways or—"

"There are no brave men or great hunters in this forest!" Meya'kwé's voice stung out of the past. "How can there be, when in all this dark woodland there is no game worthy of a real man's efforts to hunt it? Where are the great horned bison? Where are the fleet, high-leaping antelope? Where are the tall, tusked children of Katcheetohúskw, the great stiff-legged beast my people call mammoth?"

"There are deer and moose in this forest," replied Asticou. "And caribou in season. There are fish and beaver and fat muskrats in the streams. There are birds and frogs and turtles in the ponds and marshes. I do not hunger for Grassland meat, Meya'kwé!"

"Of course you do not. And we both know why. You are afraid to hunt it!"

"No! I will not hear such words!" Asticou's explosive retort struck through M'alsum's memory like the sound of a frost wedge cracking stone in the depth of the coldest winter night. "I am not afraid to hunt any game that is worth the risk! But I see no cause to lead my people from a settled life within this forest where the forces of Creation provide so generously for all of our needs. The world is changing, woman! Why should I be content to dwell as my fathers dwelled, at the edge of the grasslands, a nomad ever in search of big meat, ever on the defense against restless tribes that have made a way of life out of raiding the hunting grounds of others? And why should I desire to seek the tall children of Katcheetohúskw? Everyone knows that wherever they once walked they sucked up all the water from the ponds and streams and shouldered down the trees to be food for them! It is no small wonder that in the time beyond beginning they were hunted and slain until now they walk the world no more! I praise the forces of Creation for the fact that no living man of your tribe or mine has ever seen more of a mammoth than its bones and tusks lying cast off along the riverbanks of a world in which its kind lives no more!"

"*I* have seen!" Again Meya'kwé's voice stung out of time, defiant, openly contemptuous. "On the grasslands! On that day when wolves and an early snowstorm drove us to ground and you, blinded and confused by snow, were separated from our band as you led me away from a gathering of our two peoples and into the forest forever. I saw the dying mammoth mired in snow! I led you to shelter against it! Together we cut open the belly of the great cow so we might crawl inside to be safe from marauding wolves. And there, close to the still-throbbing heart of the living mammoth, we ate of its fetus. And afterwards, while wolves howled near, you took your bride for the first time. Nine moons later M'alsum was born, strong as a mammoth and howling like the wolves who sang as we coupled and—"

"A story fit to heat the imaginations of gullible children or feeble old men and women on cold winter nights, Meya'kwé. I know no fear of wolves, and I have never been blinded or confused by a snowstorm in my life. It was I who led you to shelter, not against the body of a dying mammoth, but inside a lean-to I was forced to raise against the rib cage of a half-rotted bison that was the only bit of high 'ground' I could find on all of that cursed prairie. To this day I can smell the stink of it!"

"Ah, but, Husband, I tell you it is not so! We ate of the meat of mammoth, you and I! We coupled in the moist, slick heat of its blood and howled back at the wolves who dared venture near! A pity that it was not the great Katcheetohúskw himself whose body sheltered and nourished us, for it is said among the Grassland People that the one who kills the Great Beast will be Master of the Feast of Life forever, an immortal, even as Katcheetohúskw and his kind were once immortal in the world of my people, made strong and invincible by the selectivity of our kills and by the fires we set to burn back the forests so there would always be browse for his kind. Ah, but look around you, Asticou! No mammoth could long survive in this dark forest, where even trees need not wait for mammoths to shoulder them down as they wither and die for want of light. How can men choose to live where they cannot see the sky? And how can a hunt chief of any worth be content to dwell forever amidst mold and shadows unless he is fit for no other life?"

M'alsum leaned into his stride, his mind boiling. Asticou had shamed Meya'kwé as punishment for her outspoken words. Before the entire band he had shamed her! He had beaten her. He had broken her fine, straight nose and split her long, soft mouth. He had dragged her by the hair into the hunt chief's lodge and, with M'alsum padding dazedly along at his heels, thrown her onto his bed furs, slapped her senseless, and, in a vain attempt to shorten the willfulness of her spirit, used the curving edge of a sharpened river shell to saw off her long black braids. This accomplished, he had straddled her, torn open her nursing dress, and taken her breasts into his fists. Informing her that they were now for his exclusive need, he had bent his head and suckled her so roughly that, when he drew away, there was blood on his face. Tucking up his loin wrap to reveal an erection the proportions of which still rose high in M'alsum's memories, he had commanded Meya'kwé to pleasure him. She had bitten him instead. Enraged, Asticou had then set himself to prolonged and violent rape. And through all of this, although Meya'kwé had uttered not a single moan of pain or cry for pity, M'alsum had cowered behind a pile of freshly gathered spruce boughs, bawled like a baby, and shamelessly pissed his loin wrap and leggings in terror.

His face convulsed as, once again, he swore as he had sworn then, "Never again! I will be brave for you, Meya'kwé! No matter how afraid I am, I will be brave! I will protect you! I will make you proud!"

"What was that you said, Brother?"

M'alsum made no reply to M'ingwé's question. His mind was lost to the present. With his hands still flexing, he could feel the way his fists had hurt and his fingernails had cut into his palms when, night after night, in a fury against Asticou's mauling of Meya'kwé, he had swallowed down his fear and flung himself onto his father's back to pummel and scratch and bite him like a screeching lynx. How many times had he been sent flying across the lodge before Asticou, rolling his eyes in anticipation of the attack, picked him up by the scruff of the neck, rolled him kicking and screaming into a caribou skin, bound him, stuffed a gag into his mouth, and tossed him onto his bed skins in the shadows of the lodge? And how many times had he wriggled within his bonds, trying to free himself, rolling off the piled sleeping skins, twisting like a furry little larva on the floor of the lodge, choking on sobs while his eyes seeped hot tears at the sight of his mother lying silent and grim-faced beneath his father's sweated predations?

"Too many!" he shouted, for although Asticou had never again been as violent with Meya'kwé as on that morning of her forced return to his lodge, would any son worth the pain of the mother who bore him ever forget or forgive his father for raping her? Or ever truly love the brothers born of subsequent maulings?

Anger flared hot at the back of M'alsum's brain. Less than a moon after dragging Meya'kwé onto his bed furs, Asticou had put M'ingwé to grow in her belly, and although the birth stressed her beyond the ability to produce milk for the newborn, Asticou had been on her again within a moon. When, nine moons later, Sac had gushed feet first from between her thighs, dragging her womb along with him, there had not been enough baneberry, shadbush, aspen root, powdered alder, or dried bumblebees in the village medicine stores to ease her hemorrhage, let alone her pain. Long had she lain near death. Although M'alsum had grieved, his spirit had soared with pride when he overheard the women of the village whispering together in awe of his mother's exemplary endurance and bravery.

"I will kill you if you hurt her again!" he warned his father.

"Kill me?" The reply came from M'ingwé, sharply, angrily. "For what? You are babbling, Brother! What is wrong with you?"

"Wrong?" M'alsum was not sure to whom he had just replied. In his mind he was still far away, sitting with his mother in front of the milk lodge, watching his siblings laying claim to her breasts, that precious territory that had once been for him alone.

"You should give these two babies away," he advised her. "You do not need these sons when you have me! If it will please you, I will break their necks and hang them in a tree to be meat for hawks and ravens as you have taught me to do with unfit pups."

"What!"

M'alsum failed to hear his brother's startled exclamation. Meya'kwé's words were flowing across time.

"Never doubt the way of my heart for you, M'alsum, my firstborn, my own little wolf, my brave warrior, my protector, chief and guardian of my little pack! Your brothers have been born of my body, but you are of my heart, the center of my life, conceived in the last moments of my happiness! Never forget this. Never! You are the one who will take me back to the Grassland of my people someday . . . or to the Dawnland of my grandmothers. You will do this, M'alsum. For that day only do I live."

Given the circumstances, it had not seemed an unreasonable request, and it seemed to him now that in the days and nights that followed he had lived for her alone. He had dreamed of the day when he would rescue her from the predations of his father. He had willed himself to be brave.

"For Meya'kwé!"

He had forced himself to be bold.

"For Meya'kwé!"

He had set himself to excel at all things.

"For Meya'kwé!"

"Our mother will not come to you in this dark wood, Brother!" exclaimed M'ingwé.

"She is always with me," said M'alsum, not knowing that he spoke at all as he remembered how, as the rift between his mother and father grew ever wider, a chasm had opened between him and Asticou. It was a dark and brooding thing across which the hunt chief made considerable effort to extend an open hand, but always in those moments Meya'kwé found a way to come close, and, guided by her wisdom and the memories of his father's violence toward her, M'alsum never reached back.

And then, under a Coming Together Moon, in the shank of his eleventh summer, when the band had journeyed to a gathering by a great lake in the hunting grounds of the Copper People, M'alsum had looked for the first time upon the Lakeland Firefly. She had looked back, and for the first time he had felt his heart touched by a female other than his mother.

Did he know that she would follow when he went from the encampment of his sleeping band to sit alone by the lake that night? Had he been waiting for her, idly skipping pebbles across moonlit waters, listening to the calling of loons as, all around, the forest pulsed with the fireflies and the sky above his head seemed alive with stars? As one born to the Forest People, never before had he seen such a high, huge sweep of open sky. He could have sworn that, with no effort at all, he could reach up and pluck the stars from the black skin of the night . . . cup them in his hands . . . watch them winking and glowing until, all powerful, he could crush them and watch their light bleeding away through his fisted fingers. Entranced by his thoughts, he had reached for the stars and found Wawautaésie instead.

He had no idea how long she had been beside him, silent, watching, waiting for what she would have of him. When their eyes met, she allowed her deerskin wrap to fall away as she knelt to display her childlike body.

"They say that in your part of the forest there is much meat and little work for women. This is true?"

He must have made some sort of affirmative rumble, for she dimpled as she told him, "I would live in such a band! When the gathering is over, you will take me with you when your people return into the deep woods?"

"Why would I want to do that?"

"For this!" she declared and turned, went down on all fours, presented her bare buttocks, and, like a little dog in heat, opened her thighs in invitation to be mated.

M'alsum caught his breath as he walked on. He could still feel the shock of ecstasy as, for the first time, he had penetrated a female and worked himself to the hot, shivering bliss of an ejaculation not born of dreams roused by memories of pleasure induced in his milk lodge days by his mother's kisses and adept, instructive hands.

He flinched, recalled other youths making their presence known, heard them guffawing like the boys they were, crow-voiced, raucous, speaking the less-than-flattering names that others of their Lakeland band called the youngest daughter of the chief.

"Trouble!"

"Likes It Too Much!"

"Spreads Herself for Trinkets!"

"Spreads Herself for Anybody!"

"Careful, Inland Boy. Sebec has threatened to brain her if he catches her at it again!"

"No! She is his favorite. Relax, Inland Boy, Sebec would never hurt her. Maybe he will brain you instead! Everyone knows that he opened her for his own pleasure long before she came to her first time of blood and would keep her for himself if he could!"

"And everyone knows that her mother and his other wives are jealous! And her mother is of a clan much stronger than our own. Her people could prove dangerous to us in these changing times. Sebec will not risk making them angry. So he has agreed to give away his Little Firefly to the first hunt chief outside our clan who will take her off his hands. That is why she spreads herself for you. To spite her father! So come, Wawautaésie, if you can open yourself to an outlander before you are given away, open yourself to us, too, as you do for your father, and we will light up like fireflies, just for you!"

M'alsum growled. He would have fought them. He would have beaten them into the ground. He would have crushed them as he had imagined himself crushing the stars, but they had sensed his strength and the extent of his adolescent anger and had wisely scampered off, laughing. Wawautaésie, pouting prettily, had assured him that they were all liars because they could not have of her that which she had so freely given to him. She cried then, copious tears, and, proclaiming that she would surely die if M'alsum could not be her man forever, had run off, leaving him in a daze, puzzling over his feelings until, at last, he had known what he must do.

In the thin blue haze of that Lakeland dawn, he had gone to Asticou. Boldly he had gone. Swallowing down his pride, he had turned his back on his gaping brothers and bravely ignored Meya'kwé's disapproving scowl as he spoke openly to his father of the way of his heart for Wawautaésie. Asticou had listened. Long and patiently he had listened. Then he had laughed in M'alsum's face.

"A boy cannot take a woman! But a man can and will take a new wife!" Smirking, Asticou had gone on to inform his eldest son that old Chief Sebec—alert to the rumor about Asticou being in the market for a warm and willing young woman to replace his cold and barren first wife—had already sought him out to detail the zeal and skill with which his youngest daughter entered into man-pleasing. "Sebec has trained her well. And now, although she still pleasures him, he finds himself with too many females at his fire. Since she is no virgin and has not yet proved herself capable of bearing a child, he has offered me a copper-headed spear if I will take his youngest daughter off his hands. This I will do! If for no other reason than to put your mother in her place and to hurt and humiliate a son who has been hurting and humiliating me for all too many years!"

And so, in the damp of that same morning, M'alsum had sought out the youngest daughter of Sebec and followed her when she left her father's lodge to squat apart from her sisters, relieving herself. Hidden amidst a tangle of flowering dogwood, woodland strawberries, ferns, and lakeside vines that in the intensity of the moment he failed to recognize as poison ivy, he had whispered of his longing, breathlessly, adoringly assuring Wawautaésie that they must run away together.

"We will make our own band!" he had proclaimed. "I will not be afraid! We will seek the distant Dawnland of my grandmother's people. We will find welcome there. What need have we of fathers who would shame us, or of mothers who would disapprove of our love!"

"Love?"

Her startled query pricked his mind as sharply as the brambles had pricked his exposed skin.

"I hold no love for you, Firstborn Son of Asticou! You are a boy! Your father is a hunt chief! He has promised my father that if, after the passage of my next moon blood, I open my thighs to please him in the ways in which he has long been denied by your mother, he will take me to be first woman in his lodge. He will see to it that my workload is light. He will give to me the prime portions of all meat that he brings to his fire. He has sworn that I will have all the best furs and skins and quills and feathers and river shells to sew into fine clothes for myself and the babies he will make on me. Long have I dreamed of such a husband! So go away, Firstborn Son of Asticou! Why should I want you when I can have your father?"

He trembled. He would never forget the agony of that moment, or the rash he had suffered in silence because of it. He would forever recall the pounding of wedding drums, the shrill scream of flutes and whistles, the hissing beat of rattles, the ululations of women, and the high, heady scent of the flesh of the bear that had been slain and roasted especially for the marriage feast at which, out of spite, Asticou had taken Wawautaésie to be his bride and, out of greed and in hope of a life of laziness, the Lakeland Firefly had taken Asticou to be her husband. In the days and nights that followed, Meya'kwé had been reduced to servitude at her own fire, and after the birth of Ne'gauni the hunt chief had never again extended a hand to M'alsum in friendship.

▼▼▼▼

The headman winced. Once again the *oo-ooh* of an owl was coming through the trees. He felt a flurry of wings pass overhead and, startled, came blinking out of a haze of yesterdays. He stopped dead in his tracks and, shaking himself violently, planted his snow walkers wide as he willed his memories to scatter like drops of water loosed from the coat of a dog emerging from a river crossing.

"We have come far enough this night," wheezed M'ingwé, pausing beside him. "Too far, if you ask me!"

"I did not ask you." M'alsum could feel his brother glaring at him from inside the dark hollow of his hood. Behind him, Kicháwan leaned on her snow walkers, hung her head, and huffed mist. Ahead, the dogs lay down in their traces. Appraising them, the headman frowned, realizing that they must have been straining through chest-high wallows for some time now, for even in the darkness he could see that the prow of the sled had pushed so much snow before it that it was going to take more than the best efforts of the pack to move it forward.

And still the snow came down.

M'alsum cursed, looked up and around, then cursed again. The ghosts were back! He growled and blinked them away. There was something about this forest, something alien and hostile and oppressive. It was claustrophic. It was unmanning. He could not wait to be clear of it. "We will go on!" he declared. "Take the snow scoops from the sled, Kicháwan. We will dig our way forward, and then we—"

"No!" M'ingwé interrupted, clearly at the limit of his endurance and patience. "I am as weary of walking as I am of holding my tongue. Stay where you are, Burden Woman! In all this snow and darkness, M'alsum, how can you be so sure that you are not leading us in circles? I, for one, have no desire to find myself back at that haunted creek. Take a good look around, Brother! The storm shows no signs of easing, and except for snowflakes, we are the only things moving within it. We must encamp now before we grow too weak to raise a shelter against the cold."

Kicháwan sank to her knees with a sob of relief.

"Get up," M'alsum ordered. "I am headman of this band. I, not M'ingwé, will tell you when we will encamp."

She moaned, clutched her head, leaned forward, and began to retch.

"Look at her, Brother," insisted M'ingwé. "She cannot go on. And look at the dogs. It is not like you to drive them to exhaustion. I do not like this forest any more than you do, but I will walk no more this night."

"I will not rest in the hunting grounds of cannibal spirits!"

"And I am too tired, hungry, and cold to be afraid of the ghosts that you have made this day."

Thunder rumbled, not overhead, and not only at the back of M'alsum's throat. It growled out of the night. It emanated from somewhere deep within the trees and the snowpack.

The headman tensed. Thunder without lightning, born of earth and not sky? Like everything else in this forest, the sound put him on edge. He held his breath, listening, avoiding the stink of Kicháwan's vomit. After a moment silence returned to the night, and he recognized the deep, somnolent hush of a still-settling storm. Hissing frustration, he knew that M'ingwé was right. Clouds would lie heavy upon the world for many hours. It would probably snow all night. To continue on was madness.

Again thunder rumbled.

And something moved within the trees through which the journeyers had just come.

M'alsum turned, heard a soft, slurring sound, a long, sustained sighing as though some huge and invisible beast had just exhaled. His head went high. The sour smell of Kicháwan's vomit was not the only stench to taint the night. There was another scent within the air, barely perceptible, but there all the same. Rank. Heavy. Subtly sweet. An elusive stink that brought to mind putrid meat and necrotic wounds. He caught his breath. It was the same scent that had raised the hackles on his skin back at the creek just before the manitous had come from the trees; it did the same now.

"The wind is rising again," observed M'ingwé. "It will grow even colder now. We must encamp, Brother, before we begin to freeze on our feet! I tell you, it is too dangerous to go on."

"And too dangerous to stay!" The headman fought back the impulse to bolt and run. Was M'ingwé as fearless as he seemed, or was fatigue making the man insensitive to danger? Or was he, M'alsum, still so shaken by earlier events that he was imagining danger where none existed? Was it possible that the elusive stench he had just caught on the night air was only the stink of his own fear?

"Come, Brother," M'ingwé was saying. "You must be wearier than you know. You have been making bad decisions all day. We will make camp now. We can take turns standing watch if you are afraid to sleep."

"Afraid?" M'alsum's hand flexed around the shaft of his father's copper-headed spear. A strange restlessness that had nothing to do with fatigue was building in him. "Do not accuse me of that, M'ingwé, unless you would have me deal with you as I have dealt with Sac."

Had he been slapped, M'ingwé's response could not have come faster or with more heat. "Be careful, M'alsum. Without me at your side you will be alone in this dark forest with only the dogs and the burden woman to protect you from your fears!"

"I fear nothing!" The lie resounded with such authority that the headman almost believed it.

"Is it so?" pressed M'ingwé, turning the words as though they were stone lancets with which he would prick and draw blood from his brother's pride. "I have stood with you today, Brother. Your choices were hard. As headman, your decisions, right or wrong, were yours to make and mine to obey. But do not stand there and tell me that you knew no fear before the dark came down this day. When the manitous came from the trees, you ran, Brother! You abandoned your woman and infant and ran like a panicked herd animal. I can still smell the stink of fear on you! As I can smell Sac's blood on us both! I do not like this smell, Brother. It worries me. It causes me to wonder what the forces of Creation may have in store for me in the world beyond this world as reward—or punishment—for obeying my headman this day. And so I have been thinking long and hard. You are my eldest brother. You alone know the way to the Dawnland. You say that you are known and respected there by many bands. Unlike Sac, I would not speak to betray your weakness to them, unless, when we reach the coast, you refuse to reward my loyalty to you in this world . . . by granting to me first choice of women and of all that we reap in trade."

There was an odd roaring at the back of M'alsum's head. "Your words cut me, Brother. Since we were boys together, I have always thought that Sac was the clever one. But in truth, M'ingwé, I never thought you stupid before now."

The younger man stiffened. "Make no mistake, M'alsum, I may not be as clever as Sac, but I am stronger. And I am no foolish youth, like Ne'gauni, to be duped into slavery, drowned, or left behind to die alone in a creek. It will prove harder for you to deal with me. I will watch my back with you . . . and my neck, eh? Deal fairly with me and I will keep your secrets. As you will keep mine. And when we at last return to the village of our father with all the wealth of the Dawnland in meat and hides, our people need never know of your cowardice or that you have abandoned one brother and strangled and dismembered a son of Meya'kwé this night."

Silence settled between the sons of Asticou, heavier than the storm, colder and darker than the night.

Kicháwan, sensing danger in it, looked up and, backhanding vomit from her face and ruff, whimpered softly.

M'alsum's head was throbbing. His pulse seemed to have slowed, and yet the roaring within his skull was more intense than ever.

"Come, Brother," invited M'ingwé. Mistaking silence for hesitancy on his brother's part, he visibly relaxed in his belief that he had just managed to shift the balance of power from M'alsum to himself. "The terrors of the trading trail have proved beyond doubt which one of us is best suited to be headman. You will feel better in the morning for seeing this my way. After you have slept, you will not remember that harsh words ever passed between us!"

"But I remember everything, Brother. Every word. Every promise. Every threat. Have you forgotten that our mother has said that my powers of recollection are a gift, a rare gift, one that assures that I will always be strong and unforgiving when I come against my enemies?"

M'ingwé snorted a rebuke. "Always with you it is Meya'kwé! What our mother says! What our mother thinks! What our mother yearns for! Maybe our father was right when he said that the way of your heart for her was not natural. And what is this talk of enemies? Surely, apart from the manitous of this forest, you have none!"

"I have you, Brother."

Again silence settled between the sons of Asticou.

Again Kicháwan whimpered.

Suddenly the dogs were up and barking and straining madly to be free of the traces that bound them to the sled.

"M'alsum . . . look there . . . " M'ingwé's voice had lost its cocky and belligerent edge; in less than a breath of time it had been reduced to a whisper of awe-strained incredulity. "Look, I say, in the trees through which we have just come!"

Kicháwan was scrambling wildly to her feet.

And M'alsum, scanning along the line of his brother's extended arm, felt his innards spasm and his heart leap into his throat. An enormous form was plodding toward them.

The headman fixed his gaze on a towering, snow-mantled presence of such overwhelming immensity that his mouth gaped wide at the sight of it. Nothing that lived could be so huge! It had to be a manitou. And yet, as it paused between the trees, he could see it breathing, inhaling and exhaling the night in a slow, even sequence that alternately created and destroyed clouds before the elongated mass of its hideous, high-domed head. The wind was blowing its scent to M'alsum. He caught the stink of old meat and open wounds, of something more dead than alive, of a terminally ill or injured animal, or of a manitou that walked in two worlds—that of the living and the dead. M'alsum shuddered. This was what he had scented on the rising wind! This was what he had sensed watching him across the miles! Not the ghosts of his slain brothers, woman, and son, but a monstrous manifestation of malevolent spirit power, a manitou unlike any other!

"Did you truly think that you could ever hope to outdistance all that you have done this day and night, M'alsum, Firstborn and Eldest Son of Asticou? Did you believe that I, or some other like me, would not come for you? In the names of Ne'gauni and Hasu'u and Sac I come! In memory of the abandoned and the slain, I come!"

"No . . ." M'alsum was shaking his head, unsure if the words he had just heard had been born of his own mind or had come to him out of the mouth of the beast.

As big as a mountain, shaggier than a bear about to enter hibernation, with tusks as thick as a grown man's thigh and as long as a young tree was tall, Katcheetohúskw—the five-legged man-crushing manitou whom Meya'kwé and her Grassland people called mammoth—was swaying on four of its stanchion limbs as, with its slender fifth leg curled upward between its eyes, it swung its great head menacingly.

M'alsum took a backward step. "It cannot be real."

"Be it real or not . . . be it mammoth or manitou . . . now *there* is an enemy for you, M'alsum!"

"Back away from it . . . perhaps it will turn and go its

own way," M'alsum urged quietly, with a calm he did not feel. It was all he could do to keep himself from turning and running off screaming into the night.

"Ah! Look at the size of him! Just like in our mother's tales, eh? Only bigger!" M'ingwé was not backing away. He had dropped his snow prods and was reaching for the triad of lances he carried beneath the shoulder straps of his backpack. "The legends do say that the one who kills and eats him lives forever! We can take him, Brother! Come! Are you not the son of Asticou our mother claims to have conceived inside the belly of a mammoth? Ha, I say to that, but here is another chance for you to prove that you are not a coward . . . as you tried to do when you shamed Sac and me into going back to the creek with you to retrieve Ne'gauni's pack, eh?"

M'alsum's head was down. Again he growled. How well his brother saw into the workings of his mind! Too well! But now, with his eyes locked on the mammoth, he shook his head to free it of potentially deadly distractions and said, "Truly you are the clever one, Brother, but just how would you have us kill that before it kills us?"

"Like this!" M'ingwé cried in a sudden fury of intent. Without so much as a breath of hesitation he took four running strides forward, then paused, levered back, and hurled a lance with all of his strength behind it.

Struck high in the face, the mammoth loosed a crescendoing cry that shook the night. Snow cascaded from the trees. A shrieking Kicháwan wallowed off into the darkness. The dogs went mad and, amidst tangled tracings, flashing teeth, spurting urine, and tucked tails, somehow succeeded in dragging the sled after the fleeing woman.

"Your spear, Brother . . . throw your spear in tandem with mine!" M'ingwé demanded as he let fly another lance.

M'alsum's hand tightened on the haft of his father's spear. He did not throw the weapon. Nor did he reach back for his other lances. He could not move. He stood as though mired in a nightmare, watching M'ingwé's second spear penetrate—not flesh, but frozen hanks of dark, ice-encrusted shoulder hair. In the next moment Death, in the guise of the mammoth spirit, Katcheetohúskw, broke into a trumpeting charge.

"Run!" commanded M'alsum.

M'ingwé did not run. He stood with one remaining spear in hand, ducking low and dancing lightly back and forth on his snow walkers, attempting to position himself for one last throw.

M'alsum was appalled. How could he flee while his brother confronted Death with such unabashed daring? Such courage! Such absolute foolishness! Katcheetohúskw was almost upon them. Its voice was a raging shriek. Its head was thrashing viciously from side to side, its tusks sweeping the night with deadly force.

"M'alsum! Your spear . . . throw your spear! Now!" cried M'ingwé as he powered back and released his last lance.

It arced high. It sang. And it struck true.

But it was M'alsum, not M'ingwé, who shouted in triumph when the stone point embedded itself deep within the mammoth's right eye. *Now,* thought the headman, *now the beast will drop and die!* And yet, impossibly it seemed, the mammoth did neither.

Katcheetohúskw uttered a high, pitiful, almost human cry, turned a tight circle on its back feet, and grasped the offending spear with the curling tip of its long, slender fifth leg. Unable to withdraw the lance, it cracked the shaft in two, then, still crying, hurled the broken half back at M'ingwé and resumed its charge in earnest.

The shout that came from M'ingwé's mouth had nothing to do with triumph. It was a screech of pure terror as the man threw himself into a desperate dive to avoid the scything impact of swinging tusks. As he hit the snow and rolled hard to his right, he disappeared beneath the forelimbs of the charging beast while M'alsum—face to face with the advancing specter of his own imminent death—turned and, losing complete control of his bladder, ran pissing and screaming for his life.

The mammoth followed.

M'alsum could feel the beast at his back. He could smell the heat of its breath. He could hear branches cracking as Katcheetohúskw crashed through the forest after him. Jolted by the shock of the monster's footfall, he gripped Asticou's spear in both hands and, holding it up and out ahead of him for balance, put all his strength behind each high-stepping stride.

Gasping, sobbing, with his snow walkers dispersing his weight and allowing him to move across the snow with the light-footed grace and agility of a fleeing snow hare, he instinctively cut a zigzag course, making his way into the densest growth of trees, hoping to slow and confound his pursuer before exhaustion overcame and confounded him.

He was not sure just when the strange, bright energy began to build within him. Born of the very terror that had only moments ago immobilized him, it burned white behind his eyes, enabling him to see his way as though by daylight, to keep his thoughts fixed so sharply ahead that, even though his limbs were afire and his lungs burned with every intake of breath, he knew that he had somehow run himself beyond the limits of fatigue.

Beyond fear!

The realization brought a new surge of energy. With Katcheetohúskw closing on him, M'alsum raced full out, no longer in the grip of mindless panic but once again in complete control of his mind and body. Following his wits, he stayed within the cover of the trees until he came to a change of terrain and, finding inspiration in it, instead of keeping to level ground, deliberately headed downhill toward the bottom of a treacherous ravine across deep snow and around outcroppings of massive boulders.

Had the grade been any steeper, it would have been vertical. Beyond terror—or perhaps inspired by it— M'alsum looked back and saw the mammoth blundering along at the top of the defile. "Come, Katcheetohúskw! Follow me, Manitou! Show me if you are as stupid as my brothers!"

The sheer audacity of the invitation emboldened him. Traversing the slope in wildly bounding leaps, he cut his way downward around monolithic boulders and across broad stretches of open snowpack. A series of bold, tension-releasing yips went out of him. He was going to survive! He was going to outrun the manitou! He knew it! Felt it! It was not likely that the mammoth would commit its ungainly girth to such a dangerous slope, but if it did, it would never again harass travelers in this cursed forest, for as he ran on to safety on the far side of the ravine, it would surely fall to its death. Exalting in his cleverness and his anticipated triumph over Death, the headman laughed as he ran.

Suddenly the tip of one of his snow walkers came up under the exposed trunk of a snow-bent sapling, and

M'alsum fell forward onto his face at the bottom of the ravine.

Stunned, he felt the footfall of the giant shaking the world. He heard its thundering cries. He smelled its stench . . . and his own. And then an anger such as he had never before experienced took hold of him. Anger at the beast for shaming him. Anger at himself for allowing himself to be shamed. And anger at the very forces of Creation for allowing such an exemplary man as M'alsum, firstborn and eldest son of Asticou, to be so unjustly humiliated.

"No . . ." The word bled out of him. "It ends here. Never again will I allow fear to shame me!" Amazed and relieved to see that he still held Asticou's spear in one hand, he forced himself to rise, turn, and position himself and the weapon for whatever must come next.

It came.

In a tumult, it came.

Screaming, it came.

Wallowing forward, its tusks extending like bone-white lances the size and girth of lodgepoles, Katcheetohúskw kept its mass of flesh and bone and hair and hide moving straight downhill.

M'alsum held his ground. He would not run! Not this time! Not ever again! If he had to hurl himself beneath the mammoth as M'ingwé had done, he would spear the beast in its gut and at least know the sweet taste of courage as he died. And yet, as he stared up in slowly dawning horror, he saw that Katcheetohúskw was no longer charging. It was slipping and sliding downward toward him on its rump. With its forelimbs braced, the mammoth fought in vain for purchase in the deep snow. If it lost its balance on the treacherous slope now, there would be no glorious confrontation, no man standing boldly to his fears, for from where M'alsum stood now it was obvious that the mammoth was about to come crashing straight down on top of him.

And then it happened.

Katcheetohúskw—head, trunk, and tusks turned skyward—bellowed as though in supplication to the storm spirits just as its front legs went out from under it. Tumbling rump over head, the mammoth plummeted over a thirty-foot drop and, as the headman scrambled madly for his life, came to rest with an earthshaking thunk on the snow-covered rocks at the bottom of the ravine.

M'alsum dared not breathe. He lay sprawled where he had thrown himself, within an arm's reach of where Katcheetohúskw had come to rest. He waited for the beast to move, to rise and come for him again, but the great mountain-of-a-manitou lay motionless, silent. After a moment, when he was certain that the mammoth was dead, the headman got to his feet, so shaken that he could not keep his trembling limbs beneath him. Lowering himself to one knee, he braced his father's spear across his extended thigh, willed himself to breathe again, and heard an owl raise its voice in lonely ululation to the spirits of the night.

A tremor of recognition shivered beneath his skin. Once again Death had come and gone its way through this haunted forest. Once again he had run from its manitou presence in blind panic, but this time he had forced himself to turn and face his fear. And Death had not taken him. He had outwitted it!

"Brother!"

M'alsum looked up to see M'ingwé sliding downslope toward him.

"That was something to see!" shouted the man, raising a snow prod and waving it until, pausing at a circumspect distance from the mammoth, he shook his head and said, "For a moment I could have sworn that it had you, M'alsum!"

The headman leveled his gaze at his brother. "And I could have sworn that I saw you die."

"As you see, I am still alive, no thanks to you," slurred M'ingwé. With his hood blown back, he knelt, gloved up a fistful of snow, pressed it within his palms, then lobbed it hard at the fallen mammoth. When the beast did not move, he eyed it thoughtfully, mumbled sourly that it had fallen on his spears, then rose and moved closer to give the downed beast a resounding kick to make certain it was dead. Confident that it was no longer a threat, he walked around it, paused to poke at the extended noselike end of its fifth leg, then climbed onto the corpse and strutted proudly atop the curve of its massive rib cage.

"Do you think it is true, M'alsum, what the legends of our mother's Grassland people say? That the one who kills and eats of the flesh of Katcheetohúskw will be Master of the Feast of Life forever? An immortal?"

"You were never one to hold much faith in legends."

M'ingwé knelt beside the horrendous eye wound and, after failing to free his projectile point from the ruined orb, bent close to lap up blood and eye fluid before leaping from the corpse and coming to M'alsum's side. "Now we will see, eh? Maybe I will be immortal! Hmm. You reek of piss, Brother, like a frightened dog. You should be grateful that our mother is not with us to see you like this . . . or to smell the stink of your shame."

The rush of adrenaline that had enabled M'alsum to win his race for life had left him exhausted. Fire spread through his blood and bones; every sinew, tendon, and nerve ending throbbed with heat. As he looked up at

M'ingwé, the odd roaring was there again, at the back of his head.

"What will the Dawnland people say when we come to them dragging the tree-trunk teeth of Katcheetohúskw, eh?" posed M'ingwé, nodding happily to himself. "Who among them will hesitate to say that I am the bravest of all men to have slain such a beast as this? And who among them will hesitate to offer the best meat and furs and women to the one whose spears have killed the mighty Katcheetohúskw?"

"Your spears may have struck him, M'ingwé, but it was I who thought to lead him downhill to the fall that killed him."

"No, Brother. I will not hear that. We both know what happened. You froze. Then you turned and ran for your life. Just as you did at the creek. It is what you do when you fear for the safety of your own skin. It seems you cannot help yourself. But I will keep your secret. You need not lie about being a coward. Not to me. While you were off on your mad run to nowhere, I put our Kicháwan to calming the dogs and setting up the lean-to. She could use our help. So get up, Brother. We will cut the tusks and tail and the fifth leg from this manitou when the storm is over. Now we both need to rest and eat and get some sleep. Come, I say! I am sure that you do not want me to leave you here alone with your many fears."

The roaring in M'alsum's head was behind his eyes now. Bright. Cold. Cutting sharp. He fixed his gaze on the lifeless form of the great mammoth, at the fallen embodiment of pure terror, and, knowing that he had faced this beast head on and outwitted it, informed his brother quietly, "I do not think I will ever be afraid to stand to my fears again, M'ingwé."

"Ha! Your words do not touch me with belief, Coward! From now on I will be headman in your place. And I think I will have our father's copper-headed spear. I have earned it! Here, give it to me, Brother. Now. You will show me a little respect for a change, for who else in all this world is left alive who knows the extent of your cowardice and will protect you from your many fears?"

"No one." With an ease that surprised him, M'alsum yielded to M'ingwé's request. He gave his brother their father's spear. Without so much as a second thought or pang of regret—in that single breath of time, a man a little less full of himself than M'ingwé might have anticipated his brother's intent and moved to avoid it—M'alsum rammed the tip of Asticou's copper-headed lance beneath the base of M'ingwé's sternum and drove the point straight upward into his brother's heart.

Chapter Four

▼▼▼▼▼▼▼

Darkness and fire.

The throbbing of a drum.

Ne'gauni moaned. He lay adrift in fevered darkness, his body aflame, his heart pounding. Somewhere beyond the blurred peripheries of his mind, an owl called. The voice of Death! Light flared behind his eyes, and within that inner light that he had yet to recognize as Vision, the youth saw his brother M'ingwé's face.

Eyes wide, pupils dilated, and mouth agape, an expression of shock and horror expanded upon the wide, sullen features until, suddenly, the man screamed and blood gushed from his throat.

So much blood!

Ne'gauni gasped. The inner light was fading. M'ingwé's face faded with it. As the youth came swimming desperately up out of the thick black soup of delirium, he could have sworn that he was back at the creek, lying sprawled, not on his back but on his belly, watching helplessly as Wíndigo, Great Ghost Cannibal, walked away from him with Hasu'u in his arms.

Across the bloodstained snow of a winter killing

ground, the chief of the manitous moved with the long, sure, confidently contemptuous stride of a conqueror. Slowly, with the copper-headed spear of Asticou gripped in one bloodied fist, he stepped over the dismembered bodies of the slain, kicked the severed heads of M'ingwé and Sac out of his way, then paused, turned his raven's head, and set small, fire-red eyes questing toward Ne'gauni.

"Come," invited the manitou. "I am Master of the Feast of Life. Follow me. If you dare."

Ne'gauni was stunned. The great black beak of the manitou was opening, gaping, revealing the wide, deep maw of a carnivorous mouth. With a gasp, the youth saw a tiny human being crouching inside that mouth, wedging up the upper beak with its shoulders, holding it open with tiny, bloodied hands as its face contorted with effort and spoke on a snarl.

"Why do you stare? Do you not know me?"

Ne'gauni felt his jaw drop. The snarling human face within the face of Wíndigo, Great Ghost Cannibal, was not the face of a manitou. It was the face of his eldest brother.

"M'alsum!" he cried. "I have been searching for you! And for the Dawnland woman. And for Sac and M'ingwé. Ah, forgive me, Brother! I did not mean to cause your death! Wait for me, M'alsum! Do not leave me a captive in the den of Mowea'qua! We will walk together in the world beyond this world, my brother! We will—"

"You are no brother of mine," sneered M'alsum. He stood erect within the mouth of the manitou and in an instant was transformed somehow. Great Ghost Cannibal was gone. M'alsum—resplendent in the black-feathered robe of Trickster—had taken his place. He had become Raven. All at once man and manitou and predator, he flew forward to alight heavily upon Ne'gauni's chest. "Die!" he commanded. He bent his raptor's head to feed upon Ne'gauni's flesh while, from out of nowhere, a pair of wolves came to hunker close, growling worriedly together as they shared in the feast that M'alsum had made for them of the youth's life.

Ne'gauni sobbed. Pain seared his senses. He felt himself stabbed beneath his breastbone, and as his heart lurched, a single bright, hot, excruciating nodule of agony burst within the core of his brain to bring him sobbing from the depths of the river of death.

"Rest . . . sleep . . . If to live and heal you are, no more troubled dreams must dream you! Weaken you they do, and cause you to bleed and thrash about and your sutures to rip and—"

"Dreams?"

"Yes, Wounded One, dreams. Bad dreams have you . . . very bad."

"Then I am still alive?"

"Yes, say I, alive you are."

He sighed, neither comforted nor convinced, but the soft, feminine voice was almost as soothing as the cool moistness of the medicine rag that was being drawn gently across his brow. He trembled. His pain was ebbing; he felt his body beginning to relax. The pungent aroma of medicinal herbs, oils, and pounded roots was in his nostrils, along with the good smell of woodsmoke and well-banked coals and of some sort of unfamiliar meat being roasted. His belly gurgled with hunger. His eyes fluttered open.

She was still there, crouching close beside him in the darkness, silhouetted against the fire.

He sighed again. She was always there, a vision born of fevered dreams. "You . . . " he sighed.

"Yes," she affirmed softly, withdrawing the medicine rag, cocking her head, allowing the combined glow of firelight and a nearby oil lamp to play across her pale features so that, within the night-black netting of her hair, the long, smooth oval of her childlike face appeared as cool and beautiful as a winter moon.

Confused and enchanted, Ne'gauni reached out to her. "Hasu'u? Is it you, Hasu'u? I have been searching for you in the dark world that lies beyond this world. There is so much that I want to say to you, Dawnland Woman. And to my brothers. There is so much that I—"

"Yah!"

The exclamation struck at Ne'gauni's senses with all the unforgiving impact of a braining club. He gasped against recurring pain. His hand fell to his side. His right shoulder felt as though a burning coal were lodged within it. His left leg throbbed mercilessly. His face ached beneath a heavy swathing of bandages. As the moon-faced girl moved away, his mind reeled. Perhaps the lovely one was not real at all? An aged specter now knelt beside him in the girl's place. He stared, horrified and revolted by the ugliness of "Mowea'qua . . . Wolf Woman . . . manitou!"

The specter hissed derision and curled back a hairy upper lip to display a ruin of timeworn teeth. "How readily you see what we would have you see! Stupid! Fearful! Credulous and hateful beast! View you the world through twisted eyes. It is the way of your kind. Abhor you all that is not like yourself . . . all that you cannot understand . . . all that you cannot control. Mmph! But ask I this of you: If manitou I am—a ghost in your eyes—what, then, are you in mine, Stranger, as in and out of the country of the dead you wander?"

"I . . . I am Ne'gauni! I am the fourth and youngest son of Asticou, hunt chief of the inland forest, only son of Wawautaésie of the Lakeland People! I am He Walks Ahead! I am—"

"He Walks Ahead? No. Never again will that name sit lightly on your bones." After a mocking snort, the specter answered its own question. "You are as good as a ghost, Wounded One, no more or less than a haunting in the memories of those who left you behind to die in the hunting grounds of Mowea'qua."

Ne'gauni winced. Although speech roused pain in his injured face, he could not do less than defend his brothers. "Of course they left me behind! How could dead men do anything else? My brothers were slain by the same phantoms who struck me down."

"Phantoms, say you? The mask wearers? Ha! More gullible are you than thought I possible! And brothers, say you? Mmph. So much for the loyalty of Strangers! By the time Young One's howls drew me to the creek, your brothers had taken for themselves your snow walkers and pack frame and, running like frightened dogs, left you to die. Saw them clearly enough did I. Ran they well and fast . . . for dead men."

Ne'gauni could not believe what he was hearing. He would not believe it. Surely the words of the specter were some sort of cruel manitou trick meant to confuse him and cause him further pain! And yet, before Mowea'qua had come to him the second time, had he not imagined his brothers bending over him as he lay helpless in the creek? Had he not heard them murmuring together, felt them pulling at him, hurting him before they had gone their way, vanishing into snow and darkness, leaving him to die alone?

He caught his breath. Hope shivered in his heart. Was it possible that they were still alive? Had they come back for him after all, only to be driven off by the manitous who now held him captive? They had the burden woman to think of. And the dogs. And the trading goods. But if they were still alive, they might yet come for him . . . and if he was still alive, he might yet find his way to them. Together they would seek the bones of Hasu'u. Together they would honor her spirit. Together they would . . .

Again he winced. Something was touching his left leg, distracting him, plucking lightly just below his knee. Gently. So very gently. And yet the resultant pain was unbearable. "Stop!" he demanded as he felt the warmth of long, moist strips of bandages being peeled away.

Whatever—or whoever—was working at his leg did not stop.

His anger suddenly cleared his head. He was the old Ne'gauni again. He would not be bullied! Not even by a pair of manitous! They were female. He was male. And he was the youngest and boldest and best of the sons of Asticou.

"Get away from me!" he commanded, trying to sit up, to prop himself on his left elbow, to pull his leg away from unwelcome ministrations. But no matter how hard he tried, his arm would not support his weight and his leg would not obey his will.

He cursed his weakness. And his leg. What was wrong with it? And what was the manitou doing to it that was causing such appalling pain?

"Leave it!" he roared. Empowered by pain and anger, he finally managed to force his elbow far enough back to support the weight of his upper body as he levered his torso upward—only to be stunned by the sudden brutal shock of air touching the exposed nerve endings of a raw and recently cauterized wound. He stared at that wound . . . at the stump of his left leg . . . and collapsed in a dead faint.

▼▼▼▼

The young one shuddered. She felt his pain as though it were her own. To her right, within the recesses of the vaulted den, the wolf had been awakened by the Stranger's shout, and she was suddenly aware of its eyes fixed upon her. With the wick of the oil lamp beginning to gutter for want of fuel, she squinted into the shadows to see the animal laying back its ears as it cocked its head and stared curiously at her from the place where she had tethered it well away from the fire pit. "The wounded one at my hands *will* heal, as you have nearly healed, dear friend," she informed the wolf. "Go back you now to sleep, U'na'li. Dream of your lost children and of how it will be when you once again run free across the snow to seek out those of your kind."

"You must also sleep," snapped Old One. Sitting cross-legged on her woven sleeping mat close to the fire pit, she reached to pinch fire from the oil lamp, then tented her heavy fur blankets around herself as she exhaled a long, dolorous sigh. "A night and a day and now most of another night have passed since foolishly we brought this wounded one here. In all this time scarcely slept have you, Mowea'qua! Nothing more can you do for the wounded one this night. Now that he has seen the worst of his injuries, die he will, of this I am sure."

"I will not let him die."

"His kami have deserted him, and his heart we have taken from him, child."

"No! His *leg* we have taken! The same it is not. And

his kami have not deserted him. The spirits of our forest have to him led me. I am his kami now, his spirit, and I will give back to him his heart to live."

"Mmph." With this single wordless articulation Old One might just as well have named the young one Fool.

Staring angrily through smoky darkness, the young one scowled at the slump of her grandmother's furred form, sensed the small, sharp eyes fixed upon her, knew that the long, wrinkled mouth would be set in a disapproving downward curve, as was her own. Annoyance joined with defiance to find voice upon her tongue. "Live he will! See this you will! When strong enough he is, we will journey together to the sacred spring. Bathe he will in the waters where clear crystals grow, and it will be as in the tales that Kinap tells. His leg will grow back, and beautiful again will his face be."

The old one exhaled a guffaw of total aggravation. "Kinap and his stories! Sacred springs! Magic crystals! Water is water. Stone is stone. The sacred spring bubbles out of your father's mind, child, not out of any place that you or I may ever hope to see. That which we have cut from this Stranger's body is gone from him forever, and beautiful his kind can never be! He will live or die not by magic, but according to the strength or weakness of his own spirit, not yours. So sleep, Young One. Rest. Soon enough dawn it will be, and his wound wrappings will once more need changing. Ah, dawn! If ever the sun we see again in all this endlessly falling snow!" She shivered and allowed her teeth to make a series of small clatterings before she whispered, "Tell you I, dear one, in the world beyond our world something has shifted. Changed. Felt this in my bones have I since before the coming of this wounded one into our den: the return of the lasting cold, the coming of the long darkness that the Ancient Ones of all tribes have foretold. It is as though I opened my eyes one morning and looked out upon the time beyond beginning . . . into a world of eternal snow and ice."

"Long winters we have before seen," the young one reminded her. "When my father comes, he will bring the sun. You will see!" Her insistent words brought a grunt of acquiescence from the old one but did little to cheer her own troubled heart. Her long, dark brows came down. The world *had* changed. She wondered what Kinap would have to say about the endless cold and about this wounded Stranger, this Enemy whom she had found abandoned in their forest. Cocking her head in the manner of the still-watching wolf, she could hear the old storyteller's voice scraping across her memories, a low, grainy rasp forced out of a smoke- and heat-damaged larynx so thickened by scar tissue that he always sounded as though he were attempting to clear sand from his throat.

"A day will come, Young One, when a gift you will find in the forest. A rare and special gift. A companion to lead you to a new life, to walk forever at your side when Old One and I are no more than dreams upon the wind of your thoughts. So carefully must you look when stalking game in the woods and setting your snares and pit traps. Under fallen bark and beneath the rain caps of mushrooms, amidst clumps of the little blue harebells that grow on the rocks close to the falls, or high above your head in a songbird's nest or down low, hiding in caribou moss, a mate will one day be waiting for you, a forest man, a mikahmuwesu, an immortal for my Mowea'qua."

The young one chewed her lower lip. The Stranger was much too big to hide beneath mushroom caps or within birds' nests or clumps of flowers, and she had seen too much of his blood and wounds to believe that he might yet prove to be an immortal. When she had seen him fall to the power of the raiders' flying sticks, Kinap's promise had been the farthest thing from her mind.

She remembered the moment with extraordinary clarity. Lying atop the snowdrift, she had observed the raid, wanting to see Strangers die, hoping the two packs of Enemies would kill each other off so that they would never again trespass in her forest. That had not happened. One pack had run. The other had set itself upon a pair of stragglers. Swallowing down disappointment, she had waited impatiently for the killing to be done and for the raiders to go their way. Although she knew that Old One would have forbidden it, she had every intention of venturing onto the killing ground to claim for herself not only the arrow that had flown wide into the trees but the arrow that had imbedded itself in the wounded one's breast. The sharp little stone projectile points that tipped the flying sticks of Strangers were invaluable for uncounted uses.

Indeed, as she watched the wounded one swept downstream by the creek, she had feared that she was about to be deprived of a portion of her booty until the outreaching arms of the fallen tree had ensnared his body. She had thanked the kami for that and, even after the raiders had gone their way with the female Stranger, had held her ground until she was certain that the wounded one was dead. She had not forgotten Old One's oft-spoken warnings about the deceptively dangerous and murderous magic of their kind.

Strangers could rise unseen to attack from mists and shadows!

Enemies could turn into ravaging beasts at will!

But the wounded one had lain as inert as a dead sala-mander and had soon proved incapable of magic.

And yet, she wondered about this now, for when she had at last dared to come close enough to look into his eyes, into his long, dark, living eyes, she had been struck to the heart by their resemblance to the eyes of the other . . . of the beautiful one, of the one whose face had seared itself into her mind and heart and spirit. It was in that moment that she had remembered Kinap's promise and known that she could not simply rip the arrow from this Stranger's breast and leave him to bleed to death in the creek.

A little breath caught in her throat. How she missed the intrepid old giant! How she wished that he were with her now to soothe and clarify the way of her thoughts! What kept him from wintering with them this year? Why had he not come tromping boldly through the forest on his enormous snow walkers, announcing his arrival as he al-ways did with high, whooping howls, his beloved face a shining knot of burn scars, his tongue quick with news of the world beyond their world, his massive shoulders laden with the many wonderful surprises that he gathered on his yearly wanderings especially to cheer her and Old One during the long, cold heart of winter?

"He *will* come!" she insisted to herself as much as to her grandmother. "He *must* come! And when he does, he will look upon the wounded one and tell you that he *is* the one promised to me, the one who—"

"Mmph! Kinap and his shining words! Kinap and his sweet promises! Always tries he to make a young one smile and ease the worries of this old one's heart! Yes, remember I his promise of one who would be your forever companion, of one who would at your side walk in the long days and

nights that must come when he and I breathe our last and
you have fleshed our bones and burned them clean and
placed them in a circle within the sacred grove. But be not
in such a hurry to flesh and burn my bones, dear one, for
although borne witness have I to the rising of many a sun,
intend I to bear witness to many another! And tell you I
now that nothing is forever. In this forest—in this world—
everything *is* changing. The past winters too long have
been. Too brief have been the summers. The trees of our
sacred grove set seed no longer; they grow old and sicken
and die around us even as the great mammoths sickened
and died in the days of my youth."

"A mammoth there *is* in our forest! The Great One!
Earth Shaker! Thunder Speaker! In the storm we heard his
voice, his great rumbling mammoth voice. And know you
what Kinap says: As long as the mammoth kind walk
within our world, we, too, will live and grow strong."

"Kinap again! Perhaps it is good that he has not come
to winter with us. His stories your head fill with nonsense.
And as for the Great One, out of the tusks and bones of his
fallen kindred have we raised this den in honor to his kind.
When walks he near, smell I the stink of sickness that eats
away at his ancient bones, and hear I rumblings of pain and
loneliness in his voice. Where are the bulls that wintered
with him in this forest? Where is the great white cow that
once walked at his side? Where are her sisters? Where are
his calves? How long can live his kind when, like the great
trees of the sacred grove, he sets no seed? Tell you I, child,
things *are* changing. All around us they change. And now
again come Strangers from the north with their masks and
their flying sticks. And out of the deep woods Strangers
venture from the south and west. What do they want in
our part of the forest? Is there not meat enough in their

own hunting grounds? Will they hunt the Great One? Will we once again by their kind be forced to flee deeper into the darkness of our world until not even you and I can see the mark of the Old Tribe upon us?"

The young one hugged herself as though buffeted by the chill of an unseen wind. Before she could think about what she was saying, she blurted hotly, "The mark is not mine!"

"What say you? Of course the mark is yours! You were born as furred as the cubs of U'na'li the wolf and will, in old age, be as furred as I. Mmph! Too long have you gone without sleep. Rest now. In the dawn light, good sense once more will you speak, Mowea'qua."

The young one cocked her head again. "The wounded one by my name calls you, Grandmother. Why does he do that?"

"Know you as well as I that to the Strangers there is only one name for the females of our kind: Mowea'qua, Wild One, Wolf Woman. Mmph. It is a name to which we have always answered with pride!"

"But speaks it he as though it fouls his tongue and sits fearsome and loathsome upon his mind. Are we so terrible to behold?"

"All Strangers see us so. As we see them. But, in truth, in all this world, they are the only loathsome, foul, and completely fearsome beasts!"

The young one turned her eyes downward to where the wounded one lay in darkness, still close to her, but not so close to the fire pit lest, during one of his bursts of delusional thrashing, he throw wide an arm and burn himself on a hot stone. "He is not so fearsome nor foul or loathsome now that we have his clothes cut away and his skin bathed. Sometimes when looks he at me, ugly I am not to his eyes. Needs me he does, Old One. As much as U'na'li needed me when the great bear mauled her and her wolf pack left her for dead. As much as U'wo'hi'li the eagle needed me when the viper struck him in his eye. And so sleep I cannot. Wake he may and call my name."

"Mmph. Calls he many times to the one he needs . . . to the one he wants . . . to the one who is not in his eyes ugly. 'Hasu'u! Hasu'u!' he calls. That name is not your name, Mowea'qua. Truly old must I be, and weak of mind, to have agreed to help you bring him here! Content we should have been to do what always we do when his kind pass through our part of the forest: wait patiently in a hidden place until they go their way, and then, only when it is safe, seek out for our own use any stone-headed flying sticks they may have left behind, and take for needles and awls the stone splinters that litter the edges of their abandoned fire circles. But no! You would seek the brightheaded lance and into our very den bring this wounded one! Ah! We should have ripped the flying stick from his chest and left him in the creek to die! Foolish! Foolish! A Stranger he is! An Enemy! In his veins runs the blood of those who have your mother slain!"

"Not much blood has he left, Grandmother."

"Bah! What if hunting him his own kind come?"

The strangest slur of emotions rippled through the young one's heart. She wondered if she had ever felt quite so sad. "Why for him should they hunt when twice they have chosen to leave him behind?"

"Because Strangers are as unpredictable as they are ugly. How could you forget this teaching, Mowea'qua? Seen by the Strangers you could have been! Hunted! Captured! Slain, as your mother was slain. And then, without you, what meaning would life have for me? You and I and old Kinap—for all we know, the last of our kind are we!"

Again the young one sighed. "Ugly the Strangers were not to my eyes, Grandmother," she admitted quietly, feeling again the painful tug at her heart as she remembered looking up from the base of the snowbank to see the master of the Strangers' pack cracking his whip, his hip-length black hair flying back in the wind, his powerful face set, so strong, so smooth, so wondrously and perfectly beautiful! A jagged breath caught in her throat. The blood of Mother slayers ran in his veins. How could she feel anything other than hatred and revulsion toward him? Why did her very being ache when she thought of him? Why did the thought of never seeing him again bring tears to her eyes?

Yearning to see him again, her hands strayed to her face, to her strong, smooth face. As confusion unsettled her, she attempted to shake it off by assuring the old one, "Careful was I. Seen was I not. So close your eyes and rest you now, Grandmother. Tired must you be. Worry no more. The Strangers are far away. He . . . they will not come here."

"Bah! How can I sleep? There is now a Stranger *among* us! In our own den an Enemy sleeps!"

▼▼▼▼

The old one was shaking. Worry no more, indeed! What sort of advice was this? The advice of a child. The advice of an ignorant, inexperienced, and all too gullible child. The advice of one who knew nothing of life or of the world beyond the forest.

She felt sick with despair. If Mowea'qua was ignorant of the world, who was to blame? Where lay the fault for the child's naïveté if not in the lap of the one who had raised her? Deep within Old One's breast, her heart made an odd, disquieting little leap. The backs of her folded knees felt suddenly weak. Her palms tingled and broke into a cold sweat. She recognized the signs of panic and, knowing how best to banish them, breathed slowly and deeply for a while, telling herself that the young one was right about one thing: She was tired, more tired than she would want her granddaughter to know.

Still sitting upright, bundling close to the fire pit, Old One closed her eyes. Years spent in hiding and on the run had taught her how to summon sleep and take advantage of it on command. It came instantly, a sudden ceasing of consciousness, a mindless state of guarded relaxation. There were no dreams within it, but there was rest. Yet it was the thin, easily bruised sleep of the habitually worried, and now the hissing of a coal in the fire pit was enough to wake her.

Her eyes batted open. Time had passed. She could hear the low, relaxed snoring of U'na'li the wolf. And she could feel a change in the substance of the night. The interior darkness of the den had thinned somewhat, and the light scurrying of tiny feet padding along an overhead beam caused her to look up.

Somewhere in the subtly graying heights of the vaulted roof, a mouse had begun to gnaw on a piece of thatching or thong, or perhaps on a seed it had carried to some secret storage place, or on a hard-shelled insect it had snatched unawares or stolen from one of the uncountable spiderwebs that gauzed the rafters. The gnawing was slow, persistent, unhurried; the mouse, it seemed, tended to the needs of life untroubled this night. Old One wished that she could say the same for herself.

A hard gust of wind slapped against the exterior of the

lodge. Cold air found its way downward through the smoke hole. She looked past the sleeping eagle and watched spiderwebs trembling as they snared flurries of descending snowflakes. Hanging baskets, hanks of dried grasses and herbs, twistings of thong and sinew and vine, air-dried cuts of meat, and the carcasses of various small birds, reptiles, and mammals swung gently to and fro from the rafters.

Chilled by the sudden bitter draft, Old One pulled her ragged sleeping skins around bare shoulders. Relaxing into their familiar warmth, she found herself gazing at the tall, conical birchbark smoker that the young one had erected with great care over the stone curbing at the far side of the fire pit. Infused with new life by the errant touch of cold air, the coals beneath the hardwood frame were swelling and glowing bright inside their blanketing of ash as the young one knelt close in attendance. Old One shook her head, worrying, wondering if Mowea'qua was ever going to sleep again. Scowling, she watched her reach for one of the stirring bones that stood upright against a curbstone and gently prod the coals to make certain that a low, even heat continued to rise under the smoker. Then, from a nearby pile of newly cut balsam tips, the young one took up a few tufts of evergreen and tossed them onto the coals immediately beneath the frame. The result was almost immediate, a pungent steam rising from the needles, a sparking of sap and oils, and then a thin blue smoke as sweet and redolent of the boreal forest as the contents of her granddaughter's smoker would eventually be.

"Ah, Grandmother, awake you are again. You have not slept nearly long enough." Mowea'qua moved back to the wounded one, shrugged off her wolfskin den cape, and lay down beside the Stranger.

Old One scowled. The young one had been bathing

him again. His bed furs had been thrown back; she could smell the pungent scent of medicinal oil.

"Come," invited Mowea'qua. "Very cold has it grown. The warmth of our bodies must be medicine for him now. Is this not what the healing ways would say for us to do?"

"It is," affirmed the old one, yet made no move to join her granddaughter. The smoke was causing her eyes to water and burn, but she could not bring herself to take her gaze from beauty and youth: the young one, so slender, with every sleek rounding curve of her body ripe with the promise of maturation soon to come; the Stranger, lying so still, breathing so shallowly that Old One was certain his life spirit was close to wandering from the confines of his body.

A deep slur of emotion troubled her mind. Long had it been since she had looked upon a naked male of his kind. She had forgotten how distracted and inexplicably disturbed she had always been by their smooth, virtually furless appearance. Her forehead creased, sending the deep V of her hairline plunging to merge with the thick, wiry tufts of her graying eyebrows. She told herself that if she were the life spirit of this injured youth, she would surely leave his body. Why stay? Two dawns ago he must have been sleek-skinned and resilient with health, as powerful and, to those of his own tribe, as beautiful to behold as a young forest lion. And as dangerous to *her* kind!

A shudder went through the old one. Now he lay torn and sundered, with his face stitched from the top of one ear to the base of the other. Beneath his bandages his features were so swollen and discolored that he was even uglier and more repellent than the painted wooden disguises worn by the masked Strangers when they came stalking through the forest, talking to each other in the voices of ravens, pretending to be manitous as they set themselves to raiding unsuspecting wanderers of their own kind.

"You shiver, Grandmother, and your face shows weary above your beard. Come, say I. Next to the wounded one lie down and rest again."

Grateful to be drawn from unhappy reverie, the old one shivered against the intensifying predawn cold and moved to settle her bony, hirsute body close alongside the Stranger. With Mowea'qua lying on the other side, she drew her bearskin and other bed furs over him, herself, and the young one.

"Still he lives, Grandmother! Said you to me that he must surely die from the shock of setting his eyes upon our cutting. But touch him. Feel him. Soothe him with your palms. See for yourself that we have killed him not."

The old one was still shivering. Against her lightly furred skin, the body of the wounded Stranger was hot and dry with fever. She sent a hand questing gently over him. He moaned. The young one was right; he was still alive. His smooth, hairless skin rippled beneath her touch, and that part of him that marked him male extended from its scant base of fur to lie warm across the upper curve of his thigh. She found her granddaughter's hand there and moved her own away.

Closing her eyes, the old one conceded that a time must soon come when Mowea'qua would have a need for this, a right to this, regardless of the cost. She did not like to think of it. Her granddaughter was still a child! But what was it Kinap had said that had so upset her before he had last gone his way? Something about the young one fast blossoming into a flower? Yes. Something about life being ultimately bearable for her only if there was some small semblance of joy and fulfillment within it, no matter how rare, no matter how fleeting? Yes. Something that had attempted to touch her old heart and make her understand that, come summer, wind-borne seedlings of flowers that would otherwise find no sustenance on the perpetually shadowed woodland floor would take root and blossom wherever thin rays of morning sunlight struck crevices in the rock and warmed them enough to nurture life.

"Life must seek life!" he had told her. "Even if all the young one is to know is one brief flowering, one single moment of sweetness, it will be enough to strengthen and sustain her for all her remaining days. You cannot deny her this, my dear old friend, for if you do, tell you I, better for her had she never been born."

The wounded one sighed.

Distracted, the old one sighed with him and was only too glad to release Kinap's words. They still upset her, threatened her already seriously shadowed sense of well-being. Moving closer to the Stranger beneath the sleeping furs, she was feeling warmer now, sleepy, her mind open to memories of other young male bodies lying warm and close against her in the winter dark.

So long ago! So far away!

Beneath her closed lids she saw herself young again, moving with her kind across a wide stony land of permafrost and stunted trees and brazen skies and endless herds of caribou . . . under the ever-watching eye of a summer sun that never slipped far enough below the horizon to fully set . . . beneath the cold sprawl of restless stars eternally hunting the moon across endless winter nights.

So long ago! So far away, so far!

Sometimes, as now, it seemed to the old one that another must have lived within her skin in those days. She had not been Old One then. She had been Kelet, a young one named Spirit, dwelling happy and content among her own kind, moving ever eastward with them out of the ancient land of their strong, sturdy, hirsute ancestors, journeying from one small family hunting camp to another, following the caribou from one killing ground to another, singing the wolflike songs of the Old Tribe, dancing their dances, playing their games, listening to their tales, avoiding their many enemies, and joyfully proving her fecundity again and again before her youth was spent.

So long ago! So far away, so far, so far!

Before that sunstruck morning at the river crossing when Strangers fell upon a gathering of her kind and claimed the ancient game route as their own. Before the slaughter of her loved ones. Before her little ones were torn from her arms and brained before her eyes. Before the whirling shaman struck upon the great drum and ate of the mushroom of madness while dancing in the white skins of winter-killed caribou and calling to new spirits in an unseen world that existed only in the sky above that place.

So long ago! So far, so far! Now lost to her and her kind forever.

Before she was raped and enslaved and, by what dark magic she still could not comprehend, pulled from her bed in the middle of the night by a giant of a youth and carried ahead of the great barrenlands fire in which all save she and Kinap had perished! Only the unborn child in her belly and poor, burned Kinap's needs had given her cause to live. For them she had survived. For them she had sought her own kind, only to blunder into the hunting territory of Strangers. They had taken her in but later, seeing the mark of the Old Tribe upon her newborn, would have killed her had she not taken her child and fled from them, long before the facial and body hair that had fallen away by her second year returned to betray her ancient lineage and protect her aging skin from the onset of an inner cold that had little to do with winter.

"His man part grows in my hand, Grandmother!"

Startled from her reverie by the young one's statement, Old One smiled despite her inner sadness. "Then take your hand away, Mowea'qua. Only the male bone of a corpse would not rise and swell to the warmth of a female hand caressing it. Let him sleep. As we both must sleep. But say I this to you now before you dream content beside him: If this wounded one lives, he will not so easily be kept caged or hobbled like one of your captive birds or beasts. A Stranger he is. Enemy he is. Say I again that it was a mistake to bring him to this place, for do you not think that when he is able, he will try to hop away after his own kind like a one-legged raven, cawing out to all, showing them the way into our forest, leading them to our den, where they will slay and skin us as reward for our kindness?"

"But why would they hate us so, Grandmother?"

"Because in our kind they see what they once were— what they still are behind their masks and inside the brightly painted and beaded skins of the beasts they wear— animals as are you and I . . . kindred to every other furred and fanged predator that walks hungry in this world!"

"Then we will make him see that enemies we need not be. He will not run. He will not hop. He will stay. Together will we make him *want* to stay."

"And if we cannot?"

The young one sucked in a little breath, not in the way of one who has been startled by a question, but as though the answer were on the tip of her tongue and she would hold it back, keep it to herself unspoken lest it win disfavor and be sullied and discouraged forever.

Once again the deep V of Old One's hairline plunged toward the wiry tufts of her brows. She sensed a secret being guarded within the confines of her granddaughter's silence. This troubled her even more than the presence of the Stranger. It was not like the young one to keep secrets. Quite to the contrary. Every thought that ran through Mowea'qua's mind, be it of hope or joy or fear or whimsical postulation, had always come bubbling from her mouth as freely and ingenuously as water welling from a spring. A coldness touched Old One's heart. She knew it for what it was: foreboding. The young one had changed since finding the wounded one. The change was not for the better.

"Mowea'qua?" she pressed. When, after a moment, no answer was forthcoming, she said pointedly, "Only one way is there for us to safely keep this wounded foundling. Much about this have I thought. Much! A Stranger he is, and although his body you may heal, he will always be Enemy to our kind. So give back to him his life if you must, but know that on the day tries he to escape to his own kind, I will fire his eyes as we have fired his wounds."

The young one sat up with a horrified gasp. "Then blind he will be!"

"Yes. But then it will be as Kinap has promised. The wounded one will have to stay. Yours will he be 'forever.' And then, perhaps, happy and content you will be."

"No, Old One, never! He could not—would not—forgive us ever for blinding him!"

"No, dear one, surely would he not. And so, say I, better that you had never found him, for be he sighted or blind, always he will be a Stranger, an Enemy, and forgiveness lives not in the hearts of his kind. He will not thank you for giving him back his life. Hate you he will for cutting off his leg and making his face as ugly as a manitou mask. And though he may well be your 'gift from the forest,' Mowea'qua, he will forever belong to the one whose name he cries aloud. To the one he loves. To this Hasu'u who lives in his heart, a heart in which he will never find space for you."

▼▼▼▼▼

The young one sat in stunned silence. Thinking hard. Harder than she had ever thought in all her life. Gripping her knees to keep her limbs from trembling, she held her mouth tightly compressed lest words spill from her lips to betray her thoughts.

Old One seemed to have been exhausted by her warnings and threats. She was curling up in a mound beneath her furs now, murmuring restlessly to herself as she made the lip-smacking noises of one who is trying hard to settle back into sleep.

Anger formed a tender spot within the young one's spirit. It fisted itself into a hot, hurtful lump at the back of her throat and made it difficult for her to swallow without wanting to cry. She did not want to withhold her thoughts from her grandmother. It deprived her of their former closeness. It made her feel sad, and small somehow, as deceptive and secretive as a little spider hiding in the shadows of intentions that she dared not share. But what choice had she? After laying out the filaments of its web, a spider had no recourse but to hide, for if it allowed itself to be seen, potential prey would not venture near its web and the spider would surely starve. If the young one revealed her intentions to her grandmother, the old one would be shocked and hurt and determined to thwart her plan by any means necessary . . . and then the young one would surely starve, of pure wanting.

The wounded one moaned softly in his sleep.

She listened, wondered when and if he would ever find peace and rest within his dreams. *Soon*, she told herself. *Soon it will be so for him. I will make it so. Old One will not blind him . . . ever!*

Touched by a sudden downdraft, she pulled her bed furs close around herself and gazed fixedly at the large birchbark smoker that she had erected with such care over the stone curbing at the far side of the fire pit. It had been no easy task to prepare and hang the contents without Old One seeing exactly what she was doing. How long would it take to cure? Surely not half as long as the wounded one would take to heal. There was time, she assured herself, plenty of time. The process must not be rushed. Skin and flesh, tendon and vein, marrow and bone must be slowly and meticulously preserved by heat and smoke before it could be withdrawn and presented as a gift of goodwill from her to the Enemy, an offering to strengthen his Stranger's heart and bring hope to his wounded spirit—and to hers—before they set off together for the sacred spring.

Her mouth compressed into a worried pucker. When would Kinap come? Without his guidance, she was not sure she could find her way to the sacred spring. And what would Old One say if she knew that it was not only the carcass of one of the slain hares that was being cured with her smoker? What if she suspected that . . .

The wounded one tossed his head, and a short little sob went out of him.

The young one's eyes moved to his shadowed form. Despite the resurgent glow of the coals, she could barely make him out in the gloom of the den. It was just as well, she thought. Old One was right about him. Beneath the bandages his face *was* as ugly as a manitou mask. Even when the swelling subsided, the bruising around his eyes faded, and his many sutures were removed, his facial wound would leave a long and twisted scar that would cruelly distort his features. It would take all the magic of the crystals that grew around the waters of Kinap's sacred spring to make him appear as he had when she had first seen him from afar, standing so boldly beside the female of his kind, the bright-headed lance in his hand, his head covering tossed back, his smooth, hairless, as yet unmarred face bared to the fading light of day . . . almost as soothing to her eyes as the face of the beautiful master of the sled and leader of his pack.

As always when she thought of the beautiful one, her heartbeat quickened. As always when his beauty filled her mind, her body warmed with a longing so intense that she nearly wept when she realized that she might never set eyes upon him again. She did not understand her feelings, for until she looked upon his face, her life had been serene and untroubled. Days and nights had come and gone in slow, sure, soothing predictability. There had been nothing she desired that she did not already possess. She had friends in Old One and Kinap, and companions in the creatures of the forest—in U'na'li the wolf and U'wo'hi'li the eagle and all the other woodland animals that presented themselves to her when they had need of healing. If now and again she found herself puzzling over why Old One and Kinap increasingly fretted together over how it must be for her if ever they breathed no more, she refused to consider the puzzle with any seriousness. Old One could not die! She would not think of it, and therefore it could not be so.

Kinap would always come to winter with them. There would always be animals to heal. And the old storyteller and Grandmother would always conspire together to make certain that there would be gifts and laughter and games and songs to fill the winter dark with joy.

Always.

And then, under lowering storm clouds, she had crouched within the little copse of birch trees and watched the Strangers emerge from the forest on the far side of the creek. And everything had changed. Everything! Her hands strayed upward to her face—her smooth, broad-mouthed, furless face—and she remembered the first time she had set eyes upon the beautiful one, and the second.

If only she had run off to the safety of the den after the attack of the masked ones, the world would still seem the ordered place it had been before. But she had not done that. No. She had howled to alert Old One of her whereabouts and hurried to the killing ground of the raiders, not only in hope of salvaging stray flying sticks and of finding the bright-headed lance but also—yes, she would admit it now—to take a closer look at the face of a Stranger. By then the wounded one's features had been slit from ear to ear. Appalled by the gaping ugliness of his wound, she would have scurried away, convinced that Old One had been correct all along in her assessment of the repulsiveness of his kind, but in that moment his band had returned to the creek.

She recalled the moment as though it were happening now. She could see herself turning and scurrying off as fast as she could. Clambering over and through snow-laden deadfall, she soon thought better of retreat and scooted back into the trees. Crouching low and downwind of the advancing Strangers, she held her ground, waiting for them to retrieve the wounded one and go their way.

There, from her hiding place, she had watched the leader of the pack searching along the creek as he made his way downstream toward her. When, with a triumphant growl, he snatched up the bright-headed lance, she growled, too, with disappointment and jealousy. Glaring balefully, hoping that the lance might yet be hers, she watched him continue downstream, wanting him to slip, to fall and drop the lance into the ice-choked waters as the wounded one had done earlier. He was far too quick and steady on his feet for that. He gripped the bright-headed lance as though it were a natural extension of his arm. With two others of his pack following close at his heels, he soon reached the place where the wounded one lay half submerged in the creek and, pausing only long enough to remove his snow walkers, upended the lance in the snow, then leaped atop the fallen birch with all the grace and agility of a forest lion.

She caught her breath, remembering how she had stared, unmoving, willing herself to remain perfectly still, allowing no mist to form upon her exhalations, making no sound, drawing in his scent, his strange, unpleasant, yet unnervingly compelling Enemy scent. He had been facing directly toward her, staring into snow and darkness, frozen in position. When his head had gone high, she had recognized his posture, sensed the tension in his crouching form, and known instinctively that he was scenting the night and storm for danger. For a moment she had been certain that she was undone, but the wind had not betrayed her.

And then, in the moment before he bent his head and turned his full attention to the task he had come to attend, the open circle of his furred head covering had fallen back.

Her long, pale eyes had always been keen; her night vision was as sharp as any wolf's or hunting cat's. Even in snow and darkness she had seen his face, and, as when she had first looked upon him from the lake of shadow at the bottom of the snowdrift, she had sensed an immediate kinship with his spirit and known that he was the most beautiful creature she had ever seen or would ever see.

It was then that the world had changed for her. It was as though the bright-headed lance had struck her through the heart. Now, as then, the young one trembled, confused and angered by a sense of betrayal so deep and hurtful that she could barely breathe.

Old One had lied to her!

The Strangers were not ugly!

The Enemies were not repulsive!

With her fingertips exploring the contours of her face, she sighed now as she had sighed then. *We are of a kind, the Strangers and I. I am one of them. I am not of the Old Tribe. The mark of the Ancient Ones is not mine!*

Another sigh from the wounded one caused her to flinch as she came blinking out of memories. She wondered if, in his fevered dreams, he saw her as Old One claimed he saw her—as a hideous and repellent beast fit only for slaying—or as one of his own kind. Did he blame her for his pain, or thank her for his life? Did he know of all she had done to keep him alive? Of the way she had tied off the great vein in his mutilated leg with a twist of hair hastily daggered off from her own head lest he bleed to death on the agonizing trek through the forest to the safety of the den? Of the way she had then burned off his severed veins, cleansing him after Old One used a pair of stone lancets to cut the flying stick from his shoulder, then stitching and salving him and packing and bandaging every sutured wound with spiderwebs, damp moss, and the soft, medicine-moistened, defurred skins of small forest animals? Did he know of how she had then lain naked over him in those first long hours when it had seemed that his heart would never find its natural rhythm, and of how—when he had at last stopped shivering and succumbed to sleep—she had placed her favorite grass-stuffed buckskin pillow beneath his left thigh and contrived a tentlike frame of bent willow twigs to keep the weight of the sleeping skins off the worst of his injuries?

Her mouth tightened. She wanted him to know all this. She wanted him to know that it was she—and not the one whose name he called again and again—who even now, two days after bringing him to the den, remained awake and alert to his every need. It was Mowea'qua, not Hasu'u, who knelt close, ready to cool his fevered skin with medicine rags. It was Young One, not Dawnland Woman, who held up his head and helped him to drink as much as he could swallow from the medicine bowl that she and Old One kept filled with a restorative brew steeped from pounded hemlock twigs, mosses, lichens, and the well-chewed inner bark of slippery elm branches.

A cascade of snowflakes found its way downward to her cheeks and the tip of her nose. She brushed them away and, squinting against an irritating increase of smoke, rose and went to adjust the nearby pole that regulated the position of the smoke flap. Finding it immovable, she knew that the woven exterior baffle must once again have become weighted by snow; if cold air and snowflakes were to be kept from the room and smoke kept to a minimum, an adjustment would have to be made from outside.

She reached for her foot liners and moccasins, put them on, and, bundling in her sleeping skin, stepped over the sleeping wolf. She ignored the gaze of the white-headed eagle as the waking raptor eyed her from its perch, ruffled its feathers, then languorously yawned, stretching its broad, dark wings and first one taloned limb, then the other. Tiptoeing to the weather baffle, she unlaced it and made her way outside.

"Ah!" she exclaimed, finding herself in thigh-high drifts. She allowed the baffle skin to fall closed behind her. Staring gape-mouthed into the snow-dappled grayness of approaching dawn, she tried to remember the last time she had seen such a snowfall. "Never!" Old One was right to be worried. Earth and sky had ceased to exist; a single mass of cloud lay silent upon the world, and out of its gray, softly undulating substance snow fell and fell until now, beyond the little lodge of bark and branch and bone, it lay heaped, burying all but the tallest boulders, weighting the trees until the entire forest seemed to be bending low beneath the press of an all-enveloping sky.

Nothing moved in such a snow.

She chewed her lower lip, worrying, hoping that the kami had been able to find the skulls and bones of the rabbit and hares that she had so hurriedly left for them in the sacred grove. In so much snow, her offerings would have been buried if the spirits had not come at once. She should have stayed longer! She should have waved the willow wands harder and howled louder! If the skulls and bones of her prey had not been accepted by the forest spirits, in the future her snares and pit traps would lie empty and her lances would not taste of meat because rabbits and hares, offended by what they would mistakenly assume to be her disrespect, would abandon their feeding grounds and nesting places and leave this part of the forest. Never again would she and Old One be able to count on the sweet red flesh of their kind to provide fresh meat throughout the long northern winter. Never again would her heart bound and her spirit sing with euphoric empathy at the sight of them leaping through her forest world. The rabbits and hares would be gone forever, and with their absence so, too, would vanish all creatures who looked to them for meat. The great Circle of Life would be broken. Then she and Old One and the Stranger would begin to starve or be forced to seek new hunting grounds in another part of the forest.

She swallowed hard. The latter was unthinkable. And yet it was all she could think about. *He* was out there, encamped somewhere in the storm—the beautiful one, the master of the wounded one's pack, the Stranger who would soon go his way and pass from her life and forest world forever. Unless . . .

Inside the den, the wounded one was moaning again.

The young one quickly sought the long, upright exterior pole that she and Old One kept near the entrance to the den, used its hooked end to loosen and scrape snow from the lodge, then, after a moment of deft maneuvering, shoved the smoke hole baffle closed and hurried back inside.

The eagle was dozing. The wolf twitched an ear but otherwise remained content with its dreams. She heard the slow, even breathing of Old One and knew that she was fast asleep. Shaking snow off her sleeping skin, then slipping out of her moccasins, she moved to the fire pit, seeking the medicine bowl, a hollow birch burl in which lay the saturated skins with which she had been wiping the wounded one's fevered brow. Fingering up a sodden skin, she twisted out excess moisture, then went to hunker on her sleeping mat next to the wounded one.

He was quiet now, so quiet that, for a moment, she was certain he was no longer breathing. Her free hand flew to his neck. Her fingertips pressed imperatively, searching for his pulse and finding it as he exhaled and sobbed softly, "Hasu'u! I would have come for you! I would! In this world or in the world beyond, I would have followed you! I would have hunted the manitous who have dishonored your spirit! But how can I follow you now? How . . . ?"

His words drifted, fell away.

Shaken, Mowea'qua withdrew her hand. She set the medicine skin aside, lay down beside him, drew her bed furs over them both, and whispered in his ear, "A way there is, my wounded one. The one you cry for walks not in the world of spirits. Alive she is! With the masked ones she is a captive now. This with my own eyes I have seen. So heal you must, for her. Grow strong you must, for her. Together we will find her and your brothers. Trust in my words, and you will at the side of Hasu'u walk once more."

His eyes opened. He turned his head and looked straight at her. "They have taken my leg, Hasu'u. How can I walk at your side with only one leg?"

"Shh." She laid her fingers across his mouth. "Wake not the old one. She will blind you if my talk she hears. Our secret she must not know. But you must know it, for until Kinap comes, you must find heart to live and grow strong upon it. Two legs have you, my wounded one! One upon your body, the other curing in my smoker for the day when we will journey together with Kinap to the sacred spring. The magic waters will heal your face and make your leg grow back. Then together run away will we. Kinap will look and look for us, but we will not let him find us. He will have to return to Old One then. This I know. He will not abandon her. Always he comes back from the world of

Strangers to see to her needs. As I must go to him, to the beautiful one who is your brother. Never again need Kinap and Old One worry about what must happen to this young one when breathe they no more. Together will we go walking into the country of your kind. You, my gift from the forest, will take me to the new life that Kinap has promised. The beautiful one will smile upon the one who has brought his brother back to him from the country of the manitous. Welcome me he will into his pack. Know he will that although I am Mowea'qua, I am not Enemy, not Stranger, not manitou, but one of his own kind. And when he looks into my eyes, surely he will find no cause to slay me, for he will know that I see straight into the way of his heart."

Chapter Five

▼▼▼▼▼▼▼

M'alsum was disgusted.

Inside the little lean-to that Kicháwan had raised against the storm, the burden woman was finally asleep. He was relieved. And annoyed. It was nearly dawn. Kicháwan had been tossing and groaning beneath their shared sleeping furs for hours. The quality of his own sleep had been ruined. He was sick of elbowing her and threatening further beatings in order to make her lie still, but now she was sucking air through her gaping mouth like a landed fish left thrashing and gasping in its death throes.

He snarled and jammed an elbow hard into the side of her bare, fleshy arm as he commanded her to silence even though he knew that, since he had smashed her nose, she could not breathe except through her mouth. He felt no sympathy for her. The woman had challenged him. She had refused to obey him. She had forgotten her place entirely. Had it not been for the welcome warmth of her big soft body and the fact that he still had need of her strength and camp skills in the days and nights to come, he would have driven her out into the storm and brained her long before now.

A smile twitched at the corners of M'alsum's mouth. It pleased him to think of making an end of her. One good smash against the side of her head with the butt end of his spear should be more than enough to finish her. But why taint the shaft of such a fine weapon with such an inconsequential killing when he could just as easily strangle her, as he had strangled Sac, or simply smother her with one of the sleeping skins as she slept? Once she was dead, he could walk confidently into the Dawnland with no one left alive to contradict his version of what had befallen him and his trading band within this haunted forest, upon this cursed trail. The latter thought produced a nearly euphoric sense of relief and satisfaction. He was no longer afraid to make the trek alone!

Katcheetohúskw was dead. And, for all intents and purposes, *he* had killed it!

Great Ghost Cannibal, winter chief of the manitous, had led his monstrous spirit band to do its worst and then gone his way again. And M'alsum was still alive!

The ghosts that he had imagined following him from the creek no longer haunted him; spawned of shame born of his own inadequacy, they had vanished in that singular moment when he had dared to look a charging mammoth in the eye and had not run away.

Ah, the tales he would tell when he reached the Dawnland! How easily they would flow from his lips! Now that he had eaten and rested awhile, the wonder of his situation was beginning to fully dawn on him, for he found it only fitting for one whose mother claimed to have conceived him within the body of a mammoth to now find himself reborn in the blood and death of another of its kind. Ah, how he looked forward to making Asticou choke on his doubts when he returned into the forest village to vindicate his mother with the trophies he would bring to her of this kill! And in the meanwhile, what a show of mourning he would make when he reached the coast. How he would wail and fast and win the sympathy of Hasu'u's father and brothers and many uncles among the coastal people before he spread wide the great brown bison hide and set himself to trade and claim new and even greater status in their eyes!

His mouth tightened. The sense of euphoria faded. Two nights and a day had passed since he and the burden woman had sought refuge from the storm. Outside it was still snowing. And he was still a good three sleeps to the Dawnland! He hissed frustration. Once the sky cleared and he was able to journey on, traveling would be slow and tedious. There was no sense killing the burden woman before he came closer to his destination. Kicháwan still had her uses, and he had to admit that, despite her weakened condition, she had done an admirable job of raising the lean-to.

The shelter was of a simple design that winter travelers through the great boreal forests had been making in snowstorms since the time beyond beginning. He had taught her to make it well: Empty the sled, back it to the wind against whatever drifts or boulders or fallen trees were available, and then, to prevent the runners from freezing fast to the snowpack, turn it on its side behind a predug snow pit; ax down enough evergreen boughs to make a soft, insulating floor at the bottom of the pit; roll out the portable lodge skins, secure them to the top of the sled, and stretch them into a single span to form a down-sloping roof; drive home a few wooden lodge stakes; pile snow and pack it down hard along the bottom edges of the skins to hold them secure; toss into the now-weatherproof hollow as many belongings as possible and then—after staking the dogs outside to tuck noses beneath tails and curl close for warmth—crawl inside, clamber out of wet clothing, pile into sleeping skins, and let Gaoh, Master of the Winds, conspire with the storm spirits to do their worst.

And so Kicháwan had done.

By the time M'alsum returned alone from the ravine carrying the tail and trunk of the great mammoth, there had been nothing for him to do. He had buried his trophies in a hastily dug snow pit well away from the dogs lest the smell of fresh meat cause them to dig for it, or draw wolves. Then he had upended his snow walkers, shaken himself free of snow, crawled into the lean-to, and, after laying the copper-headed lance alongside sleeping furs that the burden woman had already arranged for him, pulled the edges of the roof skins down to shut out the cold.

Kicháwan had lain in silence for a few moments, her breathing strained and thin. Then, "M'ingwé?" She turned his brother's name into a gasp of a query, whispering it treadingly, as though she already knew the reason for his failure to return and was afraid to hear it.

"We will now share his portion of the food and sleeping skins. He will have no more need of them," he had told her flatly. Ignoring her pained gasp, he told her to shut her mouth before she could remind him of what he already knew—that it was forbidden to take up the belongings of the dead. "I have seen to it that he will not come for these things. His spirit is cut adrift, lost forever. But since he was so concerned for your welfare, he would want you to have them. So accept them with grace, you stupid cow, and stop staring at me like that and sucking air like a half-dead bison!"

Clambering naked under the furs, he had pulled her close, not to assuage her fears, but to draw the heat of her bare body into his own as he mused over the ease with which he had seen to it that M'ingwé would never again be a threat to him, in this world or any other.

He had used his stone palm dagger to slice off his brother's hands and feet before flinging them to the Four Winds. He had gouged out M'ingwé's eyes, slit his tongue, then severed his skull from his spine with several perfectly aimed downward plunges of the copper-headed lance. The elongated metal tip had, as M'ingwé had predicted, bent back upon itself when it struck through bone, and for a moment M'alsum had cursed, thinking that even in death his brother was finding a way to mock him. But the sheer power of the blow and the finely honed sharpness of the metal spearhead accomplished his purpose, and M'alsum had used the antler-bone end of his dagger to pound the spearhead back into shape.

His brow came down. It occurred to him now, as it had then, that he should be feeling some sort of remorse or at least a small measure of revulsion over what he had done. M'ingwé had been his brother, after all. As had Sac. The act of killing and dismembering brothers should not come as easily to a man as slaying and butchering deer. But, he conceded, ever since those long-gone days of boyhood impotence in the face of Asticou's mauling of Meya'kwé, he had found surcease for his frustration and humiliation in inflicting pain and death on creatures even more impotent than he. Torturing and killing prey had become his way of releasing anguish, of alleviating shame, of claiming power in a world in which he had none.

His mouth tightened. He could not say just when he had come to enjoy killing, but he knew now that although he would mourn the loss of the easy, masculine camaraderie that he and Sac and M'ingwé had shared as youths, he would not mourn the death of either man any more than he mourned what had to have been the slow, painful death of Ne'gauni. He was glad that he had left Little Brother to be meat for the carrion eaters of the night. And he was not in the least sorry that he had killed Sac and M'ingwé; nor did he feel guilt in acknowledging the pleasure he had taken in the killings. He had offered his true brothers a new life of ease and power. As reward, they had turned on him like a pair of disloyal, recalcitrant dogs! Granted, it would not be easy when the time came to tell Meya'kwé of their deaths, but was it not their mother, in her ineffable wisdom, who had taught him long ago that, when dealing with dogs, a wise hunter must strangle any pup that showed signs of viciousness or intractability lest one day the animal put his life at risk upon the hunt or trail?

"Yes," he exhaled, releasing tension, certain that he could not be faulted in any way for the deaths of his brothers. Sac and M'ingwé had been their own undoing. They had defied him. They had mocked him. They had mistakenly perceived weakness in him and would have gone on to betray that weakness to serve their own ends. So now he felt neither sorrow nor regret nor even the vaguest suggestion of repugnance as he recalled kicking the head of his brother into the ravine and saying, "So much for your imagined immortality, Brother! Which one of us is fit to be headman now? I warned you not to goad me. As I warned Sac. You should have heeded me. It was in my heart to share the wealth of the Dawnland with you! But I see now that I should have broken both of your necks and hung you in a tree to be meat for ravens long ago!"

Thunder rumbled in the clouds outside the lean-to. It was a quiet sort of rumble, benign almost, as though some unseen giant were grumbling in protest of boredom, informing the world below to bear with its mood for just a little longer, for it would soon spend itself and be gone.

M'alsum listened. Tensed. The experiences of nearly an entire lifetime beneath the canopy of the northern forests allowed him to feel the subtle change in the pressure of the air around him. "The storm is passing," he said, less to the burden woman than to himself. "Soon the snow will stop."

Kicháwan trembled.

"Rest now, Burden Woman," he told her, not out of kindness but out of concern for her ability to complete all the work that lay ahead of her. "You will need your strength come dawn. Tomorrow we will go to the ravine, cut the tusks from the fallen Great One, and bind them to the sled. It will take our combined strength and all the stamina of the dogs to bring them to the coast. And tomorrow will be the day we journey on!"

She pulled in a troubled breath. "But . . . but what if it is still alive out there in the storm . . . not dead at all, but still following us . . . still hunting us . . . the Great One . . . the manitou from which you ran away?"

Anger broke loose within him. Snarling again, he moved to strike her across the face before he placed himself over her, levering up with his hands, glaring down at her in the darkness. "I have told you! It is dead! I have killed it!" The veracity of the statement sent a thrill shivering through his body. It coupled with the lingering heat of his violence against the burden woman to center in his loins. He felt the throbbing warmth of an erection swelling to proportions that would have impressed even such a well-endowed man as Asticou. Impelled by a need to punish and overpower and humiliate, he forced himself into the burden woman and pounded her until she wept. "Would you challenge my word again, you mewling cow?"

"No, M'alsum, no . . . but the baby . . . you must take heed of the baby! And . . . and you . . . you smell!"

The fear and pain in her voice touched no chord of compassion within him; they heightened sensation in his loins. How dare she remind him that he had pissed his garments! And why should he care about her baby? True enough, M'ingwé had been right when he said that a homely, sag-teated, aging burden carrier such as Kicháwan would be worth more to them in the Dawnland if she proved herself capable of being a life bearer, but with the tail and fifth leg of Katcheetohúskw buried out there in the snow and his trading goods intact, he knew that once the tusks were cut from the mammoth he would have more than enough to secure all that he ever desired in trade. And now, somehow, the idea of killing the unwanted spawn of this journey pleased him. He rammed deeper. Harder. Only when the burden woman cried out in pain and fear for her unborn child did release come. Violent. Explosive. Exquisite! Gratified, he collapsed on top of her and lay sated, sweated, breathing hard, deliberately stressing her with his weight until, uncomfortable, he rolled away.

He slept then, heavily, as he always did after he forced sex on a woman. It was invariably the best for him: intense, savage, thrusting and withdrawing again and again until he knew that he was causing his unwilling partner pain, denying her pleasure even as he took his upon her, hurting her as he so often imagined hurting Wawautaésie when she refused to open herself to him after agreeing to become his father's bride.

The unfulfilled need aroused him. He reached for the burden woman and used her again, handled her more roughly and hurtfully than before, thinking as he did that, in a way, he should be glad that his Dawnland woman had been taken and slain by the manitous. He had never been able to couple with Hasu'u like this lest he risk her disfavor and that of her tribe. Too much depended on their approval of him. And she had been so young, so tender, and so inexperienced in the ways of pleasuring a man of his tastes. He could still recall the way her face had paled and her passion had cooled when she joined him on his bed furs for the first time and he, proudly displaying an immensity of engorged readiness, invited her to mouth him as Meya'kwé had done when sleep had eluded him as a child, and, alone with her firstborn in the milk lodge, she had sent him into dreams on ecstasies that she alone seemed able to prolong forever.

The thought of Meya'kwé's touch brought a restless need. He took the burden woman by the hair and pulled her back and down, demanding that she ease it "Now!"

He had taught her well. She knew what he wanted and what must befall her if she denied him. Although breathing was difficult for her and every movement caused her to utter little sounds of muted protest against pain, she soon had him relaxing and sighing with pleasure.

He trembled at the warm moistness of her mouth and the skillful workings of her tongue, but sensation had been dulled by their previous couplings. Ejaculation was impossible. Annoyed, he knotted a hank of her hair in his hand and twisted it cruelly, forcing her away as he rolled onto his side and gave himself to sleep again.

He dreamed of his triumphant race with Death. He dreamed of the great mammoth lying dead in the snow. And then he dreamed of ghosts, of his drowned infant and slain woman, of Ne'gauni's body lying facedown and bleeding out his lifeblood into the creek, and of Sac's and M'ingwé's dismembered bodies somehow coming together in one hideous, gore-festooned amalgamation.

"Do you truly think that you can hope to outdistance all that you have done in this part of the forest, M'alsum, Firstborn and Eldest Son of Asticou? Do you intend to kill everyone who sees into the weakness that lies at the core of your heart . . . Coward?"

"Ah!" Sitting bolt upright, the headman awoke in a hot sweat. Shrugging back his bed furs, he swallowed down bile that tasted all too much like panic and willed himself to steady his nerves. He reminded himself that this night he had faced a charging mammoth and lived to tell the tale. After all that he had suffered and endured because of the stupidity and betrayal of his brothers, it was only natural for him to have bad dreams now and again; they would pass in time.

He steadied his breathing, looked around, and saw with a start that it was no longer night at all. The light of morning was filtering into the lean-to through accumulations of heavy snow that were causing the roof skins to sag so low that they were touching the top of his head. Ducking down a little, M'alsum knew at once that Kicháwan had failed to go outside to clear off the roof skins. Had she done a less adequate job of raising the structure, it might well have collapsed before now. He frowned. The woman was truly proving to be an irritant. "Get up and tend to your responsibilities!" he snapped at the mound of her sleeping form.

Lying with her back to him at the far edge of the skins, she made no move to obey.

He fisted her hard against the curve of a shoulder.

"Have you lost your ability to hear as well as your capacity to obey, woman? Get up, I say!"

She did not get up.

Anger caused him to break a sweat again, for the thick insulating layer of snow was proving an excellent buffer against the cold. Indeed, the confines of the little shelter captured the body heat of its two occupants so well that moisture from his breath was condensing and beginning to drip from the underside of the cold roof skins. A drop found his nose. It was warm, unpleasantly sour.

And then he caught a far more unpleasant stink.

Blood. Woman's blood. Hemorrhagic blood!

He recoiled, revolted, knowing that Kicháwan must have miscarried or issued enough moon blood for an entire month. He poked her again, hard. "Get up! Get outside! And take your fouled bedding with you! Would you unman me with it?"

She did not move.

He poked her again, harder than before.

And still she did not move.

Suspicion chilled him as he sent a hand questing across her mouth and nose. Her face was cold. She was not breathing.

"Yah!" he exclaimed.

Kicháwan was dead! Sometime during the night she had allowed her spirit to slip from her body and, by this unconscionable act, contaminated the lean-to and everything within it!

Horrified, M'alsum bolted stark naked for fresh air and sunlight.

He found both.

Cold, clean air stung his skin as he threw himself headlong into massive shouldering drifts of soft white powder. He gasped against the cold. He rolled in it. He took up armfuls of whiteness and rubbed his flesh with snow until, skin burning and shining red, he arose and stood, shivering, looking at the well-risen sun, at the glorious and golden and welcome sun.

The storm was over at last!

M'alsum threw back his head and howled with relief and joy until, unable to keep his jaws from clattering, he knew that he must reclaim his clothes or die.

It was not until he turned and was about to reenter the lean-to that it struck him that something was wrong.

The hackles rose on his already cold-hackled back.

All was still.

Utterly, completely, perfectly still.

Not a breath of wind stirred.

Not a branch creaked.

Not a bird called.

Not a single track, save long, soft bands of mauve and pink and softly blue morning shadows, marred the perfection of the sunstruck snow.

M'alsum held his breath, turning slowly, taking in the immaculate beauty of a morning that was as exquisite to his eyes as the first morning of Creation must have been to the eyes of First Man.

And then, suddenly, he realized that he stood alone.

The dogs were gone!

And now, emerging from behind a snow-grizzled stand of boulders, a giant of a man stepped into the sunlight and raised massive fur-clad arms in what seemed to be both a gesture of greeting and a statement of good intentions.

"I come in peace, Brother!" The stranger's voice belied his size. It was a harsh, grainy rasp forced out of a larynx so thickened by scar tissue that he sounded as though he were attempting to hack sand from his throat.

"I am no longer any man's brother!" M'alsum called back, instantly on the defensive as he noted with a sinking heart that while he stood unarmed and stark naked, with not a single dog left in his encampment, the giant held a pair of lances in his upraised hands.

"No brothers, eh? The same say I!" the giant called back. "No brothers! No sisters! And not a bandsman with me to ease my way or to shake a snow prod at. Was it your dogs they took?"

"They?"

"Masked ones . . . a pair of them moving behind a good-sized raiding band headed north. I saw them moving past my own lean-to just before dawn light. Laughing they were. A great prize, your dogs, for in such a storm as we have just weathered, the masked ones may well have eaten all of their own!"

"Masked ones? Manitous? *Cannibals?*" M'alsum cursed himself for sleeping so hard. He might have been slain! And if he had kept alert, the dogs could never have been taken from him unawares.

"Some would say that of them," the giant was saying. "Dangerous people, the masked ones. Dangerous! My own path has twice crossed theirs since three sleeps back. And twice I have altered my path to avoid them. If you are thinking about following after your dogs, Friend, unless you are sheltering at least three hand-counts of brave, well-armed men inside that lean-to along with the man and woman whose tracks I have seen beside your own, advise this I would not! The masked ones would as soon skin you as look at you. I have seen too much these days of what small bands of their kind have left in the wake of their

raids. If they see something they want, they take it. Good
fighters are they. Some of them seem to have made a sport
of killing, and they can strike down a man at twice a
spear's range with their bows and arrows."

"With their what?"

"A new kind of weapon. If they had wanted to kill you,
they would have done so. So best leave well enough alone.
Let them go their way back to the barrens. Maybe your
dogs will take them there faster. Maybe this time they will
not return. If you walk long enough and hard enough this
day along a shortcut I can show you, in only another sleep
you will be more or less safe from them in the Dawnland.
And you can always lay your hands on new dogs among the
coastal tribes if you are willing to work or have the right
items of trade."

M'alsum glared. "My dogs will not so easily be replaced!
Like brothers and sisters they are to me, raised by my own
hands . . . strong, fine, loyal dogs, the best and bravest
of hunters as well as the strongest of burden bearers
and . . ." The angry statement faded along with his anger
as, suddenly, the full weight of the stranger's other revelations sank in.

Was it possible? Was he truly within only a single sleep
of the Dawnland?

And had he heard correctly? Had the giant just said
that the manitous that had come from the forest on the far
side of the creek to attack his band, drown his son, slay his
woman, and shame him into running for his life were not
manitous at all, but men?

Despite the bite of the cold air of morning, M'alsum's
face flushed with resurgent anger and shame at the thought
of it, an anger made even more intense as he found himself
wondering by what unknown rule of protocol a perfect

stranger dared claim the right to address another stranger
as an equal and a "friend." He was about to say as much
but thought better of it as the man came toward him.

The headman gaped. Truly, the interloper was a giant!
With his face hidden inside a projecting cowl of wolf tails
and his body clad in the black skins of at least two adult
bears, he was enormous—easily the tallest, broadest man
M'alsum had ever seen. For all he could tell, had the giant
not spoken in the voice of a man, he might well have been
a bear standing upright in his skins, threatening, dangerous
despite his overtures and protestations of friendship.

"Stay where you are!" the headman commanded. "And
put down your lances. I have not invited you into my
camp!"

"Bah! I am Kinap the storyteller, dispenser of tales and
magic amulets to make children wide-eyed and young men
and women bold and old ones gentle in spirit as they face
the specter that must come to us all. I am welcome in all
camps! Among all tribes! Even among the masked ones.
Although, in truth, I would think twice before risking my
neck among their kind again. So look again, Stranger, and
see what is real and not a conjuring of suspicious eyes. I
have set down my lances. It is only a pair of snow prods
you see raised in my hands. I hold them upside down because I was knocking snow from the webbing when first I
saw you standing there. So be at your ease with me, my
friend, I—"

"I am at ease with no man! And I am not your friend!"

The giant stopped dead in his tracks. His head dropped.
His enormous shoulders rounded forward, and his unpleasant voice lacked any of its earlier congeniality when he
replied coldly, "When and if you reach your destination,
Stranger, do not say to those who may speak my name that

Kinap did not extend his hand to one in need. In this far part of the forest, with masked ones moving to the north and fresh sign of the Great One crossing your trail, you and those with whom you share your lean-to may well have need of a friend before you see the safe side of wherever it is you are going with no dogs left to help you drag your sled."

M'alsum, straining to appear impervious to the cold air that was now biting mercilessly at his bare skin, watched the giant turn and begin to walk away. The interloper apparently had no idea of what had transpired within this camp or in the ravine. Relief washed through him—until he realized what had just been offered, and what he had just refused: an extra pair of hands to drag the sled! A shortcut to the Dawnland!

"Wait!" the headman called. When the giant turned and looked back, he explained with an earnestness so plaintive that it actually touched his own heart, "It is more than dogs I have lost to these murdering manitous you call 'masked ones.' Two sleeps ago—or was it three? Ah, I am so stunned I cannot remember. From out of nowhere they fell upon my trading band!" It occurred to M'alsum in this moment that lies might now serve him far better than truth. "I faced them! Yes! I fought them! Boldly I fought them! But there were too many of them, a large band, as you have said. They drowned my son and slew my woman and two of my brothers. Then they followed us into the storm, tracked us like a pack of wolves until the mammoth fell upon us, but not before my last brother was slain. And now my burden woman, battered as she was by them, has just given up her spirit within my lean-to. And so, although I thank you for your kindness, Giant, I must ask you to understand why I would have you take your snow prods and leave me to mourn my dead alone."

The giant stood immobile. Clearly the story had touched him, for a long, doleful sigh escaped his hood. "It is not good for a man to mourn alone. And so, say I, before your own 'prod' freezes into an icicle and falls off in this cold, clothe yourself, Stranger, and worry not your handsome head about any harm coming to you from me. Kinap has tales to take the edge from your grief. Kinap has songs to sing the spirits of your loved ones safely into the spirit world. And Kinap has a drum whose heart will beat as your heart beats. Your dogs will know that you have not forgotten them this day!"

▼▼▼▼

Hasu'u stared at the newly arrived dogs.

The band had been on the trail since well before first light. Somehow her captors had sensed the ending of the storm, and with Amayersuk acting as an eager goad, Hasu'u had been forced to rise in snowy darkness and help to break down the lean-tos and pack up the camp. The band had moved on before dawn, eating cold rations as they walked under clearing skies. They had come far. Now the full light of noon bathed the world. She could no longer hear the sound of distant drumming and had long since stopped worrying about from where it came. She was as glad to rest as she was grateful for the beautifully carved bone eye shields that she had been given to cut the hurtful glare of day.

Even so, she squinted at the dogs, not fully believing what she was seeing. The two burly, grimy-furred, greasy-faced hunters who had just rejoined the band were being welcomed with much affectionate backslapping and rowdy words and laughter. The string of dogs they had brought back with them appeared dazed, confused, and totally overwhelmed by the enthusiastic greetings and energetic appraisals they were receiving from those who now surrounded them.

Her eyes narrowed behind her glare shields as she took in the scene before her. Her captors were keeping their own dogs well away from the canine newcomers. Although most of the recent arrivals stood with dropped hips and tucked tails, only one of them was pissing in fright, and none of the others snapped or growled or so much as raised a lip to warn of an impending bite.

Her heart sank. With the manitou infant asleep in its sling close to her breasts, she stood only slightly apart from the boisterous melee and tried not to burst into tears. The baby was no manitou. She knew that now, as she knew that her captors were not manitous. They were men! Murderous, malicious, foul, and deceitful men who donned masks to frighten and confound their human prey when they went out to steal and murder for pleasure and self-enrichment! She thought of all that she had lost to their predations—her beloved man, her drowned baby—and of poor, brave, foolish Ne'gauni being struck down and swept away by the creek.

Despite her best effort to prevent them, tears came. She let them fall. Her hands tightened into fists as anger sent a dark, throbbing haze to cloud her vision. She stared at the dogs through the haze and recalled that M'alsum's dogs never snapped or growled; it had not been his way to suffer even the most minimally troublesome animals to live. And these were M'alsum's dogs. She knew it the moment she had set eyes upon them. There was Turns in a Paw When Running, and Strong Heart, and Whines Too Much, and

Gray Eye, and Pisses in Fright, Spotted Tongue, Broken Tooth, Notch Ear, and . . ."

Amayersuk laughed at the bitterness and astonishment she saw on the captive's face. "Yes! They are 'his' dogs! All of his dogs! Ningao and Avataut thought it was a waste to leave them behind. So they went back for them. It was something to do, they said, better than passing another night of boredom in the storm camp. Even our tunraq told them that too much time had passed for them to pick up the trail of Runs and Hides, but this they did!"

Ningao, one of the two men who had just returned, came striding over to appraise Hasu'u with brashly mocking eyes. Chuckling to himself, he spoke to Amayersuk, who smirked as she translated.

"Ningao says that Runs and Hides was easy to find. His sled left a great long gouge in the snowpack that new snow did not quite fill in. Ningao and Avataut followed this path. Now they have given Runs and Hides a new name: Walks in Circles and Does Not Know It. They came across his lean-to not far from our own storm camp. He was so busy humping a woman he caught neither sound nor scent of them. Avataut came in close, tossed the dogs some fat, and they came to him like babies to the teat! Runs and Hides will now have to hitch his woman to his sled. Maybe in future days and nights he will be more careful of any dogs that are unlucky enough to come into his care."

"I am his woman! And no man is better with dogs than M'alsum!" The words tore from her throat; her anguish was so great that she could not keep herself from sobbing as she spoke them, for now she knew that he was alive, and close to her. And strong, kindhearted, plodding old Kicháwan was alive, too, easing her beloved's need for a man's release in these sad and dangerous times as was her duty. Hasu'u

felt no jealousy toward the burden woman. All the sons of
Asticou had used Kicháwan freely and openly upon the
trail, M'alsum included. It was accepted in both her tribe
and his that a man must do as he must when the need to
rut came upon him, especially since the laws of the Ancient Ones forbade him to lie upon a pregnant wife or
penetrate her body after life had come forth from it and the
blood of birthing continued to stain the mosses that she
bound between her thighs. She found herself looking
wildly around, knowing that there was a good chance that
perhaps even now M'alsum was following those who had
stolen his dogs . . . and his woman.

"Do not stress yourself in longing for him or make the
mistake of calling out to him, woman of my own kind,"
warned Amayersuk. "Remember: If for wanting of him you
fail to nourish our tunraq's son, we will hunt him down
and kill him, and if he comes for you, he will be one man
facing many. Either way, Tôrnârssuk will confront him,
and at White Bear's hands you will surely see him die."

Ningao was speaking again.

Amayersuk translated again. "Ningao says that you are
lucky to have been taken from such a man as Abandons
Woman. Two men has that one now left dead, one in the
creek to be meat for carrion eaters, the other cut into
pieces and scattered along the trail, just under the snow,
but not deep enough not to have been snouted up by
wolves and foxes! And was there not another with him? If
he was within the lean-to, there was no sign of him. Maybe
your man has killed him, too?"

Hasu'u's eyes went wide. She knew a lie when she
heard one. This one was so appalling that, for a moment,
she stood stunned by it. Then, feeling tears burning salt
into her cheeks, she pushed her eye shields down from her

forehead and let them dangle from their neck cord as she said, "Only a man of this raiding band of thieves and man slayers and baby killers and woman stealers could think of such a terrible falsehood! Never will I believe it!"

Amayersuk shrugged. "Believe as you will, but know that Ningao has also said that there was sign that the great tusked one had come from the time beyond beginning to follow the trail of Runs and Hides a day, maybe two days before. They almost turned back at the sight of this, but unlike Abandons Woman they are brave men. The Great One is dangerous. When he rises from beneath the earth, he is as big as a mountain, with shoulders that touch the sky and scatter big trees like sticks in a children's game! His teeth cut into the forest until it bleeds so much sap that injured trees wither and die! Maybe by now this great tusked one has come to crush into the snow the stink of fear and blood that Ningao and Avataut say sours the air all around your coward's camp. Maybe it has killed him as he deserves to be killed before he has a chance to abandon another woman."

Hasu'u's anger overrode her anguish. "And maybe it will follow this band instead and give you all the deaths you deserve before you have a chance to devastate others as you have devastated me!"

Amayersuk reached out and, with the heels of her mittened hands, gave Hasu'u a push to the shoulders that shoved her backward so hard she might have fallen had Ningao not caught hold of her elbow. "Never speak so!" Amayersuk was barking, showing her nasty-looking, filed little teeth. Suddenly she bowed her head, silenced by a sharply spoken reprimand given first in her tongue, and then in Hasu'u's.

"Never again strike out at the woman who gives life to my son!"

Hasu'u blinked at the sound of Tôrnârssuk's voice. The tunraq had hurled the words from where he stood amidst other raiders who were all busily engaged in assessing the quality of the dogs that Ningao and Avataut had brought to them, lifting paws, looking into ears and mouths, examining teeth, feeling around rib cages and underneath bellies and scrotums, seeking for signs of hernia or pregnancy or other weakness that would render the animals less than desirable for their purposes.

Hasu'u's head went high. She did not like the way they were handling M'alsum's dogs. As though her man would ever have chosen less than perfect animals! It irritated her to see them being judged by those whom she deemed their inferiors. The tunraq was staring at her. She stared back, wanting him to see her contempt for him and the ways of his band.

His hood was down. His brow was furrowed. The ivory labrets that he wore inserted in his lower lip to simulate the appearance of the protruding fangs of the white bear for which he was named glinted dully in the sunlight. But the broad, flat face of Tôrnârssuk, Great Ghost Cannibal, winter chief of the manitous, and Tunraq, Guide, Guardian, and All-Knowing Spirit leader of this filthy pack of murderers, showed marked signs of stress.

Hasu'u's lips quivered as she allowed herself the pleasure of a tight, downward-curving little smile at his expense. It was gratifying to know that he could feel fatigue as any other man could feel it. It lightened her heart to know that for all his obvious rank and power among his own kind, he was nevertheless a man, not a manitou. A man could die! And it was death she wished for Tôrnârssuk now as she had wished it in her dreams and in every waking, agonizing moment since he had so cruelly drowned her baby, torn her from her band, and forced her to suckle his infant as she lay trembling in fear of him in the night and walking in misery with his murderous raiders by day on a trail that must take her ever northward toward the hunting grounds of his ancestors in a land in which she knew she must surely die.

Now it was Tôrnârssuk's head that went high.

Hasu'u felt his long eyes burning into hers. She knew that he saw into her thoughts. Her chin tilted skyward. She made no attempt to mask her loathing of him, or her contempt. It was the only weapon she had against him. Feeble as it was, it was hers, and she would use it. She was, after all, a hunt chief's daughter and a headman's woman, and in this small display of stubborn pride she could at least find some measure of dignity.

With his eyes still boring into hers, he spoke to the man next to him. It was Avataut. Even clothed as he was in heavy skins, the sudden shift and rigidity of his posture evidenced the severity of the communication; nevertheless, he did not hesitate to comply with his tunraq's wishes. He, in turn, spoke to two others, and two dogs were pulled tightly by their leads from out of the pack.

Hasu'u recognized Whines Too Much and Always Pisses in Fright. The smile vanished from her face. The raiders had keen eyes. Of all M'alsum's dogs these were the only two that might be judged flawed by those who had not experienced their genial, forgiving natures and stamina upon the trail. Her breath caught at the back of her throat. She felt suddenly light-headed. She knew what was going to happen. She knew because the dogs knew. They had stiffened at the touch of new handlers, understanding a change in attitude, an undefined but looming threat. She saw the whites of their eyes, the way their lips pulled back, revealing their teeth, not in a snarl but in that strained, wild, half-mad, wolfish smile dogs smiled in the face of unspecified danger against which they knew they had no control.

Dread was in them now. As it was in Hasu'u. She saw that the dogs were doing their best to twist away from those who were dragging them off toward a long, high drift of snow that angled through the trees just ahead. As they tried in vain to brake with their feet, Pisses in Fright was living up to her name, and Whines Too Much was not whining at all; he was barking, a high, yipping plea of a bark. The pack, alerted to its brother's cries of fright, began to whine and dance about in nervous excitement. Their fear crackled in the cold air like static electricity sparking from unseen fur on the sunstruck surface of the snowpack.

Tôrnârssuk's eyes were on Hasu'u again.

She flinched against the invasiveness of his gaze and, aching for M'alsum, wished that she were stronger, braver, more worthy of the man whose honor was now being defiled once again, through her, through his dogs. They had been dragged to the far side of the drift. She could no longer see them or the two raiders who led them, but she and everyone around her heard Whines Too Much's high, startled yip of pain, and the silence that followed.

Amayersuk laughed and clapped her mittened hands together in sadistic glee and satisfaction.

Deep inside Hasu'u something turned, darkened. Although the sun was shining on her face and her eyes were smarting from the intrusive burn of snow glare, she was engulfed by shadow. It came from within her, not from without. So cold. So dark. She recognized it for what it was: hopelessness. Complete and utter despair.

Ningao, still standing close, continued to gently but firmly support her elbow as he began to speak to her.

Amayersuk did not translate.

Hasu'u understood why. She had no way of knowing Ningao's words, but they were gently spoken, and as she listened, she began to suspect that there was more than a hint of explanation, if not outright apology, in the man's tone. He was trying to soothe her—for her sake or because he was afraid she might fail to provide sustenance for his headman's son, she could not say, but she knew from Amayersuk's glum silence and resentful expression that the watch woman was not pleased by his expressions of concern.

No matter, Hasu'u thought. She was not soothed. She was shivering violently, and as Tôrnârssuk came toward her with a frightened, wild-eyed Notch Ear trotting in a tightly held lead at his side, she knew that the dogs on the far side of the snowdrift were both dead.

Without warning, the tunraq reached forward with his free hand, took hold of her swan-bone drinking tube, pulled it from around her neck, and hurled it into the snow. "You will keep nothing from your old life! Nothing! Learn from this if you would live: The dogs that have been taken from the pack had bad ways, willful ways. Now they will be meat for the others."

Hasu'u was not sure just what kept her limbs from buckling. Anger? Pride? Or perhaps her despair was simply so great that neither emotion mattered; she did not fall because he did not knock her down.

Now, with his eyes still locked on hers, Tôrnârssuk reached out again, this time to force the braided thong rope of Notch Ear's lead firmly into Hasu'u's hand. "This dog will whelp soon," he informed her. His voice had returned to that low, slow, inhumanly unemotional cadence that he used with her. "Into your care I put this dog and the pups she will bear. You are not happy in my band. This is not good for you or for my son. If you are not happy, your breasts will dry. If your breasts dry, my boy will starve. If my boy starves, both you and Abandons Woman will die. So to you I give this dog and with her the gift of life. Make of her and the pups she will bear a band of your own within this band. They will be your dogs, to carry or drag your burdens, or to eat, as you see fit. Perhaps this will make you happy since, by your past choice of husbands, you have shown that you prefer dogs to men."

Chapter Six

▼▼▼▼▼▼▼

There were secrets between the headman and the giant.

M'alsum sensed them in the cold and heavy silences that gapped between the words they spoke and the words they both were obviously withholding from one another. He told himself that this was only natural. Two solitary strangers on a lonely forest trail through which masked raiders had only recently come and gone their bloodied way dared not reveal too much of themselves. Which one of them could say with any degree of certainty that the other was not an enemy?

And so now, scowling, M'alsum looked upon the giant and felt the weight of the other man's secrets crowding close, bumping against his instincts like a gathering of invisible thunderclouds, warning him to beware of the interloper's benign and congenial manner, cautioning him to keep his eyes sharp and his tongue well leashed if he was going to succeed in manipulating the man to his own purposes.

The giant was crouching in the snow, balancing himself on the longest, broadest snow walkers M'alsum had ever seen. His hooded head was down. He was murmuring incantations in a language the headman did not know, all the while continuing to beat a low yet palpable rhythm on the odd little fringed drum he had slung from around his neck prior to beginning his promised lament for the stolen dogs.

M'alsum watched him, studied him, conceded that there was more than a little about him that remained troubling. The very fact that Kinap needed two full-sized bearskins stitched shoulder to shoulder to form his shaggy outer coat was sobering, for surely the man within was as large of bone and as powerfully muscled and—given provocation— as potentially dangerous as any bear!

The headman frowned as he noted that over his impressive bearskin coat the giant wore a hooded cape of black wolf skins, with the hood set well forward around his head and culminating in a ruff of wolf tails that completely concealed his face. At the back of the hood, the deboned face of a wolf stared outward, as though guarding the giant's back. Its hollow eyes were inset with cleverly painted bone beads, so that the face of the dead animal appeared to be staring a perpetual warning. Its long, dark snout was well oiled and sewn into a perpetual snarl. From its gaping mouth—into which its teeth had been sewn—in place of its tongue a layered cascade of the tails of many of the small animals that would have been its prey in life hung down the giant's back to below his hips. Looped around one of the giant's massive shoulders was a narrow, flattened shaft of bent wood that had been strung end to end with a taut line of twisted sinew, and slung over the same shoulder was an elongated, leather-lined wolverine-skin bag from which protruded the ends of what appeared to be feather-tipped twigs. At his bone-buckled belt, a wide strap of rawhide to which the teeth of some forest predator had been sewn in an intricate zigzag pattern, he wore an array of small skin bags, a pair of birchbark-sheathed knives, and an astounding collection of amulets and fetishes that clicked whenever he or the wind moved them: strings of minuscule shells and the tiny vertebrae and skulls of small reptiles, rodents, and carnivores, and miniature bone carvings of creatures that seemed both predator and prey, animal and man combined.

Malsum's skin crawled at the sight of the carvings. He could not prevent himself from thinking that, for all his declarations of friendship, the man who called himself Kinap was at best a thought-provoking presence. The giant had yet to reveal his face. His voice was a sepulchral rumble that sounded as though it were scraping up from the very bowels of the earth. And despite his best efforts, M'alsum continued to find the man's size as intimidating as it was awe-inspiring. Indeed, the furred mass of the man was so huge that it was easy for the headman to imagine him hefting the carcass of Katcheetohúskw onto his back and carrying it all the way to the Dawnland without so much as breaking a sweat.

Now, there was a thought to take the edge off the headman's apprehensions about the stranger. He knew, of course, that he was exaggerating the capabilities of the giant, but if Kinap was sincere in his offerings of friendship and assistance and only half as strong as he appeared to be, then M'alsum could scarcely believe the extent of his good fortune. After all that had befallen him during the last days and nights, the spirits of this cursed forest might well be looking with favor upon him once again. They had allowed him to see that his brothers were his enemies and enabled him to slay them before they went for his throat like the dogs they were. They had inspired him to lead the mammoth to its death. And now, with a companion such as the giant at his side, he had no need to lament the loss of his burden woman or even of his dogs, although he would sorely miss the latter.

His eyes narrowed. So far the interloper had proved to be as good as his word. He had honored his stated intent to raise a drumbeat that would communicate the sadness of M'alsum's heart to the stolen dogs. Indeed, the sound of that drum had been so loud and strident that M'alsum, who had just gone into the lean-to to retrieve his clothing, had burst outside stark naked with his spear at the ready. Fearing the return of the masked raiders and strongly suspecting that the giant might be summoning others of his own kind to fall upon him and steal all he owned, he had looked around in a fever of dread and ordered the man to stop drumming.

Only to discover that the giant did not take orders. He gave them.

"Bring your belongings outside where the sun may cleanse them of any lingering presence of Death. And dress yourself, man!" Kinap had boomed. "Would you freeze or take sick before you can join me in raising an acceptable lament to your stolen animals and slain kindred? The masked ones have taken what they came for. They will now be traveling north toward the Great River of the White Whales in hope of crossing to the hunting grounds of their ancestors before the ice goes out. They will not return to this camp. I know their ways. They have left us to mourn our dead and make our way to the Dawnland in peace."

Us! Our!

The words shivered hotly under M'alsum's skin as the giant's gloved hands at last lay still upon the brightly painted face of the drum. The lamentation was finished. He had begun to think it would never end. Now at last they could begin preparations to be on their way to the Dawnland. But the interloper remained as he was, shoulders stooped, hooded head bowed in obvious prayer.

M'alsum found himself scowling again. It occurred to him that he should be grateful and deeply moved by the stranger's willingness to share his grief, but since he could not understand why any man would be motivated to offer such boundless compassion to a complete stranger, he was not grateful, nor was he moved. He was suspicious.

Surely, he thought, the giant must have some deeply hidden, self-serving motive against which he must at all times remain on guard lest it prove dangerous to his well-being and a threat to his ambition to reach the coast with the tusks of the great mammoth. Deep within his spirit, suspicion hardened into resolve. Only one thing was clear to the headman now: If he was to secure the giant's help, he must maintain his sympathy. But what secrets was the giant keeping as he pretended to prayer? Might they not soon prove to be as ugly and potentially compromising as his own?

The giant was rising now, slinging back his drum over a mighty bearskin-clad shoulder, readjusting his hood so that his face remained hidden. As M'alsum had seen him do several times before giving himself over to prayer, he glanced nervously off into the trees from behind which he had first come.

All at once more wary than ever, the headman repositioned his spear as his mind filled with an earlier suspicion. "Is there something there that worries you?"

"Something?"

"Something you may have left behind . . . or hidden?"

"Hidden?"

"Yes, hidden . . . in the trees."

"Trees?"

"Yes, Giant, trees . . . the tall, barked, many-branched things that sprout needles and leaves and make up a forest and provide sap for woodpeckers and a home for birds and insects and squirrels and a stashing place for the meat of lynxes and shrikes and—"

"There is nothing about the trees that worries me. Nothing, Friend! Nothing!" The giant gave an amiable shrug. "Come! I will show you what I have left there," he invited in a tone that could not have been more enticing as he went plodding off toward the nearby trees.

M'alsum did not move. He strongly suspected that he was about to discover the giant's biggest secret—other interlopers of equal or greater size hiding in the sun-striped shadows between the trees, waiting to kill him if he dropped his guard, waiting to steal all that he owned so that they could take his trading goods to the Dawnland, where they would claim the profits for themselves. He had been alert and half expecting them to make their presence known ever since the giant had begun to beat upon his obnoxious little drum.

Kinap was laughing at him. "Why do you hesitate? Do you think I have hidden a war party of my own within these trees? Ah! Of course you do!"

M'alsum's face flushed. "It could be so!"

"If it were, you would be long dead. And I would be long gone toward the Dawnland to trade all your fine goods! Mmph! If I had a war party with me, why would my warriors be hiding in the trees from one man? And had I wanted your skin, I could have taken it with ease when you danced naked with grief and unaware of my presence until I came from the trees."

The headman knew truth when he heard it. Still, unwilling to drop his guard, he continued to hold his spear defensively as he advanced a few steps in the tracks of the giant, then took a few more steps to one side, pausing just outside the striking zone of any unseen enemies. He was now able to see into a stand of snow-bent young spruce trees.

"Behold!" The giant's voice had an almost giddy edge as he gestured downward, drawing M'alsum's eyes to a pair of joined caribou skins that had been thrown over what appeared to be a jumbled pile of personal belongings. "You see!" he said, lifting the hides to reveal what lay beneath. "It is just my pack frame and bedroll and a few bags and parfleches and skins and snare lines, nothing worth hiding from you or any other man who is not of a mind to steal them."

"I am no thief."

"Nor am I. But a man must be wary of strangers, say I . . . as say you, yes?"

Again M'alsum felt his face flush, but his cheeks had cooled by the time he came forward to see for himself that the giant had spoken the truth. A pack frame and bedroll. A few bags and parfleches. Assorted skins and snare lines. Nothing at all threatening or even unusual except for another narrow, odd-looking length of bent wood, smoothed to a fine dark sheen with a tautly stretched piece of twisted sinew attached at each end. Whatever the thing was, it looked like a weapon, but it was obviously of no threat to him now. M'alsum relaxed.

Until the furs moved.

He stared.

The skins writhed.

His eyes widened.

Something was wriggling at the bottom of the heap.

Alert and wary, he instinctively stepped back and might well have plunged the copper head of Asticou's spear into the pile had one of the giant's hands not come up to stay his intended blow.

"No, Stranger, please. These are prime winter skins! Would you slice through them and ruin them? What wriggles beneath is only a little muskrat that I am bringing as a gift to a friend in a far place. I have hobbled it and tethered its foot to my heaviest shoulder bag so it cannot run away, but it likes to burrow beneath my things when it sleeps. I would fish it out and bring it into the light of day so you may see for yourself that it is no threat to you, but it is a snappy little beast and may well take a nip out of me, so I would just as soon leave it where it lies. And, forgive me, but I would prefer that you not touch it or any of my things with your unclean flesh or belongings . . . for if you do, you will contaminate it and all that I own."

"I . . . contaminate a muskrat!"

"Please, Friend, I mean no offense. Until you have mourned your dead and cleansed yourself and your encampment of blood, you will contaminate all that you touch. This was the main reason I left my belongings here. I dare bring them no nearer. So please, Friend, leave my muskrat to his dreams and let us return to your sad camp and attend what must be done."

M'alsum rolled his eyes. Muskrat, indeed! What cared he for rodents when he had slain Katcheetohúskw? What cared he for attending to the dead in his miserable little camp when the Dawnland was only another sleep away?

There was a mammoth to detusk! And this he must do before he could pack up his trading goods and be on his way to the coast. "I would leave this place of death as soon as I can," he declared on a wave of overwhelming impatience. "I will mourn my dead as we travel together to the Dawnland of my woman's people. But first you and I must—"

"Clearly you are in shock, Stranger, not to remember the ways in which a man must honor his dead. Especially his females! Now that you have clothed yourself, you cannot just walk from your camp in a daze. We are not of the same tribe, you and I, but surely among your people there are customs to observe if you are to mourn your dead in a way that is acceptable to the spirits. This woman who lies in your lean-to—surely you cannot mean to go on your way and leave her behind unshrouded and unlamented?"

"The female in this camp was not my wife. She was only a burden woman. And why do you keep hidden from me within your hood, Giant? It is distracting to converse with a man who owns no face that I may see. The wind is down. The snow has stopped. The warmth of the sun is sweet upon my skin. After so many days of storm and bitter cold, why do you not wish to enjoy the same sweetness upon your own face?"

"Better, say I, that you may know Kinap by his words and deeds before you are dazzled and disconcerted by his appalling beauty!" He grated a laugh at what he evidently found to be some sort of joke, then offered an amiable, apologetic shrug. "Forgive me. A time it is not for jests. The corpse that the masked ones have made, the dead one who lies within your lean-to, may have been only a burden woman in this life, but she was some man's daughter and some mother's child and, if not a wife to you, a woman all the same. You must sing her praises to the Ancestors, Stranger! You must fast! You must dance in lamentation of her passing until you grease her road into the hunting grounds of the spirits with your tears and sweat! This you must do unless you would have her haunt you forever and speak your secrets to your enemies in this world and in the world beyond!"

The words were sobering. "No," said M'alsum. "I would not have her do that."

"Then together we will raise her final resting place high. We will cleanse her body, bind her tight within her robes, lay her upon a bier of fragrant evergreens, and cover her with a shroud of the same. Beneath this we will raise fire. Smoke will take the smell of her death to the sky. And when we have gone, no wolves or bears or lynx or other eaters of flesh will easily find her. Yes, say I, you will make her proud to have lived, even if it was only as a burden woman. Together we will sing her on her way to the spirit world. For four days and nights we will do this, and then, on the fifth dawn, when her shade lingers no more in this camp, we can go our way."

"Four days! And as many nights!"

"It is the customary length of time."

For M'alsum the warmth had suddenly gone from the sun. How could he spend four days and nights mourning the death of a woman he cared nothing about when the Dawnland lay so close? His brows arched. How could he not? Annoyed, he asked, "Her 'shade'? What is this term? I do not know it. Everything casts a shadow, Giant, even a corpse long after the spirit has left its bones. If we wait for my burden woman's shadow to disappear, we will be here forever!"

"Ah, Stranger, it is not the same! The shade of which I

speak is not a shadow. The masked ones even have a name for it. It is inua, the lingering presence of all that makes a living being. It is pure spirit. It is the unknowable power. It is that which causes an infant to gasp and draw breath at the moment of birth. It is that which impels the heart to beat and commands the blood to flow. It is that which sends our thoughts opening wide within our minds like blossoms expanding in the light of the sun. And it is that which fades within us as we grow old or sicken or fall to the savaging of wounds. No man, woman, or child can see the shade, Stranger, unless they be shaman. But know I this: At death it can be heard whispering as it escapes the body, and after death for four days and nights it can be felt lingering about the corpse trying to decide if it should crawl back inside through the nostrils to make that body live again. Sometimes it happens. Sometimes a shaman can make it happen. Most often not. But always, on the fifth dawn, for reasons no man or woman or even a shaman may know, the shade of the dead body is felt no more upon the earth, for the spirit of life has gone elsewhere, to live among the clouds and winds and shimmering sky rivers until it is called to be reborn into the world again."

"A pretty tale. My mother would approve."

"No, Stranger, although I am a storyteller and with my amulets and many tales of joy and sorrow and ancient wisdom earn welcome among all tribes, the shade of which I speak is not a story. It is not a tale told to win the approval or disapproval of women. It is not meant to make a child smile in wonder or to soothe old people into slumber. It is truth. The shade is real! And the woman in your lean-to— be she a burden woman or a shaman or a hunt chief's most favored wife—she has cast her shade upon this world, and

Kinap will walk with no man who cannot see that her life and spirit are worth honoring!"

▼▼▼▼

And so the sound of stone axes was heard in the forest.

Soon a bier was raised, a simple scaffolding of notched and thong-laced saplings placed high above the snow-covered ground and lashed to the outreaching branches of an ancient fir. Fragrant boughs of freshly cut spruce and balsam were laid as both mattress and shroud over the snow-scrubbed, fur-wrapped body of the burden woman. Her few belongings were placed around her: her bag of female things upon which no man dared look for fear of emasculation, her woman's palm knife, her fire drill, and her sewing bag with its well-worn bone needles and punchers and awls and neat rolls of sinew and fiber thread.

"No bag of rendered, scented fat with which to soothe her skin and oil her hair . . . no paint to make her face bright in the light of your campfires . . . no pretty things at all . . . no quillwork . . . no shells or feathers or beads or adornment of any kind," observed the giant, *tsk-*ing and shaking his head.

"She was only a burden woman," M'alsum reminded him. "Have you no such females among your own people?"

The giant pulled in a breath; there was sadness in the exhalation, and in the words that followed. "I have no people, Stranger, no band to call my own. Someday you will meet upon future trails those who will know my name. Speak to them of Kinap, and they will tell you that I am like the elusive fisher of the forest deeps . . . a solitary animal . . . preferring to make my way alone by night under the all-forgiving light of the moon and stars, keeping my secrets, hunting snow hares and porcupines—the hares for their sweet meat and soft pelts, the porcupines for their quills. In all my days I have not met a woman who did not rejoice in a fresh supply of prime hare pelts for her little ones or in quills ready for dyeing and sewing into beautiful patterns on the clothing of her loved ones. So it is that I bring pelts and quills as gifts to the women who now and again ease my life and whose hearts I may only hope to touch through my stories and expressions of kindness. It is a sorrowful thing for my eyes to behold a woman whose life has been taken from her in a camp where her only possession of beauty was her own spirit. But then, say I, since the qualities of our individual spirits are in the end what define the worth of our lives, who am I to say that this woman needed more beauty in her life than she already possessed?"

M'alsum would have liked to inform the giant that as far as he was concerned, Kicháwan was lucky to have had a life at all. No skin-softening oils or body paint or pretty shells or feathers could have made beautiful a female who appeared to have been spawned of a bison wallow. Such a big, homely woman was fortunate not have been brained at birth! But he had not missed the pointed, albeit polite rebuke in Kinap's remarks concerning the poverty of Kicháwan's possessions. This, coupled with the giant's easy talk of a preference for solitary wanderings, cautioned him to keep his own tongue well leashed. If he expected to be given a hand with the sled and shown the shortcut to the Dawnland, he must maintain the man's sympathy. So he responded evenly, not with an apology but with earnest self-justification. "I will tell you this, Giant: Before I traded much prime meat and many fine pelts for the use of this burden woman, her life was a sad thing at a fire circle around which her man gave her neither gifts nor comfort. This woman was strong, but this woman was also barren.

Among my people a barren female is granted no respect, but on the trail, as headman of my trading band, I saw to it that she was kept warm and well fed and that there were always dry mittens and moccasins for her so she would be able to perform her duties well and without complaint. For a woman who was not a life giver, she was treated better than most and given much in the way of consideration by me and my brothers. It could not have been otherwise for her in the company of the sons of Asticou!"

"Mmph. From the clotted blood upon her furs I would say that the sons of Asticou gave her more than consideration. We have two lives to mourn in this camp, Stranger. How is it that you did not know until we drew the bed skins from the lean-to that the woman was not barren after all? That there would have been a child born of her body had she not first been beaten into the world beyond this world by the masked ones?"

"I knew." M'alsum's admission was as tight as the tautly stretched skin that covered the face of the giant's drum. He was finding it increasingly difficult to maintain patience with Kinap's unsolicited insights and observations. The shadows were growing long. The air was growing cold. All too soon night would come. A full day's worth of mourning would be lost and the journey to the Dawnland delayed even longer. "Yes, I knew," he repeated in as good an imitation of remorse as he could muster, then went on, confident that truth would sheath the lies so that not even Kicháwan's lingering spirit would hear them. "In my grief, I had forgotten."

Because I did not care!

"It was such a new and tender life, Giant!"

And so totally unwanted by all except its stupid mother.

"After all that has befallen me within this forest, upon

this trail that was to have led to all good things, another loss, another spirit to mourn was . . . was . . ."

Was too unimportant to remember!

"Ah, Giant, I tell you, it has all been too much for one man to bear!"

The giant laid the vast, mittened sprawl of a consoling hand upon the headman's shoulder. "We will bear it together, Friend. Yes, say I, we will bear it together!"

▼▼▼▼

And so, together, they dug a shallow circular pit in the snow beneath the bier. Into this they placed a layering of green balsam boughs and, over these, a large bed skin, fur side down. On top of this they made fire out of branches cut from standing deadwood. While M'alsum nurtured the flames and laid cuttings of green wood upon them so that the fire would smoke and drive back the stink of death, the giant left him to feed the captive muskrat and gather from his belongings a few small things.

Of these he made gifts to Kicháwan, climbing the tree and placing them on the bier with reverent words. First, a fluffy white rope of twisted hare pelts, each stuffed with moss and goose down. "Of this may the spirit of the woman . . . what was her name, Stranger, and yours?"

"I am M'alsum, firstborn son of Asticou, hunt chief of the people of the inland forest, and eldest son of Meya'kwé, daughter of the Grassland and Dawnland tribes. The burden woman was Kicháwan, once woman of Nul, daughter of . . . I do not know."

"Mmph! I give this fur rope as a death gift to the burden woman of M'alsum, to Kicháwan, whose name, I believe, means Strong Running Woman in the language of the forest tribes. May it be so for her in the land of the spirits! May all know of the strength and endurance and loyalty of Kicháwan! And with this twisted fur and skin of the fleet hare, may she sew a shirt to keep her unborn spirit child warm as she runs with him along the shores of the Great Sky River!"

M'alsum frowned. The giant's eloquence and generosity were growing tedious; both demeaned him in subtle ways that he could neither measure nor define. And the man was not yet finished with his words or gift giving.

"And this also I give to Kicháwan." The giant placed upon the bier a wrapping of matched quills and a miniature woven pine-needle basket filled with tiny, perforated river shells and polished teeth extracted from the jaws of small animals. "May Strong Running Woman take these quills! May Kicháwan accept this basket! May she use her sewing tools and sinew, not for the adornment of others in the world beyond this world, but to sew these quills and beads of shell and teeth onto her new cloud garments so that the Ancestors will see her beauty shine!"

M'alsum rolled his eyes. *Hide her homeliness is more like it!* he thought.

And now, as his last gift, the giant raised high a string of painted and feathered deer-hoof janglers. "Accept the hooves of the swift deer, Strong Running Woman, so that when you ride joyous and beautiful upon the back of the Four Winds, those whom you have left behind in this world will hear the clacking of these janglers and know that you are near and watching over those who must surely have loved you in this life!"

M'alsum managed not to roll his eyes again.

The giant was looking at him now, waiting, expecting some sort of reciprocating gesture of respect and statement of gratitude, if not outright affection, to the corpse.

It was almost too much for the headman to stand. He uttered an inaudible groan and ground his teeth until he thought he must surely crack a tooth. What would the giant say if he were to discover that it was M'alsum, and not marauding manitous, who had beaten the burden woman? That, although he had not intended to kill her, he was not in the least sorry that she was dead? What would the giant say if he knew that, left to his own devices, M'alsum would have made no fire, raised no bier, offered no gifts, and surely not even have considered lifting a praise song to the dead burden woman's spirit, much less danced in pretense of mourning over her? That, had he been given a choice, he would have hacked Kicháwan into pieces and scattered her parts to the Four Winds as he had scattered Sac and Mingwé so that their deceitful spirits would be forever sundered, incapable of following or threatening him in this world or any other, canceled, as though they had never lived at all?

M'alsum lowered his eyes. He did not want the giant to see into his thoughts, or to glimpse the smile tugging at the corners of his mouth. He pressed his lips against his teeth, once again reminding himself that he must placate the man and secure his friendship to ensure his continued assistance. Nevertheless, the giant was beginning to amuse him. As big and overbearing as he was, Kinap brought to mind the captive bear that M'alsum had seen long ago in the Lakeland village of Sebec deep within the western forests. Toss the tethered animal a scrap of meat or a kind word and it had been so grateful that it forgot the miseries and threats inherent in confinement and happily sat up and begged for more! On the dawn of the wedding of Asticou and Wawautaésie, M'alsum had seen that bear led passively out on a lead to be brained and butchered and roasted for the marriage feast. The comparison threatened to revive his smile. The giant, in his apparent hunger for companionship, was full of questions, but M'alsum had only to toss the man a reply and Kinap gulped it down whole and digested it unchallenged. And so, with an exhalation that was certain to pass as a heaving sigh of profound melancholy, the headman obliged the giant's need to witness his bereavement.

Without a word, he went to where he had dragged his trading goods well away from the lean-to, thinking as he did that the spirits of the forest were surely smiling on him once again. By the laws of his tribe, once Death had entered the little shelter, everything within had been contaminated and must now be abandoned. But the giant, unaware of this tradition, was confident that fresh air, sunlight, and a few incantations and waftings of smoke would be enough to purify the corruption. M'alsum, grateful, had no intention of disagreeing with the man.

Now, looking down at his belongings, his glance caressed the thong-wrapped curve of the great brown bison hide and the familiar shapes of the parfleches and smaller packs that he had brought so far at such terrible cost. In his mind's eye he could see all the many wonderful things he had traded for so diligently among other bands before assembling and packing them with care, confidence, and anticipation of all that they must soon achieve for him. As though he would ever leave them behind!

Longing stirred in his heart. M'alsum could imagine himself standing proudly before his precious trading goods on the pale, lichen-scabbed bluffs upon which Ogeh'ma, Hasu'u's bandy-legged father, chose to encamp with his people, sons, and many daughters at the edge of the forest above the vast salt sea.

He could see the smooth curve of the horizon bending away to the north and south of forever, and the smooth pale dome of the nearby mountainous island where the mysterious shaman, Squam, made his residence with his woman and holy people. There was the river where Ogeh'ma and his people speared migrating salmon in early summer. There were the wild tributary creeks that the caribou forded in autumn, and the beaver pond and pool, and, beyond, the marsh where he and Ogeh'ma and Hasu'u's brothers and other men of the band had taken moose. He could see the tidal flat that, come summer, would cool the bare feet of the people as they dug for shellfish and carried it off in dripping baskets to be wrapped in sea grass and cooked in stone pit ovens on the grassy fringes of the wide sandy beach that welcomed the kiss of a gently rolling, white-lipped surf. And as he looked at the deeply indented sweep of the bay, he knew that, even now, the strange, fat, deformed dogs that the coastal bands called seals would be whelping their huge-eyed, white-furred pups on the late-winter ice beneath an open sky that stretched eastward beyond the limit of his ability to comprehend such enormity of space.

Drawing in a deep and steadying breath, M'alsum filled his lungs and nostrils, not with the acrid stink of the smoke that was rising from green wood and slowly burning hide beneath the bier of the dead woman, but with the conjured sweetness of the cool, moist air of the coast. He savored the remembered gray pungency of fog, the subtle dark, earthy scent of the estuarine marsh, and the stark, cold, bitter-clean smell of granite and salt and pack ice floating upon the bay in huge broken plates that made him think of the sloughed skin of the white whales that came in season to bask and feed in those rich and often turbulent waters.

He shivered a little, wanting to be away from the snow-bound confines of the forest deeps, yearning to once again dwell beneath the open sky in that healing, meat-rich land to which he ached to one day bring Meya'kwé and his people.

He closed his eyes, visualizing himself dropping to both knees before Ogeh'ma and his band. He bowed his head. He imagined himself accepting the solicitude of those who had adored Hasu'u and would no doubt adore him. How could they do otherwise when he told them of how he had risked everything and nearly perished along with his unfortunate brothers in his valiant and selfless attempt to wrest their Dawnland daughter from the murdering manitous so that he could bring her and her newborn son safely home to them? With no one left alive to contradict him, they would have no cause to question anything he chose to tell them. And he would tell them anything necessary to further his own position within their band.

They would weep at his words. Hasu'u's people wept easily and just as easily forgot their tears. Then they would mourn and fast, and when the mourning and fasting were done, they would marvel not only at the many trading goods that he placed before them on the shining brown bison hide, not only at the mighty tusks and hairy tail and nostriled foot of the fifth leg of Katcheetohúskw, but at the man who might now prove to be immortal.

He opened his eyes and, staring at the hide, smiled as he thought of the priceless little chunks of copper that lay secreted within, of the exquisitely woven cedar pouch of mano'min seeds, of the nodules of white quartz from the far western hills, of the prime pelts and healing fungi and bark and leaves and tubers, and of the makuks and cones and duck beaks filled with the sweet crystallized sap that the people of the Dawnland so craved that they would barter away their sons and daughters to possess it.

"Well?" pressed the giant from his perch in the boughs. "What gift will you give to your Strong Running Woman to please her spirit in the world beyond this world?"

M'alsum winced at the barb. Not sure Kinap had intended the slur or not, he ignored it as he knelt, rummaged through the parfleche nearest to him, and, knowing that it contained the least valuable of his goods, came up with a small packet of medicinal leaves and dried fungi.

"Mmph," said the giant when advised of the contents. "I doubt she will have need of medicine now. Better think I if you have any beads or feathers or copper trinkets or even small pieces of copper rock that the thunder beings might be persuaded into pounding into adornment for her. She would like that! And what about sweet sap? Yes, say I, I think she would like that, too. Traders journeying north or east to the Dawnland usually carry more than enough of that magic confection to seduce young girls of the coastal tribes into spreading themselves in exchange for a suck . . . if you will excuse the comparison. But you are a trader, are you not?"

"It is so! And yes, I do carry copper, but not enough to spare. And yes, I carry sweet sap to bring smiles to the faces of the many *children* of my slain wife's band, and for the old men and women whose gums are in need of soothing and who can taste little else of sweetness in their failing days. But surely, Giant, in the world beyond this world the dead do not eat!"

"Who can say? From what little you have told me, the life of your burden-carrying woman was shadowed and bitter. So offer her the brightness of copper! Give sweetness to her now in amends for all the sour she has had to swallow from others who have not been as considerate of her needs as the sons of Asticou. And perhaps her lost spirit child will smile at a taste of sweet sap. Especially if you carry any of it preserved on teething sticks in the pliable hollow beaks of young ducks. Everywhere little ones love ducksuckles!"

"Yes, of course I carry ducksuckles, but in the Dawnland children and old people are many. I will not have enough to go around if I part with any of them here. And it is well known that unborn and unnamed dead babies possess no spirits to squander sweetness on."

The giant heaved a ponderous, remorseful sigh. "Again say I: Who can say? It seems a harsh judgment upon those least responsible for their own destinies. A tender little stirring of life in a mother's belly, a heart beating or a heel or knee or elbow kicking hard against a father's questing palm—this has seemed proof of life and spirit enough for men when once it seemed that all the hope and dreams of the very future of my loved ones were growing in one unseen little form. Had she not been born, had she perished with her mother, somehow her spirit would have lived on, in my heart at least. Do you not know this truth when you feel the pain of the loss of your own drowned little son?"

The only pain M'alsum was feeling now was over the loss of even the smallest portion of his trade goods. He grimaced as he worked to untie the thongs of the great bison hide, reminding himself that if the sacrifice of a small share of his copper and a sweet ducksuckle or two was required to assure the sympathies and cooperation of the giant, he would part with them with no regret. With Kinap at his side, he would soon have the tusks cut from Katcheetohúskw and be on his way to the Dawnland. Without the man's help, he might well be mired in the snow of the inland forest for weeks.

And so, with well-masked reluctance and irritation, M'alsum offered up his gifts of precious copper and sweet sap to Kicháwan and her miscarried infant. As he began to speak the required words of praise and gratitude and, yes, even of affection and profound regret over their passing, it occurred to him that the moment might well be yet another gift from the spirits of the forest. Since the unexpected appearance of the giant had prevented him from mutilating the burden woman's body, Kicháwan's spirit was free to journey to the spirit world, where she was likely to speak unkindly of him to the Ancestors and from where she could return at will to haunt him. It would have been foolish not to make an attempt to pacify the dead woman! Only fatigue and the frustrations and trials of the trail had kept him from seeing this before now.

"Let the spirit of Kicháwan, Strong Running Woman, hear the lament of M'alsum, headman of this band and firstborn son of Asticou of the inland forest and of Meya'kwé of the Grassland and Dawnland peoples!" He fairly sang the words, then thought, *Let the "shade" of Kicháwan—if the giant is right about the existence of such a thing—look favorably upon my pretended sorrow and believe that, at the end of her pitiful life, there was at least one man to mourn her passing and care that she ever lived at all.*

The words flowed on, impassioned now, not for the woman but for himself. The spirit of Kicháwan must smile upon him when she reached the country of the Ancestors. She must put aside recollections of beatings and insults and rape and remember only that on the day she died he spoke well of her strength and skills and tenderly of her unborn child. Perhaps then she would be content to remain forever in the realm of the sky spirits? Perhaps . . .

"And to think I took you to be a quiet man!"

The giant's comment brought an end to M'alsum's lamentations. He looked around into settling dusk, startled to see the first stars of evening glinting in the cold northern sky.

"You will dance now," said the giant. "I will keep the fire. I will beat the rhythm of mourning for your Strong Running Woman and her lost child . . . and for those lost lives for which you have offered no lament: your drowned son and the brothers and woman you claim to have seen slain along this Dawnland trail."

There was no missing the strong, dark undertone of disapproval and perhaps even of suspicion in the giant's voice. "I . . . I mourned for them before you came!" he lied, cursing himself for his careless oversight. "And you must believe me, I saw them die!"

"Must I? Did you? Mmph. So say you, Friend, so say you. But now you must dance. The spirits of your dead command it."

▼▼▼▼

And so he danced.

Not out of grief over the deaths of Kicháwan and the unborn baby or in sorrow over the loss of his slain brothers and woman and little drowned son.

He danced for himself, for the favor and sympathy the dance would win him in the giant's eyes.

Slowly, surely, sidestepping in a circle, defining the pattern of the eternal cycle of life as it moved inexorably from life into death and then back into life again, he danced.

Like a somnambulist swaying to rhythms as ancient as

the earth beneath the snowpack, over which the giant spread wide the roof skin of the lean-to so that the headman's moccasins would remain dry throughout his ordeal, M'alsum danced.

He did not hold his spear.

He did not look warily toward the trees.

He robed himself in trust, for he was now confident that the giant was what he claimed to be: a solitary, wandering storyteller, long-winded but wise and kind and sometimes wary, one whose compassionate heart might allow him to be manipulated by a cautious and clever man, but one who would not easily be made to play the fool.

Strong in this knowledge, M'alsum danced.

For all of that long night and all the following three days and nights he danced. Never was there so solemn or outwardly sincere a mourner as M'alsum! He wailed. He moaned. He wept. He sighed and shivered and shouted the names of his dead with what any observer would have taken to be utmost love and longing.

He swayed his body to and fro to the heartbeat cadence of the drum, all the while inwardly rejoicing in the deaths he had made.

He forced a woeful grimace as he suppressed laughter at recollections of the stupidity and gullibility of his brothers.

He threw back his head and, while intoning chants of grief, sent unspoken but passionate thanksgiving to the forces of Creation for freeing him, not only of the liability of his brothers but of responsibility for a pair of women and infants he cared nothing about, and for placing upon his path a giant of a man who would soon help him cut the tusks from the great mammoth and show him the shortcut to the Dawnland!

"Ah yah!" he cried as he circled and bowed, imagining

the way it would be when he and Kinap came to the coast dragging a sled heaped high with valuable trading goods and crowned by the massive tusks of the legendary mammoth.

"Ah yah hay!" he exclaimed, anticipating his glorious arrival in the Dawnland, where, after the obligatory display of sadness over the untimely and unavoidable death of Hasu'u, he would reaffirm his admiration of her father and brothers. They were good men, trusting men, amiable men who, in the short time he had lived among them, had proved incapable of deceit or avarice, or of suspecting either such virtues in the motives of others. They gave generously to all who passed their way and were unstinting in their annual offering of tribute meat and pelts and the occasional young girl to the shaman who dwelled with his woman and attendants on the sacred island. Squam's magic powers were believed to bring game to the land and fish to the sea, and although the Magic Man had not come from his sanctuary in more winters than anyone could recall, no one found cause to question him. What a trick! M'alsum had thought then, as he thought now. To take meat without ever having to hunt for it! To accept adoration without even having to show one's face! He had left Ogeh'ma and his people with a promise to return with gifts from the wealth of the inland forests, gifts to make them and their holy man smile. Soon he would make good that promise and, with only a minimum of manipulation, have them exalting him as Mammoth Slayer and Bringer of Good Things to the People! What would old Squam have to say about that?

"Ah yah!" he shouted to the Four Winds as he envisioned his eventual return as a hunt chief—and, yes, perhaps even as a Magic Man—to his father's miserable little village, where he would spit Asticou on his own spear and at last be able to bestow upon his beloved Meya'kwé all the many rewards she had already secured for herself within his heart.

On and on he danced.

Under a cold and brilliant sun.

Under night skies strewn with stars and slashed by the white-hot tracings of meteors, he lost all track of time. Once, brought short by what he could have sworn was a low, ursine huffing, he paused, tense, expecting to see a bear recently emerged from winter sleep invading the mourning camp. But there was nothing threatening within the night. All was still. The giant appeared unperturbed as he sat by the fire, bundled in his furs with the odd length of wood across his lap, his hooded head high, his great mittened hands keeping the slow, inexorable rhythm of the drum. And so M'alsum danced on and on, stopping only when he found it necessary to relieve himself or when his muscles cramped and, trembling with fatigue, his limbs would no longer support his weight.

Only then did the drumbeat stop.

Only then did the giant come close, swooping near like some huge forest bat to drape warm furs around the headman's body and massage his aching muscles. Offering melted ice to assuage the dancer's thirst as well as to pacify his hunger, he encouraged M'alsum to rest as long as he had need.

"But not too long, lest the spirits of the dead hold even the slightest rancor toward you and decide to come to you in your sleep for the purpose of sucking your spirit from your head and claiming it as their own!"

In the light of recent events, M'alsum found this to be a far more unpleasant prospect than the giant could possibly have guessed, but since he had already gone to great lengths to eliminate any threat from the spirits of his slain brothers, it was only Kicháwan's ghost that worried him. And, considering the inordinate amount of time he had just spent placating whatever animosity she might hold toward him, how much of a threat could the spirit of the woman be? Nevertheless, with the giant's warning in mind, he willed himself to sleep only in fitful spurts, dreaming occasionally of a bear prowling close, and grateful to find Kinap hovering near when he awoke, always ready to help him drive off any spirits that might have come for him and to extend encouragement when he once again began his dance. Indeed, he would have had to be blind not to notice that the giant left his side only to beat upon the drum, empty his bladder, and see to the feeding of the captive muskrat.

"I am grateful for your consideration, for surely I would not be able to mourn my beloved dead without you," M'alsum told him, thinking that it was a good idea to grease the man's pride, as well as to express a growing concern. "You feed your muskrat with care and constancy, Giant, but I have not seen you take so much as a single bite of food since my fast began. You must not deprive yourself of meat and strength because of me!" *Or you will be of no use to me when the time comes to cut the tusks from the great mammoth and drag my sled to the Dawnland!* "Truly, Kinap, there is no need for you to fast and mourn with me."

"Ah, but, Stranger, there is," the man replied in his low, deep, grainy rasp of a voice. "I have learned in my wanderings that, despite what some would say, the Circle of Life encloses us all. Since the time beyond beginning, of man and beast—indeed all living things, even lichens and fungi and water and stones—none may stand outside the sacred Circle. All must live out their lives in the way of their kind until Death comes to transform them, to reshape and redefine their purpose within the sacred Whole. And yet, once within the embrace of Death—although they remain forever within the Circle, contained always within the Whole—they are lost to us forever in this life, for the Circle is always turning and the sacred Whole is always changing."

The giant paused, moved restlessly within the heavy fall of his hood and garments, then heaved a sigh that sounded as though there were a smile in it. "Ah, Friend, it is not all sadness, this Death and dying! Which one of us can say how long the spirit of your Kicháwan will run with her unborn child upon the back of the Four Winds once her shade has left this earth? How will she be transformed by Death? Will she seek the spirit of a newborn baby into which to be born again along with her unborn infant? It could be so! Or perhaps she will live again in a nestling or denling spawned of the birds or animals whose flesh made up the substance of her last or most favored meal. Or maybe she will be transformed into mist or fall as rain into the cool waters of some inland creek over which you may stoop on a hot summer day to slake your thirst, only to be blessed by her loving spirit. Mmph. I find it a soothing thought. Yet still Death must bruise the heart with longing for those who are forever lost to us in this life. And so, say I, the grief that one man feels at the deaths of his loved ones is the same grief that all men must share. We walk the rim of the Sacred Circle together in this life, my friend. It is a tenuous walk at best, for the Circle is always turning, always moving forward, never back, and so we are each destined to see our beloved women and children and parents and friends all fall away into the Great Whole to be transformed before we, too, must join them. And so, as I have told you, we will bear this together. It is not good for a man to mourn alone."

M'alsum forced a wan smile of appreciation. He was finding the giant's tendency toward philosophical pronouncements increasingly irksome. Long and heavy words might well prove food for the minds of some, but they did not sit well on an empty stomach. The headman had never had patience for pontificators; they always proved to be men of hesitation rather than determination, and, always, he had been able to override their will to serve his own. In the giant, however, he had met a nearly immovable object.

It was all he could do to maintain his smile. Had it not been for his need of the giant's strength and knowledge, he would not have cared whether the man ate or not. Or whether he mourned with him or not. Or whether he kept the fire burning or continued to beat out the rhythm of his mourning dance upon the discordant little drum. He cared only that Kinap remained strong and faithful to his promise to help haul the sled and show him the shortcut to the Dawnland.

And so, staggering to his feet, M'alsum saw to it that the dance of mourning went on. And on. He closed his eyes, sent his thoughts drifting into a soothing black limbo of mindlessness until the trumpeting of a distant mammoth brought him back to reality with a start.

He stood dead still, listening, looking around. As when he had imagined the huffing of a bear, all was quiet save for the sighing of the wind in the trees and the slow, unbroken beating of Kinap's drum. Whatever he had heard, if indeed he had heard anything at all, was silent now. He told himself that he must have imagined it; the only mammoth in this forest, or perhaps in all the world, lay dead in the ravine.

Above his head, a meteor streaked the sky. M'alsum looked up. The pale, watery blue luminescence of an aurora was shivering across the night. He scowled. What night was it?

Third night? Fourth?

"Ah!"

Surely it must be the fourth night! Soon the fifth dawn must come and the cursed dance could end. Soon!

"Soon!"

But when? When?

He had no idea. And so he kept dancing.

To keep himself awake, he pinched and slapped at his furs until his skin smarted. He tried to keep his eyes open by every trick he knew, counting stars, trees, observing the giant's massive hooded form hunkering close by Kicháwan's bier, endlessly beating his cursed little drum, tending the fire. Once, half stumbling on his feet, he came blinking into wakefulness in time to see the giant amble off to send a steaming stream of urine into the snow, squat to defecate, then move off to fumble amidst his belongings for food for the unseen muskrat.

For a moment, as the man walked off toward the trees, he could have sworn that when Kinap looked back over a shaggy shoulder, the auroral glow illuminated the elongated face of a hideously scarred bear. M'alsum closed his eyes and shook his head to clear it of the impossible image. When he looked again, Kinap was bending over his belongings with his head shrouded in his hood again. Although M'alsum was a good distance away and viewed the world through the fogged blur of extreme fatigue, he saw the muskrat peering at him from around the side of one of Kinap's massive legs.

Pinch-featured as a fox, the little rodent was much larger than any muskrat M'alsum had ever seen. He saw the flash of its black eyes and white dagger teeth as it snarled and chewed on whatever it had just been given. Then the giant shoved the animal under the caribou skins.

He was glad. There was something about the muskrat that both rankled and disgusted him. He could not understand his reaction any more than he could understand how any man would want to make a gift of such a creature, unless perhaps it was being fattened for skinning and roasting. But even then its fur would make an unsatisfactory pelt, and its flesh would not provide enough for even a dog to eat with any satisfaction.

He closed his eyes again and, as he danced, imagined himself crushing the little bog rat under his heel. He found it a pleasant conjuring. Had he not feared winning the giant's disapproval, he might have allowed himself a smile as he thought of how satisfying it would be to feel the bones of the little rodent cracking and the organs collapsing beneath his weight. Then, without warning, the muskrat turned to savage his heel with its needle teeth as it hissed,

"You stink of the musk of your lies, M'alsum, Firstborn Son of Asticou! Do you truly think that you can ever hope to outdistance all that you have done in this forest? I see and know you for what you are! And no matter what you do or say or where you may go, you will never be able to kill me!"

M'alsum shook himself as, with a start, he realized that he had fallen asleep and been dreaming on his feet. He dropped to his knees from sheer exhaustion. He did not have to look to his moccasined heel to know that the muskrat had not bitten him. It had not spoken to threaten him. It was still off in the trees, most likely asleep or gnawing away on whatever scraps the giant fed it, keeping itself warm under Kinap's prime caribou skins, where it seemed content to secrete itself from the light of both sun and stars.

M'alsum hung his head. He rubbed his temples with the tips of his mittened hands. He knew that the voice he had heard had come from within his own skull. He recognized it for what it was: the voice of a guilty conscience. He cursed it, considered it a weakness, like green mold eating away at good meat in a cache pit, softening the flesh, breaking it down, taking away the essence of blood and strength until it was fit only to be fed to old men and women whose teeth and gums had gone pulpy and tender. He shivered with revulsion. Despite his gifts and chants and endless dancing the ghosts of his dead brothers and women were still with him, tangled within the very substance of his soul. He cursed them all. He would not hear them! He was glad they were dead!

He shivered again. Looked around. Scowled. Night seemed to be thinning. The world had gone blue; snow and trees and boulders all appeared bruised in the light of the fading aurora, all tinged a bilious algal yellow and pink along the eastern horizon. He cringed. It *was* haunted, this forest! It had a way of eating at even the best of men. If only he could be on his way to the Dawnland. If only . . .

"Arise, Dancer!"

M'alsum flinched. Squinted. The giant was striding toward him from where he kept his belongings among the trees.

"The fourth night has passed!" announced Kinap. "It is the fifth dawn, my friend! You have mourned long enough!

And by your expressions of sorrow and the agony of your dance you have shown me the way of your heart! Only a good and caring man would have endured all that was asked of you. So now it is time for you and me and Musquash, my muskrat, to prepare to journey on."

"You will show me the shortcut to the Dawnland?"

"And help you to drag your sled, as I have vowed."

The headman rose. It was no easy feat. He was weaker than an infant and as unsteady as a newborn fawn. Yet he managed to stand, still scowling, surprised to see the muskrat riding high upon the giant's shoulders with long, skinny, fur-legginged limbs wrapped around the man's neck. M'alsum gaped. The rodent was no bog rat! It was a boy! A small, scrawny, pinch-faced, black-eyed boy of no more than six winters, wearing a traveling tunic of mismatched skins and, as a hood, the joined pelts of muskrats with the whiskered head of a single rodent facing forward over his brow.

The giant laughed at the expression of amazement on the headman's face. "M'alsum, son of Asticou of the Inland Forest, it is time for you to meet Musquash, son of Kinap. There is not yet much meat on these little bones, but there will be someday. The boy may not look like much, admit I, but he is as bright and quick and resourceful as a little bog rat. If only he could speak, he would be a perfect son, but then his mother would not have parted with him and he would not be mine to bring as a long-promised gift for a lonely child!"

"You will give away your own son?"

"He will be in better hands than mine."

M'alsum met the fixed and hostile gaze of the boy and decided that, were the child his, he would not keep him either.

In the fading light of the blue aurora, with dawn now glowing bright at his back, the child seemed edged in golden fire as his black eyes narrowed, his white little dagger teeth showed in a snarl, and he hissed at M'alsum like a riled gander.

Stunned, M'alsum took an inadvertent backward step and discovered too late that his limbs would no longer serve him. He went down with no warning and found himself on his buttocks, splay-legged and leaning back on his palms, staring up as the giant shook his hooded head.

"Forgive the boy. He has been given good cause to be distrustful of strangers. And as for you, Friend, you must rest now. You are dead on your feet."

"I am that weary," conceded M'alsum. "But, in truth, I am not sure I can die."

"Mmph. We can all die, Friend! Especially if the bear that has been snuffling around this camp returns and decides to make meat of us."

"Bear? Then it *was* real? Why did you not warn me?"

"Of what? She came, sniffed us out, and went her way with no trouble offered. A big bear, too big for two men to eat or transport. Since neither of us has need of her skin or plans to return to this part of the forest, any meat we would cache would surely be wasted. Besides, she may have cubs around. It would not be a good thing to kill a nursing sow. But, by the forces of Creation, although I am grateful for the smoked meat and fat that I carry in my traveling pack, what would I not give for a slab of meat cut fresh from a big kill!"

"There is meat, big meat," said M'alsum. Certain now that all his hopes for his future in the Dawnland were about to come true, he told the giant of the great mammoth that he had brought to its death in the ravine.

Chapter Seven

▼▼▼▼▼▼▼

Old One caught her breath.

Something had just changed within the world, shifted, turned sharply and ominously toward darkness. She could feel it, taste it, sense it in every fiber of her being.

Something.

But what? She had no idea; it was simply a knowing, a sudden sensation of dread so intense that she dropped the bed skin she had been shaking and airing in the cold, clear light of dawn.

The wolf, tethered outside the den, rose and stared at her nervously.

Old One took no notice of the animal. Her hands flew to her chest. She pressed inward in a vain attempt to steady the leaping of her heart. A cold sweat dewed her brow. Her heart was dancing, that odd, disconcertingly wild and arrhythmic dance that it had taken to doing so often and without warning these past few days.

The world seemed to sway beneath her feet. She willed herself to stand steady as her thoughts swam outward to a place that she had no wish for them to go. It was no use. She could not prevent herself from suspecting that the change she had just sensed within the world was, perhaps, not within the world at all, but within herself.

The ground beneath her feet had stopped swaying. If, indeed, it had ever swayed at all. She shook her head. She was old. No—she was ancient. To sum her years she needed to twice sum the digits of both hands and feet and add a single full hand-count plus one thumb more.

Forty-six!

Was it possible that anyone before her had ever lived to be so old? It seemed unlikely. Her teeth were worn. Her gums were tender. Her beard had gone white. The calluses on her elbows and the heels of her hands and feet were like nodes of solid bone. Despite Mowea'qua's childishly stubborn insistence to the contrary, she knew that she must soon die. But she could not understand why the knowledge always seemed to take her by surprise. Surely Death was no stranger to her. Indeed, she could not remember a day on which she had not expected to meet that specter and fall prey to his insatiable and pitiless appetite.

So long ago.

So far away.

She trembled to think of it. Always Kinap had been at her side in those long-gone days to see to it that, somehow, against all odds, Kelet managed to survive to see another dawn. And another. As she had healed him and given him back his life, so he had done for her. Like a son he had been to her! She had lived for his sake and for the child, for Pi'jiu, her only surviving child, the offspring of rape, the little one who would grow to one day become Mowea'qua's mother.

"Ah!" Her spirit bled. The memories were too painful to recall, and yet far too precious not to remember. She had been young in those days. So young! And although she had seen Death walk in and out of the encampments of her loved ones, always he left her behind. After a while she had begun to wonder if he would ever call her name.

Again she trembled.

With her heart pounding, her head swimming, and her beloved giant far away, the possibility of her own death seemed very real to her now.

The wolf lowered its head.

Old One took no notice. She spoke Kinap's name, reached out to him, wanting him to steady her on her feet, wondering where he was and why he had not come and how much longer she could brazen out her feigned lack of concern for his welfare and whereabouts so that Young One would not know just how much she worried about him. How she ached for the familiar warmth of his rough embrace! How she longed to hear the low rumble of his laughter and the gentle distractions of his wondrous stories! How she yearned for the very essence of his maleness and strength within the lodge!

"Ah!" Her heart leaped, fluttered madly, then leaped again. If Kinap did not come, it was because he could not come. If he could not come, he must be dead. And if Kinap was dead . . . how long could she endure without him?

Feeling suddenly weak, light-headed, and more than a little nauseous, Old One knew that her heart was failing. Indeed, were it not for the almost constant ache of anguished worry within her breast, she might well have suspected that her heart was no longer a heart at all. Sometimes, as now, it felt as though it had transformed itself into a little bird that was frantically fluttering its wings in an attempt to be free of her chest.

"Mmph! As though you could live apart from me," she muttered in droll but short-lived bemusement as a swoon dropped her to her knees in the level clearing that she and Young One had labored to dig from thigh-high drifts two days before.

The wolf uttered a low, worried sound, neither bark nor growl, as it pulled against its tether.

With her head spinning, Old One was aware of the attention her behavior was winning from the animal. As she braced herself on outstretched hands, she was wary of the wolf and glad that the young one was with the stranger within the lodge and not beside her to witness this moment of appalling weakness. Slowly, forcing herself to breathe deeply and evenly, she did her best to drive back dizziness and nausea. At last, with a sigh of relief, she felt clearheaded again. "Better . . . yes . . . better now," she whispered to herself, then added to the wolf as though she had every reason to expect a reply, "Would you attempt to console me for my weakness, U'na'li? Or would you set yourself to eat me if you could be free of your tether now?"

The wolf tucked its tail and lay down.

"Mmph!" Old One eyed the beast and saw no threat in it. The rhythm of her heart slowed, evened. She knew that she was not going to die. At least not in this moment. Grateful, she raised her face to the gently swaying crowns of the evergreens and, seeing faint wedges of high-fleeing geese migrating northeastward in the open patch of sky directly above her head, was certain that she had never seen a more beautiful morning.

Winter would soon be over. The passage of the geese declared it. The great, garbling, pinioned bands would be seeking open water and greening grass in the thawing marshlands and estuaries of the coast. The birds knew when to begin their migrations. The stars told them, as the stars told all who looked to the sky for wisdom and direction in this life.

Late last night they had spoken to her. She sucked in a ragged little breath, recalling how she had gone from the den, vexed as she always was by her increasing inability to hold her water until dawn. She had refused to acknowledge the infirmity of her years. She would not remain in the den and use the gourd to empty her bladder as a sickly child or dying elder would be expected to do. No! Indeed, she would be dying before she would yield to such shame! And so for a long while she had squatted defiantly in the snow, warm within the circling spread of her sleeping robe, breathing in the hot clean scent of her own urine until, after a while, soothed by star glow and transfixed by the pale light of a blue aurora, she had lost herself in memories of other star-strewn skies and auroras beneath which her band had followed the caribou back and forth across the vast and glorious desolation of the far northern barrens. Gradually, awash in the blue light of the ever-shifting gossamer light of the auroral veil, she had become aware of the Pleiades. The little star cluster hung so low in the western sky that, had it not been for its unique multicolored brilliance, she would never have noticed it sparkling between the trees that obscured the horizon. Its position in the sky had been a sure sign of the coming of spring.

Now, as then, a sob welled in Old One's throat, a sob of joy, of sorrow, and of recognition. In the star stories of her kind, the Pleiades were always the Little Lost Children. And last night, under the cold and brilliant sky, she had known that they were *her* children. Her slain babies, her slain daughter Pi'jiu. As she had watched them slipping slowly away toward the east, she heard a sound that she had not heard in over half a lifetime, a sound that now lingered in her mind: the thin, high song of the aurora.

She closed her eyes. *Yes!* She could still hear it! So rare! So delicate! So ineffably beautiful! A long, threnodic whispering, a sighing that somehow skeined itself into the blue substance of the aurora as it wove through the Old One's mind to communicate an understanding that was so wondrous and so painful that she wept.

"Do not forget us, Mother," implored the Little Lost Children in the song of the aurora. *"And do not mourn for us. Soon we will walk forever together in the ever-circling star tracks of the Great Bear and the star Brothers who hunt him. But for now there is still a Lost Child who looks to you for guidance. For the sake of that one bright star you must remain strong! You must live! For Mowea'qua you must see and savor the certain advent of spring."*

She opened her eyes.

The geese had passed from the sky above her head, but, to her surprise and delight, Old One saw that the treetops were alive with squirrels. She smiled and snuffled back tears. Here was yet another sign of spring!

Only yesterday, while working with Young One to spread a carpet of freshly cut spruce boughs across the clearing so they would be able to venture in and out of the den without wetting their moccasins, they had been happily distracted by the chattering, paw-pounding antics of the little red tree dwellers as they scampered madly about the branches in search of nesting materials. Soon the chittering of juncos and chickadees had drawn Old One's glance to the unmistakable track of a skunk winding across the drift tops just beyond the clearing.

Again she smiled. There had been no need to tell Mowea'qua that when Skunk came from his winter sleep under a forest canopy alive with squirrels, surely spring was bound to follow, for the words had been on Young One's lips even as U'na'li the wolf had suddenly caught scent of the skunk.

Old One could not keep from laughing to herself as she thought of how, as the one-eyed eagle watched from the outside perch to which Mowea'qua had tethered it, the wolf had bounded forward with the speed of one of the masked Stranger's flying sticks. Mowea'qua had called the animal back to no avail, and although the girl had scrambled after it, the wolf all too soon learned of the danger inherent in skunk hunting.

She chuckled. U'na'li was still watching her. She sensed concern in its eyes and dejection in its posture. All Mowea'qua's rubbings with snow and all the wolf's frantic rollings in the same had failed to remove the stink that U'na'li's disobedience had won for her.

"Fail did your wolf mother to teach you a basic lesson, my friend," Old One informed the animal. "Skunk may not be as quick on his short little legs as his weasel cousins, and easy is he to be found in his messy little grass burrows beneath fallen trees or in the hollows of bigwood stumps. Lazy his cousins may call him, and not much of a braveheart as he sleeps through the winter during which they must hunt or die. But clever is Skunk! When he is awake, roots he for his food—grubs and bird eggs and insects and scraps of meat and bone that bolder hunters sometimes leave behind. So although again you may cross trails with Skunk, U'na'li, respect him you must and leave him at peace, for in his cleverness a great weapon has Skunk! And now that he has used it against you, do not think that you will be welcomed back into the den until the stink of it is gone from your fur. No! With one who smells of the spray of an angry skunk, not even your own kind would dwell!"

The wolf dropped its head and crossed its paws over its snout.

Old One laughed. She was feeling better now. Much better. She saw the wolf's misadventure with the skunk as another affirmation that the long, cold winter was, indeed, fast passing away. The gashes, gouges, and broken ribs suffered by U'na'li the previous autumn during its mauling by the bear were healed. A night would soon come when the wolf would awake to the howls of her own kind and know that it was time to make her way in the world as a wolf again.

Old One one sighed. She would miss U'na'li and could not understand why Mowea'qua, who invariably settled into a protracted mood of sadness whenever it became apparent that one of her wounded foundlings was about to leave her care, expressed only gladness to see the wolf on the verge of being able to make its own way again. Indeed, as they had resumed cutting spruce boughs to replace the old floor covering of the lodge, the young one radiated a glow of transcendent happiness as she expressed her longing for spring and her certainty that, even as she spoke, woodland caribou were anticipating the coming thaw and leaving the frozen inland lakes to follow long leads of soft new snow northward to their ancestral calving grounds.

"Wolves will follow the caribou, Granddaughter," she had chosen to remind the girl. "It is their place in the Circle of Life, as it was once ours. U'na'li will hear the summoning of the pack and seek to join once more with her own kind. Will you not miss her?"

"Ah, but say I, Grandmother, that U'na'li must walk with her own kind. The forces of Creation will call to her when and as they will. Stop her from answering I can and will not!"

The response, so out of keeping with the young one's usual desire to hold her foundlings near as long as she could, set a note of warning throbbing within Old One's head. Only her own aching desire for the warmth and sunlight had allowed her to overlook it when the girl had distracted her with happy babblings about the coming spring.

Mowea'qua's voice had fairly sung as she spoke of how deep within the forest to his springtime feeding grounds the Great One must already have moved, because they had not heard his thundering voice in days. And surely, she had said, even as the great mammoth walked his way, within wind-sheltered stands of black spruce and tamarack, deer and moose must be casting their antlers as, weary of their winter diet of bark, twigs, and evergreen tips, they were beginning to venture from their winter refuge, hungry for the succulent sweetness of swelling redbuds.

She spoke, too, of how she and Old One would soon be taking up their snare lines, lures, fishing spears, and moss-lined egg-gathering baskets. Together they would go downstream of the falls to do a little ice fishing in the broad, deep pool where trout often rose hungry to their lures in the last days of winter. The wounded Stranger might enjoy a freshly caught and roasted trout. And after setting a few snares in hope of catching a grouse whose flesh might heighten the wounded Stranger's appetite, Old One would fish with both spear and line while Mowea'qua scanned the trees for jay nests. Climbing high, she would seek and, if luck was with her, gather spotted green-gray eggs recently laid by the bird women of Wiskedjak and his thieving, cocky band of gray jays that often came to perch on the den top, screeching for scraps in the dead of winter or brazenly pilfering whatever meat they could carry off from the spring and summer drying frames.

Later they would spread mats of woven grass upon the hard surface of a diminishing snowpack. Awash in the wan light of spring and in the reflected ruddy glow of birch trunks blushing with the first rising of sap, they would listen to vocalizations of newly arrived songbirds as they ate fish and sucked jay eggs, setting some aside in their baskets for the wounded Stranger. They would thank Trout for agreeing to become food for them, and although they would apologize to the gray jays for stealing and eating their unborn children, Old One would nevertheless congratulate Young One for once again being clever enough to steal from Wiskedjak and the other thieves of his feathered clan, for surely the sly, cocksure birds deserved this retribution! And if, after dozing awhile before checking their snares, they decided not to return immediately to the den but chose instead to enjoy the fine open view presented by the marsh below the beaver pond, they would walk the short distance there together and be sure to see gougings in the snowpack where moose would have hoofed out hollows in hope of feeding on the first tender shoots of wetland grasses and reeds and the crisp uncurlings of tender new ferns.

Old One exhaled a sigh of yearning for the sweetness of the first fern curls of the season. Hungering for the myriad fresh green tastes of spring, she found herself glad to concede that Mowea'qua and the geese and squirrels and skunk and Little Lost Children among the stars were right. Spring was coming! She would live to see it! She must!

Renewed and invigorated by the assurances of her thoughts, Old One rose shakily to her feet. Squinting, she looked around. The morning was so bright, so beautiful, so perfect in all ways. If only Kinap would come to her through the trees—big and strong as ever, laden with gifts, filled with new and wonderful stories and news from beyond the forest! If only she could see his dear face and hear his beloved voice, all would be right with the world once more!

But it was not the voice of Kinap that she now heard coming to her across the clearing.

It was the voice of the Stranger.

"Stay away from me!"

The wolf raised its head and laid back its ears.

Old One growled at the sharpness of the wounded one's command. It angered her. How dare he command anyone! And how could Young One ignore his rudeness as she doted over him as though he were one of her injured animal foundlings?

"Bah!" Old One shivered to think of it. He *was* a foundling. But he was no animal. He was a Stranger, an Enemy, and now, more than ever, Old One wished that she had never agreed to bring him to the den. What had she been thinking? Or *not* thinking? Why had she not simply let him die? It would have been so easy. Mowea'qua could never have brought him from the creek by herself, much less carried him through the forest to the den. It was long past due for her to stand up to the increasing willfulness of the child. And yet now, as she hugged herself against an inner chill, she knew Mowea'qua would not remain a child forever. As with the wounded Stranger, all the tender signs of impending maturity were there upon her face and form for anyone with even half an eye to see.

"Bah!" she exclaimed again. How she wished that she could turn back time. How she wished that Kinap were here to strengthen and advise her. And how she wished that neither she nor Mowea'qua had ever set eyes upon the Stranger or any of his Enemy kind!

A wave of weariness washed through the old one. She had lived far too long to believe for even a moment that the mere act of wishing could ever accomplish anything more than the guarantee of eventual frustration and disappointment. Besides, if Strangers had not fallen upon her band, if she had not been raped and impregnated by them, her daughter would never have been conceived, and Mowea'qua, her granddaughter, would never have been born.

Old One's heart began to race again.

She forced herself to her knees, drew up the sleeping fur she had earlier dropped, and held it close as suddenly, without warning, it was there again: the sense of change. The sudden and terrible knowing. The sense of dread that was so pervasive that it paralyzed every fiber of her being. Death was near for her . . . as near as the Stranger within the den.

She shuddered. "Maybe, after all, it is just as well that he lives. For if I die—*when* I die—if Kinap does not come, who else in all this world will there be for Mowea'qua?"

"You must now about him tell me all things, Wounded One!"

"Him?"

"Yes, say I! The beautiful one! The brother you name M'alsum when out of your dreams speak you."

"I have told you, he is dead."

"No! Dead he is not! Believe this will I not! Nor must you, *never*! When last saw him I, alive he was! And beautiful! So beautiful!"

Ne'gauni offered no reply to the girl's impassioned response. Everything about her peculiar way of speaking irritated him. Besides, it hurt him to talk. And he did not
believe a word she said; if M'alsum had survived the raid,
he would not have abandoned his youngest brother to die
alone in the creek.

"Tell me of him," urged the girl again.

He held his tongue. Clearheaded for the first time in
days, he suspected that she was deliberately taunting him
with false hope so that she could inflict further pain upon
him by dashing it again. Had it not been for his pain, he
would have been unable to keep himself from screaming in
rage every time he heard her voice or looked at her face or
at the bandaged stump of his left thigh and knew that the
worst part of his nightmares was not a dream. She and the
bearded old hag had cut off his leg!

"Smooth your bed furs now will I, Wounded One, even
if talk to me you will not."

"Leave them!"

"Will not I! Care for you must I! How else will heal
your wounds?" She was emphatic as she continued to fuss
around him, straightening his blankets and propping his
head on a newly fluffed buckskin pillow.

He wanted to bite her. A good, hard, vicious, skin-
breaking, bone-bruising bite! But could the flesh of a manitou—if indeed she was a manitou—be broken and bruised?
There was only one way to find out. Maybe, with a quick
snap of his head, he could tear into one of her fingers and
rip it off! Then he would just begin to be on the way to
getting even with her! Unless, of course, her flesh proved
to have some magical way of regenerating itself. How he
ached to find out! But his tightly bandaged face prevented
him from acting on his impulse, and although he longed to

strike out at her, he had already discovered to his chagrin that he was too weak to do more than give her a feeble shove. This he did even though he knew it would cause him pain and prove a useless gesture. If he had learned nothing else since regaining consciousness, he had learned that the girl would not be distracted from her constant ministrations to his every need, no matter how much she hurt or humiliated him.

As she was humiliating him now.

He lay still, determined to ignore her as she gently but deftly drew back his bed furs and set herself to help him relieve himself into the hollow gourd that she and the old hag used for this purpose. He gritted his teeth. There was no sense trying to fight either of them when it came to this; he had neither the strength nor the resolve to override the pain or degradation that another insurrection would win for him. One way or the other, he would be humiliated no matter what he did: submit to their handling like a helpless infant or void as he would and lie like a smelly babe in his wet and soiled bed furs. And so he lay motionless, allowing the humiliation and loathing the girl for subjecting him to it.

"Soon better you will feel when water you have made," she assured him breezily.

He would not dignify the moment with a reply. He glared past her, pretending she was not there, attempting to distract himself by scrutinizing his surroundings through eye slits in the moist, medicine-saturated, oily-smelling, defurred hare skins that bandaged his face.

The room in which he lay was more or less as he remembered from his nightmares: the huge, unidentifiable bones arching upward to support the high curve of a good-sized roof of bark and moldering thatch; the snow walkers of varying styles upended against a curving wall; the big woven fishing trap hanging with folded snare nets and lines from a tritonged antler mounted to the cross-bracing of a wall; the neatly stacked rolls of furs and hides close by a large fire pit surrounded by blackened stones, with a smoker at one end and baskets and cooking implements of varying shapes and sizes piled nearby; the great ball of twisted willow twigs tied and ready to be used for kindling.

He turned his head slightly, carefully, not wanting to rouse the ache that tightened and burned across his face whenever he moved his facial muscles. He was looking for the wolf. When he had first come from his dreams, he had not been sure the wolf and the girl and the hideously bearded old hag were not somehow one and the same beast. He knew better now. At various times all three of the impossible creatures filled his vision at the same time. And the wolf was there now, watching him out of yellow eyes from where it lay in the open entrance to the lodge, its snout resting on its crossed forepaws. It was not as big an animal as he remembered from his dreams, but even with the full light of morning streaming across the fur of its back, it was darker than he remembered. A black wolf. A nightmare wolf. Except in his dreams, he had never seen another like it.

Above Ne'gauni's head and slightly to his right, the white-headed eagle was dozing on its perch. In the spiderwebbed vault he could see the eviscerated carcasses of the small birds and beasts that he recalled from his dreams, all hollow-eyed, defeathered and defurred, smoked, it seemed, from the look of them: squirrels and rabbits and grouse; stringers of dead songbirds, frogs, and salamanders, all hanging upside down by their feet from crudely hewn rafters; braids of sweet grass, bunches of dried leaves, ropes of shriveled mushrooms, berries, and dried blossoms; the carapaces of small woodland turtles; and what appeared to be the cocoons of some sort of moth or butterfly.

Ne'gauni cringed. Somehow the collection seemed even more grotesque in the light of day than it had by night. He could visualize himself hanging upside down between a grouse and a squirrel, as dead as they, looped up by his one remaining ankle, his arms dangling, his body skinned, gutted, and desiccated, his skull gaping, eye sockets empty and staring down at some new and equally helpless victim in mute testimony to the fate that was about to befall them.

He closed his eyes. Perhaps, he thought, when he opened them again, with any luck at all his situation might yet prove to be a dream. There would be no collection of dead animals, birds, and reptiles hanging upside down from the ceiling above his head. There would be no girl holding his penis to a gourd, no wolf staring at him, no eagle dozing in the rafters. And his face and shoulder would be unbandaged, and his left leg would be whole and strong!

Let it be so!

He sent the unspoken imploration upward in anguished hope and absolute desperation. It was a test he had been performing whenever he could not find escape from his intolerable new reality into the sweet mindlessness of delirium. A small voice inside his head kept telling him that what he was asking was absurd as well as unjustified. He was where the forces of Creation had put him, where he deserved to be as punishment not only for calling the manitous upon his loved ones but for failing to protect them when the phantoms came. Still, he had never been very good at listening to opinions that did not serve his will and could see no reason for starting now. This lodge, the girl, the wolf, the haggard old woman, and all the grotesques hanging from the web-gauzed ceiling might well be his fate, but although there might be no escaping it, it was not within Ne'gauni's nature to do less than try.

So, with his eyes shut tight and his hands clenched into fists at his sides, the youth did his test again. What harm could there be in it? If it failed, he would be no worse off than before. If it succeeded, when he opened his eyes, he would find himself back at the creek.

It would be the moment before the manitous broke from concealment within the cover of the trees on the far embankment. His brother's beautiful Dawnland woman would just have knelt to drink. He would be listening to the cawing of Raven. He would hear the great roaring in the forest. He would recognize the stench of Danger in the wind. And this time he would not fail to do what must be done. He would take hold of the straps of Hasu'u's cradleboard and pull her to her feet. He would force her to obey him. With Death on the heels of the trading band, together they would flee with the baby in the sled tracks of his brothers. He would shout a warning to M'alsum, Sac, and M'ingwé. They would listen. He would *make* them listen! And this time, when Wíndigo, Great Ghost Cannibal, winter chief of the manitous, and his murderous band of phantoms came bursting through the trees, the sons of Asticou would be ready for them. They would not be taken by surprise! They would stand to the attack. The flimsy little flying sticks of Great Ghost Cannibal would be useless against the more powerful stone- and copper-headed spears that would surely send the manitous running in fear for their ghostly lives.

Let it be so!

Let it never have happened as I have dreamed it!

Let me be well and strong and whole! Let my band be alive—M'alsum, Sac, and M'ingwé, and Kicháwan, and the dogs, and the baby! And Hasu'u . . . beautiful Hasu'u, my eldest brother's Dawnland woman!

Let it be so!

Please!

Let it be so!

Ne'gauni opened his eyes.

It was not so.

A long sigh of disappointment went out of him. He was still lying on his back in the lodge of his captors. Cold clean air and sunlight were streaming into the shelter through the open smoke hole and the weather baffle. The girl had moved away to take the gourd outside; he had been so focused on his longings that he had not noticed. Now she was returning to his side.

He watched her as she stepped over the wolf and came toward him. Rays of sunlight bathed her slender, fur-clad form in a transparent striping of alternately soft and brilliant yellow. He glared, hated her, and was certain that she was the strangest-looking creature he had ever seen.

"*What* are you . . . *who* are you?" he asked as she knelt beside him.

She cocked her head and replied simply, "What you see, this am I."

A frown brought a deep, dull ache moving across his features. Just what did he see? A manitou? Perhaps. He was not sure. When viewed in the light of day out of eyes no longer dulled by fever, she appeared human enough. A child? No. A girl, almost a woman, with a wild black tangling of unnaturally fine, wavy hair falling loose around the elongated oval of a pale face made strangely angular by the rise of broad cheekbones and the graceful arch of thick dark eyebrows set high on a prominent brow ridge that framed wide eyes the color of mist.

Instinct warned him to look away, for surely any creature whose appearance was so far beyond the range of normal experience could well yet prove to be a manitou! But even so, what could she possibly do to him now that would be worse than what she had already done? Cut off his other leg? An arm? Both arms? Or maybe his head? The latter would be a mercy! Sooner or later, if he was not already dead and by some perverse magic of the spirits being tricked into believing himself alive, he was certain that he was going to end up hanging from the rafters along with the rest of her collection. Unless he regained his strength and managed to hang her and the old hag first!

Her head cocked to the other side, as was her way when his manner perplexed her. "Full of unspoken and angry thoughts are your eyes, Stranger."

He held his gaze steady on her face. Whatever she was, human or manitou, she was the fate that he had called upon himself. He would not, could not, turn from it now. And there was something about her eyes that held his own. Mist-colored eyes! Never, outside of his recent nightmares, had he seen the like. They were as rare and unnatural as the pallor of her skin and the wave of her hair. Neither a rich, loamy brown nor a shining black like the eyes of the People, her eyes were a composite of every imaginable variation of gray, dark and light combined in intricate striations, with an occasional fleck of green, brown, and amber that made him think of autumn leaves strewn across granite, or of tiny pebbles glistening like brightly painted stone beads on the gray-graveled bottom of the cold, clear stream that ran close to Asticou's forest village.

It occurred to him in that moment that, although unusual and therefore disturbing, the eyes of the girl were beautiful. As she was beautiful in a way unique to herself. Compelling. Enchanting. Beguiling.

A tremor went through him. Aghast, he realized that, truly, she must be a manitou! She had bewitched him! He closed his eyes against the power of her spell and turned his head away, reminding himself that she had worked together with the old hag to cut off his leg. She would never be beautiful in his eyes. *Never!*

"Look away from me why do you, Wounded One? Am . . . am ugly I to your Stranger's eyes?"

"You are the one who is strange! And, yes, you *are* ugly to my eyes!"

"Ah!"

A quiver of pleasure went through Ne'gauni at the sound of the abject misery he had just heard in her gasp of dismay. He wanted to hurt her, as she had hurt him. "Go away, Ugly One. The sight of you sickens me."

"Cannot I," she told him on the saddest of sighs. "Tend you must I."

"For what purpose?" he sneered.

"To make well and strong again your body!"

Anger touched him. He turned his head and looked at her again as he demanded in a fury of righteous self-pity, "For what purpose? You have not left enough of me for even such an ugly manitou as you to worry over!"

Her face went white. "One leg! So much it is not to have taken! If with two legs had left you I, dead would you now be! Alive with one leg are you! Alive! Enough this is for you, and for me, say I! Grateful must be you! Grateful!"

"Then give me a knife, Ugly One, and I will hack off one of your legs so we may be grateful together!"

Her long, soft mouth compressed. She cast a quick look

over her shoulder toward the entrance to the lodge, then turned her attention back to him, leaning closer, lowering her voice to confide in the tone of an eager conspirator. "Grow back your leg will, say I!"

"On the day I learn to fly!"

"No. Jest not. Soon better will be you. Old One would not believe that this could be. Said she that die you would. But knew I that it would be not so. Strong are you! And young! Like me, yes! Death to you will not so easily come. Not when with you I am always ready to drive him away! It is good, say I, yes?"

"It is good, say I, *no!*" Ne'gauni mimicked nastily. "Go away! I told you, I am as sick of the twisted sound of your words as I am of your ugly face!"

The statement obviously stung her, for her shoulders stiffened and she held her head erect, but in some way that Ne'gauni had no hope of understanding, it must also have pleased her. Her mouth parted in a smile that put dimples in her cheeks and revealed her small white teeth. "Sick will you not be soon!" she proclaimed. "For the first time since Old One and I brought you to our den, no longer walking in and out of many bad dreams are you. Know now you what is true and what is imagined. Good this is. Very good. Even if ugly find you me."

Ne'gauni did not know what irked him more: the girl's impossible and sometimes nearly incomprehensible placement of words, her happy enthusiasm, or the fact that she had made him feel guilty about calling her ugly. She deserved no kindness from him. He could see nothing good in his situation. And he did not like the look of her teeth; the canines were abnormally large and distended, pointed, like the eyeteeth of a fox or dog or . . . wolf.

His gut tightened. His glance slid to where the wolf lay

in the entranceway to the lodge. It was still there, taking in
the sun, guarding its den from intruders . . . or blocking
any hope he might entertain of escape. The animal's head
went up. It was staring fixedly at him now, not merely
watching but taking measure of him as though attempting
to decide whether to rise and come to claim him as a meal.
Ne'gauni swallowed, made a gulping sound, and succeeded
neither in clearing the sudden tension in his throat nor
relieving his rising uneasiness as he recalled the legend of
Mowea'qua, immortal wolf woman of the northern forests.

It was said that she denned with wolves. It was said that
a great dark wolf roamed ever at her side as guardian, and
mate. It was said that she named wolves Brother and Sister,
Mother and Father, Uncle, Aunt, and Child. It was said
that, in the dark of the moon, she became a wolf and ran
with them in pack, hunting in the way of their kind, howling with pleasure in her kills, seeking always her favorite
meat, the flesh of unfortunate hunters among the People
who wandered lost and unwary within the haunted forest
where she had been prowling Ne'gauni's nightmares, unbidden and unwelcome, for far too long.

"Think you that ugly he also will find me?"

"What?" the youth asked, startled from his unpleasant
reverie by the questioning girl, if indeed she was a girl and
not a shape-changing apparition. She was still smiling at
him, somewhat wistfully now, still showing her pointed
little eyeteeth. Anger stirred in him again. How could she
smile when he had lost everything that ever meant anything to him?

"Think you that ugly he will also find me?" she repeated.

"Who?"

"The beautiful one! The one who is to you a brother. The one name you M'alsum."

Had she driven a stone awl into his spirit, the pain could not have been greater. "I have told you. He is dead, slain by the masked manitous along with my other brothers and their burden woman and—"

"No! This believe must you not! Alive he is, and with him the others you name Brother. With my own eyes this have I seen. Together again with them will you one day dwell, say I. Rejoice will they to see you alive and walking once more with them on two strong legs!"

The wanting that filled Ne'gauni in that moment was a terrible thing. It rose as an ache at the back of his throat. It burned his sinuses and welled as tears in his eyes. He tried to blink it away and swallow it down, but his eyelids would not hold back the liquid expression of his grief, and his throat grew even tighter as a ragged accusation escaped his lips. "Liar!"

Once again she cast a quick look over her shoulder toward the entrance to the lodge and, seeing only the wolf lying there, turned her attention back to the youth. "Grow back your leg will, say I. It will! I am making special magic for you. Very special. When Kinap comes, go we will together to the sacred spring. There is power there, true magic there! All will again be good for you. Grow back your leg will! Healed will your wounds be! And your face will be almost as beautiful as his face! See this you will, say I. See this you—"

"He will see nothing ever again if you try to take him beyond this part of the forest, Granddaughter!"

Ne'gauni and the girl turned simultaneously to stare toward the entrance of the lodge, where the old one had come to stand beside the wolf, growling in at them.

"Grandmother!" the girl exclaimed and was on her feet in an instant.

Ne'gauni stared. The morning sun was at the hag's back, but there was more than enough light filtering downward into the shelter through the open smoke hole to allow him to see her only too clearly. A spasm of revulsion shook him. The same yellow rays of sunlight that only moments ago had illuminated the beauty of the girl were now illuminating the ugliness of the hag. With her time-worn face, wispy gray brows, white beard, mustache, and wild hair bursting outward from her scalp like an explosion of tree moss, she was even more hideous than in his dreams. Surely she could not be human!

"Mowea'qua!" He spoke her name as he had spoken it before, in recognition, revulsion, and no small measure of fear.

The wolf rose to stand beside her. She laid a gnarled, hairy-backed hand upon the animal's dark head and snorted a reply, not to Ne'gauni but to the girl. "Mmph! See you, Granddaughter, how to that name a Stranger cannot refrain from recoiling and imputing ugliness!"

"Ugly not are you, Grandmother!"

"To your eyes not, dear one, but to their kind we are always that. Everything that they do not understand and cannot control is always that. Ugly! Feared! Reviled! To be avoided! Or to be hunted as wolves and bears and lions are hunted, not only for meat but because they believe that by the eating of our flesh they may steal our power for themselves. And so they call us Mowea'qua! Yah! Wild wolf woman! Eater of the flesh of the People! Yah!" She looked straight at Ne'gauni. "It is your foul race that has pursued and devoured ours ever since our ancestors first followed the game into the face of the rising sun! And why, say I?

Because our infants are furred and our old ones grow beards? No! Because your kind will not share your hunting grounds with any not born to your own tribe! Yah! Are we not all the children of First Man and First Woman? In the time beyond beginning were not the People and Animals all of one tribe? Yes, say I, yes! But your kind has forgotten this in its lust to make itself chief over all!"

Ne'gauni was stunned. Never before had it occurred to him that it might be possible for Manitou to revile Man for the very same reasons that Man reviled Manitou. And so, for the first time, he looked at the old hag and was amazed to see that her face was drawn, haggard, her small eyes sunken into bluish swellings of skin in the way of a frail, sick old woman who had not been sleeping with any regularity. Perhaps she was only human after all!

"Come, Granddaughter!" she commanded impatiently. "Time it is for us to take the wounded one outside into the healing gaze of the sun. Bring the oil of winauk and the large porcupine quill. His wounds must be bathed and irrigated. Expose them we will to cold clean air and the sun allow to touch and heal them in its special way. After all that you have done to so foolishly save him, I would not have his flesh turn green and give off a stink that will our den foul even more than his presence has already done!"

"Your 'den' already stinks," Ne'gauni snapped in self-defense. "It stinks of you, Old Hag!"

"No," she countered. "It stinks of you, Young Stranger. And of the long confinement of a winter that, until this dawn, thought I would never end. So careful be you, Loose Tongue, if live you would to see the spring."

"I *will* live to see it!" he vowed, with absolutely no certainty but out of a desperate need to at least stand up to her with words since he could never again hope to do so on his own two feet. Besides, he had remembered another vow, one made to another manitou in another part of the forest. Ignoring the pain in his face, he told her, "I will live to seek my eldest brother's Dawnland woman! I will live to find and gather her bones! I will live to make lances of them! And then I will hunt those who have slain her! In the name of Hasu'u, this I have vowed! This I will do . . . in this world or in the world beyond!"

"Will you?" she slurred, a dangerous and provocative taunting. "Mmph. By now are her bones broken and scattered by the flesh eaters that have cracked them for marrow as they devoured her . . . as one day will I see your worthless bones broken and scattered if leash your tongue you do not with me!"

Never had Ne'gauni been so thoroughly riled. "You ugly old woman, if indeed you *are* a woman, how brave you are to threaten me as I am now! Why do you stand so far away? Do you need the wolf to protect you from a one-legged 'wounded one'? Are you not a wolf yourself? Come, Mowea'qua, attack me with more than insults if you dare, but I warn you that I am Ne'gauni, youngest and, yes, now surely the boldest and bravest and best of the sons of Asticou. Even with the use of only one good arm I will give you a fight that will cause you to regret ever bringing me to your den, you stinking, hideous, hairy-chinned old hag!"

The wolf was growling low in its throat as it raised a quivering upper lip in response to the open hostility in the youth's tone.

But, to Ne'gauni's amazement, it was the girl who bristled. "No more such words, say I! Ugly you may call me, Wounded One, but while lives Mowea'qua, my grandmother will hear from your mouth no insults, not from a Stranger, not from an Enemy whose life she has saved for me with her knowing of the healing ways of the Ancient Ones! Speak you with respect to Kelet, who is Spirit of the Old Tribe and grandmother of Mowea'qua, or speak you not at all!"

Ne'gauni was astounded. Never would he have thought the girl capable of such an intense flash of fire. "*You* are Mowea'qua?" It seemed less likely to him now than ever before. She was not smiling, so he could not see her odd, wolfish little teeth, and surely—although he would have submitted to death before admitting his thoughts to the girl or the old hag—with her gray eyes flashing and her pale cheeks flushed, Mowea'qua was easily the most beautiful and compelling creature he had ever seen. Not even Hasu'u could come close to matching Mowea'qua's beguiling loveliness.

"Yes, say I," she answered softly. "Mowea'qua is my name."

For the second time this morning, a tremor went through Ne'gauni. Compelling? Beguiling? The words snagged in his brain. By the forces of Creation, of course the girl was capable of being both if she possessed a manitou's power of enchantment! Only another of her own kind could say with any certainty just what she really looked like. Visualizing a younger version of the old hag and certain that he had betrayed the memory of Hasu'u, the youth fixed the girl named Mowea'qua with hostile eyes and conceded to her the one point he was prepared to yield to her. "You do not always look like a wolf," he told her.

Her chin tilted skyward and wobbled a little as she said, "Wolves are ugly never!"

"Exactly," said he as cuttingly as he knew how.

"Mmph!" The old one's utterance was sharper than

Ne'gauni's, and the expression on her face was one of spirit-curdling disapproval as she appraised the twosome from beneath speculatively lowered brows. "Beware, Stranger," she warned. "Enemy are you still in my eyes. When rises the moon full and then goes dark again, I may yet deal with you as I have vowed. And if I do, assure you I that I will give you *both* cause to howl!"

Chapter Eight

▼▼▼▼▼▼▼

There were tusks to be cut from a mammoth.

But first they would have to drive the she-bear and her yearling cubs from the body of Katcheetohúskw. Or kill them. M'alsum cursed the animals for wasting his time as he stood with Kinap and the boy at the top of the ravine.

"No wonder she did not return to trouble us," the giant was saying quietly. "She has come early from her long winter sleep and will 'camp' here awhile. Her cubs will grow fat and strong on so much meat. Come. We cannot linger in the hunting grounds of Bear. And the mammoth you have brought me to see cannot be Katcheetohúskw."

"Why? How can you be sure?" demanded M'alsum. When no answer was forthcoming, he protested, "I tell you, the bear did not kill the mammoth! I did! There . . . do you see . . . over there by those boulders on the far side of the ravine, that is where the raiders cornered Kicháwan and slew my brother!" How easily the lie came to him. He had no reason to believe that the giant would not gulp down every word. "It happened exactly as I told you. They violated my burden woman and cut my brother to pieces before my eyes. I tried to stop them. It was no use.

And then the mammoth came. The raiders turned and ran. I stood my ground. To save Kicháwan from being trampled, I hurled a spear, and another, and another after that! I struck the beast! Yes! Again and again I struck it! Yet still it came for me. On and on it came, forcing me to race ahead of it so that my burden woman had a chance to run to safety. Ah! I can still see it! As tall as a mountain! Roaring like thunder! Shaking the world beneath my feet! Exactly as it was in the tales my mother used to tell me. It *was* Katcheetohúskw, Giant, I know it was! No other beast, be it animal or manitou, could be so huge! There was no escaping it! Not until, at the very last moment, I had the good sense to run downhill of it and cause it to fall to its death. And that is the truth of it! As you see!"

The giant shuddered.

M'alsum was trembling with elation as he waited for words of awe and adulation to come scraping from Kinap's mouth. The giant had been listening in rapt silence, staring down, his perpetually mittened hands clenching and unclenching at his sides. Now, without a word, he turned and began to walk away.

Perplexed, the headman asked, "Where are you going? Back to the mourning camp? Good! There are extra hunting lances amidst my belongings: a good pair with heads of gray stone, hard gray stone from the north, not as fine to the touch or beautiful to the eye as my copper-headed spear, but the best of their kind."

The man made no reply but kept on walking.

M'alsum was on the giant's heels. He had eaten just enough of the traveling rations that the giant had insisted they share to feel relatively strong and fit again. "The day is still young. As long as the bears stay at their feeding, we will have the high ground when we return. If we can kill the sow, the cubs will be no threat to us as we cut the tusks from the great mammoth. And steaks. Many steaks. Together, before the sun goes down, we will share the meat of the great mammoth. If it *is* Katcheetohúskw, it may well give voice to your son! Among my mother's Grassland people it is said that there is magic power in the meat of the—"

"My traveling rations suddenly seem sweet to me," the giant interrupted sourly. With his great hands resting on the crossed ankles of the boy, he spoke not another word as he plodded back to the mourning camp, where he swung Musquash to the snow-covered ground and commanded the boy to help gather their belongings together.

M'alsum stopped beside the giant, puzzled and almost painfully aware that things had suddenly changed between them, and in no way for the better. The man was not rummaging through his bags and parfleches in search of butchering tools; he was obviously gathering his things preparatory to moving on. "What are you doing, Kinap? We cannot go on just yet! There is a bear to kill, my friend, and meat and tusks to be cut from the mammoth."

"Are you a friend, then?"

M'alsum found the question as sobering as it was confusing. "Have you not named me as such?"

"Mmph. I have also promised to show you the shortcut to the Dawnland. I will honor that vow, for I would have no man say that Kinap is not one to keep his word. But I will slay no bear or make orphans of cubs for no cause, and never will I butcher a mammoth. Especially not *that* mammoth! So load your sled, Stranger, if you would have me lend a hand with it. We will journey on. *Now*."

"But you told me that you had a hunger for meat cut fresh from a big kill!"

"Not from that kill."

M'alsum could see all his fine plans for a glorious entry into the Dawnland dissolving around him and could not understand why. "I tell you, Friend, that *is* Katch-eetohúskw lying out there at the bottom of the ravine! How much bigger could any kill be? It would be an offense to the forces of Creation to just walk off and leave it! True, it may not be as fresh a kill as on the night I led the mammoth to its death, but the flesh of that beast has lain blanketed in snow these past days and nights and, once we cut through the frozen parts, will still be red and sweet. Come, Friend, we will feast as we work together to bring the tusks and as much meat as we can carry to share with the Dawnland people of my slain woman. It is the least I can do for them after all that—"

"The Dawnland people have meat!" snapped Kinap. "They have the meat of seals and fish and wintering marsh birds and deer! And they have tusks—the big teeth they cut from the jaws of wi'pitcó, the legless swimming mammoths they call walrus."

M'alsum huffed contempt. "I will bring them *real* tusks! *Mammoth* tusks! And I will bring them the meat of mammoth! All know that it has special power, that it is—"

"Forbidden."

"What?"

"It is forbidden to hunt mammoth. The meat of their kind is forbidden meat."

"To whom?"

"To my kind, Stranger, as it should be to all. There are so few mammoth left in this world that to kill even one of them risks all of their tribe."

M'alsum was fast losing patience. "As far as I know, Friend, the mammoth in the ravine *is* the last mammoth!

Abandoning its carcass will not bring it back to life or bring others of its kind back from the spirit world! So why should we leave its meat to be food for bears? Why should we not feast upon it and take the power of its flesh into ourselves? I did not hunt the mammoth. It hunted me! Indeed, since it was not actually slain by my spears, you could say that when the mammoth followed me and tripped and fell into the ravine, it killed itself!"

Now it was the giant who huffed contempt. "Mmph!" He rose in a single angry sweep, leaving the boy crouching within the fall of his towering shadow as he pulled off his mittens, left them dangling by their neck cord, and said, "I think, Musquash, that perhaps it is time for the Stranger to behold the face of Kinap!"

The boy did not flinch as the giant reached up and folded back his hood.

M'alsum gasped. He knew that he was gaping like a stunned fish. He could not help himself. Now, for the first time, he saw the giant's bare hands. From wrists to fingertips, each was white and shining with scars from some terrible burning. And his face . . . his face! Never had M'alsum beheld such appalling ugliness. The giant's entire head was scarred, as though his flesh had melted and oozed downward over his skull before being carelessly smeared back into place and allowed to heal into a cruel parody of what had once been a human face. He had nostrils, but not enough of a nose to call a nose. He had ears, but they were merely holes cupped within distorted lumps of purplish flesh. He had eyes, watering, lashless, staring from beneath the smoothly distended skin of a hairless brow that was somehow attached to the outer edges of his upper cheeks. And, as though to emphasize the shining horror of the man's disfigurement, a long and lustrous braid of thick black hair hung from the single spot high at the back of his skull where the hair follicles had not been burned from his scalp.

"You are no man!" M'alsum exclaimed in shock, revulsion, and no small measure of fear as, taking a backward step, he swung his copper-headed spear into a defensive position. What a fool he had been! How had he not guessed the truth of the giant's identity before now? How had he not even suspected it? After seeing Wíndigo, winter chief of the manitous, with his own eyes! After being charged by Katcheetohúskw! He should have known that, in this haunted forest, the one who called himself Kinap was "Djeneta! Ah! You are Djeneta! A manitou giant! And the boy is no boy at all! He is Djigáha, one of the demented manitou dwarves who keep company with the man-eating—"

"Deformed giants of the ancient winter tales? Bah! It seems that some men will believe anything! I will concede that, big and ugly as I am, I could pass as a horror from the winter tales, but do not position your spear against me, Stranger! I assure you that I am only a man, not a manitou, as the boy is only a boy. For were we of the ghost tribe, we could long since have slain you and even now could be using your finger bones to pick our teeth clean of your shredded flesh!"

M'alsum flinched as a massive fur-mittened hand suddenly swiped out like the paw of some huge animal. In an instant, before he could do no more than blink, the spear was snatched from his hands and broken across one of the giant's quickly upraised thighs.

"There," said Kinap with no attempt to conceal either the scorn or irritation that curdled his mood as he threw the larger half of the hardwood shaft aside and placed the shorter half, with the copper projectile point intact, into M'alsum's hands. "Take this back as a gesture of my goodwill! And as a statement of my intent *not* to have you for my next meal! You can rehaft it later, Mammoth Slayer, if you value it so much, although why you prefer such a spearhead to one of stone when copper bends and breaks so easily is a mystery to me. Most would say it is fit only to be pounded into trinkets for women!"

M'alsum was shaking. He was furious, frustrated, and flushed with embarrassment. Kinap had just echoed the opinion of his slain brothers. It was as though they were mocking him out of the mouth of the giant. With no effort at all he could imagine the pair of them alive again, standing before him again, impugning his judgment again, shattering his sense of self-worth. As he stared down at the fractured end of all that was left of the exquisitely painted shaft of Asticou's spear, the odd roaring at the back of his head was there again.

It would be no easy task to replace such a fine length of hardwood. This late in the year, he doubted that he would be able to find an adequate cutting of second-growth oak or ash or any other suitable hardwood; if he was to judge by the severity of the past storm as well as by the lengthening days and the positions of the stars the past few nights, all conditions were right for sap to be rising in the trees.

He trembled. Soon, deep within the inland forests, the People would be hurrying to tap the sweet clear blood of maple and birch trees before prolonged spring rains and thunderstorms combined to warm the air and sour the sap. In the village of Asticou, men and boys would be tying on their snow walkers and preparing to go out from the village to check the supporting posts, roof coverings, and contents of the nearby sugaring huts. Women and girls would be happily trudging after them, carrying rolls of fresh birch-bark to replace or strengthen the old roof coverings beneath which they stored their sugaring troughs and tools along with great stacks of birchbark buckets and bowls and cone-shaped molds. Perhaps, even now, little ones and old ones were daydreaming of ducksuckles, while all through the forest the winter encampments of nomadic woodland hunters were being broken down and transported to their own sugaring camps, dragged by dogs on sturdy sleds and toboggans. Soon the fires of the annual spring-sap thickening would burn bright, and the woodlands would be fragrant with the sweet scent of the many forms and colors of sugar and syrup and candies that were to be savored by all.

M'alsum growled as he thought of the precious duck-suckles that Kinap had forced him to squander in the wasteful mourning ritual for Kicháwan. Soon other trading bands would be journeying out of the hardwood forests with fresh supplies of granulated sweet sap. His own would not be nearly so valuable then. And he had so hoped to be the first to reach the coast with them!

His growl became a snarl as his fingers flexed around the hard sleekness of the small portion of the spear shaft that remained. Any wood that he would gather now would be sappy and sure to swell and split during the lengthy smoking process by which unwanted insects and grubs were forced from the slowly seasoning timber.

M'alsum could feel his face burning a deep, hot red as he ground his teeth to keep from hurling a curse or a fist at the giant. How he ached to stab him with the point of the spearhead, to ram it through his furs and bury it in his belly, or at least to strike out at him for what he had done, to slash and inflict further damage to his already hideously maimed face! But as he glowered up at Kinap, M'alsum knew that, although he had been a fool to think the man a manitou, there was no denying that he was a giant. Attacking him was a far from prudent idea. Besides, he still had need of the man.

And so, after drawing in a deep breath to cool his temper, he forced himself to speak with an amiability that almost gagged him. "I must inform you, Friend, that this copper-headed spear was my father's most prized possession. It was a gift given by him to me as a token of his deep affection and concern for my safe return when I led my trading band from his village. Nevertheless, although you have shattered it, I will not forget your kindness to me in other matters. It was wrong of me to position it against you. I ask your forgiveness, and your understanding, but your appearance does put a man on his guard, you know. It was the same with the mammoth. When it came through the trees, I had never seen anything like it. I . . . I was afraid. Yes! Truly I was. And so I threw my spears. You cannot fault me for trying to save my life. And on the honor of my mother, Kinap, when the mammoth ran and fell, I did not kill it. It killed itself!"

The giant's face twisted. "Did it?" The query was lightly spoken, but the words that followed were tainted by a grim and merciless irony that contorted Kinap's lipless mouth as they rasped from his scarred vocal cords. "Then let me ask you this: Once there was a grass fire. Long ago. Far away. The flames were not set by lightning, nor by a spark gone wild in the wind after escaping from an ill-tended campfire. No. This grass fire was set by men in hope of burning alive all those with whom they had no desire to share their hunting grounds. I was forced to flee ahead of the flames. Unlike another who managed to escape, I was caught by the fire, and as you see, I was burned. So tell me, Man Who

Leads Mammoth to Suicide, whom do I fault for my burning? Do I fault the ones who set the fire and drove me ahead of it, hoping that I would be consumed? Or do I blame myself for my lack of speed and my poor choice of an escape route?"

M'alsum felt his face flush hot again. He had not missed the sarcasm in the giant's voice, or the point of his query, but he was finding it difficult to keep his eyes fixed on the man's face without yielding to an almost overwhelming need to retch. "By the forces of Creation, Kinap, how could any man have found the heart to survive such a burning?"

With a shrug the giant said, "A manitou could have leaped ahead of the flames! A Djeneta could have set his giant feet striding across the prairie until he came through the conflagration unscathed, to turn and blow the fire back into the ranks of those who set it! Ah, now that is a thought to bring a smile to even such lovely lips as mine! But, as I have said, Stranger, a giant I may be, but I *am* only a man. I am alive by the grace of the kami. I have maintained the heart to keep on living because of the loyalty and love of an old friend. And I stand before you as I am, fully blaming for my 'beauty' those who chose to set the grass fire that drove me from their hunting grounds and scarred me forever. As I blame you for choosing to run the mammoth to its death!"

"But—"

"No!" Kinap reached up to pull forward his hood, concealing his face within the ruff of encircling wolf tails. "With all the boulders and trees in that ravine, a man not bent on killing the object of his fears could have found a way to stand aside until the old tusker went thundering on his way. Old and sick and half blind was that mammoth.

No man not wishing illness on himself would ever eat of such meat! Even with so much snow blanketing his body, I knew him at once by the stink of illness on him, and by the dark color of his coat and inward curl of his right tusk."

"Katcheetohúskw!" The name of the legendary monster exploded out of M'alsum's mouth. "I knew it! It *was* the Great Beast! That manitou has walked my dreams every time I heard my mother tell of him, or listened to the tales of the old men in the winter dark or to the stories of the traders who passed through our woodland, tales of the five-legged, man-eating, man-crushing manitou as big as a mountain, with teeth so long and sharp they could skewer a double hand-count of hunters at one time. Tales that even as a boy I only half dared to believe!"

"Then you are only half a fool!" barked the giant. "The mammoth you have brought to its death is obviously no more a manitou than the masked raiders who attacked your band." He paused, looked around, then, with a new tension in his stance, lowered his voice and said, "And as for Katcheetohúskw, do you truly believe that it would be so easy for a mere man to trick that one into falling to his death? No! It could not be so! I will not believe it! All men know that in the time beyond beginning that one was born of a lightning bolt in the far northern hunting grounds of the Seven Thunderers! That one towers as high as a summer thunder cloud and is as white and dangerous. That one comes and goes as he will across the world, seeking the bones of his kind, burying them when they have not been laid out upon the earth with honor, and searching always for the living among his kind to protect them from those who would hunt them."

M'alsum's blood was rising; he felt his knuckles whiten

around the broken spear shaft. "Then you have actually seen him!"

"Mmph. Among all tribes·there are tales of him," replied the giant, his tone hushed, reverent, yet hinting strongly of evasiveness. He hunkered down beside the boy and spoke, not to the headman but to the child. "By many names is the greatest among the Great Ones known. And always his names must be spoken with respect. Always. Lest he overhear and be offended. Within the inland forests and the Dawnland he is Katcheetohúskw, Stiff-Legged Beast More Powerful than Bear, or Ktci'awa, the Great Beast who appears to men as a warning that they are soon to meet with Death, or he is Par'sar'do'kep'piart, a name whose meaning has been lost in the time beyond beginning. Some tribes call him Destroyer, Eater of Forests, Taker of the Water of Life from the People. Out at the edge of the barrens he is Thunder Speaker, Earth Shaker. Many in those far lands call him Life Giver and will tell you that his breath can be felt every time a warm wind gentles the earth after the long hard days of winter. Among the masked ones he is Rises from Below, for their shamans say that he lives beneath the earth and dreams of the flesh of the People, yet is doomed to die and leave his bones for us to find when he comes hunting us and breathes the same air as man."

Musquash gulped audibly. The boy seemed to have shrunk inside his furs. His head pivoted. His eyes were enormous as they took in his surroundings, as though he expected to see the awesome subject of the conversation standing within earshot.

"Yes, Musquash, he could be there," the giant assured him. "He could be watching us, listening to us, deciding if

we—who have chosen to walk with a mammoth slayer—
are worthy of life."

M'alsum bristled. "I have told you! The mammoth
charged me! I did not hunt it. It—"

"Yes, yes, I know! It killed itself!" said the giant dis-
dainfully. "But will Katcheetohúskw see the death of one
of its own kind as you see it—as a necessary ending of one
life in order to prolong another? Or will he see it as I see
it—as a waste and a desecration?"

"Different eyes may see the same things in different
ways! I cannot be held responsible for that!"

"No. You are right. Perhaps you cannot. In one part of
the forest the elders will tell you that Katcheetohúskw is a
force for good; in another they say he is a force for bad.
Some say that he died long ago. Others say that he cannot
be killed. In the Grassland I have heard it said that he can
be heard roaring in the whirling wind and that the man
who dares to enter the heart of a tornado to kill him will
live forever. And in the Dawnland it is believed that the
man who kills him *becomes* the Great Manitou himself, and
the elders there will tell you that a single whisker from the
slain mammoth's chin or a hair from his tail will bring
great power to those who possess these talismans. But the
truly wise men among all tribes know this one ancient
truth: On the day the last mammoth looks upon a world in
which there are no more of its own kind, it will lie down
and die. And on that day the world as we know it will
change forever. And so you see, Stranger, that the mammoth you led to its death in the ravine cannot be Katcheetohúskw, for the world is as it was, and, not unlike me,
that old tusker has been wintering with its kind in this
forest for as long as I can remember."

"Then my mother was right! There *are* still mammoth in the world!"

The giant was very still. Then, "In all of my days I have only seen them here. A small herd. A threesome of bulls, one old, two young, wintering together, leaning against trees as they slept, keeping each other warm under the Cold Moon, telling tales to one another in the language of their kind, tusking out browse and trunking down boughs for winter fodder, nosing up enough water from the spring to drown the earth if they all chose to piss at once, and no doubt dreaming of their cows and calves and of how it would be when the need to mate drove them to seek their mammoth women once again. But these last few winters, the one you have slain has come alone into this part of the forest."

"What happened to the others?"

"Who can say? Perhaps they met other M'alsums atop other ravines in other parts of the forest? Perhaps, even now, their tusks and bones lie bleaching in the sun for the eyes of other half-believing boys to see? But I will tell you this: From the smell of sickness and death rising from the ravine, this mammoth was dying when you met him. He was making his final journey to that secret place where his kind have been laying down their bones since the time beyond beginning. It must have been no trick at all for you to lure him over a deadfall that he probably could not see until it was too late to turn away. Yet I must ask you, for what purpose, Stranger, other than to seek the thrill of power that some are said to feel when outmaneuvering and killing an animal more dangerous than themselves?"

M'alsum's jaw tightened. "Surely you cannot tell me that a man of your great size and strength has not felt the thrill that comes to a hunter when he faces big, dangerous, man-eating game!"

"I kill to eat and to secure skins with which to warm my body. This is a man's place within the Circle of Life. I see no cause to either lament or rejoice in it. I have been born to live as a predator. Perhaps in the next life I will be prey. Who can say? But, Stranger, in this life mammoths do not eat men."

"They did in the tales my mother told!" M'alsum was angry now. Whether the beast in the ravine was Katcheetohúskw or not, it was a mammoth. And he had stood to its charge, lured it to its death, and lived to tell the tale! But there were to be no words of awe or adulation from Kinap. Instead, the giant was impugning his judgment and chastising him for making an unnecessary kill. He might just as well be standing before Sac or M'ingwé, or Asticou! "I have told you, Kinap, as a wise stag runs from wolves or lynx or bear or lions, I ran from the mammoth lest I be slain and eaten. If the beast had turned from the chase and chosen to go on its way, we would both still be alive."

"And I have told you, Stranger, that mammoths do not eat men."

M'alsum choked off further words. He was too close to losing his temper. And he was suddenly aware of the boy staring up at him. He looked down. He had almost forgotten about the child. The little bog rat's eyes were fixed upon him. In speculation or accusation? Or perhaps both? The headman could not tell. The child's mouth was pressed so tightly against his teeth that his lips were bloodless, and the lower edges of his nostrils had turned blue. M'alsum felt his own mouth tighten. He disliked children; he found them noisy and smelly and intrusive. And there was something about this child that unnerved him in ways he could not quite understand.

"What are you looking at?" M'alsum snapped. "Have you not been taught that it is bad manners to stare? Be careful before you judge me with your eyes, Musquash. Maybe there *is* another mammoth out there in this dark forest waiting for you. A big mammoth. A white mammoth. Maybe we will see how you behave when it comes to crush your bones into the earth so it can suck you up into its mouth with the tip of its man-eating fifth leg!"

The boy's eyes widened, and his face blanched.

M'alsum wondered if he had ever been so stupid. He had forgotten that the bog rat was the giant's son. Truly he must be more fatigued than he knew! But before he could voice an apology in hope of appeasing Kinap, he was taken aback by the giant's reaction.

Kinap laughed. A deep, sonorous laugh. "Fifth leg indeed! Truly you are one to believe everything you are told! That which projects from the middle of a mammoth's face is no leg. It is an arm, the most amazing and glorious arm in all Creation, for it carries the mammoth's nose and two strong wide fingers at its tip! With my own eyes I have seen mammoth tear down trees as thick as my thigh with that third arm. And I have seen mammoth reach down to finger up a single tender new blade of grass. But never have I seen a mammoth suck anything but water or air through its nose. So do not listen to the Stranger, Musquash. He has suffered much these past days and nights. And he is obviously a good and trusting son who believes everything his mother has ever told him. Tales of man-eating mammoths! Tales of man-eating giants! Tales of man-eating manitous! Everything is a threat to his kind! Everything! Maybe when he walks with us awhile, even on our short journey to the coast, we can convince him that this need not always be so!"

"When those who have hurt and threatened me are no more!" declared M'alsum. "When bears and masked raiders no longer steal what is mine! When mammoths no longer break through the forest to run me to my death! When—"

"When the women of your tribe grow beards!" Kinap broke in. "Bah! There has been more than enough talk between us. Your kind and mine will never see the world with the same eyes!" He eyed the sky and, drawing in a deep breath of the morning, declared, "The days and nights of winter are nearly at an end. I smell a change of seasons in the air. Come! I am anxious to be at my ease within the forest lodge of an old friend before the coming of the first rains and the rising of the Mud Moon makes travel a misery. So gather up your belongings, Stranger, and prepare to travel on. Now! Or Musquash and I will go our way and leave you to haul your sled and find your way to the Dawnland alone."

▼▼▼▼▼

They journeyed eastward into thickly forested hills. The giant set a sure, steady, relentless pace across the hard, gleaming surface of the snowpack. He was in a solemn, contemplative mood, and when the hills shouldered abruptly southward, he followed without so much as a word of explanation, keeping his eyes fixed on the way ahead and the boy trotting at his side, leashed to a tether knotted to his belt.

M'alsum refrained from asking the giant why he found it necessary to leash his son as though the boy were an ill-trained pup who might run off otherwise. It was good to have the man silent for a change, and in truth he did not care what Kinap did with the little bog rat. As he walked beside the giant, he was confident that the man knew the way of the trail, although, straining forward against the drag lines of the sled, he grimaced against the increasing difficulty of the terrain and tried to keep his mind fixed ahead on one thing: the Dawnland.

Tomorrow!

A smile expanded across M'alsum's face. He was keeping another secret from the giant now. A secret that pleased him immensely.

Kinap had forced him to abandon the tusks and meat of the mammoth to bears. So be it! In order to keep the man to his word, a compromise had been called for on M'alsum's part. But what would the giant, to whom the flesh of the great tuskers was forbidden, say if he knew that the man with whom he traveled, the man whom he now called Stranger instead of Friend, carried the tail and the largest portion of the nostriled "third arm" of the dead mammoth wrapped in a bed skin and hidden amidst his trading goods?

M'alsum almost laughed to think of it. It had taken more than a little finesse to dig his treasures from the snow without the giant or the little bog rat noticing that he was not removing and wrapping for transport just any kind of temporarily stashed trail meat.

Now, with his spirit singing, the headman came close to matching the giant step for step as he recalled Kinap's revelation that in the Dawnland it was believed that even a single chin whisker or tail hair plucked from Katcheetohúskw would bring power to whoever possessed it. Even without the tusks and meat of the great mammoth, prestige was certain to be his when he returned to Hasu'u's people with these talismans in his possession!

Ah, the tales he would tell to explain and justify her death! Ah, what a hero he would make of himself in the eyes of the Dawnland tribes! Ah!

Tomorrow!

He nearly sang the word in joyful anticipation of the day until, suddenly, worry took the song from his heart and the smile from his face.

The giant will dispute your claim to having slain the Great One. He will point to the color of the hair of the animal whose parts you bring and say that the beast that lies dead in the ravine is not Katcheetohúskw!

M'alsum was scowling now, assuring himself that Hasu'u's guileless, greedy, easily manipulated father would surely accept the word of a gift-bearing son-in-law over that of an itinerant tale teller with nothing of value to trade and an appearance as frightening as a Djeneta giant conjured from nightmares born of the winter tales.

The headman cast a speculative sideward glance in the giant's direction, then turned his gaze down, tucked his mittened thumbs into the shoulder straps of his pack, and leaned more aggressively into his stride.

What happens if the giant proves to be known and respected among the Dawnland People? He has made no secret of the fact that he makes his way in this world by trading his stories and amulets for meat and comfort. His face may be as ugly as one of the eight-legged hairless heads that crawl about on the rocks in the tide pools of the coast, but when he speaks, although he is as long-winded as a gassy moose, he is wise and eloquent, a master of words, of nuances . . . perhaps even a master of the minds of men who are less wary than I?

Indignation and resentment made a bitter brew in M'alsum's mouth. He spat it out. He was at last within reach of the Dawnland! Had he come all this way, risked all that he had risked, and done all that he had done only to find his reputation and ambitions jeopardized by one who was little more than a stranger to him?

He mumbled a curse. He had made certain that neither Sac nor M'ingwé would ever again speak to impugn his judgment. Hasu'u and Ne'gauni would never have a chance to question his bravery or the quality of his leadership. Even big, stupid Kicháwan was silenced and, he hoped, pacified in the realm of the dead. And yet, walking at his side was one who was sure to ruin everything.

Unless . . .

An idea flared brightly in M'alsum's brain. It put the song back into his heart and the smile back on his face even though the trees stood close around him now and broken ground cover mounded high beneath the snowpack, making travel increasingly difficult. Nevertheless, the way ahead seemed clearer to him now than it had since the great roaring had come from the forest and the manitous had broken from cover on the far side of the now-distant creek.

The traders from whom he had obtained the small packets of fish poison that he carried along with his other trading goods had demonstrated how, when diluted in water, the powders released invisible killing spirits that took the breath of life from fish.

Big fish and little fish alike!

Perhaps, when the way to the coast had at last been made clear to him, he might see how well it worked on small boys and giants.

"Yes!" he vowed.

Tomorrow!

▼▼▼▼

The sun stood high in a white and frozen sky.

They kept on their way, slowly now, moving steadily uphill through mixed stands of conifers and old-growth hardwoods so savaged by past storms that the resultant blowdowns would have made further progress impossible had the overlying winter snowpack not provided occasional broken avenues of solid footing across which they were able to drag the sled with caution, if not ease.

"This is your shortcut?" panted an incredulous and openly irritated M'alsum as they were forced to pause and take off their snow walkers lest the webbing be completely ruined or the frames be cracked.

"One of them," the giant confirmed, slinging his snow walkers over a shoulder as he shook back his hood and scanned the surrounding woodlands out of knowing but troubled eyes. "It is a steep and twisting passage at best, but it is the safest way for us now, and as you will see, it will cut in half the traveling time to the coast."

"Safe? Safe from *what?*" M'alsum made no attempt to disguise his growing impatience.

The giant sighed as he stared across the tangled deadfall that littered the steep incline they had just ascended. "One can never be sure just what may be afoot in this part of the forest," he replied obliquely.

"Mmph!" M'alsum was startled to hear himself use the giant's usual wordless exclamation. Annoyed, he snapped, "Whatever walks in this part of the forest needs wings! *When* will I see the coast?"

"In truth, Stranger, I knew that the way would not be easy for us with a fully loaded sled, even with one as flexible and well designed as yours, but I must admit that since the last storm the blowdowns are worse than I have ever seen them. The journey will take considerably longer than I thought. Two sleeps, not one, think I. But that should sit easier on your mind than the three or four sleeps you were expecting before we met, eh?" He shook his head as he continued to observe his surroundings. "Each winter it seems that the hardwoods in this part of the forest die and fall away to rot in greater numbers. It would not surprise me if someday they ceased to grow here at all. Perhaps the forces of Creation no longer welcome oak and ash and hemlock, or even pine, this far north. We do live in changing times, and now, with the mammoth dead in the forest, who can say what is their will? Who can say? But come. Shadows are lengthening, and the way is not as precipitous up ahead."

▼▼▼▼

They put the westering sun to their backs and stepped resolutely out into the fall of their own shadows.

Soon Kinap was proved right. The land leveled out beneath their feet, and before they knew it, the maze of deadfall was behind them. When they paused to don their snow walkers once again, the boy tugged at his tether and made noises to indicate his desire to rest, but neither M'alsum nor the giant was in a mood to stop. Kinap put the boy onto the sled and led the way across open snow and around tall islands of fragrant conifers, setting the pace with a low, droning chant that evidently eased the drudgery of the trail for him and soon had M'alsum remembering the way in which his lost Dawnland woman had filled nearly every waking hour with song.

"Hasu'u." He was only half aware of speaking her name.

For the first time, he felt her loss as the softest slur of sadness passing through his heart, shadowing his spirit with regret. If only he had listened when Sac had noticed that she and Ne'gauni had fallen behind! If only he had stopped and looked back and called out to her to hurry on! She *had* been such a pretty little thing, so quick to smile, so eager to please. She would have obeyed him if he had taken the time to command her.

"Do you not sometimes wonder if maybe, somehow, she could still be alive back there . . . with them? After all, we did not actually see her die."

He stopped, shocked by the sound of M'ingwé's voice.

"What is it, Stranger?" asked the giant, brought short beside him.

The headman did not hear the question. He was staring back along the wide gouges in the snowpack that the sled had made, back at the evergreens through which they had just come.

The ghosts were back again!

M'ingwé and Sac were leading them, holding their hollow-eyed heads under the crook of their right arms, their sundered hands and feet dangling like grotesque hunt trophies around the stumps of their necks.

M'alsum's eyes bulged.

Would he never be free of them? He would not allow himself to believe what he was seeing. His brothers were dead. With his own hands he had killed and dismembered them! Without eyes to see their way, Sac and M'ingwé could not possibly be following him! Yet there they were, with Ne'gauni trailing behind. Kicháwan was with them, not walking beside them but riding with Hasu'u and Ne'gauni on the great domed head of Katcheetohúskw as the mammoth raised its maimed trunk and bellowed in anger,

"*I will have the third arm that you have stolen from me, and I will have my tail with which to flick flies from your corpse in the world beyond this world! Do you truly think that you can outdistance all that you have done in this forest, M'alsum, Firstborn and Eldest Son of Asticou? The white mammoth has seen what you have done to me! The white mammoth will follow!*"

The hackles rose on M'alsum's back. "I will not listen!" he shouted. "Go back to the land of spirits where you belong! You are dead! Soon I will be in the Dawnland! Soon all this will be behind me!"

"Yes, say I, yes, and soon," consoled the giant as he swung a broad, avuncular arm around M'alsum's shoulder. "Be at peace with your grief, Stranger. It is only natural for you to imagine that you see your slain loved ones when longing for them is still strong in your heart. In time the great wounding of your sadness will heal. Until then you must not look back upon your sorrow. You have mourned. You have chanted. You have offered gifts to the spirits of the dead. You can do no more for them than you have already done. A new wind is rising. I, too, hear it calling in the trees. It is an east wind. It blows from the coast . . . from the Dawnland!"

M'alsum came blinking out of a daze to fix his gaze on the giant. "The Dawnland?"

"Yes, say I!"

The ghosts vanished.

"Then why do we linger here?" M'alsum turned his face into the east wind and breathed it in as though he could not have enough of it. The giant was right! He could smell the sea! The long journey to the coast was nearly over!

▼▼▼▼

They went on.

The east wind dropped, veered briefly, then dropped again. The tantalizing smell of salt vanished from the air. M'alsum ground his teeth in frustration as he stomped on. For a while, with the scent of the sea in his nostrils, he had been convinced that at any moment they must come through the trees to find themselves on the headlands. In his mind's eye he had seen the coast spreading out before him. He had heard the crash of the surf, the screaming of seabirds, the barking of seals and camp dogs, and the welcoming shouts of the Dawnland People. But it was not to be.

Not today.

Not even tomorrow!

Two sleeps, the giant had said when they had run afoul of the maze of deadfall. Two sleeps, not one! And had not Kinap said that he was a man of his word?

M'alsum mumbled against what he could only perceive as yet another turn of bad luck. At last, in the heavy gray gloom of gathering dusk, he was too tired to think at all and could only sigh with relief when Kinap announced that it was time to upend their snow walkers beside the sled and prepare to rest for the night.

A new mood was on the giant. He continued to be unusually quiet, introspective, but now he was obviously ill at ease. At his insistence, they made no fire. M'alsum was too tired to argue the point.

They shrugged off their packs and, although they each replenished the precious tinder in their fire-carrying horns with small branch tips broken off from whatever deadwood they could find, beyond this they were too weary and footsore to do more than rub their aching feet before hacking down a few spruce boughs upon which to lay out their sleeping skins. This done, they changed into dry moccasins and—after Kinap slung the odd-looking piece of sinew-strung wood from his shoulder, laid it across his lap, and advised M'alsum to keep his spears near at hand—settled down to share a meal drawn from their dwindling supplies of jerked meats, pemmican, and suet cakes pebbled with dried berries and grubs.

"What worries you, Giant?" asked the headman. "And why do you always hold one of your lengths of bent wood when you are at rest? What are they?"

"They are called bows." From the lightweight bag he habitually wore slung over his right shoulder, Kinap pulled a feather-tipped flying stick. "And this is an arrow. When mated with a bow, both become a single weapon. I have fashioned the two you have seen after the style of those carried by the masked ones. In case one is overstressed and cracks, I have the other to take its place. If I were not so tired, I would show you the way of it. Now I suggest that we eat our fill and take turns sleeping. As I have said, one never knows what may be afoot in this part of the forest."

M'alsum looked around. The surrounding woodland seemed neither more nor less threatening than any other part of the forest through which he had been traveling since leaving the now-distant creek. Nevertheless, he was glad that the giant had chosen to rest on high ground amidst a sheltering copse of young birches, and it was comforting to have the sled at their backs.

They ate without speaking, as weary travelers often do, and while Kinap chewed his food and eyed the encircling woods out of wary eyes, the boy noisily wolfed down every morsel of the minimal meal as though certain that he would never receive another.

M'alsum watched them from beneath guardedly lowered lids. The boy ate like a ravenous little animal. And even in encroaching darkness, with his hood folded back around his face, the giant was a revolting freak. The headman found himself hungering for the mammoth steaks he believed himself so unjustly deprived of, and his mouth twisted and curled downward as he ate. Were they a day closer to the Dawnland and he did not need the giant to help him haul his load, he would not wait to test the efficacy of his fish poison; he would use it now and watch the grotesque twosome die before the dark came down. True, he would then be alone in the forest, but whatever might be lurking out there in the trees could surely be no more dangerous than anything he had already faced and survived, and no more of a threat to him than the giant's loose tongue.

Tomorrow night, he vowed as he raised the last strip of his share of the pemmican to his mouth. *When the way to the coast is shown to me, I will—*

A small hand shot forward to snatch the pemmican from the headman's fingers.

M'alsum was not quick enough to snatch it back before the boy stuffed it into his own mouth. "Why, you greedy little bog rat!" he exclaimed.

"Mmph," snorted the giant. "You must excuse the boy's lack of manners. He is not sure just when or where he will find his next meal . . . because he is foolish enough to believe that I do not know that he plans to slip his tether and run away as soon as you and I are too groggy to notice. But as I have said, Stranger, you and I will take turns sleeping tonight. One or the other of us will keep watch. Musquash must *not* run away, for his own good and ours."

"Ours?" M'alsum had not missed the warning in the giant's statement and would have pressed for an explanation had the boy not recoiled, then spat the half-chewed fragments of the pemmican into the giant's face as he leaped to his feet and stood with his mittened fists clenched and his dark eyes glaring.

Despite his dislike of the child, M'alsum raised an appreciative brow. There was no dismissing the boy's ferocity. And his open display of hostility toward Kinap struck a surprising note of empathy. "Your son seems to hate you, Giant. Why is that?"

Kinap did not reply. He drew the boy's tether into a loop, then half jerked the child off his feet as he pulled him so close that the two were glaring at each other eye to eye. "You do not know who truly cares for you and who would happily see you dead and rotting on the beach of the sacred island!" The declaration made, he pushed Musquash down and gave him an admonishing poke to the shoulder. "Now you will sit! Now you will obey! The least worthy of the Stranger's stolen dogs was better trained than you! And to think that some believe that the blood of . . . of the Ancient Ones is in you! Bah! Lie down and go to sleep. And do not shame me or yourself again before a Stranger!"

The child did not lie down. He was obviously not about to go to sleep. He folded his arms across the now disheveled furs that covered his meager chest, stuck out his chin, and glowered defiance at the giant.

"Mmph," snorted Kinap again. As he fingered spittle and fragments of pemmican from his cheeks, he explained to M'alsum, "Musquash is not happy with me for taking him from his mother. If I am to judge by words that you have spoken about your own mother, I would take you to be a loyal son. Perhaps you will understand how it is with the boy. I, for one, do not!"

M'alsum, seeing hatred for Kinap burning in the child's eyes, felt sympathy for the boy. So had it once been between him and Asticou. So would it always be. "It is not good to force a son from his mother's arms, Giant."

"You would not speak so if you knew this son's mother."

A sound came from the child's throat. Not a cry. Not a moan. It was a low utterance that racked his entire body as his small mittened hands clenched and unclenched around some sort of pale talisman that he wore secured around his neck by a finely plaited length of sinew.

"By all the powers of the forces of Creation, boy, how did you get that away from her?" Kinap's exclamation fairly cracked the air around him.

M'alsum's eyes were drawn to the object. He had not noticed the amulet before. The fall had evidently freed it from the confines of the boy's furs. The headman instinctively knew what it was. "A gift from his mother?" He was barely aware of turning the question; there had been no need to ask it. He, too, wore such a memento, a small gift from Meya'kwé given to him almost a lifetime ago on the night after that terrible morning when Asticou had dragged her into the lodge to cut off her hair and shame her.

M'alsum's right hand strayed upward to press against his caribou-skin traveling coat. Just below his throat he could feel the small, painted leather pouch hanging softly against his skin from its circlet of thong. Inside was the slender curl of precious braid, his mother's hair, a part of her. He had only to touch it to remember Meya'kwé, to imagine the sweet, musky scent of her, to hear her words, to see her kneeling before him, loving him with her eyes, imploring,

"Wear this always, my own most precious son. Never forget the shame that Asticou has brought upon me . . . upon us. You are the one I love! Not him! Never him! You are the one who will take me back to the Grassland of my fathers or to the Dawnland of my grandmothers. You will do this, my firstborn, my guardian, my protector, my M'alsum, my own little wolf! You will take me back into hunting grounds where the People live proudly under the sun, as they have done since the time beyond beginning. For you and for that day only do I live. Never forget. Never!"

He caught his breath, blinked himself back out of time to see that it was the boy, not Meya'kwé, who was looking at him, communicating not love but loathing. "It is nothing of any importance," Kinap was saying of the amulet. "Just a worthless trinket. Tuck it back away inside your furs, boy, and go to sleep, say I! You have annoyed me and the Stranger enough!"

▼▼▼▼

Darkness came down upon the world.

At the giant's insistence, M'alsum slept first. He offered no argument. He was exhausted.

He was not sure what roused him.

Wind?

Wolf song?

The troubled sighing of the boy as he lay tethered close at the giant's side?

The sound of Kinap snoring?

Or the trumpeting of a distant mammoth . . . a trunkless, tailless mammoth? Or a white mammoth as tall and massive and threatening as summer thunder clouds billowing high over the hunting grounds of the Seven Thunderers?

Suddenly wide awake, M'alsum propped himself on his elbows. With his stone-headed spears near at hand and his body tense and ready to spring into action at the slightest sign of danger, he looked around. Kinap had fallen fast asleep. The camp, such as it was, was unguarded.

But all was quiet. Almost unnaturally so. No wolves howled. No mammoths roared. No wind stirred the treetops. The little bog rat had not run away. And none of Kinap's unseen and unspecified perils had come through the trees to menace them.

A meteor streaked across the sky. Distracted, M'alsum turned up his head to stare through the treetops at a moonless night strewn with stars that were faded into inconsequence by the shimmering light of an aurora that seemed a rebirth of the previous night's bruised blue glow.

His brows drew together. He did not like the look of the sky. Back in the more southerly forests that surrounded Asticou's village, auroras were rare and always red. Invariably they were a sight that had his mother portending doom while his father smiled and instructed his sons to remember that when they saw the Great Sky River burning red in the night, it was a sign that the Ancestors were using the stars for stepping stones across the sky as they held their torches high to give light and assurance of life everlasting to the People in the world below.

M'alsum sat up. He pulled his sleeping furs around his shoulders. Always Asticou saw light where Meya'kwé saw darkness. Always Asticou spoke of the future while Meya'kwé spoke of the past.

He scowled. What was it Kinap had said about the Circle of Life? Something about it always turning forward, never back? The observation was unwelcome. It seemed a judgment against Meya'kwé. He would not consider it! His mother was wise to look back upon the proud bright days of her youth in the hunting grounds of the People of the Grasslands. She could not be faulted for yearning to return there any more than she could for longing to journey to the sunlit coast of her grandmothers, where the People of the Dawnland had dwelled with pride since the time beyond beginning. It was Asticou who was the foolish one, foolish and stubborn to imagine a settled future for his band in the dark confines of the inland forest! As a trader he had learned that his mother was right when she said that it was not natural for the People to settle in one place. Since the time beyond beginning they had followed the great herds, moving with the seasons, always one step ahead of the game. Winter camps. Fishing camps. Feasting-after-the-big-kill camps. Only Asticou chose to permanently encamp. Only . . .

Another meteor streaked the sky.

M'alsum's eyes narrowed. His thoughts constricted. As the sole surviving member of his trading band, he knew that he must live in the moment if he was ever to return to his father's village as he intended and, by dealing with the past, fulfill his vow to his mother and accomplish their shared hopes for the future.

The future.

It seemed so far away!

Tomorrow, he assured himself. The future always began with tomorrow. Yet, somehow, his eyelids felt weighted by the thought of it; he closed them. Mother, father, brothers, the inland forest, youth, vows, plans, all drifted away . . . away. He let them go. They seemed unimportant now. Tomorrow lay ahead. Why go back for Yesterday? Why not make a new life for himself in the Dawnland, as though all that had gone before in the miserable, dark village of Asticou had never been?

He opened his eyes. His thoughts astounded him.

Above his head the Great Sky River was no longer blue, nor red. It was shifting toward green, a soft, grayish, somewhat gangrenous green with undertones of watery, purulent yellow; a necrotic sky, it seeped light in the same way a festering wound oozed the pus of corruption.

The headman cringed at the comparison. All around him the forest was washed in the colors of the aurora. Again his thoughts constricted. His brothers were out there in the night, his dead, dismembered, decomposing brothers. He would not think of them as ghosts! Ne'gauni must long since have become food for carrion eaters; fresh meat did not long lie exposed under a winter sky. Scavenging carnivores had no doubt found the remnants of Sac by now. And, despite his occasional nightmarish visions, he knew that M'ingwé lay in pieces back in the distant ravine beneath snow so deep that it nearly concealed a fallen mammoth. It would be well into spring before his parts were exposed to the light of day.

The wind rose. Softly. Quietly. No more than a light, transitory breeze sighing in the treetops, it whispered briefly and then was gone as quietly as it had come, like a gentle and benign spirit caressing the night.

A coldness walked in M'alsum's bones. The night was now so still that he could make out the barely audible sound of water flowing sluggishly somewhere deep beneath the snowpack. Winter was almost over. And the Dawnland was near. Only one sleep now! Only one sleep! He thought of Kicháwan lying out there in the dark upon her bier, and of Hasu'u, and of the unborn and unnamed infants. All spirits now. All dead along with his brothers on this long and torturous ghost road upon which they had followed him so trustingly toward the coast.

A wolf raised a long, low ululation. Another wolf answered. And then another wolf replied. Soon the deep, ascending monotones seemed to be coming from all around.

M'alsum sat tense, listening, trying to place the direction and distance from which the sounds were coming.

Nowhere near.

The headman relaxed, but only a little; there was something dark, elemental, and mysterious about the singing of wolves. The sound never failed to stir a deep chord of undefinable restlessness within him. He closed his eyes, remembered Asticou telling him that he had been named M'alsum, Wolf, because he had come howling into the world from between his mother's thighs and because a father could wish no finer attributes for a firstborn son than those possessed by the wolf, who was valiant and cautious and lived always for the good of the pack. Meya'kwé, on the other hand, had sworn that she had chosen the name to honor the wolves that howled on the night she conceived her firstborn inside the belly of a dead mammoth.

"M'alsum, my own little wolf! My guardian! Protector of my pack! You will bring me to the Dawnland someday. For that day only do I live!"

The memory roused a resentment he had never felt before. It drifted with the howlings in his mind until, unbidden, sleep came to him again. Heavy. Dark. And slowly, within the darkness, an old legend came to life—that of a wild woman, a wolf woman, a manitou beast who ran with wolves and called to men in the dark of the winter moon, hunting them in the forest deeps, seeking to mate with and then consume them. She was alive within his dreams, running behind him on silent paws as he looked back and saw her . . . a furred and fanged beast that snarled at him out of the face of . . . his mother.

▼▼▼▼

"No!" M'alsum fought free of his dreams and, with the nightmare name on his lips, awoke with a start. "Mowea'qua! Not Meya—"

"So you know the name of Mowea'qua." The giant was kneeling beside him. "And fear it," he said quietly.

M'alsum looked around. The aurora had faded. The stars were shifting toward dawn. The wolves were no longer singing, but the wind was sighing once more in the treetops, and against the predawn sky the forest stood like an all-encompassing black phalanx of ghosts swaying against the darker substance of the night. Impenetrable. Menacing. Spectral. The headman shivered, pulled his furs closer. "I was dreaming," he said. "About one of the old winter tales. Yes. I know 'her' name. And has ever a man passed through this cursed forest who has not feared it?"

The giant uttered an exhalation redolent of irony, sadness, and regret. "You are of a strange breed, M'alsum, Firstborn Son of Asticou and Meya'kwé. You are brave enough to set forth into a haunted forest on a trading venture that risked your life and the lives of your brothers and women, to stand to the attack of marauding raiders, to face down a charging mammoth, to take up with one who could well have proved to be a cannibal manitou giant—and to raise a spear to a bear many times your size. And yet now you cry out in your sleep in fear of—"

"It is wise to be wary of the unknown," M'alsum interrupted defensively.

"Yes. And since the time beyond beginning all men fear the wild wolf woman in the legend of Mowea'qua. Mmph. Let me tell you this, Stranger: That name was born in the nightmares of the first man to abandon a female infant under a Starving Moon! 'Maybe the infant will not be eaten,' he would say to his grieving woman. 'Maybe, instead of being torn to pieces by wolves, the infant will be suckled and raised by the very beasts to whom she has been offered as food.' Now that is a thought to take guilt from the mind! But what if the child who has been suckled by wolves *becomes* a wolf? What if that wolf child then sets herself to hunt and devour those who have wronged her? Mmph! Now that is something to worry about! And so, in the minds of men, Mowea'qua is no longer an outcast to be pitied, but a manitou to be feared. And what men fear, they flee from or hunt and seek to kill before their fear unmans them!"

"And so!" affirmed M'alsum.

"Mmph! And so Mowea'qua is hunted! And so, in the winter dark around the lodge fires of the People, the story is told again and again of the solitary hunter who happens upon a wild girl in the forest. A beautiful girl! A wild and irresistible girl! He mates with her only to discover, too late, that she is a wolf and that his offspring by her are furred and fanged. What man may abide such children? He must kill them! And then he must slay their wolf mother, for surely she will devour his pride! But, say I, Mowea'qua cannot be so easily slain. She runs. Like a wolf she runs! She hides. Clever and wary as a wolf within her secret den in the black heart of the haunted forest, she hides! And although the hunter tracks her with spear and blade and braining club and, yes, even with fire, he cannot drive her from his world, for he has tasted of her wildness and she has become a part of his spirit. And so now, as it has been from the time beyond beginning, in the dark of the moon men dream of Mowea'qua. They hear her song in the howling of wolves and know that she is calling out to them in her loneliness and in lamentation for her slaughtered children. By all the forces of Creation, what else would you have her do?"

M'alsum was stunned by the vehemence of the giant's words. He could not even begin to understand why the man was so angry.

The boy was sitting up, rubbing sleep from his eyes, staring from giant to man, from man to giant.

Kinap rumbled in profound irritation. "Mmph. And so the story goes! Look around you, Stranger. Soon it will be dawn, but now it is still the dark of the moon. You are right to be wary. Mowea'qua *is* out there. And say I this to you, even now she waits for one of her own kind to come to her, to walk with her, to be her mate forever in the black heart of a forest that is haunted only because men like you have made it so!"

M'alsum did not know what to say. He pulled in a breath of the dying night in hope of being soothed by its coolness, but the air was as heavy as the giant's words. It was dank, cold, turgid, like an invisible river settling down around him. There was rain in it somewhere. M'alsum could smell it. And something else.

"The sea!" He snapped to his feet. "I can smell the sea! And the air . . . it has the moist, heavy feel of—"

"The Dawnland," injected the giant. "I have fulfilled my promise to you, Stranger. We have been in the hills inland of the coast for some time now. My muskrat and I dare journey with you no farther. Tomorrow, if the day dawns clear, you can set your feet in the path of the rising sun, and by noon you should be able to see the Great Salt Water. If the day is clouded, you can follow the tops of the big hemlocks, and, for reasons I do not even begin to understand, the bare branches will point the way to the coast. By sunset you will be raising a driftwood fire along the shore! Another day's walk east should bring you into the hunting grounds of the tribe you seek. You are strong and in your prime and should be able to journey the rest of the way alone without undue difficulty. If not, you can cache your sled and hope that it remains unseen by travelers less honorable than yourself while you bring others from the coast to help transport it. I have no doubt that you will soon find willing hands even if you fail to offer a fair trade in exchange for labor. A handsome and clever man like you can win the minds of others and lead them in ways that he would have them go . . . as you have been trying to do with me since I first saw you dancing naked beneath the sun."

"I . . ." For the second time in less than a few moments M'alsum could find no words. He was grateful for the darkness; he knew that his face had gone white.

The giant laughed congenially. "You are shocked, Stranger! Why is that? There was a time when I, too, was young and walked the world with a face as fine as yours, a face that made the women and girls smile and the men and youths of my own age scowl in envy even as they chose to walk in the fall of my shadow, as though I exuded some sort of luck that might also be theirs. Mmph! There was little that a well-placed smile would not win for me in those days. But that was long ago, and although you have obviously thought otherwise, I am no fool, Stranger. Scald a fox and, even though his fur and flesh may forever be singed, he will nevertheless forever remain a fox. You have named me Friend in hope of securing my help and knowledge. I hold no rancor toward you for this. A man must do as he must to survive, say I! And you have suffered much. It has lightened my heart to ease your way. So go to the Dawnland in peace, Mammoth Slayer, keeping your secrets as I will keep mine. May the forces of Creation smile upon you in the days and nights that lie ahead for you. But before we go our separate ways, it is time for you to have this!" He rose and reached into his bearskins. "Here. Take this as a gift from Kinap to brighten your journey in the days ahead!"

M'alsum caught the slender object that was tossed his way. As his eyes fixed upon it, the world seemed to drop away beneath his feet, then rise again. He swayed a little, but did not fall.

"It was your woman's?"

M'alsum's fingers curled around the swan-bone drinking tube that he had fashioned for Hasu'u as a bride gift. "It was hers."

"I found it in the snow not more than a half-day's walk from where you and I first met. It is a pretty thing, like the one who wore it—a small young woman with a bruised face tattooed in the way of the Dawnland, on the eyelids and across the brow and lower lip. She was wearing a white bearskin and had an infant at her breasts as she walked north with the masked ones and your dogs."

The odd roar was there again at the back of M'alsum's brain. "You saw my *dogs!*"

The giant was openly taken aback. "I saw your woman *alive!*"

"And were close enough to see the Dawnland tattooing on her face? And not once spoke of this to me as you beat upon your stupid drum and told your endless stories and allowed me to think of my wife as slain while you forced me to mourn and fast and raise a bier for a dead burden woman?"

"A man must mourn his dead in the way of the Ancestors, or the spirits will forever darken his life and the lives of those who fail to help him fulfill his obligations to the dead. I have told you that your dogs can be replaced in the Dawnland. And what good would it have done to tell you that you were wrong to believe that you saw your woman slain? If you knew she was alive, you would have insisted on going after her and expected me to go with you into an encampment of masked ones to win your woman back, regardless of the cost to either of us! I would have refused, and you would have cursed my name as you went forth to be killed! And for what? I have told you that in my travels I have camped with masked ones. They are men, these false faces, not manitou. They have taken to stealing women and meat and furs when it pleases them, and if one of their females dies along the trail and leaves a hungry infant bawling in their camp, they will steal another female to use as a milk woman. This is why your wife was taken, Stranger. Do you imagine that the false faces would give her back in exchange for a few trading goods when they obviously have no milk woman to take her place? Mmph! Why do you think they took her from you by force in the first place? Because they knew that your kind would never offer to share the breasts of one of your women with a child not made from the spill of your own loins. They would have made you fight for her. And while you were fighting one of them, they would all have named name you Fool as another struck you down from behind."

It occurred to M'alsum in that moment that, for one who thought himself clever, the giant *was* a fool! He might well have faced down a charging mammoth to save his own skin and been anxious to spear a bear from high ground to protect the meat of his kill, but if raiders had come forth upon the trail to confront the firstborn son of Asticou with a request such as Kinap had just surmised, he would have commanded Hasu'u to open her nursing shirt and bare her breasts to their infant. After all, the woman had two teats! And if they had then insisted on taking Hasu'u away with them to the north, he would have allowed it and sent them all off with his good wishes for a happy future if he thought that by sacrificing her he could save himself and his goods. Some sort of rationale could have been concocted to explain his expedience to his brothers and win sympathy for himself when he finally reached the Dawnland without her or their unnamed son. No woman was worth dying for! Unless, of course, the woman was Meya'kwé. And perhaps even then . . .

"When you reach the coast, Stranger, show the Dawnland People the gift I have given you," the giant was saying as he knelt to roll up his sleeping furs while the boy, still tethered to his belt, stood by and gloomily watched. "Make no mention of me or the boy. Tell them that she was taken from you and that you know she is alive, for a tale like that is best heard from the mouth of the one who can best verify it. And, in truth, I would just as soon my muskrat's mother heard no word of the way in which I have taken him. But with a few brave men at your side you can journey north to the River of the White Whales and try to work out some sort of compromise by which to barter your woman back. If not, fight for her! I would if she were mine! What do you have to lose, eh? Only your life. And if you still believe that the mammoth in the ravine is Katcheetohúskw, perhaps not even that, eh?"

M'alsum made no reply to Kinap's friendly goad; the man's tone was good-natured enough, but he resented the barb. Katcheetohúskw or not, the mammoth in the ravine was dead, and for all intents and purposes he had killed it. And even if he were an immortal, the last thing he planned to do when he arrived in the Dawnland was to waste his time, and risk his life, in pursuit of a woman whom he could replace far more easily than his dogs!

"Now we must go our separate ways, you and I," declared Kinap, rising, hefting his bow and rolled skins, then freeing the boy's tether and swinging the child onto his shoulders. "Long bright days do I wish you, M'alsum, First-born Son of Asticou and Meya'kwé! And a long life with your wits about you and a steady hand! And," he added with an introspective twinkle in his eyes, "hope that the old tusker in the ravine is not the Great Beast, Mammoth Slayer, for then you would live forever in a world within which you would be destined to see all of your loved ones die! I would not seek such a 'blessing.' But, say I, if you would again have your woman safe and warm and loving at your side, seek her soon, Friend—if you are not afraid—for once her captors cross the Great River and reach the barrens, you will never find her in that endless land of perpetually frozen desolation where it is said that no living thing that is not the color of snow can long survive! As for me and my little bog rat, we will think often and well of you as we seek the shadows of the deep forest. We have a long-standing rendezvous with a wolf woman and must be on our way before the coming of the spring rains."

M'alsum smiled wanly at what he took to be a joke. Rendezvous with a wolf woman indeed! His brow flexed as he realized with a start that the giant had just named him Friend again. He did not know why it pleased him so much to hear it, nor did he allow himself to wonder. Other words had come from the man's mouth, and these he could not, would not, overlook or forgive.

"If you are not afraid!"

"Wait!" M'alsum called after the giant. "Surely you cannot mean to walk away thinking that I had no intent to honor your kindness to me! I, too, have a parting gift for you. And for the little bog rat. Yes! A ducksuckle shall Musquash have from me. And for Kinap, for my friend and fellow mourner and teller of fine tales . . . a makuk of sweet sap and a packet of rare powder from the southern forests. Mixed in clear spring water and drunk down in a single gulp, this gift is said to make a magic that will heal all ills . . . forever! Share it, my friends, and be strong on your journey together into country that is unknown to me!"

The giant uttered a pleased exhalation and waited patiently while the headman hurried to the sled and, after setting Hasu'u's drinking tube aside, rummaged amidst his belongings for what he desired. It was no easy task; he had to haul off the big bison hide, untie the thongs, and roll out the massive skin upon the snow before he could reach for the parfleches of his choice.

Geese were flying against the stars when M'alsum came to stand once more before the giant and the boy, eagerly profferring up his gifts. "First, for you, Musquash, a small token of my—"

The boy hissed and backhanded the ducksuckle into the snow.

Kinap huffed annoyance as he bent to snatch up the dried, leathery, sugar-packed upper duck mandible. "Mmph! If my little bog rat does not want this, there are those who wait for me in the forest who will be more than happy to share it!" Rising to his feet, he was distracted by the distant callings of the geese and, turning his gaze skyward, watched them a moment. "Listen . . . they tell us that despite what we see and feel around us, winter is in retreat. So much snow and cold and yet still they come. Among the masked ones it is said that the leader of the goose flock is a shaman flying through the sky on a magic sled. He is strong, this goose shaman. He is wiser even than the great shaman, Squam, who dwells on the sacred island. Since the time beyond beginning he leads his tribe to all good things, forever following the greening of the world, guiding his kind to make their home in the air, on the water, and on the earth, Masters of the Feast of Life in all three 'lands.' "

"And when brought from the skies and water and land by the birding slings and spears of men, always their kind are good eating!" added M'alsum, straining to maintain patience with the man's endless babblings.

"Mmph!" Kinap was nodding to himself. "Well spoken, Stranger, for geese are vulnerable only when they walk or fly or swim unwary, or when they shed their flight feathers in the spring and are impelled to mate and nest and guard their young from all who would devour them. Remember this moment, Friend. The geese have been a sign to you. Walk wisely and warily into the Dawnland, M'alsum, Firstborn Son of Asticou, and in these changing times be careful just when and where you choose to shed your 'feathers' among Strangers like yourself! Think often of the geese. And may all good things come to you in the days and nights that lie ahead!"

"May it also be so for you, Friend," replied M'alsum with a smile as the giant accepted the gift of Death from his hands and turned away, unknowing.

The headman watched him go. A giant bear of a man carrying a bog rat of a boy. In moments they were gone, faded away into the darkness between the trees, like a phantom pair of Djeneta and Djigáha born of nightmare tales told in the depth of the winter dark. They had come into his life, shared it briefly for his betterment, and now gone their way. Already they seemed hardly real to him. And soon, with any luck at all, they would both be dead.

A thrill went through M'alsum at the thought of it until,

Do you truly think that you can ever hope to outdistance all that you have done in this forest, M'alsum, Firstborn and Eldest Son of Asticou?

His smile vanished at the prod of the all too familiar inner voice.

The first glow of dawn was beginning to leach darkness from the eastern sky. Above his head geese were still skeining northward across the fading stars. He imagined hunting and eating them and scattering their feathers to the Four Winds, and slowly the smile returned to his face. He was M'alsum, firstborn and now *only* son of Asticou! Winter was nearly over. By noon he would be in sight of the Great Salt Water, and this cursed forest would be at his back.

The Dawnland lay ahead.

He would go there now.

With his copper spearhead and ducksuckles and all his fine trading goods he would go! With his tall tales of heroism overcoming tragedy he would go! With the tail and trunk of a dead mammoth that he could now openly claim to be Katcheetohúskw he would go! As Mammoth Slayer and Man Who Brings All Good Things to the People he would go!

Who was left alive to name him Liar?

"No one! I have seen to that. As Kinap has said, 'A man must do as he must to survive.' "

He was smiling again as he turned, went hurriedly to the sled, tossed Hasu'u's swan-bone drinking tube impatiently away, and set himself to rolling up the great brown bison hide. A new life of honor and glory awaited him on the coast if he remained cautious in his affiliations and bold in the way he framed his lies. Why should he care that Hasu'u was still alive? He had mourned his dead. And he would not risk himself to win her back from marauding raiders who were even now taking her north and out of his life forever. She had chosen her fate. As he had chosen his. He would put her from his mind as he went forth to dwell once more among the living. The Circle of Life must turn forward, never back . . . at least until the time was at last right to return safely to the village of Asticou and bring his mother home.

"And perhaps not even then!"

He caught his breath. The statement had come unbidden to his lips. It was both startling and troubling.

"I will not forget her. Cannot forget her. Not Meya'kwé! She lives only for me. Only for me! She . . ."

The wind was rising around him, turning, blowing hard out of the inland forests. Somewhere far off within the trees into which the giant and the boy had disappeared, an owl called and wolves began to howl.

M'alsum tensed, listened, and for a moment he could have sworn that he heard the trumpeting of a distant mammoth and the ghostly lamentations of the dead.

Do you truly think that you can outdistance all that you have done in this forest, M'alsum, Firstborn and Eldest Son of Asticou? The spirits of those you have slain and abandoned will not forget you! The white mammoth will follow you! And I,

Katcheetohúskw, will take back the third arm that you have stolen from me and the tail with which I will flick flies from your corpse in the world beyond this world!"

"No," he snarled. Hefting his load, he turned his back to the trees and walked on toward the Dawnland.

The winter forest *was* alive with spirits, but M'alsum had come much too far to heed or listen to them now!

Part Two

MASTERS OF THE FEAST

▼▼▼▼▼▼▼

"When Our Creator was looking over the
newly-made world he was glad to see that
everything had come just right. So as he was
walking along he met the False Face and asked
him, 'Where did you come from?' The False
Face replied, 'I made the world.' 'No, I don't
think so. I think I made the world,' said Our
Creator. . . . 'It would be better if you went
away . . .'"

—MRS. JOHN L. BUCK
Midwinter Rites of the Cayuga Longhouse
by Frank G. Speck

Chapter One

▼▼▼▼▼▼▼

Arrows flew.

Caribou fell.

Hasu'u winced.

It seemed that only a moment had passed since she and her captors had trudged over the crest of the broad, stony hill to be brought short by the sight of a small herd of forest caribou clustered on the frozen surface of a circular little bog lake in the heavily treed river valley that lay below.

She was so fatigued that she had been only half aware of Tôrnârssuk raising his hand. Somehow a command had been communicated, and now arrows were flying, dogs were *yarfing*, and in the river valley caribou were stampeding in panic into the trees, too late for some: Two cows were already down on the ice.

And still arrows flew.

Another cow went down.

And another.

A fifth, struck in the throat, dropped to her fore knees.

Hasu'u gasped. The skill, speed, and deadly accuracy with which her captors propelled their stone-headed flying sticks from their curved hardwood bows sent a shock through her body.

They were using the big arrows today, not the shorter, slender, untipped shafts she had seen them use to bring down grouse and rabbits and the occasional squirrel. The sounds of the hunt were as lances to her senses: the hiss of arrows slicing forward through thin air! The snap of sinew bowstrings against the leather arm guards of the archers! The thin suck and pull of the hunters' breathing as they reached back again and again to pull one flying stick after another from their quivers before nocking them, then sending them flying unerringly forward to their prey!

All this set her blood racing and her heart pounding.

Now, at last, she understood the true power of her captors and knew why men feared them. Against skilled archers, men who relied on spears or stone hurlers or braining sticks were all but defenseless. Not even the finest, most massively headed lance hurled by the most skilled and powerful hand—with the aid of the most perfectly balanced spear thrower—could match the speed, distance, and accuracy of a well-shot arrow! A bowman could hunt from cover or not, stand close to or at a great distance from his prey. He could bring down birds or small game, or even take fish with a single arrow, or gather together with other archers to wound and weaken bigger, more dangerous game with many arrows and later move in for the finish with lances.

Ah, she thought, watching them now, when M'alsum came for her he was sure to be killed unless he came by stealth, unless he was wary, unless he was wise and as clever as the wolves for whom his parents had named him.

Hasu'u pulled in a ragged breath.

Why has he not come? Why? Why?

Each day she looked back along the trail for him. Each night she lay awake beside another man with a dead woman's infant at her breast, waiting, yearning for M'alsum, wanting him so much that her entire being ached for him . . . and yet loving him so much that, afraid for him, she hoped that he would not come.

Notch Ear nuzzled her hand. Hasu'u looked down. She was not surprised to see that the dog had come to her from the sled upon which Tôrnârssuk insisted Notch Ear ride with the seven pups the dog had whelped only the day before. Notch Ear seemed to sense her moods as keenly as the raiders sensed the changes in the weather. The Dawnland woman's head went high as, appreciating the dog's effort to console her, her fingers stroked the side of the animal's head.

Her nostrils tightened. She caught the acrid scent of adrenaline mixed in with the stink of her captors' unwashed bodies and garments as they stood close around her, each man as tautly strung as his bow, and as dangerous.

Hasu'u frowned as she knelt and, sensing that the men were about to break ranks and run forward to finish off their prey, slung an arm around Notch Ear's neck to prevent the dog from bolting downslope with the hunters. She counted ten caribou down or staggering on the ice. The fallen and wounded animals—caught dozing and cud-chewing in the open as was the way of their kind when migrating and wishing to avoid an ambush by wolves—did not stand a chance against the human predators who, at another unspoken signal from their tunraq, now broke ranks and raced downslope, yipping and howling.

Hasu'u shuddered. She remembered the way these same men had come from the forest to fall upon her own band.

She watched them descend upon the downed and bewildered caribou, each hunter seeking to retrieve his own arrows, finishing off his kills with bone lances while a yowling Avataut leaped upon the shoulders of the throat-shot cow, pulled back her antlered head, then reached around to open her throat with his stone skinning dagger.

Even from the crest of the hill Hasu'u could hear the bawling of the dying animals and see the frozen surface of the lake going red with blood. Her mind filled with images of the distant creek and of the way the ice had darkened with Ne'gauni's blood just before it had cracked wide and the youth had been swept away.

Little Brother! Ah! Long has it been since I heard you call my name! Are you still alive? My arrogant and brash Ne'gauni, how bold you were for my sake! What I would not give to walk with you again under the warming winter sun!

Again she pulled in a startled breath. The sun had been ascending and descending across a cloudless sky for days now. The air she breathed into her lungs was still winter cold, but the watching yellow eye of Halboredja, the wandering sun, was a subtle and awesome power in the world. Hasu'u knew that just as it had thinned the ice that had sheened the surface of the now-distant creek, so must it also be working on the ice that overlay the little bog lake and the wide arm of the river just beyond.

Break, Ice! Shatter, Ice! Open, Lake, and drown those who have taken me from my people! Then I will tear off this baby carrier I am forced to wear and throw it away into the water, drowning the infant of Wíndigo as my own wonderful child was drowned! And then, somehow, I will find a way to be free of Watchdog Woman who stands at my side!

"Look there," said Amayersuk. Leaning into her browband, she readjusted the weight of her backpack with an upward heave and then a sideward shake of her shoulders. "The hunters are already dragging the caribou off the ice. Come. We must follow. There will be much work for us now."

Hasu'u stood unmoving. Staring down into the valley, she wanted her death wish for the raiders to be fulfilled so badly that, as her eyes remained fixed on them, she imagined the ice opening beneath their feet. She saw them falling into dark water. She saw them waving their arms. She saw them bobbing to the surface like seals swimming in open water. But, weighted as they were by their heavy packs and furs, the raiders could not swim and, one by one, they began to drown.

Hasu'u smiled.

They were shouting now! Crying out for help! Her smile broadened. She would not help them. She would not!

"Women, come!"

"Why do you stand there?"

"Come!"

"Amayersuk!"

"Hasu'u!"

"Come! Join now with your men! There is much for you to do!"

Hasu'u flinched. Ningao and several others were loping back up the slope toward her, waving, calling out, saying that they would bring the dogs and sleds while the two women went ahead of them into the valley. Her smile turned upside down. Disappointment flooded her veins as she saw that the frozen surface of the lake was not breaking wide. It was holding the weight of the hunters as they dragged their kills across it toward the far shore. The men on the ice *had* been calling out for help, but they had not been drowning; they were simply shouting for assistance with the work to come.

"Our men need us now," observed Amayersuk. "Come. We will—"

"They are not my men!"

Ningao came to stand before her. Noting the hostility in her voice and upon her face, he shrugged affably as was his way when choosing to overlook her occasional outbursts, then lifted Notch Ear into his arms and, after exchanging a few words with Amayersuk, carried the dog to the sled where the ever-hungry pups lay in need of their mother.

Hasu'u rose to her feet. A great sadness filled her heart as her eyes strayed downward to the carrying sling that held the tunraq's son close to her breasts. She was doing all that was required of her to keep the infant nourished, clean, and warm, but, deprived of the familiar scent and loving arms of its true mother, the infant was not thriving. Tôrnârssuk had not failed to notice his son's increasing lethargy. Nor had Amayersuk.

Her mouth tightened.

If the baby dies, you will die!

Strangely, her recollection of the threat failed to move her. She could be forced to supply the child with the milk of life for as long as she had milk to give, but the tenacity to go on living was something that she could not give the infant any more than she could long continue to maintain it for herself.

A soul-numbing wave of apathy swept through Hasu'u. If M'alsum did not come for her soon, a day would come when she would simply drop to her knees along the trail and allow her captors to kill her.

If you die, the baby dies!

She sighed. Tôrnârssuk would not allow anyone to lay a hostile hand on her as long as he needed a milk woman for his son. Unless, of course, she killed his son. Again she sighed. Despite her intent to remain aloof toward the tunraq's infant, the increasing frailty of the baby roused pity in her. The emotion was unwelcome. The child at her breast did not even completely resemble a baby of the People. Its skin was unnaturally pale, and its face was flat. Its eyebrows were thicker than those of a normal child, and its eyelids were lost to view beneath long, taut spans of skin that ran from the bridge of its tiny nose across the tear ducts to its temples, giving it the appearance of squinting even when there was no sun or snow to make it do so. It had its father's eyes. Manitou eyes in a raider's face. And it was the cause of all her sorrow.

Now, as Hasu'u looked up to see Notch Ear settling down on the sled to nurse her pups amidst the furs that had been provided as a "nest" for her, she envied the dog. Notch Ear had lost a mate in the death of Whines Too Much, but the animal still had her own children to suckle. "This baby I carry will never be my own," she sighed mournfully and thought, *I should kill it. I should plug its nostrils with moss when no one is looking. It would not be so hard to do. And then soon I would be at peace, sent by Tôrnârssuk's hand to the world of the spirits to walk with the Ancestors.*

Amayersuk was *aaw*ing an openly mocking parody of sympathy. She laughed, then clucked her tongue nastily. "Poor sad Hasu'u! How well you continue to play Noqumiut! No wonder the men have all begun to call you this! Our tunraq has said that it should now be your name, for you are no longer Hasu'u, Woman Who Sings Always. You are Noqumiut, Hang-Headed Ghost, a silly, mindless, unappreciative shadow of the woman he once thought worthy of us when we first saw you walking so strongly and proudly with your baby in the forest!"

Hasu'u glared at her with undisguised loathing. "Your tunraq has killed my baby! Is it not enough for him that I am expected to suckle his child in place of my own? Am I now required to thank him and smile happily in appreciation of my captivity as well?"

"Stupid Woman, look around! Life is good for you! Forget what *was!* Savor what *is!* The milk of your body now flows in the blood of your tiguak. That suckling even smells of you now! This dawn I saw you smile when his fingers curled around your own. Soon you will laugh when he laughs. Soon you will cry when he cries. Soon you will take pride when he raises up his arms and reaches out to you before all others. Soon you will name him Son and forget that you ever had another. Then he will begin to thrive again. You will see."

Hasu'u went rigid. "Never."

Ningao and the others were talking to the dogs as they began to move the sleds forward and down into the valley.

"Come," said Amayersuk to Hasu'u. "Much work lies ahead for us. Ningao has told me that our tunraq wants to transport our kills to a butchering camp he will make on the far side of the river. We will rest there awhile. The flesh of the caribou will be lean this late in the year, but we will make much meat and feast on it. This food will strengthen us for the long journey north to rejoin those who wait for us at the big hunting camp on the River of the White Whales."

"There are more of you?"

"Those of our band who chose to winter on the river. Women. Children. New babies now, I think. And the men who were selected to guard and hunt for them. Maybe others of our tribe. Different bands. Who can say? Many choose to journey south in these days of increasing cold, for where the game of our ancestors walk, there, too, will we journey. But whoever awaits us, they will all be eager to hear the many tales our tunraq will tell of our adventures among the strange people who dwell in the dark forests! And we are eager to look once more upon the Great River and to eat again of the meat and skin of white whales."

"Whales . . . *white* whales?"

"Yes, Noqumiut! You have probably never seen the like! But I tell you now that we have a feast to look forward to that is well worth trudging our feet into blisters for! So rich! So fat! And the sinews of the white whale are so long that your eyes will widen with disbelief as you try to imagine the many fine things you will sew in the winter dark when we are at last encamped on the barrens of our tunraq's ancestors. He longs for them now. Avataut and some of the others have said that they will stay on with their women and little ones to make a camp along the Big River, for there is game, much game, to be had year round in the surrounding woodlands, but this will be Tôrnârssuk's last journey into the land of endless trees." Her face contorted into a smug smile. "Enjoy these days, Noqumiut, for they will be your last in the hunting grounds of your people."

▼▼▼▼▼

There was blood on the snow.

And everywhere the stink of hot meat and butchery.

Hasu'u stood back, appalled, for although she had participated many times in the orderly butchering of forest caribou and many other types of game, the men of Tôrnârssuk's band would allow no female hand to touch their kills before they had skinned and opened the carcasses themselves.

Although Tôrnârssuk led them in a brief prayer of thanksgiving to the slain animals, Avataut led them to fall upon the meat like hungry wolves. Anyone watching them would have assumed that they had not eaten in a moon! There was no apparent order to their feeding frenzy. Using their stone palm knives, they slit open the bellies and throats of the caribou, bent to drink blood hot from the severed arteries of their kills, gouged out eyeballs, and tossed one each to the women—a generous sharing, to hear it from Amayersuk as she eagerly pierced hers with her own palm dagger and proceeded to suck out the warm black fluid within.

Hasu'u found no appetite for what she would, under other circumstances, have considered as much of a delicacy as the soft, acidic green pudding that packed the intestines of the downed caribou. As she stood by watching hearts, livers, tongues, intestines, and fetuses being cut and pulled free from the bodies of the caribou in a fury of ravenous intent, she was sickened by the barbarity with which each man either pushed his face and teeth into a choice portion or sliced off what he would have of it, gulping down mouthfuls that should have choked him on the spot.

At last, sated, the hunters handed to Amayersuk and Hasu'u prime cuts of liver and small fatty "woman" glands that they had cut from above the kidneys of the cows. Then, after relaxing and belching and cutting much wind for a brief period, they set themselves to skinning each animal before gesturing the women forward to begin the intricate task of extracting precious sinew.

Later, in the camp they made upon high ground on the far embankment of the river, they fed the dogs the most prodigious meal the animals had known in days, then settled down to gorge themselves on meat, both raw and roasted. Tôrnârssuk insisted that Hasu'u eat heartily of blood-rich liver and use the marrow scoop he handed to her along with a cracked and fire-singed joint bone.

"You will eat! Blood meat will make you strong! Hot marrow will make your milk flow warm and rich! Eat! Not for yourself, Hang-Headed Woman, but for my son! I will not have you make a ghost of him!"

Hasu'u did not eat.

"If you do not eat, I will brain the dog you call Notch Ear and feed you her pups!" he threatened.

She ate. For Notch Ear's sake. Sparingly she ate. To spite Tôrnârssuk. To spite them all.

They recognized defiance in her eyes. Avataut snickered and said something to the tunraq. They all laughed. Except Tôrnârssuk.

"Avataut says that we had better reach the River of the White Whales and find another milk woman soon," Amayersuk told her, translating Avataut's words. "For surely the milk from your breasts will sour our tunraq's son and make him a stubborn, hang-headed man for the rest of his days."

Anger sparked within Hasu'u. Looking around the campfire, appraising the dirty, bloodied, greasy faces of her captors, she had no appetite for anything but freedom. Or for death.

Her head went high.

She sat motionless.

The baby was asleep at her breast. She closed her eyes

and willed herself to escape from the moment in the only way possible to her.

She slept.

▼▼▼▼

Two days later a little family wandered into camp: a wizened, middle-aged man, a homely, gap-toothed woman, and an even homelier girl, all three as guileless and wide-eyed as young seals newly whelped onto the ice of the bay in spring.

Hasu'u, kneeling before the tunraq's lean-to, where she had just finished changing the baby's swaddling, rose to her feet with the infant in her arms.

They were of the People!

She could scarcely believe her eyes.

Amayersuk, fleshing a caribou skin nearby, looked up at the newcomers in amazement. "Well, what is this?"

Hasu'u could scarcely find her breath. The patterning of the family's facial tattoos was not specific to any coastal affiliation that she knew of, and the man carried no staff, either of wood or bone, to indicate rank or tribe.

The raiders were talking amongst themselves, standing before their lean-tos, or rising from where they had been lounging around the morning's fire. The dogs were all up, curious, too logy from the previous night's feast to utter a bark.

The head of the little family spoke up. His voice was sharp, grating, simultaneously whining and wheedling and demanding.

Hasu'u could barely make out his dialect, much less his name, if, in fact, he gave it. She thought that he said something about his good fortune in stumbling upon a feast. About taking meat. About others being obliged to share. And about getting married?

She frowned, giving up on understanding his words, knowing that he must be one of the many independent heads of single-family bands that, for one reason or another, broke with their own kindred to make their way in the world alone. Her father had never had anything good to say about such people; Ogeh'ma claimed that they were usually unfit or unsavory in some way, unwilling or unable to live productively within an established, smoothly functioning community. Their appearance confirmed his opinion.

They were dressed for traveling in molting, carelessly matched, shamefully ill-sewn clothes, and they stood to one side of a far too heavily laden pole-drag that was pulled by the scrawniest, mangiest, most cowed and exhausted-looking dog that Hasu'u had ever seen. Their backpacks were sloppily assembled. And they were rudely and aggressively pointing to the meat-laden drying racks, nodding and grinning and all but salivating as they spoke loudly and excitedly among themselves.

Avataut said something to Tôrnârssuk.

The tunraq's eyes narrowed as he stared fixedly at the family.

The wizened traveler met Tôrnârssuk's gaze and, radiating excitement and eagerness to please, shouted at the homely girl as he shoved her forward, made lewd pumping movements with his hips, and gestured to the drying frames, then to the girl as he shoved her farther toward the raiders.

Hasu'u did not need to understand the man's words to understand his intent: He was offering the youngest of his two women—perhaps his daughter—in exchange for fresh meat.

Avataut spoke again, eagerly.

The raiders at the fire were all on their feet now.

Tôrnârssuk exchanged a few words with them, then shook his head, shrugged, walked to the fire, and deliberately turned his back on the little family.

Hasu'u never knew who drew or loosed the arrow.

One moment the leader of the family was grinning his gap-toothed grin and pointing to the drying frames; the next he was clutching his throat. Dark blood was gushing through his fingers. Arterial blood. A steady rush. He staggered, turned, made terrible noises as he plucked at the arrow that had just impaled him.

The gap-toothed woman was waving her arms and shrieking. The homely girl stood like a stunned caribou, all eyes, her face spattered with blood, her entire being communicating disbelief and slowly dawning horror. The man went to his knees. Choking. Dying. As Tôrnârssuk remained where he was, facing away from what he had reluctantly sanctioned, Avataut led the raiders to circle the women while the mangy, trail-weary pack dog looked on.

Amayersuk wiped her fleshing dagger on her leather palm pad and uttered a low, malevolent laugh at Hasu'u's expense. "Maybe they have found another milk woman and will now have no need of you. Maybe this camp is your last camp! Maybe you will not live to complain about suckling our tunraq's son again."

It was not to be.

The gap-toothed woman was past the age of bearing, and Avataut, first to force penetration of the homely girl, howled with delight when it became apparent that she had never before been mated. For the next three days and nights, when the raiders were not eating or sleeping or reworking their assemblage of weaponry and hunting tools, they took turns on the women. Amayersuk brought warm fat to the captives and showed the girl how to slather it within her newly opened woman place to ease the pain of repeated rape and make mating more pleasurable. And then, aroused by her own advice, she hefted up her garments, greased her own genitals, and danced around the camp singing lewd songs and eagerly opening her tattooed thighs to the ruttings of the fevered men.

Hasu'u gritted her teeth and said nothing. As though a little warm grease could lessen the agony of the degradation the women were enduring! She kept her eyes downturned, not only to avoid shaming the new captives by observing their humiliation but also to draw no attention to herself. If she could have found a way to make herself invisible, she would have done so, for she lived in fear that in this camp of blood and lust and lechery Tôrnârssuk would catch the fever to mate and stop brooding over his dead wife long enough to realize that his captive was a female as well as a milk woman. He would force himself into her then and perhaps even stand aside, holding his son, while his fellow raiders took turns on her as they did with the others.

She shuddered to think of it. When the two new captives were not being used, they were put to work with her and Amayersuk, fleshing the newly taken skins, preparing meat to be carried on the long northward journey. Neither spoke; the homely girl stared blankly and drooled as she sat on her heels, working herself from side to side in silent misery as she tried to ease her pain, while the gap-toothed woman mumbled and swore under her breath in her unintelligible dialect, no doubt cursing the man who had led her into such a camp and to the fate that had befallen her.

Only Tôrnârssuk and Ningao showed no interest in the women. Hasu'u was grateful. Indeed, Ningao's only concern seemed to be the skinny dog. Although it growled at him and showed him its teeth and bit him more than once, he kept it with him, away from the rest of the pack, feeding it scraps, picking vermin from its coat, and carving a comb out of a piece of caribou bone with which to card the mats and tangles from its fur.

"He is the only one among all of you who knows the meaning of kindness," said Hasu'u, watching the raider, unaware that the tunraq had come up beside her.

"Is it kindness to take pity on a broken and injured thing, Noqumiut, if that thing refuses kindness and will not allow itself to be healed?"

She looked up at him. "That 'thing' is a dog. A living creature. You, I am sure, see it only as something to be used and would brain it. As you will brain me if I fail to keep your child alive."

He looked down. "Then do not fail," he told her quietly and walked away.

▼▼▼▼▼

The next morning they broke camp and moved on toward the distant River of the White Whales. The past days of relative rest and the fresh meat of the caribou had revived Hasu'u's body, but not her spirit. The land was rising beneath her feet, but the infant at her breast was more lethargic than before. Nursing as she walked along beside Amayersuk, a new and ever deeper dread began to form in her heart as the woman spoke on and on about the gathering of the raiders' people at the great hunting camp on the River of the White Whales.

At last, pausing to rest on the high flank of a hill as the rest of the band trudged ahead, Hasu'u, her heart heavy, asked Amayersuk, "This River of White Whales that you speak of, is it so wide that men cannot see across it at its mouth, and does it sometimes taste of salt and boil with fish beneath high cliffs—"

"Where else this far south can our men hunt the white whales that nourished their fathers?"

Hasu'u held her tongue. She dared not allow herself to answer the question.

Amayersuk was staring at her. "You know this river? You have been there before?"

"No!" Hasu'u spoke out sharply in righteous indignation. "You speak of the hunting grounds of my most northern cousins! Many times I have heard them tell of this place at our clan gatherings. You have no right to hunt the white whales or anything else in the country of my people's many encampments! Since the time beyond beginning they have—"

Amayersuk made a rude noise; anyone hearing it could easily have assumed that it had come from her buttocks instead of her face. "The time beyond beginning has come again, Stupid Woman, only now it is a *new* time, a *new* beginning, a time to follow the most ancient of all teachings—to learn new ways or die! All across the high barrens snow stays longer and lies deeper on the ground. On the coast the winter ice-pack drifts farther south each year. Tôrnârssuk's people follow the ice as the great white bears follow it. We hunt and journey where we will. Who is to stop us? Your weak and woman-bellied men who have no knowledge of our weapons? Have you not seen with your own eyes that all we need do is don our masks, pretend to be manitou, and set our arrows flying in order to send your people running before us to disappear into the forest like frightened deer? Or how we can simply sit within our hunting camps and wait for little bands of your foolish people to walk in among us? We kill their men and take their women and belongings and dogs if and when we want them!"

"How brave you are!"

"Mock me if you will, Gullible Woman, but soon your people will vanish forever into the shadow world of trees. Who will miss them? Not I! Everywhere the northern forests are dying, opening up the earth to the sky, welcoming my people. Our hunting grounds will be wherever we choose to make them, following the caribou if we so choose, or making our camps at the edge of the world, at the rim of the sea where seals whelp on the pack ice in early spring and great whales swim and sound under early summer moons while the little white whales that sing like birds come eagerly into the shallows to give up their meat and fat and skin to be food for us!"

A disturbing quiet settled upon Hasu'u's spirit. "My people *are* your people," she reminded Amayersuk with grim emphasis, knowing even as she spoke that the woman would again respond with a rude and dismissive noise. She was not mistaken. And so, offended, it pleased her to press hurtfully, "What kind of woman walks willingly with her enemies? What kind of woman stands aside gloating while these enemies make prey of her own people?"

"*This* kind of woman!" snapped Amayersuk. All mirth and mockery were now gone from her face. Her dirty, tattoo-blackened features were engorged with anger, resentment, and pure, vicious, unadulterated spite. "My enemies dwell in the camps of the weaklings who gave birth to me!

It could have been my own father I saw struck down in our last camp, so like him was he! And so I do *not* merely stand aside and gloat when my people make prey of those who traded me and my young sister Waseh'ya to raiders in exchange for their lives! Gullible Woman, it was *I* who snatched your baby from your arms and threw your child away into the creek to drown. Our tunraq might have allowed it to live had you been given time to prove to him that you had milk enough, but why should any baby of yours share the milk of life with his child, with my sister's child? And why should you have two babies when I have none!"

Hasu'u was so stunned by the woman's revelations that she had to will herself to breathe. There was something in Amayersuk's eyes that she had never seen there before. It was wild, feral, something dark and dangerous waiting to leap out and hurt her. She could see jealousy in it, and hatred born of that, and something else that eluded definition. Never before had Hasu'u looked into the eyes of madness.

Amayersuk made her rude noise again. "Stupid Woman! Why do you look at me like that? Do you not yet know why I am called Amayersuk? Has Tôrnârssuk not told you the meaning of my name? While he stands alone, mourning and brooding over the death of his Waseh'ya, my name is a great cause for amusement among the men who walk with him. Do you not wish to ask me why? No? Then I will tell you anyway:

"I am called Amayersuk because I have been named for Woman Who Steals Babies in the old stories of the north. Amayersuk is strong, as I am strong. Amayersuk is brave, as I am brave. Amayersuk knows how to make meat and sew clothes and please her men, as I please each man in this band. But Amayersuk can have no babies of her own, as I can have no babies, and so she is also dangerous! Why? Because Amayersuk walks around with a big hole in her back, always waiting for her chance to steal and stuff the babies of other women inside. The stolen babies die in that dark hole in Amayersuk's back. Does Amayersuk weep for them? No! The flesh of the little dead babies feeds her spirit and makes her smile. As your drowned baby made me smile! As I smiled when, after a raid long before I ever set eyes on your baby, Avataut gave me a dead woman's infant to hold. There were no milk women for it. It felt good in my arms. I held it close. I sang songs to it. I changed its swaddling. The men of the band laughed when I put it to my breasts to suckle even though I had no milk to give. Our tunraq was not pleased, but I am his Waseh'ya's sister, and for her sake he did not speak against me when I kept the stolen baby and stuffed its mouth with moss so no one would be offended by its cries as I carried it from camp to camp until it died.

"It was then that our tunraq named me Amayersuk and made me turn around so all could look and see if I had a hole in my back like Woman Who Steals Babies in the stories. All laughed and were glad to see that I did not, but when the band moved on again and Avataut told me to feed the dead baby to the dogs so its life would not be wasted, I did not obey. I have no hole in my back, but I *have* been named Amayersuk, and I do not give to dogs the babies I take from others! No! I crushed in its head and cut it into pieces and cooked it in my boiling bag so that its flesh would be meat for my spirit! As your drowned baby would have been had the creek not swept it away."

"Ah!" Hasu'u exclaimed in revulsion. Instinctively she drew the infant at her breast into a protective embrace as she clapped a hand to her mouth to keep from retching at the horror of what she had just heard.

"Ha! Do not look at me as though I were some loathsome thing you would step over upon the trail and leave behind you if you could. I have been set to guard you and keep ever at your side and see that no harm comes to my tunraq's child. Ungrateful Woman, you should be glad that I only drowned your infant and did not eat it, for surely if the baby at your breast was not my own dead sister's child, neither it nor you would be safe alone with Amayersuk!"

Distraught and frightened, Hasu'u held the baby close as she looked around and realized that while she and Amayersuk had been talking, the others had crested the hill. Tôrnârssuk alone stood apart, his body taut, his bow held at the ready as he stared toward her and her human watchdog.

Hasu'u swallowed down rising panic. She was alone with Amayersuk! And, from the tunraq's posture, she was certain that he was afraid for her and his child. With a quick, shallow intake of breath, she began to move forward toward him, toward the tunraq, Guide and Guardian and All-Knowing Spirit, headman of the raiding band that had destroyed her world, toward Tôrnârssuk, White Bear, Wíndigo, Great Ghost Cannibal—Slayer of Youth, Slaughterer of Wayfarers, Destroyer of Dogs, Stealer of Women, but no longer Drowner of Infants in her eyes. Never until this moment had Hasu'u been able to see the man as anything but Enemy; now he seemed a refuge, and for the baby's sake, if not her own, she would flee to his side.

Amayersuk reached out, took hold of one of Hasu'u's elbows, and jerked her hard around. "Where do you run to, Gullible Woman? And whom do you fear now? Look at you! Your face is as white as new snow! And blue at the corners of your mouth! You have swallowed every word I have spoken, half choking on my story, believing it as you once believed that the men who have taken you captive were cannibal manitous!"

Hasu'u stared. Her mind was spinning. Mirth and mockery were back in Amayersuk's eyes. There was sadness in them now, too, and regret, but the feral madness that had fired her gaze only moments ago was gone. "What are you saying?" She barely managed to choke out the words. "That you did *not* drown my baby and eat another woman's child?"

Amayersuk made another of her rude noises. "Did I drown your baby? *Yes!* Of course I drowned your baby! For the good of my tunraq's son and to assure the life of my sister's child, I snatched your suckling from your arms and threw it away to a sure, quick death. On the long winter trail through the forest to the River of the White Whales no mother could long sustain her own strength, much less continue to provide the milk of life, if she tried to feed more than one infant at the same time!"

Hasu'u was shaking as she continued to hold the fussing infant safe within her arms. "Shh . . . shh, little one, shh," she crooned, rocking the child, unaware that she was doing so.

Amayersuk laughed. "Are you afraid to ask again the second question? Did I eat another woman's child? Ha! If I thought for a single moment that this might give me a baby of my own to love and nurture as you have been given your tiguak, yes, I would do even as terrible a thing as that! But look, do you not see how the terror of my tale has made you hold my sister's little one differently against your breast? Now that you imagine it threatened, your body seeks to protect it and your spirit names this baby yours even though your lips have yet to do so!" She paused, drew in a deep, deliberate breath, then shook her head and said, not unkindly, "Speak lovingly to the baby you hold to your heart, Fortunate Woman, for an infant cannot survive on milk alone any more than the little one I failed to nourish could live only on my love. That child lies buried out there in the dark forests beneath a mound of stones in the way of our tunraq's people. A dog lies buried with her, a big, strong dog whose brave spirit has guarded and guided her on the long journey into the spirit world, where her mother and the others we killed among her band must surely have been waiting for her."

Hasu'u's throat constricted. This tale, in its simple statement of love and loss, made her weep . . . for the dead baby, for her own lost son, and, to her astonishment, for the woman who stood before her, for any woman who would never know the bittersweet joy of birthing and nurturing a child . . . any child.

"Come," said Amayersuk, tossing her head to indicate that the time for talk was over. "We have a long walk ahead of us to the big hunting camp by the River of White Whales. Maybe along the way we will come across other bands of your fearful people, and our tunraq can steal a baby for me . . . and perhaps another milk woman to take your place, if you remain unwilling to love his child!"

Hasu'u flinched. Had the woman mocked or threatened her? Both. As she fingered tears from her eyes, all sympathy for Amayersuk vanished from her spirit. On the crest of the long wide hill, Tôrnârssuk was gesturing impatiently, and the men, captives, and even the dogs were looking back.

Hasu'u stiffened as Amayersuk began to move on ahead. She remained motionless. The morning sun was in her eyes, still rising bright out of the east, its rays angling across other hills that shouldered away into distant gray mists. She swallowed hard and looked away.

The Dawnland lay out there in those mists!

How many days' journeying? She had no way of knowing. But what matter? She had no hope of ever seeing it again.

Unless . . .

Her heartbeat quickened. Once the mists cleared, she would be able to see all the way to the Great Salt Water, and, if only she were free, she would look to the sky and follow the seabirds home!

Home!

If she were to break and run, if she were to cast away the baby at her breast, if she were to turn and race eastward into the forested land, she might yet make her way home to freedom!

The thought was so overwhelming that she nearly cried aloud with the sheer joy of it. Nearly. Hope shriveled within her. She knew that it could not be.

They would follow.

They would hunt her.

They would not allow their tunraq's baby to starve. No matter how far she ran, no matter how clever and convoluted her trail, they would be on it like wolves after a deer. They would find her. They would put the infant to her breasts again, and if she were so foolish as to lead them into her father's hunting grounds, they would drive her people from their lodges, slaughter any who dared to stand against them, and take another milk woman captive to nourish their tunraq's child. They would kill her then; Hasu'u was certain of that.

And then, at the foot of the hills, across the wide, eastwardly sloping plain where late-summer blueberries

stained the moccasins of all who ventured there, Tôrnârssuk and his followers would stand on the tawny cliffs
above the immense blue bay where seals came to whelp on
the ice in late winter and white whales came to feed and
molt and play with their calves before giving up their meat
to be food for the people.

She trembled. Tôrnârssuk would need only one good
look at the intricately carved, whale-tooth-studded totem
posts around which her people danced in thanksgiving at
the end of each whale hunt to know that here—not only
in the Great River—was a place where the white whales
swam.

Hasu'u reached up again to wipe tears from her cheeks.
She would not lead him there! She would not bring devastation and death to her people! A small glimmer of hope
rekindled in her heart as, for a moment, it crossed her
mind that if she were to kill the infant before she ran away,
the raiders would have no need to follow her. Hope faded
as quickly as it had flared. She laughed bitterly at herself,
knowing that they would hunt her anyway, even if only to
make her pay with her life and the lives of her loved ones
as punishment for what she had done.

The baby yawned and stretched and flexed its tiny fingers into the soft skin of her breast. Hasu'u looked down at
the waking child and reached into the sling to place a
nipple into a disinterested little mouth. When it began to
suck, an all-pervasive feeling of tenderness toward the infant expanded within her spirit until she thought she must
choke on it. She could not kill this baby. Not now. Not
ever! And she could not run away and leave it behind as
long as this meant placing the already frail child at risk of
starvation. Too long had the little one been at her breast.
Amayersuk was right. The milk of her own life now ran in

the veins of the tunraq's son; the baby had taken on her scent, and the scent of the other, of the poor drowned and most wonderful child whom she would never again hold in her arms.

A sob ripped from Hasu'u's throat. Tôrnârssuk was coming toward her now. His stride marked his mood. He was angry. She was causing delay. He said as much as he came to stand before her.

"You will join the others now!" he commanded. "For the good of my son, you will not stand outside the protection of the band. It is not safe!"

Safe.

The word stung Hasu'u. Irony twisted her mouth as she said, "Another once spoke so to me. And then you came. Ne'gauni was right to warn me of his fears. It was not safe for us to stand outside the protection of our band in a forest within which Tôrnârssuk was hunting, wearing the mask of Raven, pretending to be Wíndigo, winter chief of the manitous. But tell me, White Bear, Guardian and All-Knowing Spirit, Slaughterer of Wayfarers, Destroyer of Dogs, and Stealer of Women, what can you, a wise and benevolent tunraq to your people, possibly fear in this forest that you have made your own with your arrows and masks and willingness to kill all who cross your path in possession of anything that you would claim for yourself?"

"I fear the specter of hunger that will fall upon my son if you do not maintain milk enough to feed him. As you should fear it. As you have been told, if he dies, you die. So come! We journey north. My spirit is weary of the darkness of your endless forest and of the darkness it brings to the spirits of those who have chosen to walk with me!"

Hasu'u hung her head.

She would not tell him how close he was to the Dawnland, to open skies and the broad stretch of the sea, where, in keeping with the traditions of his ancestors, he would find seal and walrus and, in time, the flesh of white whales.

She followed him down into the valley, nursing the baby, singing softly to the child as she felt it dozing contentedly while it sucked.

> "Hay ya, ya.
> Sleep, little one, sleep, sleep!
> Hay ya, ya.
> Father walks ahead, but Mother watches over you!
> Hay ya, ya.
> Sleep, little one, sleep, sleep, my own precious child . . ."

Hasu'u choked off further verses of the old lullaby along with the flood of memories that came with them. Tears were again welling hot beneath her lids as she whispered to the baby, "We will not tell the tunraq about my people. We will let him go on his way north across the high tangled hills and beyond to the gathering of his kind along the shores of the River of the White Whales. Even now M'alsum may have reached the coast. Even now he may be counseling with my father and brothers and many cousins. You did not ask to be the cause of my grief, and so I will live for you, my little tiguak, my adopted son, until they come for me. Surely my M'alsum has not forgotten those who have drowned his son. He will not allow that death to go unavenged. He will come for his woman. Yes! You will see! The strongest and bravest and boldest of the sons of Asticou will find his Dawnland woman and bring me safely home!"

Chapter Two

▼▼▼▼▼▼▼

There was joy in the forest.

Ne'gauni felt none of it.

Kinap was back!

Old One laughed aloud and wept with delight when she saw him come stomping into the clearing on his enormous snow walkers. Mowea'qua leaped to her feet, dropped the rabbit she had been skinning, and ran to hurl herself into his vast embrace. The eagle, jessed to its outside perch, danced back and forth restlessly as it ruffled its feathers to make itself look larger, in case the gargantuan interloper proved a threat. And the wolf, already alert to the sound of someone coming through the trees, took one look at the giant and ran off in the opposite direction.

Ne'gauni's eyes narrowed. He envied U'na'li. Of late the girl had tethered the animal only when it was inside the lodge at night, to keep it from nosing into the stores, chewing on the stacked rolls of sinew and rawhide, and helping itself to the painstakingly maintained contents of her smoker while she slept. Now, as he watched the dark lithe form vault off and disappear into the trees, he ached to follow and was glad that Mowea'qua and the old hag were so taken with the arrival of the giant that they failed to notice that the wolf had gone.

Heartened, the lethargy that had been on him for days was suddenly gone from his spirit as he gritted his teeth against pain and, unable to stand on his own, did his best to crawl away on his side after U'na'li.

His best was not good enough.

The eagle shrieked when the youth accidentally bumped his heel against the base of the pole that supported its perch.

He had the full attention of the others now.

"Yah! Stop him, child!" The old one was screeching at Mowca'qua like a riled crow. "Quickly! Warn you did I not that he would not so easily be kept caged or hobbled like one of your captive birds or beasts? Look at him! A Stranger! An Enemy! Ah, Kinap, see you how I am without you to guide me? I must have lost my head to have allowed the child to bring him here! But warn her I did! Yes, say I, I did! And now it is just as I feared! Look at him trying to escape! Today writhes he like a worm after the rain, but soon will he take up the crutch that she has been making for him. When least we expect it, he will try to hop away after his own kind like a one-legged raven awaiting the chance to caw out to all who would listen! Bah, say I, give him half a chance and caw out will he to our enemies and lead them here to our den, where slay and skin us they will as reward for our kindness to him!"

"Mmph, Grandmother, you are the only one cawing!" Mowea'qua reprimanded her, on her knees beside Ne'gauni now, trying to fix an arm firmly under his left shoulder as she struggled to help him back to where he had been sitting propped against her backrest in the sun outside the den. A shadow fell upon them.

Ne'gauni looked up, startled, as he was swept up into the arms of the giant and carried off like an infant while Mowea'qua fussed along in the behemoth's wake, instructing him to gently place "her" wounded one down.

Ne'gauni would have corrected her. He would have told her that he was not hers any more than the wolf or the eagle was hers. She might well have found them injured in the forest as she had found him, taken pity upon them, carried them to her den, fed them, healed them, and named each of them Friend, but she had only to loosen the jesses that bound the eagle to its perch and the raptor would fly away to freedom among its own kind as surely as the wolf had run. As surely as Ne'gauni would run if he could! Or drag himself back through the forest in search of his own kind, even if he died along the way, on his own terms, alone if need be, before he ended his days gutted, hollow-eyed, and hanging upside down from the rafters of the old hag's den, as he still suspected that he and the eagle and wolf would do in time.

Run fast and far, U'na'li! He willed freedom to the animal. *And do not come back into the realm of the manitous, Wolf! Ever!*

But Ne'gauni did not speak his thoughts aloud. He could not bring himself to breathe, much less utter a word. The giant was standing over him.

As big as a bear and as broad of back and limb, the man wore the shaggy black skins of two such animals, and was unbent under the elongated bulge of the biggest pack the youth had ever seen. But it was not the man's size that took the youth's breath away, or the collection of bones and amulets and grotesque fetishes that hung from his belt. The giant was scowling down out of the shadowing encirclement of a fur-ruffed hood, appraising Ne'gauni with hard, dark, piercingly inquisitive eyes. As the sun's rays struck straight into the giant's cowl, it was the face of the man within that stunned the youth into silence.

Only in nightmares—and not even then—had Ne'gauni imagined that such scarring was possible. Like rendered fat that had spilled from a soapstone lamp and run down the convex sides to congeal in cold air, the giant's flesh appeared to have melted and then coagulated over his skull in an amalgamation of lumps and rivulets and wider, shinier spaces that lay almost transparent over the bone.

Ne'gauni was sickened. Unknowing, he sent his hands drifting upward to his own face. As he gingerly fingered the long, still-tender gash that had sliced open his features from the top of one ear to the bottom of the other, a strange, sinking feeling made him light-headed. His facial wound was beginning to heal. The swelling was down; the skin itched a little and was no longer as sore as it had been only yesterday, but it was beginning to pull up along the left side of his face, distorting his nostril and mouth, and now the fine sinew sutures tickled beneath his questing fingertips like black whiskers in need of plucking.

Dread settled in his belly. The giant was still scowling at him. Was it possible, Ne'gauni wondered, that without his bandages he was as ugly to the giant's eyes as the giant was to his?

Kinap seemed to read his mind and rasped a droll, rumbling reply to the horror that he saw in the eyes of the youth. "No! Think I not! You may have lost a leg, Whoever You Are, but the wound on your face will not leave a scar that will in any way match mine. The 'beauty' of Kinap is legendary and remains unsurpassed! If you would equal it, you will have to dance in the embrace of Fire as I have danced. Kelet will heal you. As she has healed me. And then would we not be a pair of lovelies, hmm?"

Ne'gauni recoiled.

The giant grumbled a mirthless laugh. "Be content with your little gash, young Stranger, now that you have looked upon the face of Kinap!" He turned to the old woman. "Just who *is* this wounded one, Kelet, and by all the forces of Creation just what is he doing here? Surely, after all that we have endured together, you know better than to—"

"Mine he is!" Mowea'qua declared with the proud ferocity of ownership as she snapped to her feet and stood tall beside Ne'gauni.

The youth was livid. He found his voice and shouted a protest that fully equaled the ferocity of the girl's. "I am *not* yours!" Then, to the giant, "I am Ne'gauni, He Walks Ahead, only surviving son of the hunt chief Asticou of the inland forest. I was struck down along with my brothers' trading band by marauding manitous. These two found me and cut off my leg and made a mockery of my name! But I do not belong to them—not to an old hag, nor to a young . . . young . . . whatever she is!"

"Mmph!" Mowea'qua's exclamation rang with her determination to tolerate—if not overlook—the open insult to her grandmother and the implied insult to herself. Nevertheless, her tone was rapturous as she looked up at the giant with open adoration. "Sharp is his tone, Kinap, as sharp as the blades and awls that Old One and I have used to heal him after in the creek I found him within howling distance of the sacred grove. But heal he will! And the edge of his tongue will soften. He is the gift from the forest, Kinap! The one you promised to me! He will—"

The giant raised both hands in request for silence. Then, kneeling, he looked even more closely at Ne'gauni as he asked quietly, "A masked one's arrow did this to your face, here, in this part of the forest, so close to the sacred grove?"

"Yes, say I!" affirmed Mowea'qua before Ne'gauni could open his mouth. "And another struck him in the shoulder. That flying stick had to be broken before we could from his flesh remove it, but the other have I retrieved! Old One and I will of the stone heads make much good use."

The giant was not listening. He was nodding to himself, and when he spoke again, slowly, in a deeply troubled tone that was addressed more to himself than to his listeners, he continued to scrutinize the youth. "Yes . . . I can see him in you . . . in the curve of the hairline at your temples, in the arch of your nose and the lines of your mouth. Mmm. A pity for you to have been wounded so. Even with only one leg, you would have matched him in looks one day. Yet, although scarred, yours will be a strong face, as his is strong."

"His?" Ne'gauni could not bring himself to flesh out the query. He held his breath. Hope was stirring in his heart. He dared not give it voice, dared not give hope space to grow, for this time, if it was shattered within him, he knew that his heart would be irrevocably shattered with it. This time the river of death would claim him, and there would be no swimming back from its black depths.

"You are not the only surviving son of Asticou," revealed the giant somberly.

A gasp went out of the youth as, trembling, he still feared to speak his hope aloud.

M'alsum! His thoughts went wild. *The giant has to be talking about M'alsum! Only my mother ever denied that I had the look of him. M'ingwé saw it, and Sac, too. Ah, M'ingwé, strong, wry, surly M'ingwé! I do not think he really hated me.*

And Sac, clever, cautious Sac! Sometimes he was not completely hostile. Let the giant tell me now that they live . . . all three of my brothers . . . and Kicháwan, too! Homely, kind old burden woman who never had a bad word for us even when—

"Ah!" Mowea'qua's exclamation of delight cut off Ne'gauni's thoughts as she clapped her hands together before her face and, beaming, cast a smug and all-knowing look at the youth. "Kinap has the beautiful one seen! Told you I that alive he was, but you would not believe that I had seen him, or that Old One and I both saw your brothers escaping from the masked ones—"

"Be silent, Mowea'qua," Kinap interrupted without rancor, his voice still quiet, more somber than before. "I have mourned and camped and walked with a trader who gave his name as M'alsum, the Wolf, firstborn son of the hunt chief Asticou of the inland forest. He was alone. There were no brothers. All were dead. Slain by the masked ones. Except for the woman."

"Kicháwan is alive!" Ne'gauni was overwhelmed by a rush of conflicting emotions: gladness for the burden woman as he now realized just how deep was his affection for her; sadness at the loss of M'ingwé and Sac; regret because he would never have a chance to win their approval or beg their forgiveness for having unwittingly called the manitous down on them; and guilt, a startling and disconcerting guilt born of a sudden understanding that, deep down, he would not really miss M'ingwé or Sac at all. Unlike M'alsum, whom he had adored from a distance and emulated since earliest childhood, M'ingwé and Sac had only briefly been more in his eyes than a pair of eager lackeys to his eldest brother, and that had been when M'alsum had been away from the village. During his absence they had made no pretense to liking him. And now, remembering their many jests and jibes, he experienced a disturbing recollection of the pair of them bending over him as he lay helpless in the creek, murmuring together, pulling at him, hurting him, and then leaving him to die alone.

"You are wrong," the giant was saying. "The burden carrier, Strong Running Woman, was among the dead in your brother's little storm camp. Together we mourned her and her unborn child. I beat the drum and kept watch with my bow while M'alsum danced and offered gifts and sang the spirits of his loved ones to the world beyond this world in a way that did them all great honor. It is the other woman who survived. The Dawnland woman. Hasu'u. One Who Sings Always. His wife."

"The beautiful one cannot a wife have! She is the one my wounded one loves!" cried Mowea'qua with such obvious pain and disappointment that Old One raised her grizzled brows and harrumphed in surprise as well as disdain.

Ne'gauni took note of neither Old One nor Young One. "It cannot be," he said to the giant. Somehow, scarcely knowing that he spoke at all, he told him, "I saw Hasu'u die. At the creek. Before the big storm came down upon the world. It was late in the day. She had fallen behind the others. She wanted to drink. There was open water showing at the edges of the stream, and no one in the band had enjoyed fresh water for longer than any of us could remember. And besides, the baby made her thirsty, I think. So I stayed close to her while M'alsum and the others drove the dogs and sled ahead. I told her to hurry. M'alsum had warned us that there were manitous in the forest, *cannibal* manitous. And then they came. Out of nowhere they came. As though I had called them upon us with my careless words. I wanted to help her. I would have given my life in exchange for hers! But, as you see, something cut my face, and I was struck in the shoulder by one of their flying sticks. I fell. Hard. The ice broke beneath me. I was swept downstream. And still I would have helped her, but I could not move my legs, and so I lay in the creek and saw the manitous drown her baby and carry her off, bloodied, dead, no more to them than meat to be devoured. No more than that! And I could do nothing. Nothing!"

The giant reached out to lay a consoling hand upon Ne'gauni's uninjured shoulder. "Let me tell you what I told your brother, young Stranger: I saw the Dawnland woman alive, walking as a captive in the skin of a white bear with a raiding band of masked ones, carrying a child . . . days after the worst of the great storm was over. She lives! But for how long, who can say? Your brother M'alsum will seek her now. Together with her Dawnland people he will try to bring her back into the hunting grounds of her own kind. He should be at the coast by now. The way will be difficult for him, and dangerous, but—"

"He will not be afraid," said Ne'gauni.

"Mmph!" Old One interjected sourly. "It takes a brave man to leave a youth to watch over his woman in the country of the manitous while sees he to the protection of his dogs and sled!"

"He is the boldest and bravest and best of the sons of Asticou! He . . ." Ne'gauni's words faltered, broke, stumbled on. "He trusted me! I failed him! I . . ." The youth closed his eyes. He had not intended to bare his soul; now it bled onto his checks as tears.

Old One harrumphed again. "Look you at that, Mowea'qua! Your 'gift from the forest' like a baby cries! Fit he is not to live among those of the Old Tribe. He is—"

"Is not what the girl has proclaimed!" declared Kinap irritably. Rising, he slung off his pack and set it down firmly but gently upon the bough-covered snow of the clearing. "Kelet, you and I have much to talk about, for I have come to you through a forest filled with danger and rife with portents that even now I tremble to think of. But first, for Mowea'qua, among the many gifts I bring to you both, a special gift. A long-promised gift! Here, girl, come! Stand close as I loosen the ties that bind this roll of caribou skins. Just before entering the clearing I paused a moment to wrap it up for you, as all worthy presents should be wrapped. So here, child, behold! Look now upon your gift from the forest!"

This said, he knelt, ceremoniously loosened the thong ties, then rolled out the caribou skins and lifted by the scruff of the neck the captive boy. Dangling from the giant's hand, the child took one look at Ne'gauni and then at the bearded hag and began to screech and flail in terror until Kinap quickly bound him up in the caribou skins again.

"Is that a lynx or a boy you have brought us? An *Enemy* boy!" exclaimed Old One, aghast.

Ne'gauni could not help but notice that the old hag regarded the child with the same measure of contempt with which she regarded *him*. He did not know why he should find this gratifying, but he did.

"In time he will calm down," Kinap assured them, stroking the caribou skins and the boy within as he might have done to soothe a captive animal. "I explained to him where I was taking him, but I doubt that he could imagine, much less believe. Do not be offended, Kelet. He has never before seen a bearded woman . . . although he has seen much worse."

"I do not want him!" declared Mowea'qua. "He is not what you promised! He is not a mikahmuwesu!"

"Mmph!" Old One was shaking her head. "As though she could tell! And now not one, but two Strangers have I in my den! See you where your tales have us gotten, my old friend. Every word has our young one believed, every word, say I!"

Kinap was very still. "We cannot always have what we want, child."

"I am not a child!" Mowea'qua pouted.

"Nor will this boy be a boy forever," said the giant. "And there may be a little of the blood of the Old Tribe in him. It is hard to say these days, but there was one who was sure of it."

"Mmph! He is as much a Stranger as the wounded one, Kinap!" Old One was openly distraught. "Have you forgotten our blood? That we are forever Enemy to his kind and he to ours?"

"His kind! Our kind!" The giant was clearly angry. "Here in this dark forest, Kelet, what does it matter? The girl must have someone of her own, someone to care for and be cared for by when—"

"No! Hear it I will not!" Mowea'qua was shaking her head. Her mouth was pressed so tightly against her teeth that her lips had gone white. Tears brimmed in her eyes. "Always will Old One be here! Always will Kinap come to winter in the forest! And want I do not this gift from the forest that he has brought to me! I have found my mikahmuwesu! No other will I have."

The old hag rolled her eyes, straining for patience as she gestured toward Ne'gauni. "This torn and broken thing is what she believes by magic you have wished for her . . . this sharp-tongued, scar-faced, one-legged—"

"Not *him!*" Now it was Mowea'qua who rolled her eyes and snorted contempt. "It is the other I will have! The *beautiful* one. The one called M'alsum! The one Kinap has said is called Wolf in the tongue of his people, as Wolf am I called in the tongue of mine! Of a kind are we, he and I! Knew I this the moment his face I saw when came he driving his dogs fast above my hiding place in the snow. He is the one I will have. The *only* one! Work for me your magic, Kinap! Go we will to the sacred spring. Make will you the wounded one's leg grow back. Together will we go the Dawnland. M'alsum will at Mowea'qua look and forever love the one who back to him brings from the country of the dead a wounded one who will hold out his hands and name him Brother!"

Ne'gauni saw a look of amazement cross the old hag's face as surely as he felt a similar expression expand across his own. He had heard Mowea'qua make the pronouncement before, in soft whispers, but only, he thought, in his dreams. It was difficult to believe that she truly meant what she was saying. He felt a little sorry for her when he said, not unkindly, "There is no magic in this world that can make my leg grow back. And my brother could ever love a strange and ugly thing like Mowea'qua! Have you not heard the giant say that my brother has a wife? The Dawnland woman is alive! In all of this world and the world beyond there is none to equal Hasu'u."

"Then dead do I wish her!" cried Mowea'qua. "May her captors eat her and throw her bones away across the world so you and he can never find them! *Never!*" With that she was gone, off into the den in a squall of sobs.

Ne'gauni saw the giant and the old hag exchange meaningful glances.

"Know her not do I these days," said Old One, clucking her tongue and shaking her head.

"She is a woman waiting to happen," observed the giant with a bitterly nostalgic sigh. "And it seems that she has felt the pain of love and of wanting that which, in her heart, she knows can never be."

Ne'gauni was startled to hear himself harrumph in the way of the old woman. Angrily he blurted to the giant, "Use your 'magic' to make my leg grow back, Kinap, and I will ram it down that girl's ugly throat and choke her with it so she will never know the pain of anything ever again!"

The giant fixed the youth with lancet-sharp eyes. "How can such as you find her ugly?"

Ne'gauni shrank back. A shudder ripped through him. The man's question had pinioned a truth he had almost forgotten. Remembering his maimed face and mutilated form, he hated the girl all the more. "For what she has done to me and for what she has just wished upon the Dawnland woman she will always be ugly in my eyes!"

"She has worked with Kelet to save your life," the giant reminded him. "Never forget that, Wounded One, and do not hurt her again in my presence, or I will see to it that whatever pain she feels at the sting of your words you will in your own flesh feel twice!"

"Your presence?" Old One exhaled a long and mournful sigh of resignation. "And just how long with us will you be this time, my dear one, before your way you go again? I have the winter spent preparing many healing things for you to take back through the forest to those you deem worthy of the magic of the Old Tribe. Turtle shells, dried salamanders, bats and frogs and fungi and many good things. Although why our kind should care about the welfare of Strangers remains to me a puzzlement, and why insist you on returning to them, never will I understand."

The giant started to speak, thought better of whatever he was going to say, then smiled sadly as he continued to stroke the caribou skins within which the fractious boy now lay still, murmuring wordless but dwindling defiance. "There are some, the children among them, who have touched my heart. Too much, think I!" Kinap said. "But in truth, dear friend, I have seen too much of the world beyond this forest . . . too much of Man . . . too much of Change . . . and far too much of Death."

He paused and shook his head as though to clear it of a nightmare. "Too many lies have I been forced to tell in order to survive among Strangers! And too many lies have I suffered in silence as I have made my way home to you!"

Ne'gauni frowned, startled, as the giant rose in a sudden towering sweep and all the strange and disturbingly grotesque amulets and fetishes at his belt jangled and clicked and swayed as though in a passing windstorm.

"I am weary, Kelet," said the giant, his scarred face working with emotion. "I have come far through a forest that is no longer what it once was to us, no longer a refuge, no longer a shadowed haven in which I dared leave you and Mowea'qua for long moons alone. Strangers cross our old hunting trails at will! Snow stays too long upon the land! And everywhere the great trees are dying! The world is changing around us, Kelet. Everywhere. Everything! Even the People are changing. In little ways. In subtle ways, crueler ways, think I, and yet there are good hearts among them. Truly so! Ah, I do not pretend to understand it. Nor can I make peace with it even though I risked much to make a forbidden pilgrimage alone across the Dawnland ice to seek the counsel of a shaman on a sacred isle. It was said that he is the wisest and most powerful of all men, but in truth he is old and nearly blind and, in his very weakness, gave me the answers I sought, for what I found on that island awakened old nightmares and further set my heart to stone against the world. And so I tell you, dear one, that I have come home to stay. I will not leave you unprotected in this forest again. But if our Mowea'qua is to have a future worth living for, you must open your heart to the 'gift' I have brought to you. Use your healing skills to give to him the gift of speech, for although he is a Stranger born, truly he is more than he seems and with a little kindness and affection may grow to be a man of great worth to us in this dangerous and changing world."

"Mmph! Your words send shivers up the hairs on my spine, old friend! A Stranger for our Mowea'qua? Too long have you been among our enemies, Kinap! Too long, say I! And what about him, the wounded one? How do we keep him from hopping off with Mowea'qua and the boy to seek his brother and betray us to our enemies?"

Again Ne'gauni shrank back. The hag and the giant were staring at him, so fixedly that he felt skewered.

"I can blind them both now," said Old One. "It was what I planned for the wounded one before you came."

Ne'gauni was so stunned that he could not speak. She would do it! He knew without the slightest doubt that she would *enjoy* doing it!

"No. There is another way." The giant knelt again and, leaning toward Ne'gauni, said coldly, "Look at my face, Wounded One. Look long and hard at Kinap . . . and see a reflection of what your people will see when they look at you if ever you return to them! Your scarring may not be as impressive as mine, but believe me when I say that it is ugly enough to make your mother weep and your father mourn! Would you inflict such pain upon them, to allow them to see what you have become? Mmph! Youths who were once your hunt brothers will cringe at the sight of you, as you are now cringing at the sight of me. And although your scar will not be quite so 'lovely' as mine, I have two strong legs to carry my ugliness boldly wherever I dare! None have ever been foolish enough to laugh at Kinap! But children will taunt He Walks Ahead on One Leg and try to trip you so they can mock you when you fall! Elders will pity you and welcome you to the fires of the old and infirm! And no woman will have you, not a one-legged man who cannot hunt for himself, much less provide for a family! But a life you can have, Stranger, with Kelet and Mowea'qua and Kinap and the boy here, for although there is no magic that will restore your face or limb or shattered dreams, I can teach you the use of a weapon that will make you the equal of any two-legged man when it comes to protecting the family that you will have made within this forest. And though you may never see your people again, you will be able to take comfort in the knowledge that those who love you will never be brought to grief by the sight of what has become of you. And you can rejoice in this: One of your brothers survived the attack of the masked ones. M'alsum lives. He will seek the Dawnland woman. If any man can bring her back from captivity, he will be the one to do so, for I fear that your brother has slain the last great mammoth in this forest. And even as our lives must now fade away within our changing world, M'alsum may find that his own has only just begun."

Chapter Three

▼▼▼▼▼▼▼

He returned to them with the sun, on the day the seals appeared at long last in the newly opened leads in the ice-choked bay.

They named him Manitou.

Bringer of Meat!

Mammoth Slayer!

One Who Brings Good Things to the People!

All along the coast word went out that the great mammoth, Katcheetohúskw, had been slain and now walked among the Dawnland People reborn in the flesh of the man who had fulfilled the ancient legend by drinking the blood and eating the flesh of the Great Beast, Life Giver.

"M'alsum has returned!" they cried. Although all mourned the death of a daughter and grandchild of Ogeh'ma, it was as M'alsum remembered: Hasu'u's people wept easily and just as easily set aside their tears. Even as the lamentations and fasting went on, they ogled his bison hide and heavily laden sled and marveled at the hairy tail and nostriled fifth leg of Katcheetohúskw, and at the man who might now prove to be an immortal. Upon every headland and in every winter-lean encampment within every sheltered cove, the Dawnland people whispered in awe of the returning trader who had come to them with the sun and the seals. And everywhere the wondrous story that M'alsum, only surviving son of Asticou, hunt chief of the far inland forests, had told to Ogeh'ma and his people on the day he was at last reunited with Hasu'u's Dawnland band was repeated again and again for the edification of all.

A tale of his suffering at the murderous hands of the cannibal manitous who had fallen upon his trading band in the haunted forest.

"Ah!" murmured the old women. "Few have ever suffered as M'alsum has suffered!"

A tale of his heroic attempts to save his woman and child, his brothers and burden woman and dogs from phantoms who, in the end, devoured them all before his eyes even as the Great Beast came through the haunted woodlands to destroy him.

"Ah!" exclaimed the grandfathers. "Who among us would have dared to stand to such enemies?"

A tale of his transcendent bravery in the face of the Great Beast and of how, unafraid, he had slain Katcheetohúskw with a single thrust of his father's magic copper-headed spear, the broken head of which he now wore attached to a thong looped around his neck as a shining talisman and memento of his moment of glory.

"Ah!" sighed the hunters. "Who among us would not have turned and tried to run away!"

As if all this had not been enough to spellbind his listeners, M'alsum had finished off his tale with an account of his long, perilous, utterly selfless and solitary journey through the haunted forest—not back to his own inland tribe but to the people of his beloved woman and child so that he might bring to them, above all others, the gifts of power that had been bestowed upon him when the Great Beast consented to die at his hand.

"Ah!" whispered the children. "Who among us would have dared to make such a journey alone!"

"Mmph!" brazened M'alsum, only momentarily taken aback by his unintended use of Kinap's favorite exclamation. "I have dared! I have eaten of the heart of the Great Beast! Behold! I fear nothing! And as proof of my word, I bring before you the tail and fifth leg of Katcheetohúskw! Who among you has ever seen such wondrous and terrifying things?"

No one.

The bold lies and grandiose embellishments of the truth that underlay each word had been so thick and slickly laid that, looking back, M'alsum wondered how his tongue had not slipped on them, run back down his throat, and gagged him on his own audacity. But not one of his fables had stuck in a single throat other than his own. So, although the tail and grotesquely nostriled trunk of the dead mammoth had begun to smell even though he had slit both down their backs and defleshed them as best he could, he made a point of displaying them whenever he went among the Dawnland people. He wore the tail as though the appendage were his own, looped to his belt by a braid of its own hair. Of the trunk he fashioned a massive and impressive adornment and wore it, along with the copper spearhead, as a breastplate over the new hunting shirt that Hasu'u's mother had given him, a shirt pieced from the prime white belly skins of winter-killed caribou and sewn for him in the long, dark, storm-riven days of the past winter when she had hoped that the eldest son of Asticou might yet return to her people as he had promised, bringing her daughter, Hasu'u, home to the loving embrace of her parents and band once more.

Each night, alone in the little tent-lodge that Ogeh'ma's people raised for him so that he could mourn his woman, child, and brothers in solitude, he raised a small fire and worked to remove the stink from the mammoth trunk and tail. He rubbed both with ashes, smoking them as best he could over a frame contrived of his crossed lances. Gradually both began to cure and lose their stink, and while he feigned grief with much loud sighing and occasional dolorous moans, he contemplated his good fortune as he thought of the plump, pretty, unmarried daughters of Ogch'ma and Scgub'un and wondered how long he must wait before the time would be appropriate to express his need to come into a woman once again. It had not been necessary to wait long at all.

"It is not good for a mourning man to be without a woman," Ogeh'ma told him. "Generous have you been with us, husband of my slain daughter. You honor her memory. Now honor her people by choosing from among our women one or more who will distract you from your grief. There is not a man here who would not be proud to know that Mammoth Slayer has come into his woman!"

Such generosity! Such inestimable kindness! How could he refuse? He could not. He did not. The women he selected came flushed with pride to his lodge eager to peel up their tunics like fat little rabbits skinning themselves for his pleasure. And each morning when he emerged, sated and refreshed, he was greeted with much enthusiasm by all.

"Behold!"

"He comes forth!"

"M'alsum, Mammoth Slayer, Bringer of Good Things to the People, dwells among us!"

The unmarried daughters of Ogeh'ma—Chi'co'pee and Ane'pemin'an and Nee'nah—rejoiced at the sight of him and, each openly courting him as an all-the-time man, vied with one another to win his favor in countless little ways, bringing him offerings of food and drink and small trinkets of adoration: a sealskin band studded with seal teeth, this for him to sew into his hood to bring luck when sealing; the fine white pelt of an ermine, complete with head and black-tipped tail and sunken eyes jeweled with beads of painted stone, this to be stitched onto the back of his traveling coat so that on future journeys he would be as fleet and clever and successful a hunter as the ermine; the head of a tern and the claw of a black bear, both to be sewn into his inner hunting shirt so that under the Spearfish Moon he would find only the best places along the river in which to net and spear salmon, the best fish of all.

Already Ogeh'ma had sent runners to neighboring bands to announce the return of the seals. The winter camp on the bluffs was growing day by day. Hunters were out on the ice braining seals, especially the first of the white seal pups that were being born on the breaking floes, to be food for the People. Ravens, hawks, white-headed eagles, and seabirds of all kinds were gathering along the shore by night and winging overhead in the misted skies by day, impatient and ever ready to share in the leavings of the hunt.

Everywhere M'alsum went within the encampment, at Ogeh'ma's insistence relaxing and recuperating from his horrific ordeal, women would look up smiling from their communal butchering, and men and children would thank and praise him for using his manitou powers to remind the ice to open and allow seals to swim up through the leads.

"There was so much ice we thought they would not come to us this year!" said one.

"The grandfathers and grandmothers were reminding Ogeh'ma that we must be ever ready to move on in changing times," revealed another, "for in the days of their youth ice was rarely seen in this bay. The mother seals who bear the white pups did not whelp this far south, and no seals of any kind were taken here in numbers big enough to justify making a camp in this place before the time of the Spearfish Moon."

And yet another said, "There was talk of gathering many gifts and sending an emissary across the ice to Squam on the sacred island to ask him if, with his shaman's eye that sees through the power of the sacred stone, he had seen into the heart of the forces of Creation and determined why they were confused. But Squam no longer seems able to see with spirit eyes. So why waste meat and women when we can remain just as confused without his magic!"

"Be careful of what you say of shamans, Ko'ram—one never knows what their spirit ears can hear! But in truth, M'alsum, Ogeh'ma was ready to pack us all inland to seek sign of moose and deer, for surely we were beginning to grow hungry before you came and told the ice that it was long past time to open and allow the seals to swim up through the leads!"

"Grateful are we, Mammoth Slayer, for we know that you could have returned to your own people and shared your magic with them instead of us!"

"It is so," he assured them.

"The space in your heart for our hunt chief's daughter must have been great indeed for you to have chosen her people over your own! If only the Great Beast had fallen upon you and allowed you to slay it with your father's magic spear before the cannibal manitous attacked your trading band, you could have used your manitou powers to repel the deadly flying sticks of your enemies . . . and ours! And then your brothers, burden woman, and the daughter of Ogeh'ma would still be alive to speak out in affirmation of your brave and selfless heart!"

"It was not to be," he had replied emphatically, defensively, looking around to see who had spoken, for the voice had come from within a small crowd of recently arrived, ornately clothed, spear-carrying travelers who were only now unpacking their sledges at the fringes of the ice-locked cove. And the voice had come from the mouth of a woman.

"Ah!" exclaimed Ko'ram. He was obviously startled by the presence of the one who had spoken, for when next he spoke, his tone was nervous, tightly strung. "How fortunate we are, Puwo'win, to have you among us again! And M'alsum, too! Both of you on the same beach under the same sun! No wonder the seals have returned! Come, Woman of Squam, behold Mammoth Slayer, and see how generously he has come to share with the members of the Council of Many the magic hairs that he has plucked from the sacred tail of Life Giver! We must be grateful and not offend with questions One Who Brings Good Things to the People!"

"Offend? I?" Again the female voice. Low. Slow. Mellifluous. Mocking. "Why, Ko'ram, old man, I am certain that in the waning wisdom of your years you have no wish to insult my dignity or impugn the unending grace and generosity of Squam, especially not in the presence of one who claims to have slain Katcheetohúskw, banished winter, and brought the seals to be meat for the people!"

"Claims?" M'alsum could still taste the anger he had felt as he turned the word. He bristled against the obvious challenge. Until that moment the accolades he had been receiving had been more nourishing than meat, and his mood had been as benign as the moment.

Then Puwo'win stepped through the crowd. It was as though the wing of some great dark bird had passed before the sun to shadow the earth below. And somehow, in the midst of the shadow, Puwo'win had become the sun. A white sun. Her face was fleshless, glaring, a thing of polished bone, the eyes hollow, a skull's eyes, the lipless mouth drawn wide and the teeth showing in a span consisting entirely of canines. M'alsum caught his breath. Stunned. Until she drew the bone-and-ivory mask away. Not since he had looked for the first time upon the Lakeland Firefly in the distant hunting grounds of Chief Sebec of the Copper People had the firstborn son of Asticou felt his senses so shaken and his spirit so touched by a female other than his mother.

The power of Puwo'win—woman of the great and eternal shaman Squam of the sacred island—was legendary. No man journeyed to the sacred island unless invited by emissaries carrying her mask and staff of rank. No man looked upon the face of Squam without her permission, and so rarely did either the shaman or his magic woman come among the People to demand tribute and slaves that when M'alsum had first traded among the Dawnland people, he had come to assume that all he heard about the pair of wizards was spun of the same fibers as the legends of the great mammoth.

But the woman who came toward him was of flesh and blood, and his reaction to her was no boyish enthrallment. It was as though ice water had been thrown against his suddenly fevered flesh. As though a braining club had been brought hard against his skull. As though a burning brand had set fire to his loins and enflamed his soul.

The crowd parted before her as reeds bending back from the hand of an unseen reaper. When she paused in front of M'alsum and looked him straight in his eyes, it was as though the sun itself had positioned itself before him— daring him to refute the absolute power of its presence.

A cold sun.

An aging and dangerous sun.

A sun as tall as he, and as good to look upon, Puwo'win stood as straight and strong as the antlered, mask-topped staff of shamanic rank she carried and—with her long, shell-festooned hair as gray as sea rime and her tattooed face painted bloodred with sacred ochre—spoke in a voice that had none of the warmth of the sun. It was as a wind murmuring amidst icy caverns beneath the sea, hushed, cold, yet as powerful and redolent of warning as the voice of the sea itself might have been had it a tongue with which to speak.

"Mammoth Slayer?" Her painted eyelids narrowed as the eyes within fastened on his mammoth-trunk breast-plate and the gleaming copper spearhead that hung as an amulet from around his neck. "Word of you seeps up and down the coast with the coming and going of the tide, word of the one who claims to have slain Katcheetohúskw with a magic spear and has managed to make his way alone through the forest to the Dawnland with gifts and magic for the People in these dark times of raiding manitous and endless winter."

"I claim nothing," M'alsum had replied, knowing in-stinctively that if his lies failed to stand to the questing surge of her queries, all his hard-won, newly acquired status would be swept away. "All that you have heard is so!"

"He is the one who has brought the sun!" declared Kanio'te, eldest son of Ogeh'ma.

"And the seals and a sled laden with many gifts, gray-headed stone spearheads from the far northern quarries, and ducksuckles from the more southerly forests for the children and elders!" added Onen'ia, Ogeh'ma's second son, with great enthusiasm.

Puwo'win quashed it in an instant. "He has also parted the leads so that it will not be easy for me to return across the ice to Squam on the sacred island."

There was silence at that, until Ogeh'ma spoke out.

"I do not know why you have chosen to favor us with your presence after all these many long, cold moons, Woman of Squam, unless you have come to seek tribute for the great shaman in the fresh red meat of seals—and this you shall have, of course, even though another's magic has secured this meat—but the leads are yet narrow, and if you return soon and quickly across the shallows of the bay, your journey back to the sacred island should be smooth and nearly unbroken. If not, my hunters will be honored to drag out one of the larger dugouts and row you safely and quickly home."

Puwo'win's eyes had gone as hard and sharp as stone awls. The bandy-legged little hunt chief's suggestion, although offered in a manner so deferential as to be obsequious, had been a clear invitation to take what she would have and go on her way back to her island and leave him and his people alone.

A murmuring had gone through the crowd assembled on the beach.

"I will have what I will have and I will return to the

sacred island when I choose and not before," Puwo'win informed the hunt chief with a cold dismissiveness that should have served Ogeh'ma as a warning but did not. "I have come to your miserable encampment to speak to the one who claims to have come alone from the forest strong in the power of Katcheetohúskw." Her eyes had returned to M'alsum's breastplate and copper spearhead. "You killed the Great Beast with copper?"

"With a single strike to its manitou eye!" he lied boldly, without hesitation. He was so good at it now that he almost believed his own words.

"And that dark, shaggy thing you wear across your chest and hanging downward to your feet is the legendary facial appendage of the Great Beast?"

"It is!"

"And yet the legends do tell of a white mammoth."

M'alsum did not even blink. "As the legends of Squam and Puwo'win tell of shamans who are eternally *young!*"

Had he struck her across her extraordinary face, the woman's reaction could not have been stronger, or more guarded: a tensing of body, a whitening of knuckles, a tightening of mouth and brow.

Their eyes met. Held. And in that moment M'alsum had known that she would never again underestimate him. He had found the weakness in her, her pride, her woman's pride. And yet, wishing to ally himself to the power that she held in the eyes and minds of others, he salved the wound that he had made to her arrogance. "The seasons must turn as the great Circle of Life must turn, ever forward, never back, one moon following another, winter into spring, spring into summer, summer into fall, and fall into winter again. Yet, as Puwo'win's magic keeps her ever young and beautiful to the eyes of all who behold her, so

the Great Beast has worked a magic of his own! Like the
ermine, he has changed his coat at winter's end so that he
might wander through the snowy forest deeps unseen. But I
have seen him. I have slain him with the magic copper
spearhead of my father, Asticou, hunt chief of the far inland forest. I have survived the wrath of Gaoh, Master of
the Winds, and of Windigo, Great Ghost Cannibal chief of
the manitous, to come at last to share all that I may own
with the Dawnland people of my slain woman and of the
grandmothers of my mother's tribe."

"And as you have been slaying and surviving and making your way through the haunted forest deeps, have you
seen a giant and a small boy?"

Taken aback, M'alsum hesitated, but only for a scant
second, before realizing, from the fixed intensity of
Puwo'win's tone, that he must secure this one small lie lest
all the other larger, more important falsehoods also come
into question. "I have told you. I have come through the
forest alone. I have seen no one!"

"Pity. The boy I seek is my son. The only son of Squam.
I and those loyal to me have been searching for him and
the scar-headed monstrosity who stole him from me. He
has taken something of greater value than he knows! I offer
much in the way of meat and hides and magic to anyone
who finds the boy . . . and brings me the head of the
giant to prove that he has paid for the seriousness of his
offense to Squam."

M'alsum almost laughed out loud. So this was the giant's secret! He was a storyteller, all right! A liar! And a
thief! No wonder the boy hated him. The man was not his
father; he was his abductor! This was why Kinap had insisted on building no fire in their final encampment. The
giant had known that he was being hunted. M'alsum's re-

spect for the man increased a thousandfold, then collapsed
entirely as he realized that Kinap had risked himself and
his enterprise in order to help a stranger mourn his dead,
drag his goods, and show him the way to the Dawnland.
Only a fool would have been so generous or have imagined
that the risk to himself could possibly be worth any gain
the boy would bring if sold off as a drudge to some far-flung
band!

His brow furrowed as he met Puwo'win's gaze. Her eyes
were like dark, surf-washed stones glinting on the beach at
dawn. He doubted that any man would ever come out well
in any bargain struck with this one. "I need nothing from
you, Puwo'win, nothing that I, as Mammoth Slayer, do not
already possess," he told her.

"No?" Her question had been one of pure provocation
as her eyes conveyed to him what her mouth had no need
to express. *You do not possess me . . . yet!*

Raising her staff and gesturing forward what could only
be described as a spear-armed bodyguard of grotesquely
masked men attired in the finest furs, she announced, "I
will stay and share the meat of seals with the people of
Ogeh'ma this night. To do otherwise would be a statement
of ingratitude to the spirit powers of the sea. We will raise
the feast tent! We will feast and sing and dance in celebration for many days. For truly, Ogeh'ma, the forces of Creation have brought this M'alsum—this Mammoth Slayer,
this Caller of the Sun, this Banisher of Winter, this Bringer
of Seals—back alone to the Dawnland through the dark
and haunted forests to be hunt chief over your people and,
perhaps, over us all!"

Ogeh'ma had not flinched at her open refutation of his
authority, nor had he paled or shown offense when his
people cheered the woman's words. Ogeh'ma had smiled.

He was a man well past his prime, and although his wisdom had combined with the strengths and skills of his sons and bandsmen to maintain his people at more than a modicum of prosperity for many years, he apparently felt no compunction to speak out in defense of his reputation or to credit himself for a lifetime of successes. Nodding amiably to Puwo'win, he had simply shrugged his shoulders and announced to her and to all within hearing that the forces of Creation were ultimately responsible for all things. A fat camp or a lean camp, a long winter or a short one, ice in the bay or no ice in the bay, whales in the cove or salmon in the estuary, a lost son or a found son, one headman or another—all were the same in their compassionate, and compassionless, eyes.

M'alsum shivered with elation whenever he recalled the moment. Never had he imagined that his ascent to power and authority within the Dawnland would have been so easy!

Only a double hand-count of days had passed since he had come through the forest to the coast, still dragging his sled, cursing its weight and blessing his ability to maneuver it even though it raised welts on his shoulders and caused his forehead to bleed beneath the stress of his browband. As Kinap had foretold, by sundown of the day of their parting, he had stumbled out of the woods gasping and bleary-eyed with fatigue. He had raised a driftwood fire upon the shore and collapsed in a seated position close to its warmth, knees to chest, too tired to eat, huddled in his furs, staring out to sea, breathing in the cold salt smell of it, listening to the soothing suck and sigh of the waves and the crackling of ice breaking up on the rocks. Eyeing the shoreline, he had watched the dark come down, and by the time night engulfed the world, he had known by the lay of familiar promontories and the shape of offshore islands that the giant had again been right. Another day's walk up the coast and he would be in the hunting grounds of Hasu'u's band.

Another day!

He had not been sure that he could drag his sled another pace, much less the untold number of paces that would bring him within hailing distance of Ogeh'ma's camp. Exhausted, he had tented up his furs around himself and, with his stone-headed spears close by, put his head down on his folded forearms and slept.

With the sea before him, the forest at his back at last, and the open sky above his head, for the first time since he had turned his back on his woman and slain his brothers, M'alsum had not dreamed of ghosts.

He dreamed, instead, of Hasu'u, of small, pretty, trusting little Hasu'u, alive out there within the blackness of the forest deeps, far away, a slave now, lying beneath the bed furs of another man, suckling a stranger's child, opening her thighs to the press of another man's need, no longer singing her light, endless little songs but crying softly, wondering when he would come for her . . . if he would come for her . . . or if he was even still alive to think of her at all.

Mmph! he had thought in his dreams, echoing, as he often did these days and nights, the speech pattern of the giant. *It is all her fault. She should not have fallen behind. I am M'alsum, the best and boldest and bravest of the sons of Asticou, and now that I am his only son, I have better things to do with my time than waste it worrying over a woman . . . any woman.*

Guilt had pricked him in his sleep. His dreams shifted away from it, drifted off through long tides of surging, whispering darkness until he saw his mother, frail and growing old now within the dark and distant forest deeps.

"Never doubt the way of my heart for you, M'alsum, my firstborn, my own little wolf, my brave warrior, my protector, chief and guardian of my little pack! You are the one who will take me back to the Grassland of my people someday . . . or to the Dawnland of my grandmothers. You will do this, M'alsum! For that day only do I live."

His mouth turned down. He had not protected her little pack; he had slain her other sons to a man! What would she say to that? She need never know; he need never tell her the truth. And yet, perhaps, even if he did, he wondered if she would not understand and even approve.

"Your brothers have been born of my body, but you are of my heart, the center of my life, conceived in the last moments of my happiness! Never forget this. Never!"

How could he forget? She had pounded the words into his head again and again, as surely as she pounded tough meat into tenderness, using words and loving embraces in place of pounding stones to pulverize his spirit into submission to her will.

Still again the dream had shifted, the darkness thinned, the colors of a red aurora swam beneath his lids, and for a while he was a boy again, walking with his father in the dark forest beneath the light of the Great Sky River, ignoring Meya'kwé's cries of doom, listening as Asticou pointed skyward and told him not to be afraid, for the Ancestors were afoot, using the stars as stepping stones across the sky as they held their torches high to give light and assurance to the People in the world below.

He had scowled in his sleep, remembering that Asticou always saw light and hope where Meya'kwé saw doom and darkness. And as he had thought these thoughts, his dreams had shifted yet again, and he had seen himself running along the edge of the Circle of Life as it turned beneath his feet. Fast and far he ran, with the Circle turning, turning, forward . . . never back . . . never back!

His mother was old. She might even be dead by now. If he was here, far from the forests they both so loathed, safe once more beneath the open sky on the shores of the Dawnland of Meya'kwé's grandmothers, it was not his fault that she was not at his side! She was the source of his initial inspiration to turn his back on Asticou and journey away to a new life with northbound traders. He had asked her to go with him. He had begged her to go with him. But Meya'kwé had chosen to stay behind. "Asticou would surely follow me and force us both to return into the darkness of the trees. I dare not walk with you, my son. So go!" she had insisted. "Go now! And quickly! When you have made a new life and assured a place of honor for me in the country of our ancestors, come back for me, my wolf. For that day only will I live!"

So he had gone with the northbound traders. He had not had the heart to bruise her already savaged pride by telling her that his father would not come for her any more than he would pursue a despised son—not for an aging wife, not for Meya'kwé who saw into the heart of his weakness and held him in open contempt, not when Asticou had the Lakeland Firefly to warm his bed furs and eagerly and expertly maintain the hard, hot fire of aging manhood. Not when he had Ne'gauni to eclipse all his other sons in his eyes! And when M'alsum had at last returned with his Dawnland bride into the forest in the company of other traders, bringing gifts and tales of high adventure, he had returned for Meya'kwé, to restore her pride by proving to his father that he had found success, a wife who was more than an adequate replacement for the Lakeland Firefly, and that—despite Ne'gauni and whatever small affection the aging hunt chief might have felt for Sac and M'ingwé— M'alsum, as his firstborn, as Meya'kwé's pride, was still the boldest and bravest and best of his sons.

Asticou had not been impressed. He was happy in his forest. He was content with his unambitious people and his mindless Lakeland Firefly, and he remained obsessed with adoration for the obnoxious son she had borne him. And so M'alsum had conspired with his mother and brothers to take that son away, to sell him into slavery in the Dawnland, to build new lives on the profits they would make from their half brother and all that Asticou had entrusted to them to trade in his name. What a joke it would have been! If only Meya'kwé had not changed her mind at the last moment! If only she had trusted him to take care of her on the long journey ahead! Old and weak as she claimed to be, she should still have been willing to risk leaving his father's village for a new life with him.

I have led a great mammoth to its death. I have come through the haunted forest to the Dawnland at last. Is my life never to be my own? Is it always to be hers? I have slain the sons of Asticou. All of them! Why return to punish my father and his Lakeland bitch with death? Better to let them wait for the return of their precious son! Let the days and nights and seasons slip away, and as the women of Sac and M'ingwé mourn for their lost men, as Asticou grows ever older, let him fear for them. Let him wonder if they are dead, or, better yet, let him go to his death believing that they have all forgotten him! As it is time for me to forget my mother! Why should I risk myself again when she may well be dead and gone from my life forever? And as for Wawautaésie, let her live out her days a widow longing for her lost son and all the fine gifts from the

Dawnland that might have been hers had she only said yes to me and not been loyal to my father!

The dreams were sweet, so sweet.

And yet, sometime just before dawn, M'alsum had been awakened by the trumpeting of a mammoth. A white mammoth. His gut tightened. If that one came for him from the realm of legend and nightmare, would he have the courage to face it and slay it before its manitou presence refuted the charade with which he planned to win his way among the Dawnland People? Yes! What he had done once he would do again! Still, facing down one charging mammoth in a lifetime seemed enough for even the boldest and bravest and best of the sons of Asticou. He sat rigid, spears at the ready, looking around, only gradually relaxing and naming himself Fool. There was nothing in the night to challenge him.

Nothing.

Unless he considered the future and his own yearning to have everything go his way in the days and nights to come.

He tried to sleep again, and succeeded, but only for a little while. The deep, restless suck and pull of the tide moving beneath the ice of the bay brought Meya'kwé's voice whispering to him again.

"Come back for me, my wolf. For that day only will I live!"

Suddenly as restless and ill at ease as the tide, he came up groggy from unwelcome dreams and resettled himself within his furs. Lights were flickering far out across the ice of the bay. An encampment coming to life on a distant island? Travelers crossing the ice from one headland to another? He could not be sure. Seabirds called. A dog barked. Or was it a seal? Far away. Very far. Dawnland sounds. He threw more driftwood onto his fire and stared ahead with his spears at the ready.

Working his shoulders to get the blood flowing in his stiff and aching muscles, he thought of the giant and smiled, wondering if Kinap and the little bog rat had availed themselves of the gift of death that he had given them.

Soon!

"If only I could be there to see it!"

At first light he saw something else.

A small group of men, quiet as the dawn, sent out of Ogeh'ma's up-coast encampment. They had seen his fire from afar and, while he slept, ventured southward, traveling most of the night until, in the cold gray damp of morning, they crouched on the headlands, watching him, waiting for him to wake and rise and show his face so they could be sure, in these troubled times, if he was Friend or Enemy.

M'alsum rose.

He showed his face.

And still they did not know.

Chapter Four

▼▼▼▼▼▼▼

There was a singing in the forest.

With Kinap home to stay, it was Old One singing, a secret singing, one she was determined to offer to the spirits and savor alone.

And so she came from the den to the sacred grove. She came by herself in the depth of night, unafraid, walking in the bright pathway shed by the moon, cherishing her knowledge of the giant's permanent homecoming. It was too wondrous a knowing to keep silent in her heart.

There was suddenly so much to be grateful for. True enough, she had been saddened to learn that yet another mammoth had died in their forest, but she could not believe that it was Katcheetohúskw. As she had reminded Kinap, the world had been changing for many a long winter, and there had always been danger in it for her and her kind. No matter how he brooded over the death of the old tusker, he had to admit that its coat had been as shaggy and red-brown as the bark of an old cedar, and not as sweet of smell. It had not, as in all the legends of the Ancient Ones, been a white mammoth. And if, in fact, it was the same Great One that she and the girl had seen wintering in the forest before, it was old and sick and no doubt aching of tooth and bone, for all too often she and Mowea'qua had been saddened to hear its pained huffs and groanings as it made its solitary way through the forest. It had been time for that mammoth to die.

As now it was time for Kelet to begin to live again.

And so she sang as she came into the grove.

She filled the night with her singing, refusing to shadow the moonlit darkness with worry over the two sullen Strangers who now slept in her den. Kinap was keeping a close eye on them both, and if he wanted them at his side—if, in his wisdom, he could accept their kind as family—she would not question his judgment. Not now, not ever again. He was, after all, Mowea'qua's father. And for all his propensity for telling tall tales to cheer the girl and an old woman on long winter nights, he had been proved right in his assessments of life all too many times. The bedraggled, speechless little foundling was responding, albeit slowly and suspiciously, to care and kindness.

And Kinap had certainly been proved right about the girl. Mowea'qua had not been destined to remain a child forever.

She had become a woman overnight.

A few days of glum mood and headache, a tender soreness about the chest, a pain in the lower belly and back, and then, only this morning, a scream of terror.

"Grandmother! Kinap! Forever say good-bye! Ah, Wounded One, never will your beautiful brother I see again! Die must I! Blood from me comes! Soon alive will I be no more!"

"What is this?" Kinap had rushed to the girl, then hugged her close. "Die you will not this morning, Mowea'qua! But right you are about one thing. A child you are no longer! Kelet, can it be possible that you have not explained to her about a woman's moon blood?"

"Ah, say I, Kinap, why burden a child with such things?"

"Silly old woman! As though you could stop the great Circle from turning! Or would want to!"

Old One sighed and smiled, for even now Mowea'qua glumly sat out her first days and nights of menstruation in the little den of honoring that the giant had raised for her so that she could keep herself apart during this most private of times.

"Gifts you shall have to celebrate this occasion!" he had told her.

And the wounded one, scowling, had asked why, for according to the tradition of his Ancestors the girl should be putting ashes beneath her eyes as a mark of her uncleanliness and keeping herself hidden from the sun and moon and stars lest her presence offend the very forces of Creation.

"You must eat no food. Drink no water. Sew no seam. Make no meat. You must turn down your eyes and look at no living things, for everyone knows that woman power is great at this time. Bad power! Stones will crack open at the sight of you. Pregnant animals will cast off their young unborn if they meet your gaze. Birds shall lose their feathers and lay eggs without shells. Streams will dry up. Buds will fall from the trees. If you have to come from the blood lodge, you must cover your head with a bed fur and call out so all may know that you are walking about, lest they accidentally look your way and be turned into blood themselves. And you must catch your water and feces in your hands and drink and eat of it lest it contaminate the earth!"

The girl had burst into tears.

And Kinap had laughed. "By all the stars in the black blanket of the night, how can anyone believe such things? When a female wolf bleeds, she is not ostracized from the pack! And have you ever seen a cow caribou driven from its herd, Wounded One, simply because she is—"

"Caribou cows keep their own herds!"

"And in this forest, I, Kinap, will keep mine! Mowea'qua will contemplate her new state of womanhood and its responsibilities in the way of the Old Tribe as she rests within the den and tends to her needs at this sacred time. And when she emerges, reborn, there will be gifts and feasting and song!"

But "then" was still a few nights off.

Tonight Old One responded to the need to make her own song.

She sang in the way of her kind and waved peeled willow wands round and round to stir the night air and send invisible currents pooling outward as though through water, this to summon the kami, to bring them near so that she could thank them for Kinap's safe return and decision to stay, for the girl's coming to womanhood, for her own change in heart, and also to honor the soul of the fallen mammoth that had once wintered in this forest and would winter here no more.

She offered her singing within the sacred spruce grove, dancing as she sang, a slow, simple side step that defined the perimeters of the sacred Circle of Life as she threw back her grizzled head and howled in the way of the singers of the Old Tribe . . . even though she had not felt younger or stronger in years.

She sang!

She danced!

On and on she danced, exalting the kami in song and singing to the spirit of the fallen mammoth, asking him to understand why she had been unable to mourn him where he had fallen as, she was certain, Kinap must have done, assuring the spirit of the Great One that since Bear had brought her children to honor him, his spirit would live on in the flesh and bones and blood of creatures that were not completely unlike himself. He would continue to be feared and honored by all who walked within the fall of the shadows of the bears that had eaten him.

"Your life has been long, Mammoth, as mine has been long. I celebrate you. I celebrate the womanhood of my granddaughter. And I celebrate the return of Kinap into this dark forest with a boy who will grow to be a mate for my Mowea'qua!"

Moon watched her dance.

The stars listened to her song.

The Pleiades walked in the sky above her head. She smiled up at her Little Lost Children and told them that they would have to be patient, for she was no longer ready to join them in their endless walk across the sky. Not yet. Not for a very long time!

Around and around she circled beneath the stars, now and then feeling the flush of happiness so intensely that she found herself high-stepping, not exactly in the way of a young girl but with all her spirit in every step. She moved her body to the ancient rhythm. She sang her song in the way that the grandmothers of the Old Tribe had taught her long ago, in great, loud, bounding howls of pure exuberance, now and then pausing, listening, half expecting to hear wolves answering her calls.

U'na'li was out there somewhere, running with her own kind at last.

It pleased Kelet to think of it; the girl had done well to heal the wounded animal. "Remember us, Wolf, and may you and your kindred find success in the hunt this night wherever you may run!"

There was no answer.

Kelet danced on, sang on, now and then laughing despite herself when first one foot and then another broke through the crust of the deteriorating snowpack and her snow walkers sagged to one side, taking her off balance. When she fell, she did not fall hard; she fell in the way of a young girl, lightly, giggling to herself, thinking how foolish Kinap would think her if he were to see her now, lying back on the snow, her arms spread wide, looking blissfully up through the trees at the stars and the pale smiling face of Moon, unaware of all but the beauty and joy of the moment until . . .

A sound.

Soft.

No more than a tangible sensation in the air around her, the gentlest of disturbances, as though something had just breathed in and was now holding its breath.

And then, as subtle as the sound, the snowpack trembled beneath her, as though something had just stepped down.

"Kinap . . . ?"

She sat up, looked around, saw nothing save the moon-lit center of the grove with the great trees standing black all around and the stars shining fixedly between the trunks and . . .

She gasped.

No! Not stars! Eyes! One pair . . . and another . . . and another . . . and . . .

Kelet stopped counting. She did not want to see more.

And yet she knew that she must see. Her life depended on it. As she squinted to sharpen her night vision, there was no denying the shapes that she saw looming in the darkness between the trees: wolves . . . black wolves . . . standing motionless at the very edge of the clearing.

"Ah!" Terror quickened in her breast. Hope followed, thin and distant as the dawn. "U'na'li? Are you out there, Wolf? Have you your pack brought to hunt in the sacred grove of the Old Tribe?"

We are the Old Tribe.

Her eyes widened. Had the wolves spoken?

Yes!

She cocked her head, saw the dark forms clearly now, seven of them, all facing her, one forward of the rest, ears high, eyes glowing like moons, and as cold. "I see none of my grandfathers or grandmothers among you!" she told them.

Look closely, Kelet, whose pack once ran with ours as we followed the caribou into the face of the rising sun in the days when the Animals and People were of one tribe! Do you not know us?

The question disturbed her in ways that defied definition. Somehow she knew the answer before the lead wolf gave it. "Go away," she told them. "I do *not* know you!"

We are the kami you summon in the night to eat of the bones of your prey so that it may be reborn through us to run forever in the great Circle of Life! Why should we go away? And why should your bones not be food for us now? Or do you, like any other Stranger, presume to position yourself at the center of the sacred Circle and dare to imagine that you are not a portion of the sacred Whole?

Kelet steadied her breathing. "I am no Stranger!"

Then run, Kelet, run or be eaten!

"I will not consent to be prey."

Strangers never do!

"I am of the Old Tribe!"

No. We are but a memory whispering in the blood and dreams of Man. You are no longer one of us . . . Indeed, in this life, Kelet, you never have been.

Old One's heart sank. The taste of fear was bitter in her mouth. The scent of it was acrid in her nostrils. She could smell it seeping through her pores and knew that if she could smell it, the wolves could smell it, too!

A cold sweat dewed her brow.

Her eyes held the gaze of the lead wolf, and in the ancient and instinctive Knowing, she understood that she was not Kelet or Old One or Grandmother in the eyes of the animal. She was Prey. The wolf was Predator. And this moment presaged the eternal dance in which Life must devour Life if it was to transcend Death. Before Kinap's return she might have welcomed this, for to be devoured by wolves was to *become* a wolf. But it occurred to Old One in this moment that she was happy in her own skin for the first time in longer than she could remember, and with the realization came a profound annoyance with her situation.

"Mmph!" she said to the wolf whose gaze she held. "Your kind has denned in my den and eaten of the meat of my kills! And if that is you standing out there in moon shadow, U'na'li, an ungrateful wolf are you! Have you so easily forgotten that you are alive only by the grace of Kelet and Mowea'qua, who have healed you and named you as one of our own kind even as we set you free to run as a wolf again?"

A wolf must be a wolf, as you must be what you are, Old Woman! Did you not summon us with your howls and wish us good luck on the hunt this night?

Kelet shook her head. This was intolerable! She would not passively sit here and allow them to make meat of her!

The wolves remained motionless.

Kelet did not. She knew now that her howling must have called them. They must have been watching her for some time. When she had fallen, she had shown weakness; weakness had made her prey in their eyes. Now, with her gaze fixed intently on the eyes of the wolf closest to her, she knew that she must show no fear as she attempted to get to her feet with dignity and strength, to show the wolves that she was in full command of herself and that they would be wise to seek easier prey.

"As though that were possible!" she mumbled to herself, for her snow walkers were making it difficult—no, impossible—to rise. Encumbered by the length and span of her footgear, she was unable to find the proper balance to heft herself to her feet. Giving up in despair, she began to fumble with the lacings that secured her moccasins to the bindings of the snow walkers. It was usually an easy task, a loop knot slipped here, the tip of a lace pulled there . . .

One of the wolves moved forward.

"Go away!" she commanded. One foot was free now.

The animal stopped. Lowered its head.

"Away, say I!" she demanded. The loop knots of the other snow walker had been inadvertently made in reverse and would not slide free.

Another wolf moved forward, then stopped and stared menacingly with its nose raised and teeth showing.

Still working at the laces, Kelet frowned up at the beast and showed it her own teeth.

And still another wolf stepped forward, one cautious paw at a time, head down, ears back.

In the moonlight Old One recognized the animal as

U'na'li. She cursed the beast for its ingratitude, threw her snow walker at it, and, utterly despairing of freeing the laces of the other, desperately heaved herself to one foot just as one of the other wolves in the pack, the first to advance, hurled itself toward her.

"I think *not!*" roared a man's voice.

Dazed, Kelet saw the wolf go down with an arrow in its shoulder as Kinap broke through the trees, releasing one arrow after another in such quick succession that the weapons flew past her in a blur. She heard the seeking hiss of the stone projectile points slicing forward through thin air even as Mowea'qua screamed.

"No, Kinap, no!"

It was too late.

Two wolves were down. One dead. The other dying. The rest had already scattered and vanished into the forest as though they had never been more than a trick of the shadowing moon.

"U'na'li!" Mowea'qua was on her knees beside the mortally wounded wolf, cradling the animal's head in her lap, smoothing the dark fur. "All right it will be, my sister. Lie still you must! Make you better will I!"

"That animal is not your sister, nor is the other your brother." Kinap's voice was heavy with reproach. "Go back to the den of woman's blood where you belong, Mowea'qua. It is time you learned the order in which our kind runs in the great Circle of Life!"

"U'na'li was only trying to win back the respect of her pack!"

"By leading them to feast upon your grandmother!"

His words caused Old One to fight back a wave of emotion in which relief, sadness, and regret were all uncomfortably intermingled. Relief for herself, for surely, had the giant not come from the forest when he had, she would now be meat in the jaws of wolves! Sadness for the girl, because she knew the extent of the affection Mowea'qua felt for U'na'li, an affection that would now be experienced all the more keenly because it would be mixed with guilt. The girl had been so taken with the wounded Stranger and overcome with happiness at Kinap's return that she had all but forgotten the animal after it had run off and failed to come back to the den. And regret because she realized now that her behavior this night had summoned the wolves, put her life at risk, and resulted in the deaths of . . .

The kami of the sacred grove!

No! She would not consider it. Kami were spirits! Wolves were wolves! And the grove would always be a sacred place, because when she and Kinap had first brought the child into the forest, the mammoths had led them here, to this perfect circle of ancient spruce, with the clearing in the midst of the giant trees, this quiet place where the kami had spoken assurances in the whispering wind that they were safe at last.

"Stand aside, Mowea'qua. I will finish what I have started and put an end to that which—"

"You will not hurt U'na'li again!" Mowea'qua's chin was up in the way it usually was when she set herself to her own purpose in direct opposition to the will of her grandmother. But now it was Kinap who was to be the recipient of her stubbornness. "U'na'li would never have attacked Old One! She is not the leader of the pack! She would—"

"She would *what?*" Kinap interrupted with an angry snap. "What do you *really* know about the workings of the minds of wolves, Mowea'qua, save what you have heard in the tales that I and your grandmother have told you?"

"Am I not descended from their kind?" she retorted hotly. "As are you?"

"Mmph!" The sound was an implosion of bitter frustration. "You know nothing, child, nothing! About wolves, about yourself, about the world beyond this forest!"

"I am no child!" Without another word the girl lifted the wolf in her arms, rose to her feet, and headed back toward the den.

Even in the moonlight the expression of anguished frustration that crossed Kinap's scarred face put worry in Old One's heart. He had changed. He looked the same, he sounded the same, and his mannerisms were all that she remembered. But something about him was different. Not since those long-gone days when they had dwelled and wandered together after the great fire had she seen him so intense, so morose, so preoccupied and readily riled. The old easygoing giant of the past was gone. In his place was a man she scarcely knew, a man with a restive darkness at his core, a man who was . . . a stranger.

"Come," he said. "I do not want her wandering in the woods alone."

Kelet shivered. She wanted to remind him that he had many times left the girl to make her way alone in the wild forest with only an aging woman to keep watch over her. Why should he be so worried about her now? Her brow came down as she remembered what he had said upon returning, words that—had she not been so overwhelmed by her joy to see him again—might have sobered her mood, for he had confirmed all her own misgivings when he said that he had come far through a forest that was no longer what it had once been, no longer a refuge, no longer a safe and shadowed haven. Strangers were moving back and forth at will across their old hunting trails! And everywhere, *everywhere*, the world was changing in ways that awakened old nightmares and set his heart to stone.

"Come!" he demanded again.

Kelet winced at the sharpness of his tone. He had slung the dead wolf around his shoulders and was watching her, waiting impatiently, scowling at her in the moonlight, his face a mask of ugliness that would have been repellent had she not known the nature of the man whose spirit dwelled behind it.

"The girl is alone, say I!" he was shouting at her. "Do not stand there staring at me, Kelet! We must follow and make sure that she returns safely to the den."

A deep tiredness filled her body. *I have been watching her and making sure of that for her entire lifetime, dear friend.* She did not speak the words aloud; it was not the time for reprimands or recriminations. He was home! He was accepting a father's responsibility for the girl at last! She reached down and made an impatient and this time successful attempt to loosen the ties of her snow walker. She worked her foot free, picked up the back end of the birchwood frame, and would have walked quickly to retrieve the other had a sudden, dizzying faintness not overcome her. She dropped to her knees as though struck from behind.

Kinap was at her side in an instant. "Kelet . . . ? The wolves have hurt you!"

Her heart was leaping, bounding, falling, stopping, then leaping up again to dance once more the wild, arrhythmic dance it had not done for the last several days and nights. Breathless, she laid a hand on the giant's forearm to steady herself lest she swoon. "The wolves of time, dear friend, not of this forest. Old grow I, so old! Forget you, think I, that you were but an amorous boy when first you chose to run with me."

"And say I now, dear one, that you will never grow old in my eyes. I have a new medicine in the lodge, a gift from the brother of the wounded one. He swore it will cure all ills."

She smiled wryly. "Since when does Kelet need the medicine of Strangers? Besides, nothing there is that will turn back the Circle of Life, dear friend, nothing." The dizziness was passing; his nearness and strong arm beneath her hand was enough to make her feel stronger. She rose unsteadily, and with his help. "Forgive me, Kinap," she begged quietly, bowing her head in assent to her own culpability. "Worry you I would not. To the grove alone I should not have so carelessly come."

"Mmph. And did you imagine that I or anyone else could sleep through your howling? No one sings quite like you, Kelet. Ne'gauni thought you were being disemboweled, and good riddance, said he! But in truth, by the time I took up my bow and made sure the little muskrat was safely hobbled, you might well have been meat, woman, had my stride not been longer than that of the wolves who—"

"Mmph! Strangers! What do they know of the song of the Old Tribe?"

"Enough to know that it is not their song, woman!" he said as he lifted her into his great arms and hurried after Mowea'qua. "Enough to know that it is not their song!"

▼▼▼▼

Ne'gauni stood in the entrance of the lodge.

The old wolf woman had stopped howling.

He stared into the night. Leaning on the wood-and-bone crutch that the girl had fashioned for him, his shoulder ached, the stump of his leg throbbed cruelly, and he could feel the eyes of the captive boy fixed on his back. He refused to turn around.

Since Mowea'qua had been temporarily banished to her own little den, the child was always staring at him. It was a different sort of stare than that which the child reserved for the girl. That was not really a stare at all; it was a wan, reticent, sometimes wistful, often confused and bashful look that ended in a blush whenever the boy's eyes met hers, and then he would look away, clearly flustered.

With Ne'gauni it was not the same. The boy's look was direct. Invasive. Sometimes he would awake in the night and find the child lying tethered close to the giant, watching him, his small hands flexed around the pale little amulet he wore. The boy's dark eyes never wavered. They fixed on his own, focused sharply—and yet somehow they did not focus at all. Disconcerted, Ne'gauni would close his lids and turn his head away, but he could still feel the stare of the child and sense his thoughts drifting in the room, wandering, journeying worlds away and yet somehow connecting to his own. It was an invasion that sent prickles running up and down his back because he could actually feel, not merely understand, the boy's need to be away, free, somewhere else . . . with *someone* else, someone whom the child loved so intensely that Ne'gauni was bruised by the passion of the boy's emotions. How could a child communicate thoughts without words? How?

Now, standing half in and half out of the den, breathing in the cold air of midnight, a part of him longed to turn around, to go to the boy, to loosen his bonds and send him on his way. At least one of them would then be free! But how long could a frail-looking little boy survive alone in the forest? He had seen his wraithlike body when Old One had stripped him for a cleansing rubdown with spruce boughs—scarred all across his back and down the sides of his arms and legs, as though someone had flayed him and held hot brands against his skin. And he had seen the convulsive expression of anger on the giant's face when he had proclaimed that this was what he had saved the boy from and what the "great" shaman on the far island had been unable to protect him from!

His jaw tightened. He knew he would suffer for his act of "kindness" if the giant ever discovered that he had released the boy. He could, of course, steal a few provisions and go with the boy, but what good would his company do either of them? His wounds were not yet healed. He grew weary far too easily. And how far could he hope to get on one leg before the giant and the hag and the wolf girl came after him and Old One set herself to blinding him?

He frowned. The movement of his facial muscles still roused an ache, but he was almost oblivious to it. His thoughts about the old hag were not quite what they once were. She remained gruff and distant toward him, but he had been amazed to see that she was almost human in her behavior toward the giant's foundling.

Although the boy was not of the Old Tribe—and Ne'gauni had yet to determine exactly what this was—the old wolf woman was actually kind and gentle with the boy, solicitous of his needs. Sometimes she even tried to bring a smile to the glum little face or draw a word from his mouth by initiating pantomimes or guessing games, or by attempting to draw him into a friendly match of hoop-to-stick-toss or toss-the-pebble-into-the-shell, or by impressing him with her considerable skill at Spider's Web, weaving a single long length of thong back and forth between the fingers of each hand until—sometimes using her teeth and even her toes—the desired patterns were achieved.

"See Grouse Tracks!" she would cry with pleasure. "Or here, see one of Mowea'qua's favorites, Summer Web with Butterfly Inside—a tricky one this, say I! Look! Web stays, Butterfly flies! Mmph. You do not want to try? Maybe this one, then, an easier one for a boy to try, a simple one. Fishing Spear—see the three prongs and long shaft?"

Ne'gauni had been impressed, and puzzled, too, because he knew most if not all of the games and pantomimes and had many times seen the women of Asticou's village work the finger-thong patterns. He even knew a few himself. The game was considered essential to mastering the proper lacing and knotting techniques necessary to web up a pair of snow walkers in the many styles used to accommodate varying types of snow, or to make a decent netting for the shovel-ended rackets used by the men and boys of Asticou's village when a game of battle ball was played. It still seemed strange to him that Old One seemed to think that so many of the traditional games of his People were unique to her Old Tribe.

And the boy's stoicism in the face of her considerable effort on his behalf was amazing. Throughout her best attempts to bring him out of his glowering, the child sat looking stoically ahead with arms crossed, determined to ignore everything except the food that was put in front of him.

The boy was stubborn; Ne'gauni had to concede him that much. But only this morning the old hag had gotten a reaction from him when she had noticed the fascination with which he was looking at her beard. What a show she had made of combing it with her fingertips and twisting it into curls and braids, encouraging the youngster to touch it if he so wished, assuring him that he would be lucky indeed to one day have a woman of the Old Tribe with a beard as fine as Kelet's—or, if he lived long enough among her kind, to one day sprout such a beard of his own! When the boy had drawn back in dismay, she guffawed in merriment, and even Ne'gauni had laughed when she roughed the boy's hair in what anyone would have taken to be a gesture of genuine affection. But the child had screamed as though scalded and then cowered as though in terror of being beaten, and she had swept him into her arms and held him close, rocking him gently to and fro upon her broad lap, crooning soft apologies for frightening him and assuring him that no one of the Old Tribe would ever strike or abuse a child, even the child of Strangers.

Reflecting on the moment, Ne'gauni was almost sorry that he had told the giant that he would be glad if the old hag had fallen prey to wolves. *Almost.* His mood darkened. She might not raise her hand to children, but he was no child, and neither she nor her mist-eyed granddaughter suffered any second thoughts about hacking off his leg.

Now, still frowning, he saw that Mowea'qua was coming out of the trees and advancing toward him across the clearing with the dark, limp form of a wolf in her arms. He barely noticed the animal. The girl filled his senses. Was it a trick of the moon? It had to be! Surely Mowea'qua was not the most beautiful girl he had ever seen!

Hasu'u!

The name of his brother's woman sang out of his soul. She was alive! He had refused to believe it, but now he knew that it was the truth, and that somehow he had known all along. She had spoken to him out of his dreams:

"Why do you call to me in the country of the manitous, Little Brother? I am still a hunt chief's daughter and a

*headman's woman! I do not stop and sing where it does not
please me to stop and sing! I do not rise and walk where it does
not please me to rise and walk! And I will not swim in the river
of death when the river of life is yet sweet and warm and
welcoming!"*

Bitterness soured his mouth. How could life be warm
and welcoming for her now? Surely it could not please her
to be a captive, as he was a captive . . . enslaved to what
were, for all intents and purposes, murderous manitous!

Mowea'qua had stopped. She was staring at him. All of
her heart seemed to be welling up in her eyes. "Kinap has
killed U'na'li!" Her voice broke.

"As I will kill any other predator who comes against my
family!"

Ne'gauni tensed. The giant was stomping into the
clearing, carrying Old One in the fold of one arm and a
dead wolf over the other shoulder. A moment later he
stopped beside Mowea'qua and dropped the wolf uncere-
moniously onto the ground at her feet.

"Put down that carcass and go into the main lodge to
straighten your grandmother's bed furs," the giant commanded the girl. "I will rouse fire. Kelet has suffered a
shock this night. A good hot drink of melted marrow and
maybe a little of M'alsum's new medicine will revive her.
You may go back to the blood lodge when you have helped
to ease her."

Mowea'qua did not move.

Ne'gauni saw the eyes of the giant and the girl meet
and hold in an open contest of wills.

The girl's chin went up. "U'na'li is dead."

"And Kelet is *not!*" There was anger in the giant's
voice.

Ne'gauni managed to step out of the way just as the

man stormed forward, entered the lodge, and, ignoring the stares of the wide-eyed boy, placed the old woman tenderly on her bedding.

"Rest here, Kelet," Kinap told her emphatically. "The girl and I will be back to take care of you in a moment. You are skin and bones in my arms, woman! Skin and bones! You must have M'alsum's new medicine! Clearly your own are doing you little good. But first there is something I must do."

In the next instant, as Ne'gauni watched, the giant went to the eagle's perch and, before the startled bird could react, took hold of its head to effectively muzzle its massive beak. In the next instant man and bird were outside, and Mowea'qua was imploring, "No, Kinap! Stop! What are you doing? You cannot mean to let him go! Barely healed is U'wo'hi'li's ruined eye, and yet have I to teach him to hunt with the others! How will he see? How will he judge distance and his way make in the—"

"Do you see yourself as kindred of eagles, then, as well as of wolves?" the giant interrupted in a voice intended to make the girl bleed with the sting of his words. "Have you grown to womanhood with no sense of responsibility to your own kind? Your grandmother needs you! Your band needs you! People need you—*not* animals. The days of the Old Tribe are no more, Mowea'qua! For your own good, the time has come for you to begin to live in the world as it is . . . now!"

"No!" she cried.

The giant raised one immense arm and, as he continued to hold the eagle by its feet, began to release its jesses with his free hand. "Fly now . . . fly high and fly far . . . seek your own kind . . . and come back never to share this lodge of mine!" Still holding the bird high, he swung his arm around and around until the eagle, feeling the movement of air against its face and in its nostrils and penetrating its feathers, hooked down its brow and instinctively began to work its mighty wings.

Ne'gauni caught his breath at the sheer glory of the moment. Man and bird seemed somehow to have become one! As he looked at them silhouetted against the moon, just before the bird took flight, he could have sworn that the two were joined—the bird linked to the earth through the stanchion-limbed body of the man, and the man reaching upward into the promise of the sky with one extended arm that bore the wings of an eagle.

With a shriek that touched Ne'gauni to his very spirit so that he echoed it and never knew that he uttered a sound, the eagle flew free of the hand of the man. The youth felt the rush of air flow back beneath the wings of the bird, heard the pinioned stroke of feathered arms seeking, finding, claiming power and buoyancy in thin air. He saw the raptor fly into the face of the moon as though impelled by the words of the man until, almost as though in defiance of that human will, it turned back, shrieking as it cut its way across the night. Over the clearing it banked and dipped a broad wing downward as though in salutation to the girl before ascending once again, winging higher, higher, into the east, until it was one with the stars.

There was silence in the clearing.

Absolute and utter silence.

Until the merest wisp of a child's voice sighed out of the lodge, so soft, so unexpected, no louder than the tenderest whispering of a flute played low, slightly off key, the notes slurred and oddly thickened, for the player of this flute was deaf to the song he played. "Whest now, Bearded Gwandmuh-thoo. Why do you fwown? Whest! You look sick. And tie-ood. Do not get up. The son of Squam will take kay-oo of you. You ah kind. Few ah kind. If you will untie my whists and hobbles, I will make fie-oo. I will bwing you food and dwink, as you bwing food and dwink to me. But do not take M'alsum's medicine, Bearded Gwandmuh-thoo. That man is bad."

Ne'gauni turned and stared with disbelief into the benighted lodge. Moonlight poured into the interior as Kinap, ducking low and backhanding him aside, came in from the night to face the child.

"Why, you deceitful little bog rat, you *can* talk!" exclaimed the giant.

The boy, staring fixedly at the giant's mouth, glowered at him with undisguised loathing. "I cannot *hee-oo* many things! Too many times has she hit me acwoss my head! My ee-oos wing all the time! But I can see and undoostand the woo-adds you make with your mouth! I *can* speak . . . to those who ah kind to me."

"I have been kind! Who else would have had the courage to bundle you up in a bag in the dead of a winter night and steal you away from the wolverine who mothered you?"

"You said you would take me to my fah-thoo on the fah side of the island! I twusted you!"

"Your father is old and blind and does not see the extent of the corruption that he has allowed to grow around him. I rescued you from that when I found you hiding from your mother in the muskrat's nest! As I only barely managed to rescue myself after going uninvited to that cursed island and witnessing the truth of Squam's lack of power! Bah! I have done with all faith in magic! You will have a good life here in the forest. Forget those from whom I have taken you. Your mother would just as soon have seen your bones heaped and hidden away forever beneath one of the grave mounds of her people! And what powers can your shaman father have if he cannot see into the manipulative heart of his own woman or bring his son to speak . . . or hear!"

The boy's chin moved downward, indicating his amulet. "The say-kwed stone of the Ancient Ones is mine. My muh-thoo is dead. The uh-thoo killed huh and took the stone from Squam. I took it from huh. Fwom Puwo'win! I will bwing it back to my fah-thoo!"

"And for that bit of thievery, boy, she will hunt us both and kill us if ever she finds us!"

Old One's hands went to her chest. "Strangers in my den . . . in my forest . . . Ah! Always it is the same! They walk with Death!"

The giant dropped to his knees and, as Mowea'qua came to stand in the entryway to the lodge, moved to his pack roll. "You will have M'alsum's medicine, dear one," he declared. It will ease you, Kelet. M'alsum said that—"

"No!" The boy shook his head vehemently. "That man is bad! Twust nothing he gives you!"

"He is my brother!" protested Ne'gauni, his mind spinning with all that he had just heard. "He is the boldest and bravest and best of the sons of Asticou."

"No," replied the child. "You ah that. Maybe the white mammoth will find your bwuh-thoo and cwush his bones into the earth as he has wished for me . . . That would be the best medicine for all!"

"There is no white mammoth," revealed Kinap on a scowl of bitterness. "That one is as much myth and legend as the magic spring and sacred stone the Dawnland people so foolishly cherish! Katcheetohúskw lies dead in the ravine where M'alsum led it to its death."

"Ah!" Mowea'qua's voice was a whisper of incredulity clarified. "Then he *is* mikahmuwesu . . . an immortal!"

Kinap expelled a noise of profound disgruntlement. "I have told you, girl, the last mammoth in this forest—in all this world—is *dead!*"

"No," said the boy quietly. "There is anuh-thoo. A white mammoth. As big as a thunduh cwowd! With tusks like lightning bolts! I have seen it."

"Only in your dreams!" rebuffed the giant.

"No," the boy again disputed quietly. "It walks in the Dawnland. It is real."

Chapter Five

▼▼▼▼▼▼▼

There was meat.

In abundance!

With a mild wind fresh off the sea ice, the sacred, whale-tooth-studded totem posts on the beach below Ogeh'ma's encampment were now slick and dark with the blood of seals and adorned with stringers of seal teeth and offerings of fur and fat and flippers.

All day the people worked outside at their braining, butchering, and rendering. At dusk several more seals were dragged from the ice. Soapstone lamps were filled with seal oil and placed at the base of each totem post as a sign of thanksgiving to the sky-wandering spirits of the slain seals.

Hunters drew lots to see which two of them would stand guard over the lamps until dawn. It was important that the moss wicks not gutter for want of fuel or be blown out in the wind. If this happened, it was sure to be taken as a sign of carelessness and disrespect by the spirits of the slain seals, who might then convey their displeasure to all the seals still living in the sea. And next year the seal kind could very well decide not to return to be food for the People.

Tonight, with the shaman Puwo'win in their camp, there was to be a great feast to assure that this would not happen. And so Onen'ia and Ami'ck, elected guardians of the lamps, took the seal meat, fat, and blood that their women had set aside for them and went to the beach without complaint. With Mammoth Slayer and the woman of the great shaman Squam in their encampment, they felt honored to have been chosen by the spirits to be guardians of the lamps on the night of such an important feast. They would do their best to keep alert, for if the camp dogs pricked up their ears and took a restless turn, they would remember their second purpose for being out in the cold at the edge of the encampment while their people were assembled inside the great tent for a night of feasting. For this they kept their best lances close: long, well-balanced throwing spears with finely edged stone projectile points the length of each man's hand, and shorter stabbing lances with slender, elongated points of ground slate designed for the close-in killing of walrus and seal. Not that they needed these weapons to fight off the wind as they guarded the flames in the soapstone lamps. No. It was equally important that they guard against another threat, a more earthly threat, albeit a slim one this early in the year. With tents and fire circles festooning the clifftop, drying frames laden with meat and skins were everywhere. A bear might well be drawn from hibernation by the smell of so much blood and, were it not for the guardians of the lamps, wander from the forest unseen to feast upon the meat and defile the honor of the seals who had not consented to die for them. With the dogs to sound the alert, the two men would be up from the beach faster than any bear could imagine. If they drove it off, they would be rewarded with the gratitude of the assembled bands and, no doubt, small gifts of appreciation. If they killed the bear, its hide and meat would be theirs to share and portion among the People. The honor would be great. The anticipation of such a windfall was worth a cold night's duty on the cliffs.

Already the great feast tent had been raised and readied.

M'alsum stood marveling at the sight of it. He had not seen its like since he had last traveled in the Dawnland many a long moon ago. It was a circular shelter well over twenty full strides across at its base, with its center post a debranched spruce of almost unmanageable height and its massive roof skin a combination of many joined hides and pelts contributed by each of the hunt chiefs of the various little family bands that had come at Ogeh'ma's invitation to join together in this one big hunting and feasting camp.

He could not help but note that all the pelts and hides of the roof covering were prime: not only sealskins but black bear and wolverine, wolf and fox and lynx, marten and ermine, beaver and otter, deer and moose and caribou, as well as the feathered skins of herons and eagles and hawks and seabirds and the scaled hides of serpents and salmon—indeed, of all creatures of the land and sea and air who gave so generously of their lives to be meat and warmth for the People.

Coveting them, M'alsum restrained a smile, for he knew from past experience among the coastal bands that each prime pelt and skin would come to the host chief when the camp was at last disbanded. No self-respecting hunter would consider offering anything less than his best in tribute to the generosity of the Master of the Feast who welcomed others to share in the bounty of hunting grounds that he could just as easily have kept to himself and his own family band. It was considered an honor—as well as an obligation—to show deference to such a considerate man by adding one's share of weight and warmth to the covering of the great feast tent that celebrated the success of the joint hunt . . . and of life itself.

M'alsum—in a beneficent mood—proudly offered up his shaggy brown bison hide to add to the weight and warmth of the other prime skins, knowing as he did so that since bison were never seen in the Dawnland, the people viewed the dark and heavy hide as a rare and wondrous thing. "Hairy moose" they called it. Or, since he had described the animal to them at great length, "the horned bear who eats grass and walks on four legs." He knew that if he were to offer it in trade, he could secure its weight and more in lighter, warmer, more useful caribou skins, but he was not in the least concerned about forfeiting it to another. Indeed, as he felt the narrowed eyes of Ogeh'ma's sons on his back, he took his time smoothing the long, lustrous hump hair of the bison hide, then took off his mammoth-trunk breastplate and laid it with much reverence atop the hide.

A communal sigh of awe and adulation went up from the assembly.

"Katcheetohúskw has been meat for this man," M'alsum reminded them, glad that he was facing away so that no one could see his smile. He knew that with this truly rarest and most wondrous of all offerings—ostensibly made to Ogeh'ma, his host and hunt chief, but in reality a statement to all of who was the greatest hunter among them—he was virtually assuring that when the assembled bands dispersed and went their separate ways with their bellies full and their sledges loaded with seal meat and fat and hides, the prime pelts and skins of the feast tent would come not to Ogeh'ma but to him. And so he added, with much emotion, "May the power of the Great Beast bring strength and the bounty of all future hunts to those who will now gather beneath its hair and hide to eat of the food provided by the Master of this Feast!"

"Mammoth Slayer and Bringer of All Good Things to the People is generous!" declared Puwo'win. Standing slightly apart with her guardians, she raised her masked and antlered staff of authority, shaking it vigorously so that all the many stringers of birds' feet and beaks and bones clattered in the wind as though to emphasize her words.

"Ogeh'ma is host and hunt chief in this camp!" sputtered old Ko'ram as he stepped forward to shake his eagle-feathered turtle-shell rattle at the woman of Squam, as though he would drive her back to her island with it. He carried no staff of rank, for he held no more status among his people than any other man. His advanced age alone gave him authority in the eyes of his people. It was proof of his wisdom and of the favor of the spirits that had allowed him to live to the brink of infirmity and still remain young and brave enough in his heart to face down the shaman woman of Squam out of loyalty to the hunt chief of his band. "It is Ogeh'ma who has chosen to bring his people to this place and to so generously summon the bands of his many kinsmen to come to his cove to hunt and share in the feast!"

"And it is M'alsum who has summoned the seals and opened the leads so that we may all eat of their meat! Have you not said as much out of your own mouth, Old Man?" The question fairly curdled the air with the contempt with which it had been posed. When Ko'ram huffed indignantly and with a noticeable measure of confusion, Puwo'win huffed back at him and shook her staff of rank in his face. "The seals did not come to be meat for the People in

Ogeh'ma's camp until M'alsum came! Who, then, is Master of this Feast?"

Ogeh'ma's face hardened as he saw his son, Onen'ia, lower his eyes and his daughters stare at their feet in embarrassment for what they obviously took to be their father's shaming. The replies of the assembled hunters and their families resounded in the night.

"M'alsum!"

"Mammoth Slayer!"

"Bringer of All Good Things to the People!"

"M'alsum is Master of the Feast!"

▼▼▼▼

They made it so.

The assembly of Dawnland People swept M'alsum before them as they gathered under the great roof of many skins and hides. They closed the entrance and the smoke hole to the tent and formed a circle, males on one side, females on the other. The shaman Puwo'win took up a smoking brand from the central fire and moved with care around the interior of the enclosure, making sure that no draft of air or smoke was free to make its way outside. If air and smoke could not escape, the spirits of the newly killed seals could not escape either. At this feast it was important that they remain within the meat until it was all consumed.

The several seals that had been killed at dusk had been dragged into the interior and arranged in a circle around but well back from the central fire. Each had been hauled by a specially made length of shell-decorated sealskin thong and then placed to rest on its back on a bed of snow that had been carried inside and smoothed down atop the floor covering of freshly cut spruce boughs until it almost resembled a sheet of pack ice. Led by Puwo'win, the People were now encouraged to greet the seals with imitative hand clapping and barking as they invited them to feel at home within the great feast tent.

M'alsum remembered the ritual, for he had wintered with Ogeh'ma's band and been with them when the seals had last come through the leads. Hasu'u, then an adoring helpmate—but not yet his bride—had eagerly explained it to him, and since the long trek through the forest had not dulled his gift of total recollection, he was not at a loss. When Ogeh'ma, now granite-faced, eyed him resentfully and asked if the Master of the Feast needed help in recalling the protocol of the feast, he was able to thank his host and then say, "No, thank you" as he proceeded without assistance, embellishing every word and gesture, no matter how tedious or foolish he found it. He would not have it said of him that, as Master of the Feast, he was not a good host to "his" people, or to the seals.

He called forth the children. It was their duty to pour seawater over the skins and into the mouths of the seals, for it was believed by the Dawnland People that when on land, whether alive or dead, seals were eternally thirsty and in need of cool liquid to drink and to moisten their skins. The children did so, using the little birchbark cups their mothers had made for just this purpose, and, smiling at M'alsum, no doubt wondered if Mammoth Slayer, Bringer of All Good Things to the People, Master of the Feast, had more ducksuckles hidden away for them among his now depleted trading goods.

Then M'alsum called forth the women of the hunters who had killed these particular seals. He enjoyed watching them as, proudly, they set to the intricate process of opening each animal and laying back the ribs with their curved palm knives. He admired the way they were able to create a neat, spillproof receptacle out of the abdomen of each animal, this to hold the blood and innards as they bent to the task of portioning meat and fat and flippers. Observing the care that the women took at their task, M'alsum was grateful that he was among Dawnlanders. A trader he had once traveled with had told him that there were hunters from the far north who had a name and specified allotment number for every portion of a seal, down to the last lower vertebra and the ends of the flippers, both front and back. The most insignificant relative and hunt parter expected to claim a share of the kill, and this share was designated, not at the time of the hunt, but sometimes even before the birth of the hunter! Hunters, he had said, were thus sometimes named by others in their hunting bands not for their special characteristics but for their designated part of the kill. A man might be called Hind Quarters, or First Front Flipper, or Second Rib. Even the dogs' portion of the feast was decided long before the seals ever appeared in the leads or at the breathing holes. Here, however, in the feast tent of Ogeh'ma's people, traditions developed in a relatively meat-rich land tolerated a more casual approach to distribution.

Soon the birchbark cups were being dipped into gaping seal abdomens, handed up, and passed around, brimful with blood. Quaffed to the dregs, they were passed back, dipped again, and raised up once more to eager lips.

Now eating knives and skewers and plates of wood and bone were handed around, and meat and fat were passed in generous portions.

First portion to the Master of the Feast. Second portion to the visiting shaman, Puwo'win. Third to Ogeh'ma, host and hunt chief of the encampment. Fourth to Ko'ram, eldest of all hunters. Fifth to the men who had slain the seals, then to all men, and, when each had received his portion, to all male children. When the men were all chewing and smiling and beginning to belch, the final portions were served by the women to the women and girl children.

To the dogs would go nothing from this feast, for this was an Eat All Feast, a Making of Seal into Man Feast, a feast to demonstrate the profound gratitude of hunters who had waited so long for the meat before them that they had begun to fear that they might not eat of it again. The bones of these seals would be pounded for marrow and then, along with their skins and pulverized teeth and skulls, burned; the ashes would be diluted in water and drunk down by all. In this way, since the seals were being consumed in their entirety so soon after being slain, even the spirits of the animals were being incorporated into the flesh and blood and bone of the assembly. From this night until the ending of all nights, the spirits of the seals would live on in these people, communicating the ways and intentions of their kind so that their cyclic and often mysterious comings and goings up and down the Dawnland coast would be understood and anticipated. Never again need the people fear being deprived of their meat.

And so they ate until they could eat no more. Flipper and flesh and fat, innards and eyes and tongues, all was meat for the people. And when they could eat no more, the women set aside the remaining meat and built up the fire, and Puwo'win went about collecting the scapulas and pelvic bones of the seals and handing them to the individual hunt chiefs, including M'alsum, instructing each man to use his eating knife to meticulously inscribe small line drawings in the bones to show the various routes they traditionally took to the sealing grounds. This done, she gave them to the Master of the Feast and instructed him to place them facedown around the edges of the fire, close enough to be thoroughly charred but not consumed. Before the feast was over, she would take them up and divine by the cracks in the bone which trails would be rich in game as the People traveled to the sealing grounds next year.

Now the dancing was to begin, to spur the appetites of the people anew. Ogeh'ma, as host chief, prepared the ceremonial song drum that hung from the center post. It was a finely made instrument, its sides painted with images of swimming seals that were, when viewed closely, also men, each image swimming after and entwining with the others, inexorably linked in the eternal circling dance of life.

From the same container out of which the children had dipped water to bathe the seals and give them water to drink, Ogeh'ma fingered up liquid that he then flicked across the rawhide face of the drum to moisten it slightly. This done, he tapped it with the wooden beater, a single light tap, and then, as he spun it around on the cord that held it suspended from the ceiling, he asked the drum if it was ready to sing for the people. When the broad surface of the drumskin returned to meet the beater in the hand of the man, the answer of the drum was given.

Now the dancing could begin in earnest.

Ogeh'ma, as host chief, yielded to tradition by handing the wooden beater to the one who had been named Master of the Feast.

As their eyes met and held, M'alsum saw within the older man's direct and unflinching gaze emotions that might have pained a compassionate man to see: battered but unyielding pride, even though he stood before one who had eclipsed his value in the eyes of his own people; resentful acceptance of this shameful usurpation; and a deep and all-abiding uncertainty.

Are you what you seem, M'alsum, widower of my slain daughter, Mammoth Slayer, Bringer of All Good Things to My People? Am I right to step aside for you? asked the eyes of Ogeh'ma as they moved intently over M'alsum's face, searching the features as though they did not belong to the face of a man at all but were a mask that he must see behind before it was too late and the true nature of its wearer prove a danger to him and his people.

M'alsum's eyes narrowed defensively. The eyes were the entranceways to the spirit. All men knew this. Ogeh'ma's boldly seeking stare was a deliberate invasion. His head went high. He would not allow the other man's trespass.

"Yah hay!" cried M'alsum as he snatched the beater from Ogeh'ma's hand and, by the sheer aggressiveness of this openly proprietary move, sent the host chief shrinking back.

Kanio'te stepped forward to stand beside his father, no doubt wishing that his brother Onen'ia had not been one of the two chosen to guard the soapstone lamps from the wind and the encampment from bears. The young man's earnest face was strained, his expression one of hurt bewilderment. He had openly credited M'alsum with bringing the sun and the seals. He had given Mammoth Slayer free use of his woman. There was no need for the Master of the Feast to demean his father and therefore his entire band before an assembly when the host chief had so obligingly stepped aside for him.

M'alsum's mouth turned down. A glowering Ko'ram had come to stand beside the young hunter and the aged hunt chief, but no one else moved. A trembling of elation went through him. He snarled at Ko'ram and Ogeh'ma and

Kanio'te. He knew that he was now lead wolf of their pack, and in the smoky, stifling confines of the heavily shadowed feast tent, the knowledge was as a rush of cold night air sweeping through his brain to clarify his thoughts and senses.

"Yah hay!" he cried again and began to beat the drum.

"Dance!" The command came from Puwo'win as she stood before the women on the female side of the feast tent, her gaze fixed on the Master of the Feast as though she had just convinced herself that he was some rare and only recently discovered type of game that she fully intended to hunt and devour.

Their eyes met. Held. Again M'alsum felt the gaze of another attempt trespass into his spirit. This time he did not lower his lids against the intended invasion. He would show no weakness to this woman. None! Let her see the carnivore that occupied his soul! Let her know that he was dangerous! They were two predators poised on either side of selected prey. Would they fight for possession of it? Or would they share in the feast to come?

▼▼▼▼

A long, broad shadow fell across open snow on the headland opposite the beach upon which the two young men kept watch.

Tall.

Tusked.

The form was enormous!

And it was of a shape that neither guardian could identify; it was the very strangeness of it that sent the cold feet of dread walking up their backs. Embarrassed and feeling like a pair of easily spooked boys, they both tried to shrug it off as they agreed that it must be a moonlit distortion of tree shadow.

But it was no use.

Onen'ia kept squinting into the darkness. "What *is* that? It is still there—do you see?—not just the shadow, but what is throwing the shadow, something pale standing back in the trees . . . watching us. Am I imagining it? Look! Quickly! Before it disappears!"

Ami'ck got to his feet and, forcing a yawn, attempted to appear unconcerned while stretching to calm his nerves. He stared off. Whatever had been on the opposite headland a moment ago, if anything at all, was gone now. He relaxed and gave a shrug. "As we said, a trick of the moon, most probably shining on an outcropping of snow-covered rocks!"

Onen'ia wanted to agree. But he remained unsure, unconvinced that he had not seen something out there in the dark. Something more than shadow, more than a trick of the moon. Something big. Something solid. Something *alive*. Indecision made him restless with worry. Maybe it was real. Maybe it was not. But whatever it was, it had enflamed his imagination as well as his fears. He tried to calm himself with the reassurance that whatever he had seen was on the opposite headland and, therefore, could not be viewed as an immediate threat. Unless . . . "What if it was . . . was the white, you *know*, what *she* said! A manitou."

Neither man would name the object of Onen'ia's fear. And neither would name Puwo'win. The female shaman was enough to raise the hackles on any man's back; they would both be glad when she had returned to her island with the silent men who were always at her side whenever she appeared.

Ami'ck was shaking his head in congenial rebuke of his companion's continued nervousness. "Be at ease, Onen'ia! Mammoth Slayer now sits in your father's place of honor in the feast tent. He has slain the Great Beast. There is no sense worrying about that one anymore, or maybe even about anything else, now that One Who Brings All Good Things to the People is to be a part of our band!"

Onen'ia held his tongue. He resented the way the forest trader had taken over the encampment. It was his father's hunting ground! Sooner or later Ogeh'ma always led the people to meat. Even if the seals had not come to the bay this year, his father would have led the band into the interior tamarack swamp to hunt moose as the big-nosed deer came clambering clumsily out their late winter yards. No doubt Ogeh'ma and his people would be feasting on that good, albeit bland meat even now! And it would be *their* meat. Ogeh'ma would not take over another man's encampment to make a hunt chief of another band feel small in his own eyes and in the eyes of his sons. And even if he were to be invited to join with others on a hunt in which he was the first to sight game, he would designate as Master of the Feast not himself but the man who had been gracious enough to welcome him into hunting grounds that were not his own.

Onen'ia frowned. He had not realized just how much resentment he harbored toward M'alsum, eldest and now only son of Asticou of the far inland forests. The man should have taken better care of Hasu'u! Ah, a man could have many sisters and love them all, but the loss of One Who Sings Always had left a wound in his heart that he was sure would never fully heal.

The wind was down.

The night was quiet save for the drumbeat that was

now coming from the feast tent, the low rumblings and creakings of the ever-shifting pack ice, and the *shhh* of the surf as it surged beneath the lips of the ice onto the pebbles of the strand.

Onen'ia wrapped his arms around his knees. He watched the water sighing forward from beneath the ice and then sighing back again. Black water, shining sleek, sparkling with stars and moonlight. It was beautiful. He sighed, closed his eyes. He had eaten all the meat and fat that his woman had given him; it sat heavy in his belly, weighting his blood, making it easy to drift off toward sleep.

Ami'ck was walking about, checking the soapstone lamps. As long as one them remained awake . . .

▼▼▼▼

Ami'ck shook his head. He and Onen'ia had added fresh fat to the lamps not long ago, and in the chill air of the windless night the moss wicks were trembling a little but otherwise burning well and strong. The dogs up on the bluffs were quiet. Whatever the two men had seen on the headlands had surely been a trick of their imaginations, but Onen'ia had not asked him to keep watch while he relaxed and took a nap on duty. It irked him to think that, as the hunt chief's son, the other man might be assuming rank.

Annoyed, Ami'ck came close to nudge his sleeping companion with the tip of a booted foot. "Wake up! I told you not to eat so much. Keep alert. They have not put us out of the feast tent so we can sit here dreaming!"

Onen'ia blinked himself awake.

"How about a game of beaver-tooth toss? That should keep us both awake," suggested Ami'ck.

Onen'ia rubbed his eyes. A line of fog had formed out

on the ice at the islanded entrance to the bay. And far out on the ice a wisp of white mist seemed to crawl up out of one of the leads and slide forward across the surface of the ice. Several sleeping seals awoke and slithered off, barking worriedly, and then all was quiet again. In the encampment on the bluff, the drum beat on and on, and the dogs were still.

"A game, then?" Ami'ck put his back to the sea and hunkered down on his heels.

"A game," agreed Onen'ia.

▼▼▼▼

The dance went on.

A celebration of meat and life!

In the increasingly hot interior, the people stripped off their garments and gave themselves naked to the dance, males and females remaining on separate sides, circling, circling, taking up handfuls of rapidly melting snow to cool their bare flesh as every now and then a hunter burst forth in song or furious pantomime of the hunt, or a woman broke from the circle to dance a pantomime of her own, a meat-making dance, or a reenactment of pounding blubber into fat, or a waiting for the men to come safely off the ice.

M'alsum was not sure just when the dance became her dance, Puwo'win's dance, but although his arms were aching from endless beating upon the drum, he knew that he must match—or challenge—the cadence of the woman's movement or be proved inadequate to the task at hand. The people stepped back and drew the children close and watched the magic woman dance the shaman's dance to assure the intent of their feast.

In all his life M'alsum had never seen a dance like this . . . or a woman like this.

She whirled.

She spun.

She threw back her head and howled, like a wolf, like a dog when something sad has touched its soul, like the wind soughing through the forest or roaring over the sea in a storm, and all the while she raised up her arms in invitation to her attendants to close in and strip away the layerings of her outer garments.

M'alsum nearly lost the beat as she whirled around him. She was nearly naked now, her pale skin all but blackened with a patterning of tattoos that replicated the lines and curves of every major bone in her body. Her only garment was a cape, a grotesquely painted cape of pale buckskin that had been worked to near transparency and cut into a deeply delineated shape that closely approximated her own, so that as she whirled, it appeared as though her own shadow whirled with her. Indeed, as M'alsum observed the garment, he could not keep from thinking that had the skin of a human female been flayed and preserved by the most skilled hands, with even the face and hands and feet flattened out and every detail embellished by the artist's genius, it could not have been more realistic in appearance than this most disturbing piece of apparel.

She danced on.

And on.

Around and around Puwo'win whirled, then dropped to the ground and, moaning, simulated the emergence of a newborn creature from a womb from which she pretended to burst forth screaming, spurting blood from little sacks that she wore attached to bands at her wrists. The children screamed at this. The men and women caught their breaths. Even M'alsum was startled, for it was a splendid trick, especially when she rubbed the blood over her body and danced on to touch the mouth of every member of the assembly with it, moving not like a woman at all, but like a seal.

She swam.

She arched her slender torso and seemed to move, not through air but through invisible tides of water, diving, leaping, swimming in and out through the crowd, touching the women and children, leaving small gifts of shells drawn from her hair with each, then insinuating herself between the legs of the adult males, brushing their maleness with hand or mouth or cheek. At last she came to the Master of the Feast.

She stood before him.

A murmur arose from the assembly.

She took his hands from the drum.

The gathering began to clap the rhythm of the dance that M'alsum knew he was expected to dance with her now. He was Man, Master of the Feast. She was Shaman, Woman transformed into Seal. To mate with her would be to become one with her; to become one with her would be to verify the meaning of the feast for all.

And so it was done.

On the cold, bloodied, now nearly melted snow that symbolized the pack ice upon which seals mated, spawned, and gave themselves to be meat for the People, Puwo'win lay down on her back upon her strange cape of buckskin and opened herself to the Master of the Feast.

M'alsum stood over her, saw her wild gray hair tangled like sea spume on the cape—as gray and beautiful as Meya'kwé's hair on the day he had last set eyes on her— saw her breasts being raised to him and her long, soft mouth whispering his name in invitation. The watching assembly roared approval of his erection, for even for a son of Asticou it was of proportions that amazed him and would long stand high in the memories of the Dawnland people. He knelt, positioned himself, and drove deep.

She arched to him, flexed around him, held him, then relaxed and flexed again and again. As he moved on her, the assembly clapped the rhythm of their joining until ejaculation came. One by one the men turned to their own women, and while the elders saw to the children, the dance of procreation went on and on.

Until, from beyond the feast tent, the screams of a man rent the night.

▼▼▼▼

Fog lay heavy upon the beach.

The soapstone lamps were out and scattered across the strand, their oil spilled upon the stones, mixing with the blood of Ami'ck.

There was no sign of the man himself, only a few beaver teeth strewn upon the beach, along with the fox-skin bag in which the young man carried his gaming pieces.

"The Great One warned us!" Onen'ia gasped. "It stood there on the headland at the edge of the forest! Its shadow must have been pointing to Death coming for us from out there on the ice! But we did not believe our own eyes!"

A hollow seemed to have opened in M'alsum's gut as he straightened his hastily donned garments and looked down upon the distraught young man. "Great One! What Great One?"

"The one you claim to have slain!"

"And *have* slain!"

"The mammoth we saw on the headland was *white*! As in all the legends! As Puwo'win said! In the dark we were not sure if it was just a trick of the moon . . . snow shining bright on rocks between the trees . . . but I tell you now that it must have been a mammoth . . . a manitou mammoth as white as the great bear that came out of the fog in silence from the sea and took Ami'ck before I could even reach for a spear!"

"The Great One is dead!" insisted M'alsum. "It must have been the bear you saw on the headland . . . or a manifestation of your own fear, a vision of Ktci'awa, the Great Beast who appears to men as a warning that they are soon to meet Death!"

"White bears have never been known to come this far south!" Ogeh'ma was shaking his head as though to clear it of a bad dream. "And no man I have ever known has seen Ktci'awa. No . . . no . . ." He was rambling, so stunned that neither his tone nor posture was that of a hunt chief who was expected to be in control of the situation.

M'alsum's jaw tightened. The white mammoth? No! Surely what he had just said to the young hunter was true! It could not be real! He would not believe it! And he dared not let the others believe it, or he would not be Master of the Feast for long. Now, remembering what Kinap had said about Hasu'u being taken north, wearing the skin of a white bear, the irony of the situation struck him, as did a recollection of something he had heard from traders who had journeyed far into northern country. "It is said that white bears are ice bears, that they follow seals that give birth on the floes. Why would they not come here? Ogeh'ma should have warned his people of this danger."

Ogeh'ma, remembering that he was hunt chief in this encampment, indignantly puffed himself up within his furs. "My bandsmen know to watch for bears!"

"But your son does not know how to defend against them!"

•

"The wind was down. The dogs caught no scent or sound of danger and sounded no alarm," Onen'ia sputtered. "And who would have thought that a bear would come, not from the forest but out of the sea . . . out of the fog? By the time I threw a spear, it was a part of the mists . . . gone into thin air and—"

"And who would have thought that a hunt chief's son would come running to his father screaming for help instead of going after Ami'ck before the bear could take a man of his band down into the dark waters and under the ice between the leads?" demanded Puwo'win with no attempt to conceal the contempt in her voice.

Onen'ia uttered a garbled exhalation of misery. There were no words for the devastation he was feeling now.

There was silence on the beach.

Out on the ice several younger men had waded through the fog and had caught up with and were grappling with old Ko'ram, who, wailing and calling out to his lost son, was being restrained by Kanio'te lest he slip and fall into the dark water between the leads and drown, or venture too far out and risk being taken by the very bear that had taken his only son—although they had all agreed that there was little chance of this now. Despite the prodigious appetite of its kind, after devouring a man the bear would probably not feel the need to eat again for several days.

M'alsum's brow was down. He knew the answer to Puwo'win's question; he could smell it. "The son of Ogeh'ma reeks of fear. He has shamed himself and his band. Indeed, he has shamed all of us who have put our trust in him this night!"

"Never have I seen a bear like that! Never! One minute it was not there, and the next minute it had Ami'ck's head in its mouth and his guts were streaming out all over the beach and . . . and . . . has M'alsum never been afraid?" Onen'ia was bereft, desperately wanting forgiveness and understanding.

M'alsum eyed the young man coldly as he lied with an ease that was second nature to him now. "I have never turned my back on a friend or run away and left a member of my band to die. I have slain Katcheetohúskw! I have eaten of the heart of the Great Beast! I fear *nothing!*" Head high, he scanned the faces of those who had gathered on the beach. They believed every word. "Come," he said, ignoring Ogeh'ma's baleful glare. Both inviting and commanding, he spoke to the assembly with the full authority of one who knows that he has succeeded in making himself chief over lesser men. "There is nothing more that can be done for Ami'ck. Now seek warmth, my people. Now seek shelter. Now seek rest. Tomorrow we will mourn."

"And Onen'ia?" The shaman's query hung in the air, as chilling as the mists that now all but obscured the beach and bay and surrounding headlands.

M'alsum tensed. He met Puwo'win's gaze. Her words had been an open challenge to him, and well he knew it. Her head was held as high as his. Her body was as tense. Her tattooed features were taut with breathless expectation. He knew that she was allowing the invasion of his stare, welcoming it as intensely as she had welcomed the penetration of his passion, informing him with her gaze that what he said and did now would determine his ultimate worth in her eyes. Once again they were as predators poised on either side of prey. And this time, even before he spoke, M'alsum was certain that from this moment they would share in the feast of power that was to come.

"Onen'ia is cast out!" he declared.

A murmur went through the assembly.

M'alsum let it settle.

"It would be kinder to brain him here on the beach," said Puwo'win, her eyes narrowed now, measuring.

"I am Mammoth Slayer, Bringer of All Good Things to the People. I will not shame my host chief by taking the life of his worthless son! This is for him to do. Or not do. But let all know now: I will not abide a coward in any encampment of mine."

▼▼▼▼

"Encampment of *his?*"

"That is what he said, my husband."

Ogeh'ma heard Segub'un's affirmation. He started to speak again but could not find his voice. He stood rooted to the strand, watching M'alsum and Puwo'win leading the people up the narrow, well-worn pathway to the bluffs. Heartsick, he watched them go.

All of them.

Except Segub'un, of course, and Onen'ia's bucktoothed woman, Goh'beet, and their small children. And Suda'li, the new widow of Ami'ck, and her now fatherless twin boys.

That was all. Save for Kanio'te and the three young men of his band who were still out on the ice with Ko'ram, these were the only individuals who had remained behind to give comfort to him in this most comfortless of moments. And now Segub'un was on her knees before Onen'ia. Her head was bent as she silently shed a mother's tears of bereavement for a son who must now be killed by his father's hand or sent on his way with his woman and little ones. As one cast out of his band for causing the death of another he would be allowed none of his belongings, and wherever he went, cautious men would shun him.

A shiver went up Ogeh'ma's back. The soft sound of his woman's crying moved him more deeply than he could afford to be moved. He needed to think. He needed to find his tongue again. And his wits! He was furious with himself for not challenging M'alsum. The man had been challenging his authority and deliberately demeaning him in small, not always subtle ways for days now. And why had he not looked the shaman woman of the great Squam straight in her avaricious eyes and told her once and for all what he thought of her shrewd and lewd pretense to magic!

"Puwo'win." The name soured his mouth. He worked up saliva and spat it from the end of his tongue to keep the fragments of its sound from contaminating his lips. He knew that he should have expressed his doubts about her long ago, when winters first began to grow long, when Squam stopped making his seasonal visits, when she and her emissaries came from the island demanding ever more in meat and hides and the occasional young girl to "honor" the great Squam's needs. The latter request always irritated him, for he knew that other bands were being asked for similar tribute, and he could not keep from wondering crossly just how many young girls were needed to raise an old shaman's hunt staff these days. More likely they were servicing the young men who guarded Squam's woman and did her bidding. But, since the families of the chosen girls made no complaints and the human tribute always seemed eager to be "honored," he had kept his thoughts to himself. After all, he had been hunt chief long enough to know that in changing and uncertain times people needed magic and ritual more than ever.

Since the time beyond beginning the People of all tribes had venerated their shamans, their magic men and women, their alleviators of boredom, their bringers of solace to wounded hearts when men died on the hunt or children drowned at river crossings or women bled to death in childbirth or infants were stillborn or the People sat silent and empty-eyed in the dead of winter with the ache of hunger feeding on their innards. And from the time beyond beginning, since First Man and First Woman were said to have made their final camp in the Dawnland on the sacred island in the face of the rising sun, there had always been a shaman in residence on the sacred island. A Squam. A magic man said to be like no other. A man capable of calling the game and banishing the Great Ghost Cannibal winter. A shaman as wise and mysterious and as giving of the gifts of life—to those who paid him tribute—as the great anadromous fish for whom he was named. For it was ancient knowledge that when the sea rose to make an island of what had been a sacred mountain, First Man and First Woman gave their bones into the care of their shaman and entrusted their spirits to the salmon so that, when summoned by Squam, they might return each year from the salt water of the sea to mate and spawn in the fresh water that poured forth from the land and yield their flesh along with the flesh of all of the animals of the land and sea and sky to sustain the life of Dawnland tribes forever.

Ogeh'ma's hands tightened into fists at his sides. He was not sure he believed any of it. By nature he was a pragmatic and observant man, and lessons learned during a long and cautiously lived life had given him no cause to place his faith in magic or in those who claimed to be able to affect the turning of the tides of life with a dance or song or the drop of a feather or the turn of a stone or the burning of a bone, or with wishes made for good or evil in return for meat or prime pelts or prime women. Better to watch the stars and the lengthening or shortening of the sun's shadow upon the earth if one wanted to anticipate the return of the game and the marsh birds and the seals. Better to mark in the mind the many trails the deer and moose and caribou made through the forest, and where they safely forded the streams and rivers, and where, each year, the People could set their weirs and nets in almost certain knowledge that the capelin would come in spring to be food for them, with salmon and char and trout soon following, and white whales! And if the fish failed to come in numbers sufficient to fill the bellies of all, better to know how and where to find other meat and how to safely procure it in a land upon which Man was not the only hungry carnivore and might well become meat himself if—like poor Ami'ck—in a moment of carelessness he turned his back to the advantage of an unseen predator.

Segub'un's sobbing had grown louder.

"Stop your sniveling, woman!" he commanded. He would not stand here and listen to her weep. It unmanned him. Onen'ia was not dead yet! And it was not right for Segub'un to be forced to mourn for him when she was still in mourning for a daughter who had been so precious to her that she had cut her hair in an agony of grief over the loss of the girl. His mouth tightened. M'alsum had failed to save Hasu'u's life. Ogeh'ma had not sent the man from his encampment! He had not demanded his life in return for that of his lost and, although he had never admitted it to a soul, favorite daughter. When the girl had agreed to go off with the handsome, clever trader from the inland forests, Segub'un had suffered in silence for endless moons, as had he. And now Nee'nah, Ane'pemin'an, and Chi'co'pee had followed the same man, leaving their mother to say her final good-byes to a brother they were not likely ever to see again. And only Nee'nah looked back! What kind of daughters had he raised? And what kind of man was this M'alsum to so easily seduce them away from those who loved them? A surge of indignation went through him. He knew what kind of man he was: a usurper. And ah, but he *was* clever!

"Not clever enough!" Ogeh'ma declared. "I have been too considerate of him. I have been too anxious to accept his every word. But I will not be shamed in my own encampment! I will not follow along at his heels like an obedient dog! No! I will not turn up my neck to him or to any other man again! Onen'ia, embrace your mother and take up your spears."

The young man looked at his father, confused, dull-eyed with grief. "I am not worthy of them," he said quietly.

Ogeh'ma was suddenly disgusted with his son, and even more with himself. "Then go out onto the ice and call back the white bear! Not to kill it, because you say you are unworthy of that, but to tell it that you will make a second portion of meat for it this night! Go, Onen'ia, go! You might as well! Because I will brain no son of mine or send from my family one who has, until this night, been one of the strongest and bravest hunters in my band. With what skill and presumption M'alsum dares to manipulate me and leave me standing on my feet before the assembled bands while he walks away with my pride! Kill a son . . . abandon a son . . . what kind of a choice is this to give to a man in his own hunting camp? If I do either, I will be a dog in his eyes and in the eyes of my people forever!"

"But, my father, I *was* afraid. When the bear came out of the fog, I could not move. I stared at it. It stared at me. And somehow its eyes seemed to tell me: 'You are not who will be meat for me unless you move, unless you speak.' And then Ami'ck looked up from the gaming pieces and saw the look on my face, and as he turned to see what I saw—"

"Do not frighten the children," Ogeh'ma interrupted sternly. The others were coming off the ice now. His face worked with emotion as he saw the way Ko'ram was being supported by Kanio'te. As they came close, he spoke to all but looked directly at the little ones when he said, "Know this, and never forget it: Sometimes when a hunter is confronted by a terrible and sudden danger, his spirit withers at the sight of it. Sometimes his courage and strength desert him. It is like reaching into icy water for something you have dropped. What happens to the skin of the reaching hand at the first shock of cold water?"

"It shrivels up!" answered one of the little ones.

"Yes!" affirmed Ogeh'ma. "It is afraid of the cold. It would turn itself inside out and hide inside the bones of the reaching hand if it could. But the hand keeps reaching even though the skin remains shriveled and afraid. Brave hand! So it is with the heart of the hunter. A brave heart must overcome the shock that comes to his body when he faces a thing that shrivels the skin of his spirit. Many times your father has done this! Many times! Tonight . . . it was not one of those times."

Ko'ram was shaking his head. "It was my fault, not Onen'ia's. I spoke badly of the shaman. She called the bear out of the fog to punish me through my son. Puwo'win's powers are great! She—"

"Would have you believe exactly that! She would have us all believe exactly that! But I tell you it was the smell and light of the oil lamps that drew the bear!" Ogeh'ma was emphatic. "If Ami'ck had not been sitting with his back to the sea, he and Onen'ia would have driven it off! As it was, it was a danger unforeseen. One that will *not* be overlooked again. The loss of Ami'ck's life will assure this! And from this night, if it is the will of Ami'ck's family, Onen'ia will hunt in his place for his father and women and children! But let no man or woman ever name a son or daughter of Ogeh'ma Coward! Bravely did my Hasu'u walk from this band with a new man who swore to protect her and bring her safely back to us. And all hunters who face the great toothed ones in the night are afraid! All! And so I tell you now, Ogeh'ma will not yield to the command of a hunt chief who says otherwise . . . nor will I walk with him, for that man is either a liar or a fool!"

"That one is no fool," said Goh'beet darkly. With a shudder she drew her children close. "He hurt me when he lay on me . . . to make me feel his power, he said. And he has made himself shine in the eyes of the shaman, Puwo'win. I think, father of my husband, that he will now be hunt chief and Master of the Feast of your band, forever."

"Only Squam lives forever!" said Ko'ram. There was bitterness in his voice, and weariness, and sadness—the deep and unutterable sadness of a father who has outlived the last of his children. Then, with a sigh, he conceded, "And the Mammoth Slayer who has slain Katcheetohúskw!"

"Who knows what M'alsum has slain?" snapped Ogeh'ma. "And who has seen Squam in nearly a handcount of winters? I say maybe there is no Squam! Maybe he died long ago and there is only his shrewd and greedy woman hanging on to his reputation and wisely linking herself with an ambitious trader from the inland forest who dares to tell tales as tall as the stories spun by the scarheaded giant who comes this way to earn meat in exchange for his stories and knowledge of the healing ways!"

"Squam will live on in his son." Ko'ram sighed the reminder. "When they find that boy, even if Squam himself is dead, he will live on, not as other men live through their sons, but completely—same man, same memories, same wisdom—a true and magical rebirth. The power of the sacred stone of the Ancestors will make it so."

"Magic stones! Magic men! Magic women!" Ogeh'ma was beyond anger, beyond patience. "What kind of magic can Puwo'win or Squam possess if they could not prevent their son from being stolen? And how could she dance as she danced in the feast tent when a child of her own body has been taken from her?"

"For the People . . . to appease the spirits of the slain seals . . . she has put aside her sadness for us," said Onen'ia.

Ogeh'ma stared at his son as though he could not believe what he had just heard him say. "Maybe she is right. Maybe I *should* brain you! If there is a brain inside the head of any man who truly believes that a woman can appease the seals through dance or that a man can actually call the game and determine the weather or that a single hair plucked from the flesh of a dead animal will give the power of that animal to the man who possesses it! No! It is *myself* I should brain for allowing you to believe these things when, in my own heart, I have doubted!"

"Ogeh'ma!" Segub'un was on her feet. "You have always led your people to a meat-rich camp. Always! Your sons and daughters are the children of a great hunt chief! We will always believe what you tell us . . . because you have never given us cause to doubt *you!*"

He stood a little taller. She was still strong and willful, his Segub'un, like all her daughters. As Hasu'u must have been strong and willful when the manitous came for her.

She must have fought them! She must have held her head high and fought them until the end! Thoughts of her hardened his heart even more against M'alsum. He had let her die! And then he had come back to her people, shamed her father, robbed him of his authority over the assembled bands, and now he actually expected him to kill or abandon one of her brothers to suit his will. His eyes met Segub'un's and held. A man could draw back from such a woman whatever pride he had lost.

"The forces of Creation have given me the eyes and the wisdom to see the signs of shifting weather and changing game trails. I need no magic man or magic woman or magic stones to show me the way to feed and clothe myself or my people! We will mourn Ami'ck. Here on the beach we will mourn. Then I will take my family and any who wish to walk with me away from this camp. I will seek the caribou. Yes! We will follow them north! Far from this encampment! Long has it been since I have visited with our cousins at the distant River of the White Whales."

"But, my father . . . I have seen Ktci'awa!"

Ogeh'ma fixed Onen'ia with hard eyes. "If you had seen the white bear in time to alert Ami'ck, I would still be your father! Now you will be Ko'ram's son. He is old. Because of you he has no sons. No family. You will hunt and care for him now. Your family will be his family. As for what you saw on the headland, I do not know, nor do I *want* to know. There will be no more talk of manitous—or of mammoths—in my encampment!"

▼▼▼▼

He had to know.

Alone in the dark with two spears in one hand and a third held at the ready in the other, M'alsum crept from the sleeping encampment, barely daring to believe that he had not awakened the dogs as he made his way off the bluff, into the trees, and toward the headland.

The moon had long since set. A light wind had risen, driving the fog before it, leaving the forest thinly veiled with wisps of mist and reeking of cold dampness. Somewhere not far away a lynx screamed. The sound sliced through every nerve ending in M'alsum's body.

He was afraid, but not of the lynx. Of something much larger and more dangerous.

His mouth was dry, his gut constricted, but he went on. He had to know just what the two guardsmen on the beach had seen.

Moonlight on snow-covered rocks? Yes! Everyone agreed that it had to have been that. Only that. Just as everyone agreed that ice bears were not known to venture into the forests, but then . . .

A wave of nausea went through him as he visualized the bear out on the fog-shrouded ice, feasting on Ami'ck in the dark. And yet it was not the white bear he feared even half as much as the other apparition that now stood at the back of his mind threatening to be the ruination of all he had secured for himself this night.

The white mammoth!

If it was real, it would have left tracks in the snow. There would be signs of its presence. He had to see! He had to know! And if the nightmare proved to be of flesh and blood, he had to obliterate all sign of it before anyone else came this way and saw the truth of his lies.

And if the mammoth is still there? Waiting for you? Following you?

He stopped dead in his tracks and, reliving the terror he had felt in the ravine, reminded himself that he had already faced one charging mammoth and lived to tell the tale. What he had done he could do again if he had to!

Could you?

"Ah!"

Never!

Nausea overwhelmed him. He dropped to his knees and succumbed to a paroxysm of retching.

"What a waste of good feast meat. A man should not move so quickly so soon after eating. The seals would surely be offended . . . if I choose to tell them."

M'alsum looked up, backhanded vomit from his mouth, and squinted into darkness to see "Puwo'win?"

"Whom else would you expect to find in the forest in the deep of the night, Mammoth Slayer? The virgin daughters of Ogeh'ma? They would come if you asked them. But I think you were seeking something else . . . something larger . . . something more dangerous. A white mammoth, perhaps?"

He went cold.

"We think alike, you and I," she said as she came toward him through the darkness, a woman all in white, her hair loose, as gray as the skeining mists, so like Meya'kwé's hair. "There was nothing on the headland, Mammoth Slayer. Only trees and snow-covered rocks. And the snowpack is free of all but the tracks of hares and squirrels and birds."

Relief flushed through him. He felt better now. Much better. He turned the spear in his right hand, used the stone head to break up the hard surface of the snowpack, then fisted up loosened snow, cleansed his mouth with it, and spat it out. Feeling at a disadvantage on his knees before her, he got to his feet and asked coldly, warily, "Why should this concern the woman of Squam?"

"For the same reason it concerns you. If the white mammoth is real, you cannot have killed it, can you? And if you have not killed it, then you are not what you claim to be. But since it was only a trick of the moon played on the minds of fearful men, we have nothing to fear."

"I fear nothing!" His gut constricted at the lie, and at something else, a word she had used. "We?"

"Yes. We. You understand the meaning of magic as well as I. You know how to turn the minds of others to serve your will."

"I am no shaman!"

She laughed softly, mirthlessly. "It is not what you *are* that matters, Fearless Mammoth Slayer and Bringer of All Good Things to the People. What matters is what others *believe* you to be!"

"And what do you believe me to be, Puwo'win, woman of Squam?"

"A dangerous man to anyone who does not serve your will."

"And what is my will?"

"To have—to take—*all*."

"No man can have or take all."

"Squam can."

"I am not Squam."

"You could be."

He laughed. Then realized that she was not jesting. "What are you saying, Puwo'win?"

"That the People could be led to believe that the forces of Creation have brought you to the Dawnland to dwell on the sacred island in Squam's place. Already they question his power. But they have found no cause to question yours. You have brought the sun and the seals! They would bring us tribute just as they have always brought it to him . . . the best in furs and—"

"*Us?*"

"Would you not be Master of the Feast of Life in all encampments, M'alsum? Would you not have all men acknowledge your strength and power as they acknowledge his? It could be said that, in you, the great Squam has been reborn!"

"Why not in you?"

"I am female. The legend does not favor me. The great Squam must be male."

Excitement was rising in him, and yet he remembered, "Your son, the one you search for. Is he not expected to take Squam's place?"

She looked at him long and hard, thinking, determining. And then, on an intake of breath, deciding. "I will speak truth to you. The one I hunt is not mine. Squam would never allow my children to live. No, the one I hunt is the spawn of his old age, born not to me but to one of the young women brought to the island from a far place as tribute to please him. Who would have thought that he would want her child when for an entire lifetime he believed that he would live only as long as no son of his was allowed to grow to manhood and rob him of his powers. But this time—old and blind and living in a cave at the far side of the island so that no outsider might see his frailty— she made him believe that no man is immortal and that he could live on only through her child, for surely he was no longer man enough to make another." A tremor of loathing and anger went through her. "She was one of *them*, one of the Old Tribe! Until her coming I thought them all dead, driven from the land, drowned, burned up in fire. But she had the mark! A small dark mark at the base of her spine. I saw it when she was wading in the surf one day. And so I killed her, as those of our kind must always kill her kind. They have *true* power. Not magic. Not pre-science. They simply see what is false in the world. They are our enemies wherever we find them. But Squam would have made her Puwo'win in my place! Imagine it! She would have made no pretense to magic. None! Who would bring tribute to such a woman or to her son? And what would have become of me and those who have served me and been rewarded so generously by me all these long years?"

"And so you hunt the boy."

"He saw me dancing in his mother's skin! He knew what it was! He knew it was a fresh skin, not the old one that was given to me by my shaman mother long ago—a sign of our power over *them*. The child attacked me and ran away. When he is found, he is to be killed . . . before he finds his tongue and tells of Squam's frailty to every living creature in this world and the world beyond."

His eyes narrowed. "You need not fear him. He is dead. In the forest. And the giant with him. Killed by the same raiders who fell upon my band."

She did not move. "You told me that you saw no sign of them."

"I saw a mother looking for her son. I had no heart to bring grief to you."

Still she did not move. "Do not lie to me, Mammoth Slayer, for I have long yearned to have a man in his prime beside me in the night again, not only one of those who serve me in exchange for the ease of life they find on the island. I would have an equal, a man who understands how easily the People may be manipulated through magic and fear of all that they may only hope to understand and control—through us. But we must come to one another in trust, M'alsum. If we are to deceive them, we cannot deceive one another. We must know each other for what we are."

"And what are we, Puwo'win?"

"We are Masters of the Feast of Life, Mammoth Slayer! We are the bear come from the sea, concealed in the fog of the People's superstitions, benign, beautiful, never recognized in time . . . until they are devoured."

"Or the bear is killed."

Her head went high at his openly cautionary statement. Was there mirth in her eyes? He could not tell. The wind had dropped. Fog was insinuating its way back through the trees, graying and thickening the darkness all around them. He could barely see her now. High above, lost in the mists, the distant callings of migrating geese could be heard; the sound was gone before he could fully grasp a fleeting recollection of something Kinap had said about the birds . . . something . . . impossible to remember now as Puwo'win reached out and laid her hands softly, seductively, upon his forearms.

"Not you, M'alsum!" she said in reply to his statement. "Never you! Have you not slain Katcheetohúskw? Have you not survived your woman and child and brothers and all who have traveled with you or passed within the fall of your shadow . . . only to have the People believe that you are invincible?"

"I . . ." Now it was M'alsum's head that went high. Puwo'win's questions had not been questions. She had made each one an accusation. As though she knew. As though she had seen straight into the heart of his lies and seen the truth. The entire tangled, bloodied truth!

And adored him for it!

"Squam is dead," she told him. "I have killed him. Now let me create him again in you."

Part Three

CIRCLE

‾‾‾‾‾‾
▼▼▼▼▼▼▼

Ho!
I am Life!
I dance! I turn! Forward! Never back!
Ho!
I am Life!
Catch me! Hold me! If you can!
Ho!

Chapter One

▼▼▼▼▼▼▼

Mowea'qua would not forgive him.

No matter how kind he was to her. No matter how many times he tried to make it right in so many little ways. No matter how often he explained his reasons. Sound reasons to Kinap were not sound reasons to Mowea'qua.

U'na'li was dead.

He had skinned the wolf along with the other he had slain and had made a New Woman coat for her. As though she would accept it! She had thrown it in his face. And then, sobbing, she had taken it back again, not to please him—she would never try to please him again—but to cherish forever the memory of the wolf who had trusted her and had come to death because of that trust.

"You could have driven her off! You did not have to kill her!"

"With your grandmother's life at risk, wolves are of no importance to me!"

Mowea'qua would not hear such ponderous logic. As though love for one canceled love for the other! She smoothed her hands over the sleek black skin of the wolf and refused to look at the wolf's killer. At Kinap. At her

no-longer-beloved giant. At her father who without so
much as a second thought had killed the wolf and practically hurled the eagle U'wo'hi'li into the night with a command never to return.

But U'wo'hi'li *had* turned. Just for a moment. It had
been enough. The great white-headed eagle had flown
back over the clearing and dipped its wings to her. And
then U'wo'hi'li had kept on flying, not in the way that
Kinap had commanded it to go but in the opposite direction. Higher and higher U'wo'hi'li had flown. Into the
stars. Into the vast dark distances that, with the dawn, gave
birth to the rising sun.

She trembled now as she remembered the moment.

U'wo'hi'li' had shown her what she must do. Yes! She
would follow the eagle! U'wo'hi'li had shown her the way
to the Dawnland, and soon she would go. She would not
spend her life in this dark forest with Kinap, caring for a
stubborn old grandmother who refused to take her medicine, and wedded for the rest of her days to a goggle-eyed,
nearly deaf boy with a lisp. As soon as she could convince
Ne'gauni to make the trek, she would give him back his
leg, and together, with or without Kinap's help, they would
seek the sacred spring, make use of its magic, and then go
on their way to find the beautiful one and—

The sharp thunk of an arrow struck her thoughts. She
looked up. Kinap was working with the boy again, and with
Ne'gauni, teaching the way of the new weapon. His stu-
dents were aiming at a target made of an old buckskin sack
tied to a tree at the far end of the clearing.

"Mowea'qua!" The giant gestured to her. "Come! Join
us! You have prepared enough rabbit skins to keep yourself
in moon-blood rags for a lifetime! Get up! You must learn
the skill of this, too. And not just for the hunt. You never

know when you will need to use it to protect your band against our enemies. I was a fool not to insist that you master the art of the bow and arrow long ago."

"The ways of the masked Strangers are not our ways," Old One mumbled.

"I will hear no more of such nonsense from you, Kelet! We live as we must live. You know as well as I that the world is changing. And the Circle of Life must turn forward, never—"

"We know, we know!" snapped the girl, in no mood for what was certain to lead into a lecture or a story full of tedious analogies. She did not think she could bear to hear another of his stories. She got to her feet and wiped the palms of her hands on her hips. Calluses were forming on the backs of her fingers and the heels of her hands, and at his suggestion she had made herself a wide leather wristband to prevent the snap of the bowstring from balding the sleeve of her hunting shirt or raising a welt on her forearm.

Now, although she stood her ground and presented a glum, indifferent face, when she picked up the ashwood bow and the quiver of arrows he had made for her, she had to concede that she was glad Kinap was teaching her the use of the new weapon. She liked everything she saw of it and marveled each time he attached a string to a lighter arrow so that he could bring down birds and rabbits from a distance and then haul them in, arrow intact and ready for another shot. She liked the way the arrows sounded when they flew, and when they landed. And she liked the feel of the bow in her hands, even though Kinap had told her that neither bow nor arrows were anywhere near what he would like for her. It was too late in the season to find suitable hardwood, but he was convinced that they were adequate for a start. The longer she worked to perfect her skills with the weapon, the more convinced she became of just how useful it would prove in the days and nights when she and Ne'gauni were on the trail to the Dawnland. Once there, the beautiful one was sure to be even more delighted with the girl who brought his brother back from the country of the dead when she volunteered to teach him the use of this wonderful new weapon! She sighed to think of it. The Dawnland woman could never give the beautiful one such a wonderful gift as this. For with knowledge of the bow, thanks to Mowea'qua, he would be able to travel through the forest unafraid, the equal of any man or manitou with his bright copper-headed spear and his sleek, deadly arrows. Never again would he be outarmed and forced to run before the predations of masked raiders!

"There is a robin bob-walking on that bare patch of earth over there," Kinap told her, pointing a good ways off. "See if you have learned anything! And remember, release the arrow from the right side of the bow so you do not have to slow its flight with the press of a finger lest the shaft fly wild. Careful. Yes. That looks right. *Now.*"

She held her breath, aimed, and . . .

An arrow loosed from Ne'gauni's bow took the robin through its throat. With a whoop of excitement Musquash practically flew forward to scoop up the prey and bring it to Ne'gauni.

"It was for me to kill!" protested Mowea'qua.

The boy looked crestfallen.

Ne'gauni eyed the dead bird, carefully freed his arrow, then gave the robin back to Musquash and, with a nod of his head, gave him permission to give it to Mowea'qua. "The kill goes to the quick, but if you want it, take it!" Ne'gauni told her sharply as the boy stopped before her, looked up at her adoringly, then handed up the bird.

Mowea'qua glared down at the love-struck child. "For yourself keep! If kill it I cannot, want it I do not! And stop looking at me like that! Yah! Now that Kinap no longer tethers you, why run do you not away?"

"He will run away when you do," drawled Ne'gauni.

The boy's face became very solemn. He moved off to sit beside Old One where she sat cross-legged on her furs, propped up against her padded backrest, smiling and welcoming him close with a hug. "I will take kay-oo of you, Bearded Gwandmuh-thoo," he assured her. "But when you ah stwong again, I will wun away. I must!"

The giant loosed one of his heavy arrows and, when it made a deep and angry *thwank* in the target tree, glowered at the foursome and said emphatically, "No one is going anywhere! We are a family now. This is our home. Here we will stay and hope that our enemies never find us!"

"My fah-thoo has enemies," said the boy. "He, too, is old and sick. Now that I am gone, there is no one to take care of him. Except *huh*."

"Then he is as good as dead, boy! Forget him! Thank the forces of Creation that you have a new life now!" Kinap strode to the target, removed the arrow, and, after staring at it a moment as though he wished to stab it back into the target, turned back to the child. "Look to Mowea'qua for your future. And to Kelet. They are the new women in your life. Good women! Kind women! And Ne'gauni here can be a brother to you. And I . . . well . . . I may not be a match for Squam, but I will not stand by and allow harm to come to you, my boy."

"I am not yohs," the child said without rancor, quietly, soberly. He looked from the giant to the others and, after allowing his gaze to hold on Mowea'qua, offered up the most melancholy of sighs as he sagged into Old One's embrace and buried his face in her lap. "The pwiddy one does not like me. She will nevoo mahwee me!"

Mowea'qua rolled her eyes. It was not true! At least the part about her not liking him. She had not cared for him at all at first, of course, but that was because of the way he had behaved and because of the shock of being told that he—and not her beautiful one—was to be her gift from the forest and her mate forever. It was still an appalling thought. But he was proving to be a thoughtful, albeit somber, little boy. And although he sometimes woke screaming in the night and messed his bed furs, how could she dislike anyone who called her "pwiddy"? Pretty. How sweet it was to hear! But she would not marry him. Ever. Her heart belonged to another.

▼▼▼▼

She came to Ne'gauni that night. Quietly, like the wraith he had first seen staring at him out of the falling snow when he had lain in the creek and given up his spirit to the black river of death.

"What do you want?" he asked brusquely. He did not care if he offended her. He had never quite forgiven her for her outburst against Hasu'u.

"Shh. Wake the boy do not. Kinap has Old One helped to go outside. Still she cannot her water hold until dawn! Maybe soon now she will better be. If your brother's magic medicine she will only take!"

"She is old, Mowea'qua. Old people drift in and out of the lodges by night. My kind or yours, it makes no difference. I doubt there is a medicine that will make her young again."

"Your brother has Kinap told that all ills his medicine will cure."

He sighed. She was in a mood to talk; there was no use trying to ignore her. "M'alsum always traded for the best." He would concede her that much.

"When stronger is Old One, we will go to him!"

"That again? He will not want to see this face, Mowea'qua. Nor will he want any part of you. He has a woman. The best of women! He will be searching for her now. He will bring her back to her people, and to ours. Perhaps he already has. And you cannot leave your grandmother, Mowea'qua."

"Kinap she has! And now Musquash, too! You so fast are healing! And every day you practice with the bow and arrows that Kinap for you has made. He says that you and the arrows seem of one mind to be. You from the quiver draw an arrow, and, even before you mate it to the bow and send it flying, knows it where you wish it to go!"

"You are learning quickly, too."

"Yes, say I. And to think the flying sticks we took, Old One and I, to use the stone heads for scrapers and awls and never their true purpose knew! But lucky are we to have collected so many. Now Kinap does not need to make new heads for the arrows he makes for us. Ah, think of how your beautiful M'alsum would smile to learn from us the magic of the bow! A brother would he welcome, and a woman, who would bring him such a gift, say I, yes?"

"Forget him, Mowea'qua."

"Never! The crutch I have for you made, with the rabbit-fur padding, and the new carved bottom leg for you to strap on and walk with, with these things you now move around almost as—"

"The stump of the leg that you have taken from me still oozes. It pains me to walk, Mowea'qua. It will always pain me to walk. And even if it did not, everything that Kinap said to me was true. I have no desire to return to my people. I am not going anywhere. For their sake even more than my own."

She pulled in a little breath, held it a moment, then blurted, "Soon winter over will be! See you will! When the rains come and the ice goes out and you bathe in the sacred spring, a new leg and a new face you will have!"

"And frogs will sprout feathers in the same pond!"

"Mock me not. Believe you must."

"Why?"

"Because true it is!"

"What is twue?" asked the boy on a yawn, peeking up from his furs and rubbing sleep from his eyes.

The weather baffle was swept aside. Kinap entered in a rush, holding his furs over his head and ushering a mumbling and distracted Old One inside.

"Make room for a pair of old wet dogs!" said the giant.

Ne'gauni smelled the fine, misty smell of a spring rain and knew that Mowea'qua was right. Winter was over at last.

Chapter Two

▼▼▼▼▼▼▼

They were talking of resting and eating again.

Hasu'u could not understand why.

They had not come far since leaving the place of the caribou kill and the little valley where they had taken the new women captives. Perhaps it was simply the surfeit of meat and the tendency to overeat and grow groggy-eyed upon the trail that slowed them down. The River of the White Whales was very far; all agreed that this was so. The travelers, while yearning for the abundance of its shores and lusting for the meat and skin of whale, had begun to take their time enjoying the meat at hand. Amayersuk told Hasu'u that there was really no reason to hurry, for the sun would have to lengthen its walk across the sky for up to a third of a double hand-count of moons before the whales came to molt in the shallows, easy meat for the hunters who gathered along the shores of the great river.

Hasu'u made no comment. What did she know about it, save that she hoped never to set eyes on the place? She did not remind her captors that, with the coming of spring, the forests would teem with blackflies and ticks, and travel would be a misery.

The days had been cold, but not bitterly so, and yesterday it had rained again, a fine, barely noticeable mist. It had jeweled the trees and dewed the rapidly diminishing snowpack but failed to do more than layer a thin sheen of moisture that quickly froze again on the surface of the small bog lakes and watercourses that remained in the hard lock of ice. Travel remained as easy for them as it did for the caribou whose trails they crossed now and then. And each dawn a dank and heavy mist lay upon the land and lingered until nearly noon.

Hasu'u breathed it in hungrily. She could still smell the sea in it. Far away now. Several days away. As she walked along, she drew comfort from thinking of her people safe in their late-winter camp on the bluffs above the sea. The seals must have come into the leads by now. Ogeh'ma and Segub'un and her sisters, brothers, and aunties would have their work cut out for them, but it would be joyous work. There would be much singing and laughter, and maybe even Squam himself would come across the ice this year. He had not come in so long! Or perhaps Puwo'win might come without him again.

Hasu'u's smile disappeared. Puwo'win's visits had always shadowed her days. The woman was handsome and aloof and a little frightening, as a shaman should be, but she put on far too much of a show with her excess of tattoos and feathers and paint and her ugly white fanged mask and all the shells in her hair. Hasu'u had seen her only twice, but each time Puwo'win made her think of something that had been washed up on the beach after a storm surf, with all the refuse of the tide thrown upon it. If M'alsum had reached the Dawnland, she wondered what he would think of Puwo'win. He would see through her wiles; she was certain of that!

M'alsum! Ah, M'alsum! Why have you not come for me?

She drew the baby close. Her little tiguak was nursing hungrily. Her smile reappeared, not for herself but for her adopted son. She had lost her own wonderful child; nothing she did could bring him back. He would live forever in her heart. But in that heart she had found room for another. And Amayersuk was right. With only a little love on her part, the baby was thriving. Looking down at the now familiar face pressed to her breast, she began to hum a soft, wordless little song to the child.

"Be careful, Noqumiut, you have a reputation to maintain!" warned Amayersuk as she walked along to Hasu'u's right.

Hasu'u looked up and turned her gaze to the other woman. "Reputation?"

"How are we to know that we have named you correctly for a miserable, ungrateful, hang-headed ghost if you smile and walk along singing like a woman who is enjoying her life?"

"Her name is Hasu'u! One Who Sings Always!" said Tôrnârssuk, overhearing the two women's words as he came up from behind them on his way to the front of the column of travelers. "It is a better name for the woman who gives the milk of life to my son. It is from her old life, but maybe, along with the dogs I have given her, I will let her keep it!"

Hasu'u was not sure if he had just offered a concession or an enticement to further good behavior in the same manner that he would have tossed a lump of prime fat to one of the dogs as reward for a good day's work. Either way, she would not thank him. She was Hasu'u, a hunt chief's daughter and a headman's woman, and although she was his slave it did not matter to her what he called her. She did not draw her sense of self-worth from him.

They reached the river, not a large watercourse compared to the river they had crossed on the day they had slain the caribou. It seemed safe enough, with the water frozen solid and high embankments shaded by spruce and balsam and white fir leveling off to broad, pebbly beaches littered with deadfall and stippled with broken stands of aspen. They took note of the downed trees, for most were flood sweeps and not deadfall, and they observed the whitened bars and scars on the aspens that delineated the high-water mark of this creek to the height of a man. Tôrnârssuk led the way with Avataut and Ningao to make sure that the crossing was solid. The skinny dog moved out ahead of them, tail high and nose to the ice, trotting back and forth and taking on a manner of much greater importance than it possessed except in its own mind.

It was a good crossing. Hasu'u did not doubt for a moment that it would be. The ice beneath her feet was firm and opaque, with no transparency and none of the gray cast that warned of disintegration.

They brought the sledges to a stop on the far shore. The sun was peeking through impending rain clouds, sending long warm rays onto the embankment where they decided to pause and rest and savor the sunlight while they could. Thunder sounded. Far away. Barely audible.

Hasu'u turned toward the northeast. Clouds were piled high above the mountains that were said to be the home of the Seven Thunderers. Black, heavy, ugly clouds. She thought that it must be snowing there now, and cold. She was weary of the cold!

"There is rain in the mountains," observed Tôrnârssuk. Nothing else was said, but everyone was suddenly working together to drag the sledges higher onto the embankment. In a short time they were all settled in the sunlight, looking down at the riverbed from about the same height as the high-water mark on the aspens.

"Our tunraq is wise. Now we can rest. And eat!" said Amayersuk.

Hasu'u made no comment. They had already stopped to eat three times since dawn. She was beginning to learn that in Tôrnârssuk's band it was always time to eat. "They should all look like walruses!" she said as she spread out a hide, then took the baby from its sling and placed it on the ground covering in the warmth of the sun.

Amayersuk chuckled and shook her head as she helped with the baby. "They can go for days with no food. No complaint. But when there is meat and no hurry on the trail . . . why not eat? Who knows if there will be food tomorrow?"

Hasu'u took up the bearskin baby bag that had been put into her care and, kneeling, began to change the infant's soiled swaddling. "We carry enough meat on our sledges to last us all the way to the River of the White Whales! But I think they will eat it all before we ever—"

"What is that?" Amayersuk turned, straining to hear. "What?"

The dogs were barking. Straining at their tethers. The skinny dog was nipping at Ningao's leggings, pulling at him as though trying to drag him off.

But to where and from what?

And then she knew.

There was a faint roar coming from upriver, and somehow it was also rising from within the ground. It was not the roar of thunder. It was . . .

"The ice goes out!" exclaimed Amayersuk.

They were both on their feet. Amayersuk stood as stiff as a strip of frozen cod. Hasu'u held the baby, and her breath. She wanted to run. Every nerve ending in her body was screaming at her to run, and yet she did not because no one else was doing so, and everyone was lower down on the embankment than she and Amayersuk.

Except the skinny dog. He had given up on Ningao and was running as fast as his scrawny legs would carry him, uphill, past the two women, and on and on.

Amayersuk placed a steadying hand on Hasu'u's shoulder. "We are not dogs to run in panic! Show faith in our tunraq's judgment. He has brought us to high ground. He was right about the rain in the mountains. He knows!"

"There is higher ground behind us! We can—"

"We are safe if our tunraq says we are safe. We will observe the spectacle! If the others are not scrambling for higher ground, what have we to fear? Winter has been long. The ice will be . . ."

Hasu'u did not know if the woman was still talking. She could not hear her. The roar was deafening now. She stared upriver and saw a wall of water coming toward them, carrying all the sharded ice of winter in a roiling, raging tumult. Her eyes widened. The wall was growing higher . . . higher . . . coming toward them . . . hurling plates and blocks of ice the size of feast tents high into the air and over the embankment, flattening trees and all that lay before it.

She ran.

Amayersuk was beside her . . . then behind her . . . The water was following . . . rising . . . alive . . . coming for her . . . to sweep her away.

She fell to her knees, held on to the screaming baby, fought her way to her feet. Something struck her. She fell again. Her mind was roaring with the flood. Someone lifted her, dragged her. She was choking, drowning, and yet still being dragged until, at last, prostrate, not sure if she was dead or alive, she found herself sprawled on high ground with Ningao beside her.

She sat up. Stunned, with blood pouring into her eyes from a cut on her brow, her only thoughts were for the infant. It was still in her arms, still screaming, its face flushed with life and outrage at the cold and wet. She hugged it. Loved it. And then saw that below her, at the base of the rise, Tôrnârssuk was fighting, not for his own life but to pull his drowning band from the raging turmoil of the still-rushing waters.

"Help him!" she demanded of Ningao.

He understood. He shook his head. He showed her that he could not. His arm was broken, the bone protruding upward through his sleeve.

"They will die!" Hasu'u cried. Realizing that he could do nothing to help them, without a moment of hesitation she placed the infant into his good arm and raced downhill.

Later it would seem a blur.

Later it would seem a dream.

Later she would sit on the embankment shaking, shivering like one of the half-drowned dogs, and Tôrnârssuk would look at her in wonderment and ask, "Why? Why did you do this?"

She thought for only a moment. She had cast off the bearskin before hurling herself into the icy water to extend a branch to Avataut before he went under for the third time. It seemed she had done the same for several others. She was not sure; it must be so. The bearskin was back around her shoulders now, and its warmth was all the world to her. She held it close, her teeth chattering when the tunraq again asked her,

"Why?"

It seemed such a waste of breath. Tôrnârssuk was a tunraq, a wise and all-knowing guardian of his people. He should know the answer to such a question. But since he did not, she reminded him, "I am a hunt chief's daughter and a headman's woman. People were drowning! And it was obvious as I watched you floundering along the shore that as a Dawnland woman I am the only one among you who knows how to swim!"

▼▼▼▼▼

The skinny dog came back that night.

Notch Ear did not, and all the pups were lost. Hasu'u was saddened by their deaths, but she did not mourn them. There were others to mourn. It did not seem right to lament the loss of dogs when three men and the elder of the two captives had perished. And Amayersuk. Greasy-faced, file-toothed, avaricious, nasty, cruel-hearted Amayersuk. And yet Hasu'u missed the older woman's greasy face and ugly, file-toothed smile. She missed her goads, her unpredictable turns of temper. She had been someone to talk to, to share her thoughts with, no matter how guardedly. Now there was no one. Except the tunraq.

He entered the shelter that he had made. It was dark. Outside it was raining. He crawled onto the sleeping skins and lay down motionless beside her. "We will rest here for five days. We will mourn our dead. And then . . . then we will honor one who has risked her life to save our people."

She lay still on her side, bundled in the great fur, holding the sleeping infant close as, tensing, she felt him draw her near.

He did not speak. His arms enfolded her. He moved onto his side and curled his length against hers.

She held her breath, felt the curve of his damp brow press softly into the hollow at the back of her neck. She closed her eyes. Now he would take her. Now the ultimate humiliation of captivity would be hers. She waited.

"Forgive me."

She shivered at his words and in anticipation of what must come to her now.

Outside in the hastily made encampment, a dog was howling in the rain and a girl was offering a low, broken chant of lamentation for her lost mother.

And in the lean-to of the tunraq—of the One Who Gives Power, of Guide and Guardian and All-Knowing Spirit, of Windigo, Great Ghost Cannibal, Slayer of Youth, Slaughterer of Wayfarers, Destroyer of Dogs, Stealer of Women—Hasu'u closed her eyes and listened to Tôrnârssuk weeping.

▼▼▼▼

For four days and nights they stayed in that encampment. Each night the raiders sang for those who had been lost. And Hasu'u raised her voice with theirs in a song so high and sweet and touchingly sad that, after a while, the others fell silent. They listened. And as Tôrnârssuk looked at the Dawnland woman with love and pride, her voice alone filled the night.

The skies cleared.

Another dog came back.

Ningao—his arm reset by the tunraq and tended by the captive girl and worried over by the skinny dog—continued to run a fever. The girl worried; she ventured timidly to the tunraq to voice her concerns about moving on when the prescribed period of mourning was over.

Tôrnârssuk calmed her fears. "We will stay in this camp until Ningao's fever breaks. And until my woman and all of you are rested from our ordeal."

Avataut was not pleased. "The captive's milk flows. Ningao can walk. If you insist on lingering here, Armik and I would move on. We have talked about this. The River of the White Whales is far, and we do not like this place. We would rejoin the others in the big gathering camp and have our own women with us again in the night."

"Go, then," the tunraq told him without hesitation or hostility. "We will follow and greet you there when all our members are well and strong."

"You are certain?" Avataut appeared almost disappointed, as though he had spent some time preparing himself for a fight in order to win his way.

"Go!" Tôrnârssuk dismissed him with a wave of his hand. "We will meet and hunt again when the white whales are many in the great river."

The two exchanged a long and meaningful glance. Then, "The journey is long. We would take the captive who sits with Ningao. You have the other to share among the rest of you."

Tôrnârssuk's eyes narrowed. "In my camp there will be no more captives. When we reach the River of the White Whales, if Hasu'u no longer wishes to be a milk woman for my son, another will be chosen, and she may return to her people if this is her desire. So it is with the other. If she would go with you, let her speak."

The girl moved closer to Ningao. "I will stay."

Avataut and Armik did not look happy, but they bowed their heads and went their way.

That night the skies cleared briefly before the rains returned. And once again Hasu'u sang. In sadness for all that she had suffered. In gratitude for all that she had survived. And, for the first time since the masked manitous had burst from the cover of the trees on the far side of the creek, with hope in the future once again.

▼▼▼▼

"Do you hear that, husband?"

Far across the rainy hills, in another encampment of northbound travelers brought to pause by the violence of the ice going out upon the river, Segub'un's question went unanswered. The little family group of outcasts had traveled far. She left them asleep and came from her tent to stand alone in the rain . . . listening . . . to a voice she knew she could not be hearing, to her slain daughter's voice. "Will a time ever come when I will stop hearing it?"

"Come in out of the rain, woman." Ogeh'ma, awakened by her cry, stuck his head out of their tent and then, turning up an ear, came out himself. "Hasu'u?"

"The spirit of our lost child sings to us in the night, my husband. Even in death she is One Who Sings Always."

Kanio'te came from his own lean-to and stood beside his parents. Soon Onen'ia and old Ko'ram and the women were all coming from their shelters and standing in the rain.

"That is no ghostly song!" declared Ko'ram. "I am near enough to walking in the world beyond this world to tell you that I would know a spirit if I heard one singing in the night. That is no ghost singing! It is Hasu'u! Who ever in this life or any other had a voice as sweet as that?"

"It cannot be," said Segub'un as the voice fell away. "I have lost my Hasu'u forever. She is dead. M'alsum saw her die."

"M'alsum!" Ko'ram spat the name with all the revilement he could enunciate. "What other lies has that manitou told to drive us from our own hunting grounds and alienate us from our own people so that he may be hunt chief in Ogeh'ma's place!"

There was silence. Absolute and complete silence. Even the raindrops seemed not to fall for that one breath of time until, from far across the hills, the song of a young woman came across the night and made the listeners look at one another in a slow dawning of disbelief and anger.

It was Ogeh'ma who tore the moment with a curse. And once again the curse was the name of a man. "M'alsum!"

"If that *is* my sister out there in the night, then M'alsum *has* lied to us," said Kanio'te. "All this time that he has led us to hunt for him and worship him, all this time that he has been taking a man's release into our women and passing ducksuckles around to pacify our children, we could have had men out searching for her, bringing the Dawnland bands together to find her and at least try to bring her home!"

"But why would he lie to us, my father?" asked Onen'ia.

A visible tremor shook Ogeh'ma. "If that is my daughter out there in the night . . . if there is even the smallest vestige of justice in the whims of the forces of Creation that are said to turn the Great Circle of Life, by the honor of the blood of my ancestors I will know! And he *will* answer!"

Chapter Three

▼▼▼▼▼▼▼

It was to be a joyous morning.

Despite the rain.

"Our giant will tell stories!" Old One declared. "When I was a girl, long ago and far away, it was always the favorite way of the Old Tribe to pass the time on a rainy day!"

Ne'gauni settled against the backrest that Mowea'qua had made for him.

Musquash did the same, eager and bright-eyed as the muskrat for which he was named. "I like stories now!" he announced. Old One had given him a special hot drink mixed with dried leaves and pulverized roots and had poured heated medicinal oils into his ears. His ears had stopped ringing, and, with his hearing improved, so had his speech. His lisp was barely noticeable now.

"I have heard all of Kinap's stories!" Mowea'qua said sourly.

"Then let Musquash tell us one you may not have heard," suggested the giant.

"Me?"

"It is time for the son of Squam to learn to turn a tale," said the giant.

"Why?" moped Mowea'qua. "If all intend you to do is keep him forever in this forest, who will want to listen to him except the trees?"

"You and me and Old One and Ne'gauni. We will listen. He will speak wisdom. He is the son of the great shaman. So come now, Musquash, tell us of the sacred stone you wear. Perhaps, being born of the far inland forest, Ne'gauni has not heard this story."

The boy sat very straight. Very solemn. "In the time beyond beginning, in the time when the Animals and People were of one twibe, when it came time for First Man and First Woman to walk away upon the wind, they gave their bones into the twust of their children. Many were their children. Like the caribou! Like the geese! Like the leaves that blow away acwoss the world in the time of leaves falling down. And everywhere they went, following the mammoth kind acwoss the world, they took the bones of First Man and First Woman with them, breaking them into smaller and smaller pieces until in this time they are divided among all of the many bands of the People acwoss the whole world. Only shamans have these bones. Good and bwave men. Like Squam, my father. And all shamans know that someday, when the world grows cold and ice walks down fwom the the mountaintops and the time beyond beginning comes again, to end the shivering of the People and Animals, the shamans will bwing the sacred stones of the Ancient Ones together in one place, and all the People will be one People! The sun will come back, and the cold times of winter will be banished forever, because on that day First Man and First Woman will be reborn!"

He paused. Sighed. And looked earnestly at the giant. "So I had to steal the stone from Puwo'win. She is bad! I saw her kill my mother. My mother was good. Kind like you." He turned his gaze to Kelet. "She was of your twibe! She told me stories about long-ago times, about following the caribou out of the face of the rising sun acwoss the top of the world to meet the sun again in a new land, where other twibes did not want to share their hunting grounds with people whose grandmothers grow beards and whose babies are born with fur. I did not believe! Not really. She told so many stories. Good stories. And at her back, low down, there was a little dark spot. 'The mark' she called it."

Mowea'qua grumbled to herself and wrapped her arms around her folded knees. "It is not mine!"

Old One grumbled back at her. "And when was the time last that could see you to the bottom of your own back?"

"Mmph!" said the girl.

Musquash smiled at Mowea'qua. "The mark is good, Pretty One! Squam said that it was *very* good when my mother came to him, because now on his sacred island there were two twibes living as one. Soon other shamans would come! From all other twibes they would come! Soon the sacred stone could be placed all together again, and never again would the cold days of endless winter return to the People." His eyes went back to the giant. "And so I must bring the stone back to Squam. It is no use here!"

Ne'gauni was frowning, trying to think if anyone among his forest people had ever spoken of shamans who possessed sacred stones such as those of which the boy had spoken. He shook his head. Shamans everywhere always claimed to possess some sort of magic talismans! And even storytellers like the giant carried amulets and fetishes that were supposed to make bad spirits go away and bring good ones close.

Old One was clearly unhappy. "The People cannot be one! They have *never* been one! The Old Tribe is the *best* tribe! We were the tribe who walked out of the rising sun with the Animals in the time beyond beginning. Not the others! Not the masked ones or the hairless ones! Mmph! Those of the Old Tribe cannot live and mate with Strangers. Better that the cold times come again and the long dark comes down upon the world and mountains of ice cover us all."

Kinap was staring at the Old One as though he could not believe what he had just heard her say. "How can you of all people say this?"

"Mmph! The People look different from the Old Tribe. The People *are* different from the Old Tribe. Forgotten have you how they deal with us? How always they have dealt with us? Forgotten have you the whirling shaman who danced and sang while my band was slaughtered and skinned like so many animals? Forgotten have you the band of them that fell upon Pi'jiu when she ran away after Mowea'qua was born and—"

"Bah!" He roared her to silence. "You have forgotten to whom you speak, Kelet! And no, old woman, I have *not* forgotten! That is why I have come back to you! That is why I tell you now that you must live protected within this forest! The whirling shaman who took Pi'jiu's skin dwells on the sacred island of the Dawnland. She wears it still! And lives with Squam! And slew our Musquash's mother as surely as she would have slain him had I not stolen him away."

Ne'gauni found himself gaping. "These shamans take human skins? They *wear* human skins?"

"They do not consider those of the Old Tribe human," answered the giant.

"We are *not!*" Old One was adamant, and indignant. Clearly she had just suffered the worst insult imaginable. She glared at Kinap, her face pale, her hands crossed and braced against her chest, rubbing her heart. "Why did you not kill her? Why? Ah! Hers is a skin I would dance in, and sing while danced I!"

"Then you would be a whirling shaman no better than any other who draws the People to celebrate life through their dark and seductive magic," said the giant sadly.

Mowea'qua's eyes had become enormous. "M'alsum has gone to the Dawnland. What will happen to my beautiful one if he meets a whirling shaman there?"

A droll rumble of a laugh escaped the giant's mouth. "Do not fear for that one, Mowea'qua. He is as wary as any wolf and safeguards his every thought and step. Even Puwo'win would meet her match in such a man as M'alsum!"

"He *is* Puwo'win." The boy shivered. "I have seen her heart beating in his eyes!"

"I will believe this never!" snapped Mowea'qua. "He is beautiful! What is beautiful cannot be bad!"

"He is the best and the bravest and the boldest of the sons of Asticou," insisted Ne'gauni and, listening to the rain, tried not to be afraid for him.

▼▼▼▼▼

Ogeh'ma knew from the start that he had set himself to a dangerous course. And it was not exactly the best of times to be allowing Onen'ia to make good on his sullied reputation. But the young man had insisted on coming along, and it was too late now to change his mind.

They crouched in heavy undergrowth amidst a broken stand of dripping balsams. Onen'ia's stomach was growling. Ogeh'ma eyed him venomously. They had brought no food; none should have been necessary, for by all of the powers of the forces of Creation their bellies were full enough of seal meat. And it was to have been a quick sortie: Advance under cover of darkness to the place where the singing came from, look around, see if there was any sign of Hasu'u, and steal her away.

Simple!

Not simple.

The source of the singing had been much farther away than they had anticipated. The sun was up! And now the growling of Onen'ia's stomach had alerted one of the dogs in the camp up ahead.

They were seen!

The raiders were up and out of their lean-tos, all of them, as one, scrambling for their bows. Ogeh'ma knew in that moment that he and Onen'ia were undone. These were men of the far north! He had seen a demonstration of their bows once, many years before, when a small band of them had stayed briefly among his people to trade. He had been so impressed that he had traded his best toggle-headed harpoon for one, but he had never been able to make a stick to fly from the thing and, frustrated, had burned the bow. Now, from what he remembered of that long-ago demonstration put on by skilled bowmen, Ogeh'ma knew that the lances that he and Onen'ia carried were useless. They were within bow range.

A skinny dog was racing toward them.

Men were shouting, gesturing to them to stand. And there, behind and to one side of a powerful-looking man who by his manner appeared to be the headman of the group, was a woman in a white bearskin with a baby in her arms.

"Well," drawled the bandy-legged hunt chief to his son, "it seems you have a second chance at a white bear, but do not throw your spear, my son! I think this one may be your sister!"

▼▼▼▼▼

Hasu'u could not believe her own eyes when she saw the interlopers emerge from the woodland.

One man. Young. "Onen'ia?" No! It could not be.

Another man. Old. "Ogeh'ma?" Ah! She must at last be losing her ability to perceive reality.

But they were both in Dawnland garb. Feathers worn with furs. She had not been a captive long enough to have forgotten what the clothing of her own people looked like. And they were holding their lances in both hands, gripped firmly at each end and held upward over their heads as a sign to the men who were advancing toward them with arrows nocked and ready that they came in peace.

As they were forced forward, Tôrnârssuk remained at her side, appraising them. "They dress as people from the coastal tribes. They do not look like much, but we will see what they have that is worth taking."

"You have already taken it," said Hasu'u. A moment later she looked into the faces of her father and brother and did not know whether to cry out in joy or terror as Tôrnârssuk spoke coldly to them in a broken dialect of their own tongue.

"What brings two such 'bold' hunters to venture so near to my encampment that you disturb my dogs and woman but do not have courtesy enough to call out in respect to ask for welcome!"

It was Ogeh'ma who spoke. Boldly. Unflinchingly. As a hunt chief should. As though he had no cause whatsoever to be afraid. "I come for my daughter and grandson. Good morning, Hasu'u. We thought we heard you singing last night. It is better and more bitter than you know for this man to see with his own eyes that you are alive, for we would have come for you long before now had we even suspected that you might still live."

Tôrnârssuk looked to Hasu'u for confirmation. "Can this be? This is your father?"

"And the other is my brother."

He stared at them. "You dare to walk into my camp? One old man and a single hunter?"

"I am not afraid!" Onen'ia defended himself curtly. "And my father may be no youth, but he is a Dawnland hunt chief, and throughout my life I have seen him dare many things. He is Ogeh'ma! And he *is* bold!"

Hasu'u was surprised to see Ogeh'ma give her brother a sideward glance that had an unusual, almost surprised look of satisfaction, as though he had not expected him to be capable of such a brave, blustering outburst.

Tôrnârssuk was speaking to his fellow raiders.

A murmuring went up. Heads were nodding. Expressions changed.

"And tell me, Ogeh'ma, father of my woman, do you expect to take your daughter back to your Dawnland hunting camp?"

"I expect to take her back. And my grandson with her."

"The infant at her breast is mine."

Ogeh'ma and Onen'ia exchanged glances.

"It is true, my father. My son . . ." She stopped herself before she told him the truth; it would be dangerous now. "My son lived a short and much-loved life. I care for this man's infant. The child is Tiguak. The man is Tôrnârssuk, tunraq, headman of these rai . . . of this band."

"You can say the word. I know what they are! I know what they have done! M'alsum told me everything. But it seems he left something out."

"M'alsum." Her heart seemed to drop out of her body. She nearly swooned. M'alsum was out there in the rain! M'alsum had come for her at last! But why had he sent Ogeh'ma and Onen'ia for her? Why—

"M'alsum!" Tôrnârssuk spat the name as though it were a piece of spoiled meat that he did not wish to keep in his mouth. "Runs and Hides? No! It cannot be! Where is he? Hiding back there in the trees? No! Even that would be too much for him. I do not believe it! Not Pisses in Fright! Ningao, take Kamak and a few others and see if he is there. Be careful when you touch him. He has no doubt soiled himself by now."

Hasu'u saw the faces of her father and brother tighten. "Do not tell them," she implored. With all her strength she cried out, "Go, M'alsum, run fast and far! Do not put yourself at risk! It is too late for you to help us now! Run, I say! Run!"

Ogeh'ma's face turned bright red. "He is a three-day walk from here, daughter. He is in the Dawnland. Enjoying the bounty in seals in my winter camp, and more. He is . . . safe."

Tôrnârssuk laughed. One spurt of sound. "You will see," he said to Hasu'u as he gestured to the others to make their search. "We have not lied to you." And to Ogeh'ma, "Your daughter has spoken of this M'alsum. Your daughter has been waiting for him. We told her that he would not come. Unlike her father and brother, he is not bold. She is a loyal wife to Abandons Woman and Never Looks Back. Runs and Hides is—"

"He is a liar and a thief," interrupted Ogeh'ma. "And if only I could hunt him, I would, for I tell you that if he were here now I would tie him to a tree and ask you to show me just how to master the use of your bow . . . using him as the target!"

Tôrnârssuk stood very still, as a hunting cat or wolf would stand if it had sighted potential and intriguing prey from afar. "Three days to the Dawnland?"

"Three days!" affirmed Ogeh'ma, looking suspicious.

"There are seals in your camp?"

"Many seals. Much feasting. It will go on for days. But it is M'alsum's hunting camp now. I will not share it with a wolf. No, with a wolf I *would* share it! There would be enough meat for all! But with a thief and a liar who has allowed me to think that my own daughter is dead, I—"

"We could hunt him together," suggested Tôrnârssuk. "And enjoy the seals. It is close to three moons before the whales come to the great river of the north. My men would enjoy a brief turn at the coast if there are seals!" He looked at Hasu'u. "It would not displease you to have your father and your brother as a part of this band?"

"You cannot mean to hunt my man!"

"It will give me great pleasure, One Who Sings Always, to hunt with your bold father and brother at my side! It is time you saw with your own eyes what this M'alsum truly is!"

▼▼▼▼

No one was in a mood for stories.

The rain stopped, but the day seemed to bleed away into a gray and dismal evening. No one was in a mood to cook, nor did anyone much enjoy their meal of yesterday's leftover hare. The dark came down. Old One could not breathe. The giant sat with her and rubbed her back until she relaxed into dreams. The boy and Ne'gauni drifted off to sleep. The giant rose and went out, mumbling something about needing to be outside for a while.

Mowea'qua sat up on her bed skins. Old One's breathing was so shallow, so quick; it frightened her. She knew it frightened Kinap, too. Chewing her lower lip, she stared off across the den and knew what she must do. M'alsum's medicine would make her grandmother well; she knew it would! The ducksuckle that he had brought had caused no one any ill even though the boy had screeched when she and Old One had shared it with Ne'gauni.

And so it was done.

She rummaged in Kinap's things and found the packet. She poured its contents into Old One's drinking gourd and crept with it to Old One's side.

"Drink, dear one. This will soothe you."

Old One drank. Deeply. Trustingly. Working her lips a little, muttering about bitterness, an unfamiliar taste, and then she lay back and slept again, still smiling.

Mowea'qua knelt back on her haunches. She set the gourd aside. She smiled. There! Old One was going to be better now! They would all see that she was right about M'alsum. They would all see! No one so beautiful could be bad! No one . . .

Kinap backhanded the weather baffle aside.

The boy stirred.

Old One gasped.

Mowea'qua tensed. "She will be well now, you will see!" she declared, so defensively that, even before Kelet's old body went into violent paroxysms and Kinap carried her outside for fresh air, the boy was wide awake and screaming as he bolted out the door after Kinap. He knew what she had done.

"She is old, Musquash," soothed the giant. "Old hearts cannot beat forever."

Mowea'qua stood with Ne'gauni. Old One was limp in the giant's arms. So limp.

"It is over," said the giant.

Mowea'qua felt the strangest heaviness within her spirit. Old One dead? Her spirit gone? No! Old One would always be here for her! Always! And Kinap would always be at her side, whenever she had need of his stories. Even when she sought out the beautiful one, they would return into the forest to visit! They would bring their children! They might even bring the Dawnland woman, if M'alsum still wanted her after he had met the one who had saved his brother's life and brought to him the knowledge and skill of the bow and arrow. Yes, she thought. They would bring Hasu'u. And if she had children, they would bring them, too. And Old One would teach them the healing ways of the Old Tribe, and Kinap would tell them tales of magic. "She will breathe again. You will see. Now she will be well and strong." And then she added, by way of assurance, for she saw no reason to deny it, "I gave her M'alsum's magic medicine."

"No magic can stop the great Circle from turning." Kinap was smoothing back Old One's hair, touching her face. "Magic! Ah, foolish girl, how can you believe in magic or in any of the tales I told you of it when they were uttered through such lips as mine? Can you imagine that if any of it were true, that if the sacred spring possessed healing powers, I would not have used them to heal myself? No medicine can—"

"Bad medicine!" Musquash interrupted. He turned, ran into the den, retrieved the little leather packet from which Mowea'qua had poured the healing powder, and came outside to hurl it away into the night.

It flew against the side of Kinap's hand, sending an explosion of medicinal residue into the air before landing on the ground next to the giant. Something about the scent of the powder caused him to frown as he reached down, picked it up, and held it to his nostrils.

Mowea'qua waited. He recognized the smell of the powder! He knew what it was. A smile bent her lips. Everything would be all right now. In a moment he would tell her that she had done well to administer to her grandmother the wonderful magic from beyond the dark forest. "It is good medicine, yes, say I!" she said eagerly and came to his side. Any moment now Old One would wake up. She frowned a little. There was an odd foam at her grandmother's lips, and blood and bile were oozing from the corners of her mouth.

The packet fell from Kinap's hand. "It is not medicine," he said. "It is not magic. It is poison!"

▼▼▼▼

He carried her into the sacred grove.

Without a word. Without a tear. He was aware of the boy at his side, and of the girl following at his heels, tugging at his tunic, telling him again and again that he was mistaken, that her M'alsum would never do such a thing.

He struck her.

She fell.

Never in his life had he struck her, or wanted to. And yet there had been a day, long ago, when he had taken her into his big hands and looked down at her furry little form and—as Pi'jiu sobbed and begged for him to kill "it"—he had nearly ended Mowea'qua's life. A single turn of his thumb would have been enough to crack the fragile infant neck. He would have done anything to please Pi'jiu. He would, after she had seen the Strangers, have taken her from the forest and risked losing her forever to see her happy and free and beautiful among those who would appreciate her beauty as much as she had been captivated by theirs. If only he could have been sure that she would not bear a child that would betray her lineage.

Had he been mad? To fall in love with Kelet's child? To imagine that Pi'jiu—the product of rape, half Old Tribe, half Stranger—might lie down and love *him* as a man and bear a child to him that was not . . .

No.

The mark had been there. As it had been on Pi'jiu at birth. Pi'jiu! His uncle's baby! The baby that the shaman of his band would have brained at birth and its mother, the captive, Kelet, too, had Kinap not snatched up the captive and her child and run from the village and his own kind in order to save them.

He trembled.

He had not intended to stay with them forever. He had found another band of their kind. He had lived with them. And then the Strangers had come. Strangers! His kind! With their whirling shamans and their lust for all that was not theirs, claiming the hunting grounds of the Old Tribe, setting the great fire that had . . .

Mowea'qua was backhanding blood from her mouth. She was looking up at him like an injured animal, feeling the pain he had caused her but not quite able to believe that he had really struck her.

The boy was at her side, glowering up at Kinap. "Those of the Old Tribe do not strike or hurt their children!"

"I am not of the Old Tribe! And do not look at me like that, Mowea'qua! For in my heart I am no better than they. Yes! I am your father. And I have hidden you here to keep you safe . . . and to hide my shame at ever siring one of you!"

Mowea'qua's hand froze.

Strange, he thought. His heart had frozen, too. "Forgive me. I should have told you long ago. For your grandmother's sake I did not. She feared and hated my kind almost as much as mine hated hers. The burns on my face made it easy for her to pretend that all that brought us together never happened. But after the fire how could I forget? I owed her my life . . . and my loss of it! I had hoped, through the boy, that for Kelet's sake the blood of the Old Tribe might be renewed through you, Mowea'qua. There is nothing left for me beyond this forest. We could have shared our shadow days and . . ."

Mowea'qua swayed to her feet. Ne'gauni had come through the trees, using his crutch. She seemed unaware of him. Her mind seemed to be working very hard, as though all the hurtful things he had just said had gone unheard. There was one thought in her mind. And one only. "If you are a Stranger and my mother's father was a Stranger, then M'alsum and I do share the same blood! We—"

"M'alsum . . ." The ice began to melt around his heart. It was bleeding now, into a numbing, blinding, slowly building rage.

"A mistake it must have been," the girl assured the giant. "M'alsum must the wrong packet have given you!"

"M'alsum makes no mistakes," said Musquash.

"Yes," said the giant. "He has made one. He has taken

the hand of Kinap in friendship and given me Death in return. I will return that gift in kind!"

▼▼▼▼

He raised a bier for her, a simple scaffolding of notched and thong-laced saplings placed high above the sodden earth and lashed within the outreaching branches of the tallest of the ancient spruces.

"This is not the way of the Old Tribe," Mowea'qua told him. "There can be no magic in this."

"I will not strip her bones and skull of flesh and lay them in a circle! I will not do that, Mowea'qua! Never!"

"Then the kami will not—"

"By all the forces of Creation, girl, it is wolves who will come! Wolves and foxes and all the meat-gnawing and bone-eating carnivores of the night! No! I will not mourn her in that way."

She cocked her head. "Then show me the way a Stranger mourns," she said. "I must learn for when I go to him and live among his . . . our kind."

"Yes," he told her and knew that he was shaking. "Observe and observe well, for when I have finished here, I will seek M'alsum in the Dawnland. And I will give you something to mourn."

Her eyes went wide. "Hurt him I will not let you."

He turned away.

Fragrant boughs of freshly cut spruce and balsam were laid as both mattress and shroud over the snow-scrubbed, fur-wrapped body of the old woman. Kinap gathered her few belongings and placed them around her.

The boy helped, solemnly, reverently. "She was good. She was kind. I will remember her always."

It was raining again.

The giant's hands lay still upon his drum. He eyed the sky from beneath his heavy cowl, then looked to the three sodden figures sitting across from him before the mourning fire beneath what was supposed to pass as a waterproof tarpaulin of laced deer gut; the seams were leaking. And it was very late. "Go back to the den. Three more nights and four days I must be at this. Go, say I! All three of you. For Old One's sake. Kelet would not want any of you to take ill because of her."

His tone allowed no disobedience. And he was too intent on other thoughts to castigate the youth Ne'gauni even though he clearly heard the youth exhale, "Mmph!"

"You would not be sitting here now if she had not cared about you," he told the youth. "Go! Sleep! And in your dreams thank Kelet of the Old Tribe for your life, and be glad that I am trying to forget that you are brother to the one who killed her."

"You are wrong about him," said Ne'gauni.

"Mmph." The giant gestured them off so aggressively that not one of them hesitated to obey.

▼▼▼▼

"Ne'gauni, wake up!"

He opened his eyes. She was kneeling over him. The boy was beside her. The thin gray light of dawn was filtering into the den. He heard no drumming from the sacred grove and was relieved.

"He has taken his bows and gone away," Mowea'qua told him.

He slumped more deeply into his bed furs. "Good!"

"Understand you do not!" Her face worked with emotion. "He has gone to hunt and kill your brother!"

Now it was the boy who said, "Good."

Ne'gauni sat up. He was bewildered. His eyes scanned the room for his crutch, found it, and then looked back to Mowea'qua. "I cannot walk all the way to the Dawnland on one leg!"

The girl smiled, a tight, nervous, somewhat distracted smile, but a smile all the same. "It is for you time to see this. To have this. To hold it close. Cut off have I a part of your leg, but I have not *taken* the leg, Wounded One! I have healed it. Strong it is now. Maybe the power of Musquash's sacred stone on this will work, and your leg will grow back on."

"My stone does not work magic. It is simply a thing that speaks for good and hope."

"Well, let it speak for good and hope this morning, Muskrat! We must stop our giant. And he has been gone a long time, probably since just after he sent us off last night."

"I do not want to stop him. M'alsum is bad. Kinap should kill him."

Ne'gauni found a birchbark packet thrust into his hands. It smelled deliciously of smoke and well-cured meat; his stomach growled. They had been fasting since the old one's death. He assumed that she was enticing him with some sort of special morning meal and was not about to turn it down. But when the last thong tie was loosed and the last turn of birchbark was peeled away, he found himself staring in horror.

"You have smoked his leg!" cried the boy.

"Told I you I had not taken it!" Mowea'qua said proudly. "Look! Perfect it is! Not even one of the toenails is burned. A little dark, maybe, and sunken in here and there, but—"

Ne'gauni hurled the leg and its wrappings into the fire pit and was sick.

"Ah, you are a weak thing!" Mowea'qua spoke with undisguised disdain. "I will not wait for you! I will not let my giant kill your brother, even if you do not care about him! Surely you are *not* the best and boldest and bravest of the sons of Asticou, but tell him will I that I have found you. Maybe glad he will be to know that you are alive, but why, I do not know!"

"Pretty One, you cannot go alone. You do not know the way."

"Kinap has probably a trail left as big as a mammoth's! Follow will I!"

Ne'gauni felt a light, tentative poke to his shoulder. "We cannot let a girl of the Old Tribe go alone among Strangers, Wounded One. The world is changing. It is dangerous, for us, for her."

Ne'gauni rolled over. Mowea'qua was gone. He glared at the boy and, as he looked into the fixed black eyes, could have sworn that he was back at the creek, seeing the raiders, seeing Hasu'u taken.

"Maybe you will see her again."

"How do you know my thoughts, Muskrat?"

The boy shrugged. "I am good at guessing. And I *do* know the way to the Dawnland." He extended a small hand. "You have your crutch. Old One has left medicines to eat your pain. We have our bows and arrows. Together we can go. We can catch up with Mowea'qua. Come. I would like to see your brother die. And you would like to save him. Who knows which of us will have our way?" He turned and brought the staff that Mowea'qua had made for Ne'gauni. "Take this. With it and me beside you, you will have two strong legs!"

Chapter Four

▼▼▼▼▼▼▼

The Circle of Life was turning.

M'alsum opened his eyes in the special tent that had been raised for Mammoth Slayer and Puwo'win. The sun would be rising soon; he could sense it in the subtly changing light of the interior. He wondered if this was the day that he and the shaman and her retainers would go to the sacred island. He doubted it. He could hear the wind tugging at the tent stakes; the roof skins were trembling. He groaned softly, trying to think if he had seen more than two consecutive clear days since he had come from the forest.

Fog and rain. Rain and fog. Fog and rain. Sometimes a little sleet. And wind, not always harsh, but changeable, and always there, a constant, like the overcast gray skies beneath which, just at dawn, the sun sometimes showed itself before being swallowed by the dank gray substance of the very air.

He exhaled in longing for the warm Dawnland sun and clear blue skies with which Meya'kwé had filled his boyhood dreams. Where were they? Had her Dawnland grandmothers misled her? Or had she simply invented them to inspire him to the restlessness that she hoped would one day take her from his father's village? Had it been like this when he had last journeyed here? Yes. Perhaps it had. But there had always been so much to do, so much to learn, so many good times shared with Hasu'u's people. And he stayed on into summer.

Summer!

He smiled to think of it. Skies would be clearer then. There would be thunderheads over the inland mountains. The bay would be blue again! Deep blue. Ice free. Several days ago—had it been a full hand-count, or more? More. Yes. He was sure it was more. Ogeh'ma and his pathetic little assortment of followers had been out of the winter camp for at least three nights when the ice had gone out on the inland rivers and the great bay had been turned into a roiling, roaring span of open water heaped with discolored slag ice. The seals that had not been taken by then had vanished; the surviving pups most likely had drowned, since he doubted they had had enough time to learn to swim within the leads. The past days of rain and wind had roused an angry surf and a white-capped sea that only a seabird would seek to cross and no man in his right mind would wish to navigate in one of the dugouts, which were designed for inland waters and calm seas.

He rolled over and slung an arm across the girl he and Puwo'win had shared the previous night. His new woman had strange tastes. She enjoyed watching him with others, enjoyed handling women as much as he, and hurting them. It was gratifying. No holding back with Puwo'win. Not like with Hasu'u. No. The shaman was a woman who howled and scratched and bit him when he came into her, and sometimes, sweating and moaning, lay on his back when he rode others, absorbing his pleasure through her skin.

Where was she now? Gone. She rose early. Painted herself in the light of an oil lamp in her own private tent. Adorned herself so that she could stand in the light of the rising sun—when and if there was any—so that the People would see her and sense an aura of invincibility about her. She said that it was part of the ritual, part of the magic, something that he must make an effort to learn as he gradually took on the identity of the new Squam.

He smiled to think of it, drifted back into the shallows of sleep, imagining the robe she had described to him, a glorious thing of raven and eagle feathers waiting for him on the sacred island. He yawned. Stretched. Became aware of the warmth of the woman lying naked beside him and ran his hands between her thighs and, when she stiffened in anticipation of pain, became aroused, reached to take her by her hair, and pulled down. Puwo'win had no taste for this, but he had taught this one as well as he had once taught Kicháwan. She knew what he wanted, and what must befall her if she denied him. He sighed and arched his hips to the warm moistness of her mouth and the workings of her tongue.

Somewhere outside the tent, someone called out to Puwo'win. A male voice not instantly familiar. The sensation in his loins was exquisite. The girl was licking, drawing. He told himself that he would have to join Puwo'win soon, paint his face with red ochre, don the breastplate, and . . . ejaculation came. The girl took it all.

"M'alsum!"

He tensed at the sound of a familiar voice. Male. A harsh call. Deep. Grainy.

"Mammoth Slayer, you must come out!"

The girl raised her head.

The tense, imperative nature of the man's command

had M'alsum propped on his elbows and glaring at a Dawnland man who had presumed to enter the tent unbidden,
an obsequious fellow whose name he could not remember
this early in the morning. "Why do you disturb me? It
cannot be sunrise yet?"

"It is, Mammoth Slayer. And something has happened
to our Puwo'win. Someone has . . . has . . ."

"What?"

"She is dead, Mammoth Slayer. Please. You must come
out."

He reached for the hunting shirt that Segub'un had
given him, pulled it on, and shoved his feet into his moccasins. He rose. The girl was already on her feet, handing
him his heavy mammoth-trunk breastplate, adjusting the
fall of the copper spearhead amulet, and handing him his
leggings. He waved them away, took up the stone-headed
spears that he kept by the entranceway, and went out.

The sun had just risen.

He stared toward the little drumlike dais that Puwo'win
had brought with her from the sacred island and upon
which she always stood to greet the sun. She was there.
Not on it. Behind it. On her back. With one arrow in her
throat and another in her breast.

Some of the people were standing around in shock,
staring. Others were just emerging from their shelters.
Three of Puwo'win's guardsmen were also down, dead. A
dog whined, but not one had barked.

And standing at the edge of the forest was the giant,
bow raised, another arrow nocked and ready to fly.
M'alsum's gut constricted.

"I was not sure if you would be here!" called Kinap.
"How fortunate! Thank you for coming out to greet me! I
come armed into your camp this day to thank you for your

parting gift to me. Imagine it! You and Puwo'win in one day! Truly the forces of Creation are smiling upon me in Kelet's name! Now, what is that I see hanging before you? Ah, of course. I should have known!"

Kinap's arrow flew.

M'alsum was struck before he could react.

And Kinap laughed to see his arrow protruding from the trunk of the mammoth with the man who wore it unhurt, staring goggle-eyed.

The obsequious little man at M'alsum's side muttered, "Bad spirits have taken over the giant's head, Mammoth Slayer. He has always been the kindest of men, always the—"

M'alsum, seeing the giant nocking another arrow, turned and dived for the cover afforded by the tent.

"Wait, Kinap! Hurt him do not!"

It was a girl's voice. High. Frightened. Wild. When she came bursting through the trees behind the giant with her own bow held at the ready, a gasp went up from everyone in the encampment.

"I do not know who she is, but I will love her until the day I die!" said M'alsum, rising and wiping the mud of the earth off his hands on his hunt shirt.

"Yah!" Segub'un's voice. "I knew my kind efforts on your behalf were wasted, but I did not want to believe it, not of my own slain daughter's husband! But did I not share the shadow of my heart with you, Hasu'u, and beg you not to marry a stranger?"

M'alsum was disoriented. Segub'un was deliberately speaking loudly enough to be heard by all as she emerged from another part of the forest that all but encircled the village on the bluffs. Had the woman lost her reason? Why had she come back? And why was she talking as though

Hasu'u was with her? Impossible! He blinked, startled to see Ogeh'ma, Ko'ram, Onen'ia, and Kanio'te and their families coming from the trees. An entire group of masked manitous was with them, all armed with bows, with arrows aimed at him. He staggered back a step and bumped into the girl who had passed the night with him and Puwo'win. He pushed her down and out of his way.

Someone muttered a muted protest, her father or brother or some other member of her family. M'alsum snarled at the sound. He had no concern for them now. The girl at the edge of the forest was staring fixedly at the newcomers. Her body had gone as taut as her bowstring. Clearly she was afraid, and just as clearly she was determined to hold her ground.

"Put down your bows, all of you! You will not shoot the beautiful one!"

M'alsum stood a little straighter. She was right about his looks, and about her loyalties. And she was not unpleasant to his eyes.

Everyone was staring at the girl.

"You cannot shoot us all, Mowea'qua," said the giant. "Put down your bow, daughter."

The odd roaring was back at the base of M'alsum's brain. Mowea'qua? The wild wolf woman of legend? Now *he* was losing his reason. The girl was a girl. Not a manitou. And even if she were the latter, she seemed to be the only one with a bow who was on his side.

"It seems we both prefer to hunt at dawn, Storyteller," said the bandy-legged hunt chief.

A bearskin-clad figure stepped forward from among the masked manitous.

M'alsum could feel the eyes of . . .

"I have brought you a white bear, Mammoth Slayer!"

called Onen'ia. "See if you can do better than I at defending yourself against its kind! Go on, Hasu'u! Let him see that it is you. Let *everyone* see!"

She stepped forward.

M'alsum stared. The long rays of the rising sun were streaming through the cloud cover. She lowered the bearskin that she had been wearing tented up around her head. He saw her face. And that she carried a child. "I . . . I saw you die! And the baby drowned!"

Someone laughed. A man's mirthless laugh. And then, from behind the face of a raven, an accented voice spoke out, clear and strong. "One truth! Look at me, Abandons Woman and Never Looks Back! Do you not know me?"

M'alsum caught his breath. The manitou was the manitou he had seen leading the others out of the woods on the far side of the creek! And now, as he stared in disbelief, the phantom gave some sort of signal, and all the manitous in his company, save two who kept their arrows aimed at him, took off their faces to reveal faces beneath . . . the faces of men.

The girl with the arrow aimed at the giant reacted in obvious shock. "Kinap! Some of them have hair on their faces! They are of the Old Tribe!"

The giant's posture changed slightly. "Maybe. Who can say? They come from a far land. But they are People, like you and I, foolish girl! Now lower your bow and let this Stranger do what he has come to do!"

"No!"

M'alsum knew the voice. Had another arrow struck him, the blow would not have been as devastating.

Two figures came from the trees: a small boy and a scarfaced, one-legged youth leaning on a crutch.

"Musquash . . ." M'alsum spoke the name of the boy,

but he could hear the race of the distant creek, feel the coldness of the water as Ne'gauni called out to him.

"Sac and M'ingwé—are they here with you, Brother? And Kicháwan?"

"Slain by raiders when they pursued me into the ravine and—" The lie had come before he remembered that the raiders he spoke of were standing before him and would certainly know that they had not followed him even as far as the creek. As would Hasu'u.

All around him now there was a noticeable restlessness in the encampment.

M'alsum snarled. "You are dead, Little Brother!" he shouted at Ne'gauni. "We left you in the creek, bleeding like a gut-wounded deer with your face half torn off and your leg broken and snared in a tree. You cannot still be alive!"

The scar-faced man dropped to the ground from what seemed to be exhaustion. And yet all heard his cry as the boy went to his knees beside him.

"Hold your arrows, Giant," said the man who had removed the raven mask. "I think we are killing him where he stands."

▼▼▼▼

And it was so.

His lies devoured him; there was no escaping them. The people of the Dawnland and those who had come from the forest surrounded him.

"Mammoth Slayer . . . Bringer of All Good Things to the People . . . Smells Danger and Runs and Hides . . . Abandons Woman and Never Looks Back . . . where are your brothers and burden woman? Where is the brave spirit of old Kelet, to whom you gave the gift of Death? Go!

Return into the dark forest and walk with them. We will take your weapons and your warm clothes. Go! Let us see if you really are immortal!"

They gave their children spears to chase the naked man for sport, and they ran him out into the dark forest from which he had come.

The women with whom he had lain in his "grief" for the Dawnland woman he had in fact abandoned followed with their husbands. Picking up the little lances as they fell when the children tired, they threw them again and again.

His wounds were many.

He fell, exhausted, many times.

And always he was prodded to his feet until, at last, the dark came down and the fog came in and, naked and bleeding, they left him where he lay.

"Do not come back!"

The voices rang as one. He knew not who spoke. Someone threw something onto his back. It was heavy and smelled of smoke and putrefying meat. He pulled the trunk of the mammoth over himself and, shivering, curled up in the mud and fell asleep.

He dreamed of his triumphant race with Death. He dreamed of the great mammoth lying dead in the snow. And then he dreamed of ghosts moving around him in the night. M'ingwé and Sac were leading them, holding their hollow-eyed heads under the crook of their right arms, their sundered hands and feet dangling like grotesque hunt trophies around the stumps of their necks. Kicháwan was with them, not walking beside them but riding with old Kelet, who held his drowned baby in her arms as she rode on the great domed head of Katcheetohúskw. The mammoth raised its maimed trunk and bellowed in anger,

"I will have the third arm that you have stolen from me,

and I will have my tail with which to flick flies from your corpse in the world beyond this world! Do you truly think that you can outdistance all that you have done in this forest, M'alsum, Firstborn and Eldest Son of Asticou? Do you truly believe that you alone among all men are invincible? The white mammoth has seen what you have done! The white mammoth will follow!"

He awoke screaming.

The fog was wafting, skeining, revealing that which he had somehow known would be there. A great white form. A mammoth. A manitou. He rose. He ran.

And did not see the dropoff in the dark and the fog. It was not a high embankment, only a small slope falling off to a stony creek bed. He heard the race of water just before he fell.

The roaring at the back of his head was very loud just before all sound ebbed away. Bright. White behind his eyes.

Had he lived, he would have told them all what he had seen. The white mammoth. Within himself. Where, perhaps, it had always been.

Epilogue

▼▼▼▼▼▼▼

The winter forest was alive with spirits. Cannibal spirits. All men knew this. And yet, although the woman's smile was sad as she sat with the others in the disbanding encampment of her father, she smiled nonetheless. Winter was over. Hasu'u was home in the Dawnland. She was no longer afraid.

"I heard your voice, Little Brother. You gave me the will to live."

Ne'gauni hung his head. He could not look her in the face and had earlier tried to borrow one of the "manitou" masks from Tôrnârssuk, but the man was so impressed by his scars and those of the giant that he could not understand why anyone would wish to hide them. "Among my people you would be considered bringers of good fortune . . . living amulets! To walk with you is to walk with those who know how to survive and endure."

Ne'gauni was heartened by the man's words, but he still felt ugly in Hasu'u's eyes. "I knew you were alive," he told her. "I do not know how, but I heard your voice in my head. 'Why do you call to me in the country of the manitous, Little Brother? I am still a hunt chief's daughter and a headman's woman! I do not stop and sing where it does not please me to stop and sing! I do not rise and walk where it does not please me to rise and walk! And I will not swim in the river of death when the river of life is yet sweet and warm and welcoming!' This is what I heard you say."

She leaned forward and kissed him on the mouth. "And now I say this. You are the boldest and bravest and best of the sons of Asticou."

"Mmph," said Mowea'qua peevishly. "He is now the only son of Asticou! And he is not only the boldest and bravest and best . . . he is to my eyes the most beautiful!"

Musquash, sitting close, looked at her adoringly. "And you are the pwiddiest girl in this camp!"

"Do not lisp! Has not my grandmother Kelet healed you? You can hear! You can speak! Talk like the son of a shaman! Remember what the servant of the whirling shaman said before he died. Your father is dead. The sacred stone of the Ancient Ones is yours now. You must honor it. Someday you will be Squam in your father's place and live on the sacred island, and all will come to worship you!"

"A lonely and loveless life for a little boy," said Ogeh'ma. "Better that he stay on the mainland with us and learn the tales of the Ancient Ones from the best storyteller we all know!"

Kinap raised his head and looked around. "And who would that be, mmph?"

"You, Old Friend. Are you not tired of wandering? Your daughter needs a home and a band. People to call her own."

"I am of the Old Tribe!" said Mowea'qua, her chin raised, her gray eyes daring anyone to speak against her.

Ko'ram shrugged and eyed the mixed assembly with a droll smile. "I think perhaps when all is said and done we are all of the Old Tribe, girl."

Mowea'qua looked at Tôrnârssuk. "You have hair on your upper lip, and on your chin, like my grandmother."

The tunraq raised an eyebrow. "And I also wear a white stone around my neck. It was my father's, and his father's before that, going back to the time beyond beginning when, according to the legends of my people, the twin sons of First Man and First Woman parted company forever, one following the migrating geese eastward over mountains of ice, the other following the caribou and the great white hare who wears snowshoes northward to where the white whales swim." He paused and turned his gaze to Hasu'u. "You are now among your own kind, One Who Sings Always. A promise I have made to you. There will be no captives among my people. Your singing and brave heart will be missed upon the trail, but if there is a milk woman in this big band of yours who would not mind journeying north with us to the River of the White Whales, I—"

Ogeh'ma's eyes sparkled. "Long has it been since my people have savored the taste of whale meat! Some of them will gladly go. My son Kanio'te was saying to me when we left here before the ice went out that he was glad for a change of scene, and his woman has milk enough! She herself could suckle a whale if it came to that!"

There was laughter.

Kanio'te's woman beamed with pride and said that she would be honored to give the milk of life to the tunraq's son as well as to her own.

Tôrnârssuk stared solemnly into the dark hollow of his own lap. "Then Hasu'u will stay in the Dawnland. She will live and dwell once more among her own kind."

Hasu'u exhaled a huff of annoyance. "I do not rise and walk where it does not please me to rise and walk! I am a hunt chief's daughter and a tunraq's woman! I will not put my Tiguak to another woman's breast when I have milk to feed my son! If Tôrnârssuk journeys to the River of the White Whales, then Hasu'u will say whether she stays or goes!"

Ne'gauni looked up at the tunraq and then at Hasu'u as, for the first time in longer than he could remember, he smiled and teased one whom he loved with all his heart. "You are very stubborn, woman. Once there was a time when, had I been bolder and wiser and not tongue-tied by a pretty female, I would have pulled you along by your pack straps and made you go where I would have had you go. And then where would we all have been?"

"Mmph!" said Kinap. "That reminds me of a story. Yes! Come closer to the fire, everyone. Come! Let it be told in the old way! Come! Listen! My story waits! Let it be as it was in the time beyond beginning, in the time when the Animals and the People were of one tribe and set out together for the River of the White Whales . . ."

Author's Note

▼▼▼▼▼▼▼

Over the last two million years, four Ages of Ice have flowed and ebbed across our planet. Some five thousand years ago the Altithermal Period, or Great Warming, came to an end. With its passing, weather patterns shifted radically and the world began to grow cold again, wetter in some areas, drier in others. Although the vast continental ice sheets had retreated to the heart of Greenland and the northwesternmost shores of Labrador, montane glaciers began to grow once more on the high peaks of the Sierras, the Rockies, the northern mountaintops of the Appalachians, and the highlands of the Laurentian Plateau. Oceans that had already risen to inundate ancient coastlines began to rise again. Pack ice drifted south from the high Arctic into bays and inlets where it had not been seen in millennia. And the great boreal and northern hardwood forests that had advanced more than a hundred miles beyond today's most northerly treeline began to die back. The Neoglacial or New Glacial Age had begun.

Time Beyond Beginning is set in this period of prehistory. It initiates a new phase in the saga of the First Americans. As in all the previous novels in the series, the storyline and characters have been drawn from extensive research into the findings of archaeologists, anthropologists, geologists, and meteorologists as well as the legends of the native peoples whose ancestors were the first Americans.

The cannibal phantoms, mysterious beasts, and "supernatural" races of dwarves, giants, and hairy people akin to werewolves were inspired by the mythology of Northeast Woodland, Canadian Maritime, and Inuit cultures. Research has led me to believe that these traditions are not born of fiction; they recount the early migrations of man into and across the North American continent and affirm the purely human propensity to demonize the unknown.

Bones of mammoths and mastodons have been found throughout the regions depicted in this novel and continue to be hauled up in the nets of trawlers fishing off the Canadian Maritimes and the coast of Maine. In 1994 Russian scientists working on Wrangel Island proved that mammoths were living off the coast of Siberia as late as 2000 B.C. And tales of Algonkian-speaking tribes from Maine to the barrenlands of Canada tell of five-legged shaggy monsters that slept standing upright, crushed careless hunters, consumed the forests, and sucked up so much water from lakes and rivers that they had to be hunted and destroyed to the last of their kind.

In *Time Beyond Beginning* tribes referred to as the People—of the Forest, Dawnland, Grassland, and Lakeland—are Palaeo-Indians. By the onset of the Neoglacial Period these descendants of the first Americans had greatly diversified their original big-game hunting traditions and expanded their hunting range across the entire North and South American continents. Small bands of big-game hunters established hunting territories—and a Maritime culture—northward along the Atlantic coast. By the time the world began to grow cold again, copper tools, projectile points, beads, and adornment were being imported from the interior Great Lakes and traded extensively along with Ramah chert, the much-coveted gray stone mentioned in this novel, a rare form of chalcedony found only in one place in Labrador—and quarried at a site occupied by a "new" race of people from the high Arctic.

It was the advent of this second arrival of man into the "new world" that inspired the summer costume of Hasu'u. Since Maritime Palaeo-Indians used sewing needles of bone, stone, and sometimes imported copper, I have shown Dawnland Woman carrying her needles in a traveling case made of a hollow porcupine quill that she wears inserted through the septum of her nose. This was long the style among subarctic Indian and Arctic Eskimo tribes, and I wanted to show the gradual amalgamation of the two cultures. Yet, although trading goods changed hands and fashion trends were copied, the legends of both people speak of a stark and often murderous enmity between them.

The masked raiders are Palaeo-Eskimo/Inuit who are advancing their hunting range southward into the cooling subarctic forests and coastlines of Canada and the United States. They are bringing with them a new weapon, the bow and arrow, destined to revolutionize the hunting techniques of native Americans as surely as the toggle-headed harpoon of "new world" invention would revolutionize their way of taking whales, seals, and walrus.

The Old Tribe is an ancient proto-Ainu race that may—or may not—have crossed into the new world at the dawn of time. Hirsutism is rare but not unknown among Inuit or Native American people. When Europeans first traveled among the Cherokee, the "Indian" men wore full beards and flowing mustaches. Since so much of Ainu ritual seems linked to subarctic shamanic cultures in the old and new worlds, and since little bone carvings of wolf women have been showing up in the Arctic for over three thousand years, I have taken the liberty of injecting this component into my storyline.

If the tale has sometimes been harsh, it has reflected what I believe to have been the lifeways and attitudes of Paleolithic man, not the intent of this author to shock or offend. Cruelty and avarice are not foreign to our own time and "civilized" lifeways. And if there were a way to write about the degradation of the human spirit in a manner that would not offend my readers, I must admit that I would not use it. Rape, murder, slavery, the killing of infants, the betrayal of loved ones to advance the cause of one's own greed: What are we if we are not shocked and appalled by such things?

I am, once again, indebted to Dr. Richard M. Gramly, curator of the Great Lakes Artifact Repository, Buffalo, New York, Clovis Project director at Richey Clovis Cache in Wenatchee, Washington, and organizer of the American Association for Amateur Archaeology, for his continued support and enthusiasm for the First Americans saga—and for packing up what seemed his entire library of rare editions on the Maritimes and sending them my way along with the extraordinary articles "North American Indian Traditions Suggesting a Knowledge of the Mammoth" and "Discussion and Correspondence—Mammoth or 'Stiff-Legged' Bear" from the 1934–35 editions of *American Anthropologist*, volumes 36 and 37.

A word of appreciation must also go to Ron Toelke,

who so consistently comes up with maps based on this author's scribbled sketches of the lands of Whatmighthavebeen.

Thanks, too, to Paul Littlecoyote and Jessie Doguiles for insights into native American history, culture, spirituality—and a great time at the Littlerock Pow Wow! To my editor at Book Creations, Elizabeth Tinsley, for her patience, keen eye, and voluntary overtime on Easter Sunday. To Sally Smith for "trucking" the disk to Bantam so the project would be on time even though its author was still doing battle with Edward A. Murphy and El Niño brownouts.

And, last but not least, my thanks must go to George Engel, president of Book Creations, whose father, Lyle Kenyon Engel, founder of Book Creations, called me one day and asked if I would be interested in putting my "time and talent to work developing a little idea" he had about doing a book on the first Americans. Thirteen years and, hopefully, an equal measure of talent later, the First Americans saga numbers ten volumes. As of this writing, two more books are slated to follow, and foreign translations of the novels are best-sellers in Europe, under my own name as well as the pseudonym William Sarabande. Lyle Engel, a master of marketing, felt strongly that I "did not write like a lady" and that my given name, Joan Lesley Hamilton, sounded as though it belonged to someone doing "romance fiction." He was convinced that the series would do better under a man's name. Now, with George at the helm of Lyle's ship and the forces of Creation turning forward, never back, it is time to reveal my identity. Thank you, George, as Lonit would say, "always and forever" for making it possible to reveal the identity of the author behind the pseudonym and letting "William" out of the closet at last.

Joan Lesley Hamilton Cline
aka William Sarabande
Fawnskin, California